SCIENCE FICTION

Winnetka-Northfield Public Library

3 1240 00529 7275

MAY — — 2015

WITHDRAWN

D1509112

WINNETKA-NORTHFIELD
PUBLIC LIBRARY DISTR.
WINNETKA, IL 60093
847-446-7220

CASH CRASH JUBILEE

CASH CRASH JUBILEE

BOOK ONE OF THE JUBILEE CYCLE

ELI K. P. WILLIAM

TALOS PRESS

Copyright © 2015 by Eli K. P. William

The quote "In the beginning all the world was America" was taken from *Second Treatise on Government*, by John Locke

All Rights Reserved. No part of this book may be reproduced in any manner without the express written consent of the publisher, except in the case of brief excerpts in critical reviews or articles. All inquiries should be addressed to Talos Press, 307 West 36th Street, 11th Floor, New York, NY 10018.

Talos Press books may be purchased in bulk at special discounts for sales promotion, corporate gifts, fund-raising, or educational purposes. Special editions can also be created to specifications. For details, contact the Special Sales Department, Talos Press, 307 West 36th Street, 11th Floor, New York, NY 10018 or info@skyhorsepublishing.com.

Talos Press is an imprint of Skyhorse Publishing, Inc.®, a Delaware corporation.

Visit our website at www.talospress.com.

10 9 8 7 6 5 4 3 2 1

Library of Congress Control Number: 2014960099

Jacket illustration and design by Sean Jun

Print ISBN: 978-1-940456-27-0
Ebook ISBN 978-1-940456-31-7
Printed in the United States of America

This is a work of fiction. Any names, locations, or references to the outside world are purely coincidental.

This novel is dedicated to Lee Maracle, for convincing me that I couldn't write; to Albert Moritz, for convincing me that I could; and to Maiko Takemoto, for her unwavering faith and support throughout its writing.

PART 1
CASH

1

AMON'S APARTMENT

A pane of darkness descended on the room for an instant, blacking out the hazy image of a man sitting in a garden, like a curtain falling on a mid-performance stage.

These fleeting slivers of absence came and went intermittently, relentlessly, and Amon Kenzaki did his best to fight them off for as long as he could bear, in the hopes of filling his bank account. But it wasn't easy, even for him.

For the umpteenth time, the man in the garden said: "Blinking is money. Blinking is choice. Blink less to save yourself, to save yourself, to save your moneeee—" He extended the final vowel, humming it in monotone until his voice grew crackly and he ran out of breath.

Sitting alone on a chair in his apartment, Amon was taking an online blink reduction seminar. By mastering this simple method, the promotional video had promised, students could reduce their number of blinks per minute and, with daily practice, retrain their eyelids until blinking less frequently became automatic.

The man in the garden was called "the guru." No one seemed to care if he had another name, least of all Amon. He had richly-tanned skin and long silken hair tied in a ponytail. He sat on an emerald green rug, his legs crossed with each foot resting on the opposite thigh, his hands stacked palms down on his lap and his eyes half-closed. A gray shawl, with a pattern of lustrous, burgundy stitching looping elegantly along the edges, was wrapped diagonally over his right shoulder and around his waist. In front of him was a still, clear pond. Behind, lush ferns bowed out of porcelain flower pots the size of kegs. The pond reflected the guru's seated form along with the garden background. The reflection and the original evenly split Amon's visual field top to bottom, forming a symmetrical double-image like a mandala. This scene was projected for Amon on his eyescreen, a display integrated with his eyes, appearing as a semitransparent overlay on the cream-colored walls of his room. Every time he blinked it disappeared for a fraction of a second and returned.

"Find the space without space where the eyelid meets the brow," said the guru. "There in the emptiness you will find the frugal mind, the parsimonious mind, the creditable mind."

Amon sat motionless on a fold-up chair with his spine straight, his feet flat on the floor, and his palms resting on his thighs while listening intently to the lesson. As instructed, he focused on the top of his eyelids. The trick was to keep the eyes open until they felt dry but close them just before they started to sting. Close too early and the time until the next blink would be that much shorter. Wait too long and the body would detect strain and compensate by making the eyes more sensitive, hastening the onset of stinging in the next blink cycle and spurring a premature shut. But with consummate timing, the duration of the dry sensation could be extended to its limit, and with successful repetition, the eyes would gradually adjust, incrementally postponing stinging and lengthening the period between each blink nanosecond by nanosecond.

After a few minutes of silence, the guru repeated his mantra: "Blinking is money. Blinking is choice. Blink less to save yourself, to save yourself, to save your moneeee—" Many voices joined in unison with the guru, layering over and amplifying his voice. Unlike the other students participating from their various locations, Amon remained silent. The website audio settings made the guru's voice loudest, and the heavily-accented Japanese he spoke stood out in the mix. It was difficult for Amon to identify what kind of accent. It might have been Indian; it might have been Chinese; it might also have been German, or a hybrid of all three. Whatever the origin, distinctive pronunciation and intonation endowed the guru with a certain exotic authority, as though coming from a distant, undefined land were a prerequisite to be an authentic master of frugality. The guru went quiet, leaving the students to chant without him. Placid intensity seemed to radiate from his tanned forehead, as though he were deeply focused on something . . . perhaps his eyelids.

"Blinking is money." Amon reflected on this phrase. The wording was a bit crude, but he had to admit the statement was true. More blinking=less money. Less blinking=more money. Like every other action, blinking was a kind of intellectual property, the usage of which required payment of a licensing fee. Every time he blinked, jumped, sang, downloaded music, played hopscotch, ate a waffle, or did anything by choice, the network of sensors and chips implanted invisibly under his skin detected the corresponding muscle movement and nerve signals. This embodied computer system—his BodyBank—then transferred the action-data to GATA, which checked who owned the rights to the action-property at that moment and gave them permission to withdraw the money instantly from his account.

A single blink wasn't all that expensive. In fact, compared to other daily actions like walking and eating, the price of each blink in the action-transaction marketplace was relatively cheap. But people were incessantly blinking, thought Amon, and the costs added up like grains of sand falling one by one through an hourglass until, before you knew it, a significant portion of creditime had been spent.

Differentiating the sensation of dryness from stinging and antici-pating the critical moment before one changed to the other required a subtle awareness that took weeks to cultivate, and full habituation of the eyes took many months more. This meant a sizeable investment of creditime, but it seemed worth it to Amon. According to PennyPinch, his accounting consultant application, the cost of tuition would be paid off in one month if he could cut down by a quarter blink per minute—a conservative estimate given that the website promotional video had promised a reduction by two.

However adept he became though, blinking costs could never be brought to zero. A certain portion of every day required the use of sight—working and commuting hours at the bare minimum—during which time blinking was inevitable; and, as Amon was pained to admit, any attempt to keep his eyes constantly peeled would be overridden by reflexes that protected them from damage. Keeping the eyes closed too long—even while resting—was equally risky in its own way, as GATA might interpret this as *sleeping, napping, daydreaming,* or some such action even more pricey than *blinking.* Amon remembered an era when *squinting* had been the trendy alternative in cost-cutting circles, but the fee had risen over the years perhaps due to increased demand, making this approach no longer feasible. Easy shortcuts were invariably false trails when it came to budgeting. The essence of deep frugality was devoted training; meticulously honing choices in the narrow realm of volition left for Free Citizens between involuntary bodily functions and the uncontrollable world, as though walking a tightrope between the twin precipices of fate.

Without changing his upright posture, the guru picked up a handful of lavender petals from a straw basket at his left side and tossed them into the pond. The petals fluttered briefly in the air as they fell, bleached almost white in the sunlight, before landing gently in the water. Circular ripples expanded outwards from each impact point, colliding with each other and breaking into fragments of intersecting arcs that wavered on the verge of dissolution. Some petals remained floating on the elastic tension of the water's surface, and others, located at the meeting point of multiple subtle waves, were engulfed by the gentle sloshing and sank slowly out of sight.

"Don't give in to the craving mind, the spending mind, the bankrupt mind. Embrace the frugal mind, the parsimonious mind, the creditable mind."

Amon had been sitting still so long there was now a kink in his neck, and his buttocks felt numb from the pressure of his own weight against the hard plastic seat, but he would not give in to the spending mind and resisted *fidgeting* even the slightest. Some tenets of the guru's philosophy, like prohibitions on eating yeast and sleeping with pillows, Amon found difficult to accept. And he felt no solidarity with the anonymous students whose voices he heard, as they seemed to believe that chanting out loud was a meritorious deed that would one day reap pecuniary rewards while Amon saw such *vocalization* as a senseless waste of money. Instead, he preferred to recite in his mind, the only domain in existence where all actions were complimentary.

Superstitions aside, the guru's techniques were great allies in the battle for thrift. He also offered a breath reduction course that Amon had completed the previous winter. With daily practice he had managed to bring his total monthly expenses down by 0.06 percent, a result he found very satisfying. He had also enrolled in the guru's voiding and urination reduction courses, but withdrew when these actions were nationalized, making them a part of the public domain and no longer subject to licensing fees. Headed by the great leader Lawrence Barrow, the ruling Moderate Choice Party was pushing for nationalization of blinking, insisting it was not truly volitional but merely an autonomic physiological function. This gave Amon some hope that all the guru's methods might one day become obsolete, allowing him to invest his creditime elsewhere. Yet fierce debate raged on with the Absolute Choice Party, which opposed such policies to increase spending and pushed instead for privatization of *heartbeating*. With no resolution to the wrangling in sight—

The guru whipped his right hand out and snatched at the air before him, as though sensing Amon's wandering mind floating there and wrenching him back to attention. The ripples in the pond had dissipated, and the few petals remaining on the surface bobbed and swayed softly.

Amon tried to dissolve his discreditable thoughts and pay attention to his eyelids, but something was nagging at him, and this time it wasn't perennial political issues. He usually took pride in his ability to focus—his concentration test score had been perfect after all, a rare achievement only matched by prodigies like Chief Executive Minister Lawrence Barrow. But today something was wrong. Extraneous thoughts crept into his mind like worms into a dark burrow. The more effort he put into blocking them out, reinforcing the cave walls, the more persistently they encroached, squirming and gnawing ravenously at whatever he paid attention to. Meanwhile, his blinks kept firing off rapidly irrespective of his intentions, like a camera shutter gone haywire.

It had been almost twelve hours since he'd contacted Rick and still there was no answer. *But if I don't hear back soon then . . . And what if he . . .* a rampant swarm of fears and apprehensions disrupted his attempts to change the mental subject and direct conscious efforts back at his blinking.

Reluctantly accepting his lack of clarity, Amon did a combination of slight twitches with his right index and middle finger. The sensors in his hand recognized the command for *close window* and the scene of the guru disappeared. All that remained was the unmade futon at his feet, the cream wall ahead, and his action-transaction readout, a small box of text in the bottom right corner of his eye that inexorably recorded his lifetime of enacted choices and their ever-fluctuating price. Without moving his head, Amon glanced at the readout:

Property	Fee	Time	Licensor
...	...	...	...
Blink	¥535	06:45:45	Xian Te
Blink	¥490	06:45:50	Xian Te
Exhale	¥1,010	06:45:51	LYS Dynamics
Close vid	¥2,354	06:45:51	Kavipal
Blink	¥589	06:45:56	TTY Group
Blink	¥535	06:46:02	Xian Te
Inhale	¥430	06:46:04	TTY Group
Check AT Readout	¥1,237	06:46:04	Latoni Sedo
Blink	¥601	06:46:10	R-Lite
...	...	...	...

He watched as the owner of blink rapidly changed hands: first it was Xian Te, then the TTY Group, then R-Lite, all within thirty seconds. These companies were based outside Japan, so the licensing fees had to be paid in their respective foreign currency. Amon kept the money in his checking account diversified, so that his smart trading application, CleverBarter, could automatically pay his bills in the currency with the best exchange rate at that moment. But Amon had set the readout to display fees in the equivalent Japanese yen value, which he found more intuitive. The price for each execution of *blinking* bounced around constantly, although for the time being it never strayed far from five-hundred yen. This was actually a misleadingly low price, Amon knew. It had to be corrected for early morning economic stagnation. By the time afternoon inflation kicked in, all licensing fees would be much higher, perhaps exponentially higher depending on how badly the morning market crashes went. Amon activated PennyPinch to help him tally his blink expenses that morning. The result appeared immediately.

His performance was poor: in fact, the blink frequency had been slightly above his average. Amon sighed.

Amon hated sighing, but whenever he failed to be frugal, bone-deep guilt and disappointment overcame him, and the urge became irresistible. *Sighing* was dangerous for him. It was an expensive act that wasted his funds and amped up his guilt further, which in turn made him want to sigh again. If he wasn't careful, he could get caught in an unending spiral of sighing about sighs about sighs that would plunge him into the pit of bankruptcy. Of course nothing approaching this had ever happened. He had never sighed more than twice in a row. Yet the downward sigh spiral was his deepest fear, something that might have manifested in his nightmares, if his sleeping life had been filled with anything other than the dream, the only dream he ever had anymore . . .

For some reason, he found himself wondering what it would be like to be the wall before him. The wall had no impulses to quell or desires to prioritize. No incentives to succeed, nor consequences if it didn't. Admittedly it also had no BodyBank, and Amon could hardly envy existence without money and freedom. (He might as well have envied bankrupts!) All the same, he found himself wishing the wall would imbibe his consciousness with just a taste of its droning, dull stasis.

Soon a circular patch of skin on the center of his belly began to vibrate and the ding of a twentieth century cash register went off, his alarm telling him it was creditime to head off for work.

2

A TOKYO SUBWAY

The salarymen and office ladies were crammed together so tight on the train it was as though their bodies had fused into one; a thousand-headed beast swaying to and fro with each acceleration and deceleration, each bump or snag on the track. Vertical poles were installed near the doors, and plastic loops hung in rows from two rails running in parallel along the length of the ceiling, but many commuters were stranded out of reach from these handholds. A cluster of them leaned on Amon for support as he stood gripping an overhead rail with two hands, his body an integral strand binding the disparate fibers of this amalgamated organism.

A foot or so taller than most, Amon looked out over a dense headscape topped with trim haircuts. The supporting necks poked up from white collars drawn tight with conservatively-patterned ties and edged with dark jacket lapels. Despite their expressions of stifled discomfort and vacant denial of their surroundings, every one of these commuters, men and women alike, managed to look exquisitely good. All eyes were clear and animated, all hair was lustrous and meticulously set, all lips were moist and vibrant, all teeth straight and gleaming white, all features in just the right proportion, size and arrangement to bring out that person's best qualities. They were so impeccably beautiful you could take any person at random, magnify their skin a hundredfold, and it would look just as glassy smooth, without bumps, misplaced hairs or even pores.

This supernaturally attractive crowd was visible to Amon by way of the ImmaNet, a global communication network that matched up the world seen by the naked eye with a veneer of graphics and information *infoseen* by the eyescreen integrated into every Free Citizen's retina. Using a kind of software called digimake, it was easy to design a personalized overlay and attach it to your body, as though sketching a portrait on tracing paper, modifying it, and pasting it atop the model. When the people around Amon moved, the ImmaNet ensured their digimade appearance moved with them, the digital world inextricably bound to its naked counterpart. There were no bad hair days, no bulging veins, no sunspots or hairy moles, no red eye, yellow teeth, dangling nose-hairs or crooked smiles, no crumpled shirts, mismatched ties or poorly-fitted suits. Average faces were coded with distinction, strange faces averaged into charm, the power of digimake cleansing the metropolis of ugliness like the alchemical light of some esthetic deity.

Yet the ImmaNet was limited to only two senses—sight and hearing—and Amon's sense of touch belied the spectacle. Nowhere could he see even a dab of fat; every office lady either voluptuous or slender, every salaryman brawny or slim. But he could feel flab and untoned muscle pressing in all around him: a squishy love handle on his side, a soft bicep on his belly, a sagging breast on the small of his back.

The air was filled with the scent of perfume, spray-on deodorant, and mild halitosis. Jets of A/C continuously blasted the top of his head, still sweaty from his walk through humid streets to the train station a few minutes earlier. This injected an almost nauseating chill into his blood, yet soothed the heat seeping from his cocoon of clammy fabric-covered flesh.

Amon had his arms upraised in front of him, his hands gripping the cold metal rail overhead. He allowed his torso to lean with the train's juddering momentum but kept his feet firmly planted on the floor, never *stepping* from his spot, while he focused on his diaphragm in keeping with the breath reduction method he had mastered. To make up for his failure at blink reduction back in his apartment, it was imperative that he utilize these spare minutes in transit effectively and limit inessential actions. Amon believed in living in the now.

Breath reduction was very much like blink reduction, in that it was all about finding the golden mean. First, he made each breath long, but not so long that GATA would register it as *deep breathing*, a relatively expensive action. A breath was marked as "deep" after a precise amount of time (specified by the definition of the action-property) had elapsed since it was initiated. Through repeated practice, Amon had drilled this duration into his nerves until he developed a visceral intuition of exactly when to stop, so that respiration would be maximally drawn out without ever quite being deep.

At the same time, he regulated the pauses between the beginning and end of each inhalation and exhalation. Once again, the trick was balance: the pauses had to be lengthened, but never so long as to be registered as *holding breath*, another expensive action. Successful pausing also required subtle awareness of air hunger. Like the sensation of dryness in the eyes, the sensation of air hunger was a sign of impending reflexes that would jack up average breath frequency and safeguard homeostasis. According to the guru, the timing of the onset of air hunger varied from individual to individual and, after months of training, Amon had finally discovered his personal ideal. He could halt his lungs right up until the moment just before the action was labeled as *holding breath*, but by about the third or fourth consecutive breath cycle, he always detected a premonition of air hunger and knew that for the next few breaths he had to stop slightly earlier. Ever striving to calibrate his respiration into a more cost-effective pattern, he manipulated the muscles around his solar plexus, gently guiding their expansion and contraction, stoppering the faintest whispers of physiological imbalance before they could amplify into profligate nervous system echoes.

All over the train car interior—on the walls, windows, and handrails; the seats, bag-rack and floor; in every space visible between, above and below the tight horde of bodies—a kaleidoscope of advertainment squirmed. In an effort to ignore it, Amon stared at the back of a woman standing a few paces in front of him. She was wearing a navy blue blazer, her light brown hair falling loose to just below her shoulders. He kept his eyes fixed on a point a few centimeters beneath the tips of her hair, pretending the light and color dancing in his peripheral wasn't there. Yet even still, he caught fleeting glimpses out of the corner of his eye. An apple with an eardrum pulsated to a silent beat; a group of women sat at a sleek white bar before dark green smoothies laughing uproariously; a penguin waddled alone through a department store with a Koku brand cigar sticking from its mouth. These myriad fragments of story and image were rendered in dynamic 3D, indistinguishable from the vistas of naked perception. They appeared within frames of different shapes and sizes that covered every inch of the surfaces, like shards of a broken mirror that had cobbled themselves together, a shuffling mosaic of jagged portals to alternate realms.

Lone tableaux and snippets of scenes leapt from their display fragments into the edges of Amon's visual field in quick succession, like lightning flashes only half seen. Two male hands shaking firmly against a tropical ocean backdrop; a tortoise on wooden floorboards watching a form hidden beneath white sheets pump up and down; the truncated, triangular squiggles of the Kavipal logo. One after the other, they tried to grab his attention, but the attempt was in vain. Never for a moment did Amon look away from the navy blue fabric, for that would have meant wasting his money. The ImmaNet was constantly detecting the focal point of his eyes and charging him for the image rights of whatever he looked at. This would have included the woman, except she had waived the licensing fees for her back unlike the advertising agencies that managed chunks of the train, as people were generally sociable and wanted to encourage friendly attention, whereas companies were confident that their content could enthrall viewers into paying their rates and using their actions.

Such confidence was misplaced in Amon's case, however, because he had configured his privacy settings to hide all his personal information. This allowed him to elude the powerful marketing algorithms that controlled how the InfoFlux presented itself from one instant to the next. Usually these programs displayed a different selection of content to each individual depending on their preferences, goals, vital signs, mood, age, job, gender. They then recorded the frequency and length of time each item was viewed, calculated viewing tendencies, and used the result to provide a new bundle of content the following second. This attention analysis loop ensured that material displayed to any one person was the best possible match for their desires at that moment. But since Amon kept marketers in the dark about who he was, their algorithms could only work with anonymous factors like location, date, and time of day. As a result, the majority of what he saw on that rush hour train was geared towards the "working professional," not specifically to him. He realized that in configuring his settings this way, he was sacrificing his chance to inhabit a personally meaningful world; a world always funny to him, exciting to him, moving to him, full of wit and art and drama, and miraculous goods he never knew he wanted. But a meaningful world was a distracting world, and distractions were inimical to frugality. By increasing the chances that things in his vicinity were boring, Amon ensured that they were much easier to ignore. Admittedly, flicking his eyes away from the woman's back to watch something—anything—would have been more interesting than the dull fabric of her blazer, but that was where willpower came in. After every exhalation, Amon checked the alignment of his eye-line in relation to her shoulders, correcting the slightest drift in any direction by bringing it back to center.

Accompanying the amorphous promosurround, a spastic audio clash—like the simultaneous playback of infinite microphones placed at every point in time and space—whispered in Amon's ears. Every second, distinct sounds would rise out of this faint infoblather and grow in volume—a syllable, a clack, a symphonic gasp—synched with the segments pelting the fringes of his vision. In the background, he could hear the people around him mumbling, and see them twitching their hands as they entered BodyBank commands, all engaged in some online diversion. Sometimes he felt their eyes on him too.

The frequent glances and occasional stares of strangers used to make Amon uncomfortable, but he was used to it now, having learned years ago to accept that he stood out, even amongst this edited crowd. This was partly because of his stature and exotic looks. Height was something difficult to fake without heels or platform shoes, since you had to pay by the millimeter to the company that owned the right to increase it, and his facial features would have been a fortune to render graphically if he hadn't been born this way. Going on what he'd heard about his origin, and that wasn't much, Amon was of Persian and Japanese descent. His dark hair buzzed short, his skin light brown, he had a softly-rounded, longish nose above a thin line of moustache. Most distinguishing of all was his combination of double-folded Asian eyelids and greenish-blue eyes, kindled with an acute, almost daring glint that contrasted with his serious demeanor. Enhanced with digimake—his joined eyebrows divided and elegantly arced, the stretched pores in his cheeks left by teenage acne filled in like potholes, his slightly off-kilter front teeth reoriented, the curvature of his cheeks streamlined for greater symmetry—Amon was undeniably intriguing.

But more than this, what most drew curious glances and sometimes stares was his uniform. Over his lithe torso and long but powerfully-toned limbs, he wore a gray suit with a gray shirt and a gray tie, as though tailored out of pure concrete. The letters "GATA" printed in jagged lavender font on the right breast. It was an oddly bland uniform for the most feared profession in the Free World, but the outfit made up for deficiencies in design with usefulness. From a distance it was inconspicuous, a shade of nethercolor the eye dismissed as irrelevant, a mere shadow of the city amidst the flood of images. Up close, when the spectator noticed that the gray was full body, it was immediately recognizable, instilling terror in those who took his presence as a sign their time had come. No one in the vicinity of Amon showed special deference, but they all knew what he was and Amon sensed their gut tension. A gray uniform meant Liquidators, and Liquidators meant . . .

An announcement politely gave the name of the next stop and the train began to slow. Amon glanced at his AT readout and had PennyPinch calculate his respiration rate. For the past several minutes it was below his average, and even approached his personal record. He was beginning to feel proud of himself for redeeming his earlier failure with blinking, when thinking about this failure reminded him of what had caused it and his mind turned again towards Rick. Anxious thoughts began to tug insistently on his focus, dragging it off his breathing.

When the image of a solar cowboy and a winged princess flickered into view, Amon turned his head up to look straight at its source, hoping that by losing himself in advertainment he might evade his worries. Emerging from a warped, asymmetrical octagon in the ceiling, the cowboy gazed at the horizon of a turquoise desert landscape as three red suns rose. He wore a leather vest over a dark green shirt, sunglasses with red transparent lenses, and a sleek blaster in a holster at each hip. The blonde-haired princess stood beside him and sprayed her bleach-white teeth with a lipstick-sized canister, the light glittering on the pink tinsel of her dress.

"I been all cross this galaxy," drawled the cowboy. "From the Dragon Nebula to the Plasma Sea, and I've never seen anything sparkle like yer smile." He looked the princess in the eyes and she smiled again, flapping her wings bashfully and giving her teeth another spray. A hyperlink for a website where the spray could be downloaded appeared in the sky above her head.

A flaming asteroid hurtled through the stars towards the turquoise planet . . .

He wouldn't seriously . . . not today . . . Amon's internal monologue interrupted. Despite his efforts to get entertained, it chattered on and on. In a last act of desperation, he tried to combine this monologue with the audio and visuals of the space opera, the sensation of cold air and warm bodies, the smell of perfume and bad breath, the feeling of eyes on him, the frustration at his failure, melding sensations and thoughts and emotions in his consciousness to create an incoherent synesthetic noise that could not interfere with the frugal task at hand. *Don't give in to the bankrupt mind!* But it was no good. His attention refused to stay on his lungs.

Guilt welled up inside him and he sighed, then immediately regretted it, as the fear of a downward sigh spiral took hold. But before a second sigh came on, the train rolled to a stop, the doors opened, and Amon felt the crowd shift around him as spurts of passengers made their way off.

When a new load of passengers had squashed him into place and the train started forward again, Amon did a few rhythmic finger gestures to pull up his contact book. A list of names appeared as faint translucent text over the boxed headscape. He scrolled down and clicked on Rick Ferro. Ignoring his friend's profile stills and description, Amon pulled up his map. When he saw where Rick was, his guilt and fear evaporated, and were immediately replaced by a new, stronger emotion: anger. On an abstract, bird's-eye-view diagram of the city, a red dot blinked over one complex. It was Rick's apartment building in Kiyosumi. He was still at home and would undoubtedly be late for work if he didn't leave within a few seconds. The very idea was outrageous, and Amon clenched the handrail tight in his fists.

In his head, he tried to roughly calculate the cost of *calling* Rick, given the current level of inflation. He knew they were long overdue for a talk, but had been putting it off and putting it off and putting it off. Whenever he thought of the immense fees just for *dialing* and *hanging up*, not to mention all the *speaking*, he froze up. As the weeks and months passed, the problem had only worsened. Finally, the previous evening he had broken down and texted him, but it had been more than twelve hours and there was still no response. Amon didn't like being ignored under regular circumstances, but today was an important day and he took this as an exceptional insult.

Amon had been waiting patiently long enough.

He traced a tiny circle in the air with his thumb and pointer finger. A keyboard appeared in front of him and he brought his right hand down from the pole to begin typing, his fingers striking air.

RCK. U THAIR? WI NEEED 2 TAWK.

When texting, Amon intentionally wrote in garbled Japanese, as the cost of proper writing was higher. All imaginable strings of text had been patented, with phrases in commonly used languages the most expensive, recognizable derivatives of these slightly less so, and gibberish the cheapest of all. To save money, Amon entered the wrong ideograms, omitted and reordered phonetic characters, mixed in Roman letters, and added redundant script as needed. Misspelling everything while still managing to create intelligible sentences required a certain knack, but was at least as fast as regular typing once it became habitual, and the cost of the occasional extra character was more than offset by the overall savings on words. Scrambling grammar too could be a bargain, but Amon usually didn't go that far, except occasionally when he wanted to make up for a particularly discreditable day.

Amon waited a few moments, but there was no response. He couldn't imagine what was holding Rick up. The man was supposed to be getting ready for work and all he had to do was send a quick response. Unless . . . anxiety gripped his bowels, and he air-typed rapidly.

DIJU FERGAYT? 2DEH IZ EVALUAYSHON DEH. AZ YER FREND & YER BAWSS, AYM BAYGIN U. PLEEZ B AWN TAIM!

After a few breaths and blinks, Amon fired off several more texts and tried facephoning him, but it just kept ringing and ringing. Having run out of options, he opened his favorite decision forum—Career Calibration—for advice on what to do next, and posted a brief query describing his conundrum:

HAI AWL,

MAI BAYST FREND & AI HAV BEEEN WERKING 2GETHER FER SEVIN YEERZ. WWE ALWAYZ GAWT ALAWNG GRAYT, & WERKT WAYL AZ AA TEEM. BUUT NAUW AIV BEEEN PRAMOTED & POOT EEN CHARRGE UV HEEM, & REESENTLY HEEZ BEEEN LAYT FER WERK & WAYSTING TAIM @ THA AWFIS. SINSE AIM HIZ BAWS, HIZ SLAKKING WIIL EEMPACT MAI PERFFORMANS EEVOWLUAYSHON.

2DEH IZ THA DEH WEE GAYT AUWR REZULTS & AI WAWNTED 2 MAYK SHUR HEEZ AWN TAIM, SOE AI TAYXTED HEEM LAAST NAIT & KALLED HEEM DIS MORNIN BAAT HI HAZNT RESPAWNDED. AI CHEKKED HIZ LOKAYSHON AWN THA MAAP & EEF HII DUZNT LEEV NAOW, HIIL DEHFINATELY BII LAYT. FER HIZ SAYK & MINNE, WAT SHOOD AI DOO NAYXT?

THAYNKS AZ ALWAYZ,

AMAWN

Responses began to pour in immediately:

WHY NOT THREATEN TO FIRE HIM! NO FRIEND WOULD JEOPAR-DIZE HIS FRIEND'S JOB LIKE THAT . . .
    IT SOUNDS LIKE HE'S A CLOSE FRIEND OF YOURS. I THINK HE'LL REALIZE IT HIMSELF. WHY NOT WAIT FOR A SHORT WHILE AND . . .

Since signing up for Career Calibration several years ago, Amon had been regularly paring down his list of friends. Only those who gave consistently useful advice could comment on his posts. Even still, he had thousands of friends and there were immediately hundreds of responses. With no time to read them all before his stop, he activated SiftAssist. This application outsourced his comments to sift teams who scanned them for redundancy using specialized search engines, summarizing and categorizing each post according to content. In their haste to skim numerous orders in a limited time frame, the poorly paid sifters frequently glossed over nuanced turns of phrase, ignored crucial passages, erroneously grouped unrelated text, and totally missed sarcasm. But when confronted with a garbage heap of noise, they did a halfway-decent job of picking out the scraps of signal. Within seconds, the application had boiled all the comments down to six pieces of advice, which he reposted on the forum to see what his decision friends would recommend. In an instant their votes had been tallied:

1. Manifest in front of him right now and tell him to hurry 38%
2. Ask your boss to transfer him to another section 23%
3. Threaten to assign him menial jobs if he doesn't fly straight 19%
4. Ask to be transferred to another section 12%
5. Let things take their course and focus on improving your results 7%
6. Other (kill your friend, quit your job, drink it off, etc.) 1%

Despite the popularity of option 1, Amon was reluctant to carry it out, and decided to consider the other alternatives before making his choice. He quickly eliminated option 2. Requesting a transfer would imply to the upper management that Rick was slacking. Amon was upset, but he wasn't about to go and get his friend fired—not yet anyways. Next he eliminated option 4. Transferring would mean abandoning his new position as Identity Executioner, since there was only one in each squad. Given Rick's personality, Amon knew option 3 would fire up his rebellious tendencies and rebound him deeper into truancy. The path of least resistance approach, option 5, was too risky and he promptly blocked the users who made suggestions grouped under option 6, which were too radical or absurd.

When he was done eliminating the other options, he reflected on 1 more carefully. At first he didn't like it. In addition to being expensive, it would require violating Rick's privacy, and that was something he really didn't want to do.

Amon knew if he clicked on one of the commuters in his vicinity, the amount of information that popped up would vary. While most Free Citizens were willing to share certain details with marketers, sharing with strangers was a different story. Some people might allow Amon access to their name and city of residence, others added hobbies and a personality description, and the occasional exhibitionist might share their nude photos, fetishes, costume of choice, and similar quirks. But Amon took his right to anonymity seriously, knowing full well how valuable personal information was on the phishing blackmarket, and refused to disclose even the bare minimum. Complete strangers who browsed his public profile would find it empty. He allowed them to access his premium profile for a fee, but it displayed only his name. His acquaintance profile additionally listed his favorite music and most-frequented websites, but also required payment. To avoid alienating potential connections, his professional profile was complimentary, but contained only his job title, qualifications, and a speech about his goals.

Yet Amon had nothing to hide from Rick. He had given him full access to his entire inner profile and Rick had returned the gesture in kind. They could view each other's LifeStream, blogs, fingerprints, blood type, allergies, retina pattern, DNA—you name it, they shared it. Such deep reciprocal trust was a rare treasure in the Free World, where information was advantage, and Amon didn't want to abuse it. To carry out option 1, he would have to use the spatial location listed in Rick's inner profile, disclosed in good faith, and manifest his perspective into his home. But Rick wasn't responding to messages, which meant he didn't want to be found. If Amon barged in to scold him for being late at a time like this, Rick might take it as an imposing and presumptuous abuse of their intimacy. Factor in the costs of the ensuing communication, and it was looking downright crazy. But the more Amon thought about it, the more he came to see 1 as the only viable plan; figuring that if his many decision friends hadn't thought of something better, it probably didn't exist.

The train slowed down with a jerk as it approached the next stop, sending Amon lurching forward in step with the bodies around him. The weight of the crowd leaning from behind pushed him right onto his toes. In that instant, he imagined himself toppling over, sinking to the floor, and being trampled under thousands of dress shoes, but quickly the momentum swung back and he regained his balance. At times like these, the spots on his body where others pressed against him felt like octopus suckers draining away his funds, and Amon was grateful that train companies subsidized licensing fees for *touching* to give passengers riding incentive. Although most Tokyo professionals did their jobs online from their apartments, the mall, the golf course, the salon—wherever they happened to be—some still had to commute to work for various reasons, and with the population of the metropolis being as dense as it was, this was enough to ensure the trains were filled way beyond capacity. Amon had been required to go in to the office ever since he started out at GATA seven years earlier, since the comparatively strict security systems only gave network access to those present inside, and when he was squashed in like this, he almost wished he could work from home like the others. But he dismissed this desire by reminding himself about the increasingly competitive worksphere, and the way it was demanding ever more commitment from telework employees. With accounting revisions urgently needed at 3 a.m., sales strategy brainstorms held on the toilet, and hourly quality control seminars interrupting vacations, corporate duties had invaded their lives so thoroughly that the distinction between private and work time hardly existed anymore. Many specialists said that this was a major factor behind the rising prevalence of mental disorders and suicides, and while the disorders were fine because pharmaceutical companies had a range of lucrative cures that would feed the economy, the suicides were considered a serious issue. All told, Amon preferred the crowds and their touching costs to such occupational hazards, and could only do his best to cope.

Reopening the map, he zoomed in on the red dot. A simplified outline of the apartment layout came into view: a living room, kitchen, bedroom, and veranda. The dot was located at Rick's front door. Amon copied the coordinates into his manifestation app of choice—Teleport Surprise—and clicked to engage.

Amon shifted his whole audio and visual feed to a graphical copy of his body that now stood in Rick's apartment: he could feel his clammy skin on the swaying warm flesh in the cold A/C'd air and smell the perfumed human stink, but couldn't hear or see any of it.

Teleport Surprise had plunked him into the living room with his back to the entrance. Walls of dark brown clay rose up from a floor covered in rugs of tightly-matted reeds. Above, a ceiling of the same clay sloped diagonally upwards to a sunroof in the dead center. Windows stretched across the far end, with curtains of brownish fur from some animal of cold climes—like grizzly or wolverine—drawn aside. Outside he could see a river lined with trees and crossed by golden bridges like rings over a blue finger. In the middle of the room was a wide sofa of purple leather covered in a dull green pattern of spear-hunting figures. A huge aloe vera plant reared its vigorously ramified branches over the sofa-back, and miniature palms in slim glass vases stood on each side, their roots soaking in a clear red liquid like diluted pomegranite juice. On the left, a fireplace of smooth, silver-gray rock holding two charred logs opened from the wall. On the right, through a crack in an open door, a haphazard tangle of sheets and pillows hung suspended in a king-size hammock of shimmering silk threads.

Amon had heard that Rick recently moved from the grimy bowels of Ueno to verdant Kiyosumi, but had never before seen his new apartment. He was both stunned and appalled by the wild, sumptuous decor. There was no way Rick could afford such extravagance on their Liquidator's salary, less so with his job on the line.

Amon bent his pinky to turn his perspective towards the front door and started in surprise, the force of his movement jostling the passengers around him. Instead of Rick there was a bundle of hair, clothing, and intertwined limbs. It was two people—not one—and Amon's surprise quickly changed to horror when he realized what their bodies were doing: they were hugging.

Rick had his right arm around a woman's shoulders, his left forearm vertically cradling the back of her head. She was a head shorter than him, and he crouched down to nestle his face into the nape of her neck, tufts of his tousled hair pointing straight at Amon. The woman, whose back was to Amon, had one arm wrapped behind Rick's chest and the other behind his waist. Amon couldn't see her face, buried as it was into

Rick's torso, but he noticed her hair: a remarkable shimmering brown. Something stirred in his memory.

Rick and the woman had yet to notice the figment of Amon standing there, and he decided to wait a few moments, hoping they would extricate from each other.

The train stopped. Amon felt bodies brush past, then space opened up around him, and a force pushed from one direction (that he guessed was of the doors) before everyone molded back into place. Still Rick and the woman clung, and listening closely, Amon could hear across the living room their deep, quivering breaths and a low-pitched *mmm* that made his spine crawl.

In his lifetime, Amon had enjoyed heaps of porn, acclimatizing him to harshly exultant panting, passionate moans, and vulgar pillowtalk. Yet the humming of Rick and his partner had an unfamiliar resonance, suggesting not lust but a kind of tenderness. To Amon's ears, it seemed to carry dangerous overtones, like a time-bomb counting down with the eerie jingle of a wind-up music box. All actions concerned with dating were expensive: the purchase of bouquets, the writing of romantic poetry, dinners by candlelight. They were so expensive, in fact, that many lovers only met online; website marriage being a common practice amongst the middle class and long distance artificial insemination popular amongst the wealthy. On special occasions when face-to-face meetings did happen, Amon thought it foolish to waste creditime on holding hands, snuggling, kissing, and other behavior with a poor cost-to-stimulation ratio. He understood the need for foreplay, but it was prudent to limit minimally arousing acts so as to reserve funding for frequent, satisfying consummation . . . and this hug was going on far too long. He could almost smell the odor of sexual frustration and monetary irresponsibility drifting through the room (even though his olfactory senses were elsewhere, amongst the perfumed human stink).

RCK! Amon typed, but there was no reaction. Amon tried again. RCK. PLEEZ!!! Still nothing. Rick's message alert must have been set to silent, meaning there was nothing Amon could do. Unless that is, he sent a message through his work account and bypassed the block. Sensing the awkward timing, Amon was tempted to leave the lovebirds alone and return his perspective to the train. That would be the polite thing to do.

But this compassionate impulse was overwhelmed by a rising panic, like acidic light congealing in his veins. *Backing off now*, said a frantic inner voice, *would mean leaving Rick in his spacious* (read "extravagant") *new apartment to hug forever* (already about one minute and thirty seconds by Amon's count) *when he was already running late for the billionth time* (on evaluation day no less). If Rick wasn't punctual, Amon might lose the respect of GATA's upper executives. He might lose bonuses and promotions. Lose his job. His dream. Everything.

RCK. KIIP YER HANZ TUE YERSAYLF. EETS TAIM FER WERK! Amon sent an official text with an emergency tag. He had wanted to be diplomatic, but the months of pent up tension had exploded. Rick's shoulder muscles bristled like a startled cat. He disengaged his arms from the woman and raised his head from her neck to meet Amon's gaze.

Like Amon, Rick wore the Liquidator uniform of concrete gray. Built like a cone stood on its tip, he always kept his long, slim legs placed close together, his hips went out slightly wider, and his muscled shoulders were the broadest of all. His hair was golden-brown, bangs swept to the right over his forehead and the sides stylishly disheveled; his long chin slightly pointed with a cute little dab of fat on the end like the pads on a cat's paw; his nose thin and longish; his eyebrows thick and straight; the white skin of his cheeks tinged with a healthy flush. Overall he was handsome, but his looks were marred somewhat by a brooding depth in his light brown eyes, always seeming to hint at some half-forgotten tragedy. Reacting to Rick's abrupt withdrawal, the woman tilted her head to look in his eyes, rippling her remarkable, shimmering hair.

"What's wrong?" she asked. Her voice, like her hair, was uncannily familiar.

AMON? texted Rick, his eyes wide and twitching with alert. WHAT ARE YOU DOING?

U EEGNORED MAI MAYSAJ LAYST NAIT & DIDNT PIKK UUP 2DEH. WAI R U STIL HEER EEN YER APPARTMAYNT? WBLOJ!* DU U HAYV–

Amon's airtyping was cut short when the woman let go of Rick, turned around and their eyes met.

He couldn't believe it was her after all these years. The petite physique: her breasts small but upright and shapely; her waist, almost tiny enough

---

* We'll both lose our jobs.

to hold in one hand, looking fragile yet endowed with a powerful core. The sharp, refined jaw-line and nose; the vivid, papaya-pink lips; the incisive dark-brown eyes that seemed to peer into the essence of each moment. And her hair . . . her one-of-a-kind hair, like mahogany laced with hot mercury; bangs making a line above her eyebrows; the rest, falling all the way to her midriff, parted back to front by her shoulders.

"Mayuko?" he said, forgetting to text.

Mayuko wore a dress with a black and white pattern of warped, squiggly checkers like a cubist painting. From a necklace of fine silver links, a circle of black beads with a white rose in the center hung to her bosom. To Amon's surprise, he had access to her inner profile just as in the old days, and could see beneath her graphical makeup to the flaws of her naked face. She looked tired in a way he had never seen in her before. The early divots of frown lines were beginning to form between her eyebrows, she had pale rings under her eyes, and there was a slight sag to her cheeks as though weighed down with resignation.

"Amon . . ." she said, a complex look of sadness, wonder, and disbelief in her eyes. "How strange . . ."

"So you finally took up my invitation to come for a visit," said Rick. "What do you think of my new place?" He gestured around with his pointed chin. His tone was indignant, but his usually flushed cheeks were almost crimson.

Mayuko stared at Amon and blinked slowly, her eyelids apparently hindered by that same resignation, and Amon stared blankly back.

Just then he felt a tingling sensation in his legs and a hoarse male voice shouted, "Your stop!" in his ear. He flicked his fingers to clear away Rick's apartment. His attention prompter—Mindfulator—had detected the arrival of his stop and delivered a mild current of electricity to his legs along with an audio warning.

Amon quickly shouldered his way to the doors, stepped onto the platform, and trudged in line up the moving lane of an escalator.

When he pulled up Rick's apartment again, they were gone.

3

CHIYODA, GATA TOWER

Amon wove down a wide hallway through a deluge of commuters and poured out with them through the high stone archway of Tokyo Station, onto the streets of Chiyoda.

Beyond the field of bobbing heads that surrounded him, he could see huge skyscrapers sprawling endlessly in all directions, their every wall and window covered in a motley sheen of entertisements: a multiracial choir sang hand on breast beneath the holy glow of an insurance brochure; a red, hazy eye outlined in infrared rocketed through tight stone tunnels; fingers tore open a teabag-sized pouch in a car and released thousands of insectile robots that swarmed over seats and the dashboard, sucking up dust. Moving images rippled up, down, and across the sleek angular contours of these many rising shafts, like shifting patterns of light on the surface of a lake. A dazzling confluence of wardrobes and slogans and machinery and wild beasts—anything and everything imaginable that could sell action—emerged and dissolved, flowed and stalled, the borders between the manifold segments so blurry they melded into one scrambled whole that pervaded the cityscape.

Peeking from slim cracks in the skyline above, the InfoSky stretched bright and clear, a cinematic quilt of promotional narratives, each patch blinking and shifting across the heavens from one channel to the next. Gangster flicks were sewn to wedding dress shoppers stitched to smiling hedge fund managers, the cacophonous burble of their ephemeral soundtracks drifting down to the city like divine revelations vying for minds.

To his immediate left, Amon could see the red-brick walls of Tokyo Station. To his right, a jam of freshly-buffed, immaculate cars inched bumper-to-bumper along the road. Ignoring the relentless barrage of sensations striking him, he kept his attention on navigating to the office and directed his gaze down to the infosidewalk. It was divided into a grid of concrete tiles slightly larger than his foot. The tiles were owned by different companies, and to help him decide which ones to step on, he used the latest version of ScrimpNavi; an application that calculated the cheapest route to any destination. Arrows color-coded according to price blinked on the ground before the tramping dress shoes and clacking stilettos that kept advancing just ahead of him. Red arrows marked the most expensive tiles, purple the mid-range, and blue the cheapest. Amon kept his eye on the blue arrows, looked to where they pointed beyond the line of advancing legs, and stepped on the ensuing tiles as soon as they appeared, careful not to land on cracks and pay double.

Each tile was overlaid with a glowing, see-through picture like an ectoplasmic spray-paint mural. The tiles on his trail displayed the proprietary images of TTY. If he hit them successively with the right timing, the pictures would animate into a continuous video, like film cranked through a projector. On the first tile, a pre-teen girl held a glass bottle filled with dense mist. In the next, she twisted off the top. Then she looked in wonder as the mist stayed inert beneath the bottleneck. Bringing the bottle above her lips, she tipped it back. The mist hit the rim threshold in slow-mo, transforming into golden liquid that poured through the air into her mouth. She wore a look of ecstasy as a nimbus cloud coalesced around her. The cloud carried her into the InfoSky. *Cloud9 Nectar*, written in clouds. An orgasmic female voice whispered *Blissing Refreshment*. The following tile indicated by the blue arrow had the same image he had started with, depicting the girl holding a mist-filled bottle. And when he stepped on it, the pattern began to repeat.

Watching the same video again and again was irking but also rewarding. Every ten tiles or so, silver numbers blossomed out of nowhere above the head of the person immediately in front of him. *10 points. 100 points. Double bonus!* Users who connected tiles owned by a particular company earned gaming currency, which could be exchanged for money. By transforming a walk down the street into a game, the companies propagated product awareness, and made using their properties fun, with rebates as an additional incentive for returners.

Now and again, tiny white arrows popped up to point his eyes away from the ground and towards surfaces devoid of images that appeared along his path: a patch of asphalt in the gutter, an alleyway wall, a storefront window. These bare spaces lacked added-value media, incurring even cheaper viewing charges than most people. He glanced at them whenever they appeared in positions that he could see in his peripheral whilst continuing to stay on course, his eyes and feet following divergent directives for the common cause of frugality.

He tried his best to appear to walk casually, so that a very slight meander was visible in his gait but, he hoped, never quite a noticeable zigzag. This was to hide his budgeting from nearby colleagues who might assume he had financial troubles, which he didn't. He was just saving up for something important—something he would even die for if need be—and every little bit counted.

The shock of what Amon had seen in Rick's apartment was still fresh in him. It lingered beneath his skin like an electric charge in metal after a lightning blast. *Rick and Mayuko. Mayuko and Rick.* Amon wasn't sure how to name what he was feeling. Jealous? Envious? Betrayed? Such petty emotions led to nothing but irresponsible spending, and mechanically obeying the guidance of ScrimpNavi was all he could do to fend them off. Putting one foot in front of the other, purposefully and precisely, helped take Amon's mind away from his troubles and kept these inchoate feelings from festering into distracting worries . . . for the time being at least.

Amon had a strong appreciation for lifestyle-parsimony apps like CleverBarter and PennyPinch, which allowed the user to save more than the cost of their usage fees and minutely subscription, but among them he particularly admired ScrimpNavi, for it showed him how to transcend brand loyalty. The simplest budgeting strategy was to stick with a single company whenever possible. That way customer-appreciation points accumulated and overlapped with gaming points, garnering bonuses and creating a kind of bargain synergy. But for those like Amon who could tolerate the harrowing exhaustion of seizing upon the cheapest option at every moment, ScrimpNavi was like having an economist devil or a Machiavellian accountant on your shoulder. When allying with one company was cheapest, it told you to do that, and when betraying it for another was cheapest, it told you to do that.

"Thirty-two degrees. Sunny. Ten percent chance of precipitation," murmured a weather diagram that popped up beside his left nostril as he continued slowly along the street. It was a hot and sticky summer day in Tokyo, the congestion of buildings, crowds, and traffic trapping the viscous humidity. Bundled up snug in his suit, Amon's face was sticky and his back wet after only a few minutes of frugal walking. He wanted to wipe the sweat gathering on his brow with his sleeve, but resisted the urge and kept on ahead. Droplets had already condensed into rivulets that began to dribble down his cheeks, dripping off his chin onto the breast of his jacket, and oozing around the back of his neck to soak his collar (a gross display digimake thankfully edited out).

Fighting off the craving to wipe his brow meant minor discomfort, but Amon could bear it since it also meant more credit in his account. If he reflected on it for a moment, he did have his qualms with some aspects of the action-transaction system (particularly when certain politicians in the Absolute Choice Party abused it). But he believed it had undoubtedly made the world a better place, not least of all by teaching humanity one crucial lesson: the difference between wastes of energy and crucial undertakings. The slimy feeling of clinging sweat, for example, gave rise to the urge to wipe. This urge—like the urge to lick the lips or rub the eyes—could be ignored indefinitely, the sweat eventually evaporating of its own accord. In other cases, as Amon knew all too well, the satiation of an urge only made the inciting sensation worse, like a maddening rash or mosquito bite that itched the more with scratching. But these were qualitatively different from urges like eating, sleeping, or responding to a business email. One could not ignore the hollowness of an empty stomach, heavy eyelids at night, or the burning need to please a company superior without palpable repercussions. By forcing everyone to constantly monitor visceral impulses and authorize or suppress them in accordance with their salary and the going rates, wearing a BodyBank made the line between pointless spasms of the unconscious and meaningful drives sharper and sharper, until all motivational glitches could be identified and patched before they manifested into superfluous actions.

His thoughts on the virtues of the AT system were interrupted when the blue arrow he was following suddenly turned red. One company had bought the tile from another and jacked up the price while he was in mid-step. His right foot outstretched, he froze and balanced on his left before redirecting his airborne foot to another tile indicated by a new, blue arrow.

He had not gone more than a few paces further when the line of legs stopped advancing, and he was forced to a halt. Looking up from the infosidewalk, he saw that the signal at the intersection just a few meters ahead had turned red. The crowd closed in tight around him as those behind continued to edge forward. Now that his commuting routine had been interrupted, Amon felt the claws of his emotions scrabbling their way to the surface of his awareness, carrying anxious thoughts with them, and he turned his gaze upward in search of inspiration, as he had countless times before.

There he saw a wilderness of kaleidoscopic concrete peaks layered against the InfoSky and rising from scattered locations in their midst, thirteen buildings taller than the rest. These housed the Tokyo headquarters of "The Twelve And One," a group of MegaGloms that together owned all domains of human endeavor. One building was for H&H Kenko, which held the rights to all actions associated with health, medicine, nutrition, and exercise. Another was for Ultimate Truth Limited (UT Ltd. for short), the proprietor of religion, philosophy, spirituality, science, and the cosmos. No Logo Inc.: protesting, subversion, counter-culture, swearing. R-Lite: the sun, energy, atoms, and everything smaller. The remaining handful were represented as well: TTY Group, Xian Te, Yomoko Holdings, LYS Dynamics, Latoni Sedo, Kavipal, XXXTrust, Fertilex, and LVR. The immensity of their buildings seemed to bespeak the strength of their influence, as they reared over the surrounding rooftops of their subsidiaries and independent venture startups no doubt destined to be their subsidiaries. From Amon's grounded vantage, the MegaGlom buildings all appeared to be of equal height and he sometimes wondered if this symbolized their equal standing in the global marketplace. Or perhaps that all thirteen were really just one; their share in each other's assets being so large and so rapidly traded that only specialists could even attempt to draw lines between them.

Whatever the significance of their height, there was another building—GATA Tower—that exceeded every other by far. It was like a swollen skyscraper gutted and turned inside out, with its frame and supports on the exterior. Tight braids of polished steel—gleaming with a subtle tinge of baby blue dappled lavender—formed pillars at the four corners, like poisonous snakes coiling straight to heaven. Reaching diagonally between these pillars, bands of the same steel wove a latticework façade, through which diamond-shaped patches of the brown-tinted inner glass walls could be seen. Where it met the InfoSky there was a thin ring of untouched blue. This gigantic fortress was sheathed in an invisible cylinder one kilometer in diameter beyond which the writhing images could not approach; an information vacuum at the epicenter of this communixchange vortex called Tokyo.

The signal finally changed green, urging Amon and his surrounding professionals across the road. On the other side, he made his way right to the next corner and turned left onto a broad boulevard where the entertisements petered out. He followed a sidewalk of glossy, transparent concrete interspersed with triangular slivers of pale topaz. Slender spruce growing straight out of this concrete lined the curb beside a four-lane road. Their threadlike roots traced a forking pattern of bright green just beneath the surface of the sidewalk, visible intermittently through the multitude of flapping pant legs and sleek calves. In the middle of the road was an island plaza of the same glossy concrete. It was topped with vacant benches, young potted ginkgo, and a fountain playing the logo of Yomoko Holdings. Sculptured spurts of grayscale fluid depicted jagged pieces of broken glass re-fusing into a mirror that reflected a black cube with one corner cleanly nicked off, this graphic-spray floating amidst the ocean of roaring cars like a castaway's desperate SOS signal. Looking straight ahead, Amon had an unobstructed view of GATA Tower. Its intricate shaft protruded from a round platform of brown marble at the end of the boulevard. It rose straight up and up and up to an overwhelming altitude, beyond the streets and roofscape, the city and the world, receding endlessly into the outer reaches.

Amon doubted if it was architecturally possible to build a structure with such a narrow base that would be stable enough to exit the atmosphere—certainly not in earthquake-prone Japan—and had always wondered about GATA Tower's naked dimensions. Maybe it reached no higher than the subsidiary rooftops? Maybe it was as monumentally tall as it seemed? Reliable information on the subject wasn't easy to come by. The GATA Tokyo website claimed it was the tallest building in the world, but so did the GATA headquarters in Seoul, Rio De Janeiro, and Mumbai, and the discussion page of the FlexiPedia article for "Tallest Building" had degenerated into a bout of name-calling between the various architects and their followers. Satellite views were equally useless, as the controversial buildings were all inexplicably blacked out from publicly affordable maps.

Amon had been tempted for a long time to try diminishing GATA Tower's overlay. Added floors and other digimade features that might have been applied—like vivid coloration and increased girth—would dissipate, allowing him to look upon the structure with naked eyes. But he had never tried, for it was financially unthinkable. Peering beneath the overlay on tangible property like buildings, parks, and clothing was a violation of the owner's image rights—that is, a credicrime. Sentences varied from case to case, so Amon could only guess at the fine for peeking at GATA Tower, but given the heated encyclopedia debate, it was probably exorbitant. The architects' bragging rights were at stake, giving them vested interest in lobbying for strict protections, and GATA would have a stake in maintaining its mystique. Amon was curious, but not enough to consider throwing away his precious savings.

Approaching the looming edifice, he arched his neck up and tried to spot the top, but it shrunk to a minuscule point inside its thin circle of ad-less sky and vanished into the blue distance. Strangely, the complex muddle of emotions that had been nagging him began to settle down, and he almost felt relaxed. Looking at GATA Tower often had this effect on him. It was as though the very inability of his eyes to fully encompass such an imposing thing brought him solace and reminded him how lucky he was to work for an organization that had reached the pinnacle of justice. Instead of fretting over some minor interpersonal problem, he ought to feel more grateful for who he was and the time he'd been born.

As he entered the shadow of the tower slanting across the root-traced concrete at his feet, Amon began to reflect with reverence on the history of GATA and the inauguration of the Free Era. To think, it was only forty-nine years ago that GATA, the Global Action Transaction Authority, had first been established. In response to the worldwide economic collapse that followed the Great Cyberwar, branches of GATA had been built simultaneously in every capital on Earth and had jointly fulfilled the roles of both domestic and international governance ever since. *What kind of world, what sick, iniquitous world had existed before?* Amon knew about credit cards and the Internet and cellphones and people *doing* things that didn't feed the economy, but he couldn't really imagine it. Now, after less than five decades of GATA administration—Amon had learned in the BioPen and at his Liquidator training—all social injustice had been eliminated, all citizens had been emancipated from financial despotism, and government interference in the market had been reduced to the minimum.

Now here he was, at the end of the boulevard, before this majestic tower, this stronghold of salvation. Here he was at the end of history, when the ideal life of humankind—the life of absolute liberty—had finally been attained, and primitive institutions scrapped in favor of fair and efficient ones: laws superseded by credilaws, courts by Judicial Brokers, police by Liquidators, criminals by bankrupts, jails by pecuniary retreats, and for the first time ever, not just war, but the very capacity for war was gone, as militaries were universally disbanded under the sway of Pax Economica—the great economic peace. All excess bureaucracy was eliminated, leaving just enough to ensure that every action was charged its due, just enough to uphold the guiding principle of the Free World:

All the freedom you can earn.

Amon recited this phrase in his mind as he went up an escalator to the round marble platform, tailing a line of his colleagues. Some were dressed in concrete gray like him, and others in the baby blue shirt, lavender tie and brown suit of the standard uniform; but everyone had GATA written in lavender on their right breast. Moving with them towards the glass doors leading into GATA Tower, he felt relief and pride wash over him. Corporate empires might fall, cherished currencies might deflate, real estate barons might lose their homes, but GATA would always be there; for without GATA there could be no empires, currency, or real estate of any kind. Being on the GATA payroll meant job security for a lifetime, and so long as he kept working hard and scrimping consummately, accumulation of savings was guaranteed. Setbacks like the trouble with Rick might occur from time to time, but if he took the long view, tried to see the metropolis for the skyscrapers, his dream—the only thing he lived for—was right there, glinting over the wildly sprawling rim of the adscape horizon.

When the elevator reached the Liquidation Ministry, Amon was pushed out the doorway by the eager Liquidators behind him. He entered an expansive concourse with a pyramidal roof made of green glass squares in an orange frame and a floor of circular turquoise tiles the size of flattened cans. In the distance he could see stores side-by-side that sold various kinds of goods: outdoor gear, shoes, bags, toys. Customers wandered leisurely in and out of the stores holding paper bags stamped with brand names. The wallpaper provided by the Liquidation Ministry changed daily. Sometimes it was a beach or a golf course or a library, other times a swimming pool or a riverside or an open diamond mine, and occasionally, like today, a mall.

The walls of the office were marked off by a faint field of white dots in the foreground of the mall. Along the edges were vending machines serving energy drinks, bottled green tea, water, and instant noodles. There was no furniture except for rows of wheeled office chairs facing away from the elevator. The chairs were distributed evenly across the whole floor, standing exactly three meters apart to form a symmetrical grid. Every five rows there was an extra three-meter space that formed an aisle and carved up the grid into five-by-five squares of twenty-five seats.

There were hundreds of such squares, each supposed to be occupied by a Liquidator squadron, yet every chair in the room appeared to be empty, like a stadium in a ghost town. As Amon edged along the dotted wall, Liquidators ahead of him took the aisle to their chairs, sat down, and disappeared from sight. The default setting in the office was to edit everyone out of the ImmaNet, turning them invisible. This way the ministry could give the staff privacy without the need for ugly cubicles, and ensure no one felt like they were being watched, even if they sometimes were (by higher management, who could make them visible with a click).

Halfway to the far end, Amon turned right and took the aisle to the square of his squad. He was about to sit down in his chair—located front and center—when two colossal men began to approach him along the same aisle, both waving to get his attention. It was Tororo Xiong and Freg Bear—two Liquidators recruited at the same time as Amon and Rick. Both were over two meters tall with huge hairy clutches for hands, round barrel-shoulders like wheat bales hoisted horizontally, and rock-hard potbellies. As if to intentionally flaunt their immensity, their Liquidator uniforms were always digimade too small to contain their bursting, fatty muscles. Although the resemblance between them was uncanny, there were a few differences. Half-Japanese, half-Chinese Tororo kept a pointed goatee, his eyes long and narrow with single-folded lids, his black hair rising in small, wispy curls; while Lithuanian Freg was clean-shaven, his eyes gray-blue, his sandy brown hair in a tall, spiky mohawk.

Yet as similar as they were outwardly, their personalities diverged. Just then, as they plodded heavily closer on stout legs like hydraulic cylinders, Tororo was jabbering excitedly, and Freg was letting out his signature laugh; a slow, rolling bass vibe. As Freg's bellowing mirth died down, the two giants stopped a few paces away, said *good morning*, and gave a slight bow, the spikes of Freg's mohawk aimed at Amon.

"Where's that scoundrel, Rick?" said Tororo with his hands on his hips in mock indignation. It was an odd gesture that Amon supposed he had picked up from American movies.

"Good question," said Amon. "I called him this morning to find out but didn't get a good answer."

At work, Amon always spoke instead of texting, using properly pronounced words (which were more expensive than *slurring*) in order to make professional communications smoother and avoid giving his colleagues the false impression that he was broke.

"Answers! From Rick?" said Tororo. "You might get better answers from a poker-shark if you asked him whether he's bluffing." Freg laughed thunderously. Amon didn't even snicker. No one except Freg ever seemed to find Tororo funny, not even Tororo himself.

"Would you like me to try calling him?" suggested Freg with a soft smile.

"No, that's fine. I'm sure he'll be here in a moment."

"Yeah, I bet he'll arrive here in a moment, just not a moment any time soon." Freg laughed again. Amon just stared blankly at them, irritation simmering under his skin. It wasn't Tororo's inane humor that was bothering him. It was that rumors about Rick's tardiness were starting to circulate.

"Feeling nervous about the evaluation results?" asked Freg, thoughtfully noticing Amon's brief reverie. "I know I am."

"You would be, Freggy," said Tororo. "Anyone as trigger-happy as you ought to be. How many dozen passersby got dusted in your crossfire this year?" Freg laughed, but this time it sounded curt and hollow.

"Come on Tororo," said Freg, almost pleadingly. "I know you're just as nervous as me. Our evaluations come together."

"To my *chagrin*," said Tororo, raising an eyebrow at Amon, and Freg gave another mirthless chuckle.

"I am a bit nervous to be honest," said Amon. "It's hard to keep pace after a promotion. I can only hope the overtime I put in will make up for . . ."

Sensing the implication of the unfinished sentence, the two giants were briefly lost for words. Only the sound of the departing nightshift's stifled chit-chat and shuffling footsteps remained.

"Well, I guess we should get to it," said Amon, breaking the silence. There were still a few minutes until start time and Tororo's lower lip quivered as though he had something to add, but Amon began edging towards his chair. Taking the cue, the two men bowed and headed for their seats.

It was 8:25 when Amon sat down. Only five minutes to go and Rick was nowhere in sight. Just to make sure he hadn't somehow arrived early and turned invisible in his seat, Amon opened up the squad attendance diagram. An aerial view of the square of chairs showed a glowing dot of light for present, a black dot for absent. In the seat directly right of Amon, there was a black dot. Rick was most definitely late.

Raised in the same BioPen, Amon and Rick had been good friends since childhood. Both were accepted into the Tokyo branch of GATA, and even ended up as partners in the same squad of the Liquidation Ministry. Their like-minded intimacy had made them an effective team. In their seven years serving as Liquidators, Amon and Rick had apprehended thousands of bankrupts quickly and discretely, earning them generous bonuses and recognition from ministry execs. Yet in the end, it was Amon who got the big reward, receiving a promotion to Identity Executioner last year. Now he had a higher salary and more authority, not to mention privileged access to the top-secret Death Codes. And now that he was Rick's boss, a strain had appeared in their relationship for the first time ever.

During their first six years at GATA, both had been diligent and ambitious workers. But ever since Amon was promoted, Rick's performance had gradually deteriorated. While Amon continued to give the ministry his all and do overtime at every chance, Rick was showing up late, sometimes dreary-eyed and lethargic, perhaps even hungover. He was calling in sick, admittedly within his assigned number of rest days, but often enough to suggest laziness. In the office, Amon sometimes caught him engaged in social communications and he frequently took extended breaks. If this slacking streak had happened last summer, Amon wouldn't have been personally offended, though perhaps concerned for his friend's job. Yet everything had changed when Amon became his supervisor: Rick's blunders were Amon's blunders, Rick's negligence Amon's.

Amon held his tongue for months as Rick's absences came with greater frequency, his arrival time later and later, his idling longer. He had finally texted Rick the previous night to ask him to be on time—just this once—to receive their evaluation results. But Rick had ignored him, and Amon was beginning to suspect that he was jealous. Whatever his motives, Rick was putting Amon's career—and thus his dream—in jeopardy. Now, in his efforts to rein him in, Amon had spent his most expensive morning in years, maybe ever. Even more disturbing, Mayuko had suddenly reappeared in his life. He couldn't fathom why she would be in that apartment with Rick, on a weekday morning, in caring embrace, and gritted his teeth when a lewd image of what they might have been doing the night before flashed before his mind's eye . . .

There's nothing to be done, Amon consoled himself and tried his best to relax in the spare minutes that remained until his shift began. He sunk into his chair. It was ergonomically molded to his contours, with armrests for his entire forearm to the tip of his fingers, so he could twitch out commands to the network for hours on end without discomfort. *Ahhhh*, he exhaled long and slow and inhaled deeply several times in succession. *Deep breathing* was an avoidable expense in principle, but Amon needed to clear his head before work. While some big companies compensated staff for all their actions on the job to keep their minds off personal accounting and on their duties, GATA only included a flat action allowance in the salary. They also offered licensing fee exemptions for cost-intensive missions, but this didn't apply in the office. Amon avoided obvious wastes of creditime like lifelogging, massaging his forehead, talking to himself, and surfing the net so as to never exceed the allowance (he had never come close). But to boost his efficiency, he allowed himself to take it easy on frugality while working, letting his eyelids blink away, using the washroom regularly, and even taking short strolls around the office. He carefully timed such breaks for when his focus was lagging and saw them not as lapses of the will, but cleverly-calculated investments that would pay off in bonuses and promotion, for he knew that sometimes one had to spend money to make it, offer up pecuniary sacrifices for the greater savings. Enacting this respiration ritual the moment he arrived each morning eased him into the workflow, and he savored every molecule of oxygen.

Eight-thirty. Shift start. Amon logged on to the Liquidator network and opened up Illiquidity Alert. A list of random combinations of letters and numerals appeared in the air about a meter in front of him. These were the names of people that Illiquidity Alert had judged to be at risk of bankruptcy and then encrypted to make them anonymous. The program sorted their alphanumeric codenames in order of bankruptcy risk, with people at high risk on the top and low risk on the bottom. Formally, the list was entitled the *Asset Integrity and Monetary Life Quality Incertitude Registry*, but Liquidators usually just called it *the Gutter*.

Amon raised his index finger to scroll down. The top of the list was not his particular concern. The names there were constantly appearing, exchanging spots and disappearing as many people stumbled into the upper range of the bankruptcy danger zone, received an automated warning notice from the Liquidation Ministry, and quickly climbed back onto sure financial footing. Ministry statistics showed that dipping into the Gutter served as positive reinforcement, with nearly 90 percent who did so going on to live long, creditable lives. The people Amon had to watch closely were a more derelict breed. Illiquidity Alert could pick out candidates for the Gutter using a formula that pitted their assets and earnings against their debt and expenditures, but it was unable to predict which ones were likely to cash crash. This required intuition and inter-pretation, something computers had never figured out. When he wasn't on liquidation missions, Amon's job was to scan the Gutter, judge which subjects were most likely to go bankrupt, and mark them as critically illiquid. This was not an easy judgment however, since Liquidators were only given a limited amount of information about the individuals by the House of Blinding. Although the technical details of how the House of Blinding operated went beyond Amon's expertise, he knew enough about it to do his job, and that was all that was expected of him.

The action-based global economy was devised at the Tokyo Roundtable, a meeting held in the aftermath of the Great Cyberwar by the Old Powers of the West and the New Powers of mainland Asia. According to the FlexiPedia article Amon had read about it, the new system promised an effective way of ensuring that owners could profit off their properties at a time when data heists, hacking, and widespread tampering with financial systems had made all assets nearly worthless. But to realize this economy in practice, the government needed complete knowledge of every bodily movement on earth at every moment. Since information about what a person was doing at any given time was itself a kind of property that each individual was entitled to hold or sell as they wished, and practically speaking the government could not be asked to pay licensing fees to all citizens for the privilege of watching them, action monitoring would amount to constant uncompensated infringement of proprietary material, or in other words, theft. To prevent the terrifying possibility of such a klepto-surveillance state, the Roundtable faced the challenge of somehow protecting property rights in general without overriding each citizen's claim to ownership of their own action-data, that is, without compromising privacy.

The result was the enshrinement of anonymity rights and the division of GATA into seven parts that performed different functions. A democratically elected parliament called the Executive Council was put in charge of drafting new legislation and performing internal oversight. The Fiscal Judiciary made sure such legislation was constitutional and gave verdicts on credicrimes. The Ministry of Records safe-kept the Archives, where AT readouts and the digital memories of bankrupts were stored. The Ministry of Access oversaw the ImmaNet network and identity registration. The Ministry of Liquidation, where Amon worked, saw to the capture of bankrupts. And finally, two independent institutions were established: the Ministry of Monitoring and the House of Blinding, which together became the central module around which the action-transaction system and the other institutions of GATA were built.

The BodyBank of all Free Citizens was assigned a unique string of characters called an identity signature. When any action was undertaken, the data gathered by the individual's BodyBank sensors were attached to their signature and sent directly to the House of Blinding. The House then encrypted this signature, turning it into a blinded signature, and routed it together with the action-data to the Ministry of Monitoring. Without any knowledge of the individual's identity signature, the Monitors matched this action-data with an action-property description saved in the Ministry of Access, and authorized the property owner to withdraw the corresponding action fee. The owner then attached the Monitor's authorization and the blinded signature to a withdrawal request and sent it to the House of Blinding. The House then decoded the blinded signature into the original actor's identity signature, withdrew the requested credit from their account, and sent it to the property owner.

The whole process usually happened in a fraction of a second when AI could handle it. If human judgment was required, it might take about ten.

This procedure allowed the Monitors to watch each citizen's every move without knowing who they were. A new blinded signature was created for every action, so that neither the Monitors nor the property-owning corporations would ever have access to the identity of the individual. They would only know that an isolated action had been performed at a certain time by an unidentified somebody guised in layers of cryptography. Moreover, although the database of all these disparate, unidentified actions had to be stored in the Archives to allow for verification of past transactions, harvesting it for marketing purposes was strictly prohibited. In this way, action-transactions could be completed without violating the inalienable right to individual anonymity and thereby opening the door to publicly-sanctioned pirating of information about each citizen's endeavors.

So although Amon was in charge of marking individuals as critically illiquid if he thought they were due to go bankrupt, he knew very little about the people he was marking. When Illiquidity Alert put someone in the Gutter, the Blinders exposed only the bare minimum about them: a blinded name, their bank account balance, the total value of their assets, their income, and their recent action-transaction readout edited to exclude personal identifiers. The credilaws decreed all other information must be hidden and the Blinders invariably obeyed.

Using these scarce, fragmented hints of a life, Amon searched for risky spending patterns. First he checked the bottom of the list for blinded names that had remained in the Gutter for a while or that kept falling in again and again, in order to locate chronic squanderers. Alternately, he looked for the plunging account balances of rampant spendthrifts on self-destructive action-sprees. Once he located a financially precarious person, Amon looked through their AT readout and bank account. By checking their action-transactions and balance fluctuations over the past few weeks, months, and sometimes years, he could begin to see an abstract picture of their routine, their job, their hobbies, and their addictions. Amon almost felt a sort of monetary personality manifesting from the vague bundle of activities like a face spotted in the clouds. From this he guessed whether they were critically illiquid and likely headed for bankruptcy, or were showing signs of recovery.

After skimming through several AT readouts, Amon picked out one subject of concern, blinded as Z98. For weeks now, Z98 had hovered just three spaces from the bottom of the list. It was miraculous that the subject had managed to stay there so long without going over the bankruptcy threshold or climbing up to a more stable slot. He (Amon didn't know his subjects' gender but had a habit of thinking of them as males) was constantly lying motionless in the bed of his capsule apartment, hardly eating, drinking, or using the bathroom. His job was blinded but Amon watched as a measly smidgen of income would roll in now and then, whereupon Z98 would go out to the local pool hall and throw it away within minutes on squid jerky, beer, and billiards, saving just enough money for the walk home. There he returned again to a stupor and started the whole cycle over.

In some ways, Z98 had the qualities of frugality that Amon admired. He was living a simple, almost catatonic life to save for his true joy: squid jerky, beer and billiards apparently. But unlike Amon, there was a desperation to it. Such gutterfolk went on action binges until the threat of bankruptcy was close and palpable. For most, it was only a matter of time until they scratched one itch too many or failed to hold in one last cascade of farts and went over the edge, although Amon had seen a few climb their way out through restraint and perseverance or the charity of a friend. At heart he was optimistic and hoped that subject Z98 might be one of those.

Amon marked Z98 as critically illiquid. He was now out of Amon's hands. The computers in the House of Blinding would automatically expose his text address and FacePhone number to action counselors, gangs of which would nudge him encouragingly towards financial recovery or thoroughly harass him as needed, like sharks that smell the red, vital liquid of unpaid loans. Since GATA was responsible for reimbursing the creditors of bankrupts for a portion of their bad debt, and dispatching Liquidators to apprehend bankrupts was costly, contracting counselors was worth the expense if they could prevent them from crashing. This meant that Liquidators could reduce government expenses by accurately distinguishing irreversibly profligate souls from temporary high-rollers and recommending contracted help only when it was cost-effective. Amon's talent in making this distinction accurately was part of the reason he had been promoted to Identity Executioner.

Amon scanned the Gutter for a few minutes more, when suddenly the huge face of a man appeared in front of him, enlarged to ten times the normal size and rendered in exquisite detail. He had long, blond curls that hung in dangling twists along the sides of his cheeks like a curtain of soft, golden candy canes, and his eyes were hazel, painted with smudged daubs that resembled the impressionistic brushstrokes of a distant wheat field. His nose was long, elegant, and smooth, with a slightly pointed tip; his jaw-line sharply chiseled; his finely-textured skin brushed into gentle grooves, like miniature sand dunes or a zen garden. Below the chin, only his shoulders were visible, garbed in a brown pinstripe jacket. There was a startling angled symmetry to his features, almost Slavic but more polished and geometric, which conveyed a delicate, masculine beauty. It was Yoshiyuki Sekido, the Minister of Liquidation.

"Good morning, Sekido-san," said Amon.

"Good morning, Kenzaki," Sekido returned. "There are some issues of an important although not yet pressing kind that might warrant an exchange of words, maybe a conversation—no, formal discussion perhaps is a more appropriate phrase—between the parties concerned: to be more precise, I am referring to you and I."

As Minister of Liquidation, Sekido's main job was to manage and coordinate the different liquidation squads. He was generally well-liked in the ministry, thought to be a diligent and reasonable overseer who was strict with newcomers but generous with bonuses, although he was infamous for a few peculiar quirks. One of these was his vague and roundabout manner of speech.

"I see. What would you like to discuss?" said Amon.

"It concerns the appraisal of certain managerial initiatives, organizational endeavors, professional practices, and their ilk within the liquidation squadron of which you are in charge, in your capacity, duly acknowledged, as Identity Executioner."

"You must be referring to my evaluation." Amon felt a stab of fear in his gut, sensing Rick's empty seat out of the corner of his eye without looking at it conspicuously and drawing the attention of his boss. "Were my results satisfactory?"

"*Satisfactory* is not how I would choose to describe the outcome of our thorough valuational assessment of the entire squadron over the last twelve months since you were elevated to a leadership role, both individually and taken as a unit, with particularly close attention paid to your records."

If the squad's performance was not satisfactory, how bad had it been? Amon wondered, his skin tightening with anxiety, as though stretched taut by invisible hands. "M-my records?" he asked feebly.

"Yes. You have displayed a certain quantity of notable promise since the day we recruited you into this indefatigable ministry, especially taking into account your perfect concentration test score, and irrespective of any variations there may or may not have been in your performance over the years, our high expectations for you have never faltered, even now that we have enough evidence to seek an appropriate confirmation or disconfirmation of our preliminary impression.

"We've been looking over your results from all sorts of angles, in order to consider the plurality of pertinent facets in correlate, and thereby analyze the variegated factors involved in the matter at hand. Your potential for leadership, if any, is of course central, but your putative skills at facilitating the training of new recruits, and whatever tact you might possess in carrying out cash crash operations—all of these have been incorporated into our calculation of your potential for integrity and future successfulness."

Sekido paused to stare intently at Amon with his wheat-field eyes. Amon waited in tense silence for him to continue. He wanted to ask directly for his results, but held his tongue; he knew that Sekido's speech got more circumlocutory the more important the news he was trying to convey, and had learned that asking questions only sent him further off topic.

"In any case, there's a new project of sorts in initial preparatory stages, an infant undertaking if you will, although whatever details I have received, which are minimal to say the least, lack the requisite precision to express to you the enormous possibilities it offers. All I can impart by way of communication at this time and date and place is that the Liquidator—if indeed it is a Liquidator, and my superiors have offered no guarantees, only highly provocative innuendo—the Liquidator who gets this job will be the envy of everyone else in the Ministry, possibly of everyone in GATA, and not unplausibly even some external to GATA who admire the services we provide. According to the specifications of the relevant human resources representative and their compatriots in that section, the ideal candidate will be quick-thinking, creditable of course, organized—although not an essential prerequisite, we would prefer someone in good physical shape—able to rapidly understand obscure and sophisticated directives and faithfully reliable."

Where the hell are you going with this? snapped an icy, bitter thought in Amon's head, but he nodded to everything his superior said with a bright, attentive expression. His stomach had gone cold with dread.

"Now about your evaluation, Kenzaki. We were very pleased."

"Is that so? Really!?" After the long, preamble, Amon was taken off guard by this sudden positive turn. "I mean, I suppose . . . that was the overall consensus then?"

"The propriety of a man of my standing misleading an inferior is questionable at best, don't you think?"

"I'm delighted to hear that my efforts have paid off."

"Well, while I do believe a celebratory mood is not beyond the pale, as it's difficult to quantify exactly how pleased we were, cautious excitement might be more prudent than delight; you can take that as a piece of advice or just casual banter as you will. You see, there are certain areas for improvement—as the saying goes, nothing but money is perfect—and I will give you a full breakdown of our suggestions in an email by the beginning of next week."

"I look forward to reviewing them."

"Yes, well. To tell you a bit more about the project, it will be facilitated by certain elite members of the Executive Council and will commence some time within the next year, give or take a few weeks. As I'm sure you are prescient, it usually isn't possible to advance straight from our ministry to a position proximate to the Council, yet that shouldn't disturb us as it won't be a direct move per say, but more of a skirt around the institutional edges, if you know what I mean."

Amon continued nodding as if he knew what Sekido meant.

"In short, I've recommended you for this position."

"That is fantastic news, sir. I almost can't believe my ears."

"Now don't forget what I counseled already about cautious excitement. According to the fruits of our implemented selection protocol, you have all the traits we're looking for—in spades—but this is a mere recommendation and other candidates may present themselves as unsurmountable hurdles or sharp caltrops on the application racetrack, if you'll allow your mind to encompass these little metaphors. That is to say, your rejection is not an unthinkable impossibility, although you may have a chance to meet with one of our internal headhunters in the near future to talk about your eligibility."

"Thank you very much!" said Amon, leaning forward in his chair to bow his head low. "I'm so grateful for this chance."

"Don't thank me. Just keep on working hard so there won't be anything to exclude you when the time comes for our meeting with the headhunter."

"Of course. I'll do my best."

"No one wants to lose you from this squadron nor from this ministry—with the exception perhaps of those hungry for your post who we can leave out of the discussion for now as the challenge they present is not imminent—least of all me, but I can't neglect my duty to ensure that GATA employees do the job that will best assist this organization over the long term. Good luck!"

As soon as Sekido's face had disappeared, leaving the quiet mall, Amon went back to scanning the Gutter, but found himself jittery with elation. This opportunity was almost too good to be true. The Identity Executioner position was known to be a stepping stone to higher levels of the organization, but Amon had been expecting some diddling secretarial post in say the Ministry of Access at best. Never had he imagined leaping so close to the Executive Council. It reminded him of the career path taken by Chief Executive Minister Lawrence Barrow. He had started out as a lowly Liquidator just like Amon, and eventually became an assistant to the Executive Council. There he got into politics and eventually rose to the top of GATA Japan, where he had proven himself a great leader. Amon didn't even care about the details of the job, so long as he could follow in the footsteps of his hero.

His thoughts were interrupted by a pulsing beep, warning him that someone in his squad's jurisdiction had gone bankrupt. Immediately, his own name flashed in front of him. Sekido had assigned him to the mission. He stood up and dashed a few steps down the aisle, hoping to get equipped for liquidation and pursue the target, when he remembered that Rick hadn't arrived yet. *Where was he?* Regulations required that Liquidators move in pairs, so Amon was forbidden from going in alone. Without Rick, he would have to decline the assignment. But that would mean giving up an ideal chance to demonstrate his prowess before the meeting with the headhunter. Even worse, he would have to admit to Sekido that Rick wasn't there and might end up looking like a lax supervisor.

The moment someone went bankrupt, they forfeit their anonymity rights, and the Blinders had already exposed part of the target's profile to Amon. He opened it and blinked a few times when he saw the name, as though that would wipe away a scratch on a blank slate. He even flicked the screen away and drew it back, but the name didn't change. It read Shota Kitao, but surely it wasn't *the* Shota Kitao? A quick browse confirmed that it undoubtedly was. Shota Kitao. Minister of Records. Bankrupt.

The target was armed and stood at a packed intersection in the heart of Tokyo. A weapon in a crowded place was a volatile situation no matter who was carrying it, but this was no ordinary bankrupt. The Minister of Records was a renowned official, making this the most sensitive mission Amon had ever been given. It would require quick strategizing and media tact if things got ugly. If he declined and the mission went foul due to the incompetence of whichever Liquidator pair inherited it, he could take the blame. If he wavered too long, this armed bankrupt could do harm to the many nearby citizens and rack up more bad debt. It was imperative that Amon decide quickly so that someone else could be dispatched.

He began reluctantly typing a text message to Sekido recommending Tororo and Freg, when Rick ambled along the aisle towards his chair, the squashed tangle of bed-head beneath his digimade face visible only to Amon.

4

SHIBUYA

Rick and Amon rode motorbikes side by side along the highway. Following the neon red navigation beam streaking in zigzags ahead of him, Amon carved through tight cracks in traffic. The vehicles he passed were adorned in a multitude of overlays, from the stylish to the surreal: sports cars with fresh, shiny wax-jobs; jeeps with tinted windows and monster wheels; an SUV composed of fused-together cat bodies formed of scrunched up laundry; a melted van with warped, lopsided wheels, its wicker-like frame of steel rods dripping plastic with exposed wires casting circles of electricity.

The meandering concrete overpass led them twisting through narrow gaps between skyscrapers. It dropped into tunnels beneath the sidewalk, and then arced up through the phantasmic dance of pale InfoSmog, intersecting and wrapping through other suspended roads like one thread in an intertwining maze of industrial tongues.

The InfoSun had emerged from the rearing concrete canopy. Amon kept his eyes on the road, never looking directly at this capsule of constant imagery embedded diagonally above him in the fluctuating patchwork firmament. Yet he couldn't stop its infolight from slipping over the rim of his helmet and striking his eyes, whereupon hazy, effervescent glimmers of an exclusive interview with a has-been teen idol appeared unbidden, as though seared into his retina. Amon couldn't remember the idol's name, but he recognized her from her media heyday a few years back. Her face was of incredible high-quality; literally iconic, a sculpted configuration of ornate lines; her hair individuated blue strands curlicueing to the height of her diamond-shaped nose; her eyes like stained-glass spheres glowing from within; her smooth, delicate ears like fragile seashells. A team of virtuoso digimakers had idealized away the particulars of a woman's face, leaving only raw feminine Beauty, before adding layers of stylizing abstraction to create a work of art, an enticing mannequin somehow more human than human. Seated in a plush lawn chair against the backdrop of an empty tennis court, she spoke of her collection of whips. Amon immediately detected this blatant, sensational attempt to stir controversy for a return to fame, yet her supernaturally emotive expressions seemed to override his intellect. Her brilliant smile of bleached jewel rectangles conjured faint hints of happiness; the movements of her facial muscles tugged on his heart like strings on a puppet's limbs, as he stooped forward gripping the steering handles and toggled lanes.

Blasting at breakneck speed between convertibles of fluttering silk and hatchbacks that jiggled like gelatine, wheeled mecha and sedan-size WWII tanks, he paid no heed to the infoscape whipping by, to the passing blur of adverpromo and datatainment squirming on the road, on highway barriers, on residential rooftops, on the windows of a looming mall. Instead he studied their target's profile in his desktop, an overlay of transparent links and text projected over everything like a thin membrane. It was crucial to learn as much as they could about Minister Kitao now that the veil of blinding was down, for there was no telling what personality quirk, what illness, what secret desire they might uncover that would make subduing him easier and allow them to minimize any risks to themselves or others.

As though they had formed a silent pact, neither Rick nor Amon mentioned the events of that morning. They were two professional Liquidators on an important mission now. Nothing personal could interfere.

"This is the worst mission ever," said Rick by FacePhone, his face a small box in the center-left of Amon's perspective. "I'm as nervous as a damn rookie. Why us?"

"I hear you. This is gonna be a tough one for sure. But I'd say we're actually pretty lucky."

"What? How?"

"Sekido gave us this job because he believes in us. Now we've got a chance to show what we can do."

"Or a chance to screw it up big time."

"Sure, but have we ever screwed up a mission before? If we follow protocol and do what we've always done, there's nothing to worry about, right?"

"Oh yeah? So what's the protocol for dealing with an armed politician in a fucking crowd then, huh?"

There wasn't any of course and Amon said nothing. Although he wasn't going to tell Rick, in his heart he shared some of his partner's foreboding. Their target was a powerful, well-connected man and there would be plenty of onlookers. But mixed with his worries was a feeling of pride. The challenge Sekido had assigned them made it clear just how much confidence he had in their abilities, and Amon was grateful for this last trial to prove his mettle before meeting with the headhunter.

Inside popsicle-colored high-definition globules that rose before Amon's eyes and evaporated rapidly like champagne fizz, an interviewer was asking the idol about an ex-choreographer's alleged sexual harassment. Her resplendent eyes began to tear up, sending Amon a vague tingle of sadness. He blinked away the infoglare and shook off the vicarious emotions as he wove through a cluster of scooters mounted by slick-haired rockabilly revivalists in leather jackets, directing his attention instead to Minister Kitao's bank account.

"It looks like he had a solid income and a big savings until recently."

"Yup," said Rick. "According to his transfer records, the government salary was only a small portion of his earnings. The majority was dividends from shares in *knitting* and electronic lubricants that he inherited from a relative."

"Can you see what drove him over the edge?"

"No, but this should help make it a bit clearer."

The small box to center-left in Amon's eye was highlighted with a white glow as Rick shared a chart with him. Amon selected it with a verbal command and a line representing the value of Minister Kitao's assets appeared. For most of the minister's life, it rose jaggedly, dropping slightly now and again from pricey action-sprees, but leaping up even higher with each salary deposit. Then about two years ago the drops in the line grew closer and steeper, his sprees gradually increasing in frequency and cost until his expenses surpassed his income and the overall trend became downwards. In the last month, the line had begun to plummet, almost totally vertical: the man was now spending more than a years earnings every day.

This pattern of oscillating financial deterioration was common for bankrupts. Amon had seen it ten-thousand times before. Yet, in this case, he found it hard to believe. Who could have guessed that an upstanding public servant with abundant assets would ever in a million years end up in the Gutter—let alone go bankrupt—while armed, on a bustling street? Amon still thought that most GATA workers were frugal and responsible like himself, and therefore immune to bankruptcy. But looking at Kitao's precipitous chart, it seemed that anything was possible; that anyone might succumb to their darkest, most exorbitant impulses.

Their navi-beam began to point towards an exit up ahead, so Amon and Rick eased off the acceleration, pulled into the left lane, and coasted down a ramp leading off the highway into the thick of Shibuya.

Parking their bikes in front of a ramen bar on a narrow side-street, they entered a mall through glass doors, took an elevator to the fifth floor, and walked over to a window overlooking the intersection where Minister Kitao awaited.

Red light: cars roared through and crowds accumulated at each corner. Green light: the crowds crossed and interweaved. Accumulate, cross, interweave, roar; accumulate, cross, interweave, roar. Traffic signals directed population clog, like router arteries pumping data clots through junctions of fiber-optic veins. Up above, a multitude of animated billboards kept blinking open in mid air and then vanishing, like fleeting windows into the city's commercial soul. A *zaibatsu* CEO sipped an energy drink that cured knotted shoulders while guiding a tour of his mansion. Runners in skin-tight gray rubber crouched at their staggered start lines around a track amidst a cratered, moonlike landscape. TV personalities used hooked poles to fish packets of longevity-enzyme-exuding air freshener off chains dangling from the necks of hungry, caged pandas.

The ecstatic faces of deep-fried sushi taste-testers. Transitory segments of these 3D marketing narratives played on walls over storefronts and floated above shopping thoroughfares, popped out of curbs in the faces of streetwalkers and rippled atop roadside kiosks, blipping in and out, sometimes never to return, sometimes reappearing in different places at fresh angles with altered color schemes, segueing into each other, trading places, blending and merging into one—existentially unstable desire-paintings on strobing display in gallery Shibuya.

Hordes of twenty-somethings decked out in the latest styles stood beside the monuments of a dog and a decommissioned streetcar in the Hachiko Plaza, a stretch of open sidewalk occupying one corner. Many of them were waiting for friends, smoking cigarettes or just posing ostentatiously. The fashion trend of the afternoon, as the surrounding billboards confirmed, was the Four Elements. Ragged leather hats ablaze with dancing flames; baggy T-shirts rippling and bulging with gusts of wind; half-pants of gray, brown, and black mineral sedimentation in fissured patterns that tremored with ersatz earthquakes; and sneakers made of two glass layers with water in between so the foot looked like it was at the bottom of a swimming pool. While Four Element attire seemed universally popular, there were variations in the intensity of the flame, in the force and interval of the wind, in the coloration of the earth, and roughness of the water that indicated clique membership, differentiated according to music genre or product preference or some other factor Amon was too socially aloof to identify.

An arrow appeared above these convening fadsters, pointing down at their target. Amon zoomed in. *Height: 2 m, 10 cm*, read his profile. Minister Kitao was extremely tall, definitely the tallest Japanese Amon had ever seen. He had long legs, long arms, long fingers, everything long except for his face, which was broad and commanding, embellished with a trim goatee. Amon remembered how the minister's great stature had always made him look impressive in the black suits he wore at award ceremonies and other GATA functions. But now, wearing a green polo shirt and brown cords, hair gelled flat to a head that loomed over the multitude of cool youth, he looked incongruously lanky. Smiling slack-jawed, he stood still and gazed about the city, his eyes glazed with a strange expression of giddy wonderment. A pocket in the crowd had opened around him, as the nearby youth seemed to be keeping their distance, but passersby took advantage of the space and streamed steadily through.

"Why do you think the kids won't get close?" asked Amon.

"How should I—" Rick stopped what he was saying, frowned, and gestured out the window with his pointed chin. "Maybe that's got something to do with it."

Kitao's eyes went wide with gleeful excitement, revealing blood-shot whites, as they tracked a stocky salaryman in a pinstripe suit just entering the crowd gap. The man was busy talking to himself (or a FacePhone friend) and was totally oblivious when the minister lunged in with his long arms and grabbed him under the armpits. The startled man sprung back and struggled against his grip, but the minister lifted him off the ground and brought his face close to the crown of the man's thrashing head. He then took a deep sniff, waving his nose about sensually as though inhaling a divine fragrance. With an expression of pacified satisfaction, the minister put down the man, who scurried off into the crowd cringing in humiliation and horror.

"What the hell is he doing?" Rick wondered aloud.

"I don't know. He—"

"Forgot to take his crazy pills maybe. I mean, did you see those eyes? He looks about ready to go berserk."

"Let's try to get in his head space before we move in. Otherwise, there's no telling what might set him off."

A few seconds later Kitao grabbed his next victim, a buxom office lady in a blue mini-skirt. Seeming to sense his strength, she fearfully submitted, not resisting even as he took a second whiff before releasing her. They watched him repeat his deranged and inscrutable routine a few more times, grabbing someone, picking them up, sniffing their head, putting them down, and then completely ignoring them as they ran off or shouted at him in perplexity and disgust, before pausing to hunt about with his eyes and starting over. None of his victims were alert enough to evade his gangly arms nor strong enough to break his clutch, and no one noticed the holster at his hip—highlighted in glowing white for Amon and Rick—or they might have been more afraid.

"His readout says he's been doing this repeatedly for several days," said Rick, "with eight hour breaks here and there where he buys a hooker and checks into a love hotel over there." Rick pointed up Dogenzaka, a hill covered in buildings with tinted windows. "But the hookers always leave after a few minutes, and then he goes straight to sleep."

"After a quick bedtime sniff."

"Sure. Why not?"

Amon pulled up a detailed breakdown of the minister's AT readout during his peak spending periods. Sure enough, there was a lot of *grabbing*, *lifting*, and *sniffing*. Kitao was re-enacting his habitual pattern of discreditability before their eyes. These intrusive actions were especially expensive since his victims had given no consent, making them credicrimes like *assault* or *harassment* depending on the verdict of the Judicial Brokers.

"We'd better figure this out and deal with him fast," said Amon, and Rick nodded in agreement.

Although stopping credicrimes wasn't the responsibility of Liquidators, bankrupts still had to be apprehended quickly. Credicrimes were just like any other action-property, aside from two crucial differences: they were owned by GATA instead of corporations or individuals, and the fee for performing them was fixed by credilaw rather than the market. When a Monitor found that someone's action matched a credicrime, the data was sent to the Fiscal Judiciary, where a Judicial Broker gave a sentence in accordance with credilaw. Judicial Brokers were so-called because they worked on commission. Every time a credicrime was enacted (committed), they brokered the deal (case) between GATA the action owner (court of law) and the customer (criminal), taking a cut of the fee (fine).

All the freedom you can earn meant that everything was permitted so long as you could afford it, and that included credicrimes. Policing died when the Free Era was born. To arrest, jail, or interrogate citizens was an atrocious obstruction of their freedom, no matter what they had done. Instead, justice was better entrusted to the market whenever possible. In the Free Era, creditable citizens who worked hard and acted within their means were granted the chance to earn limitless freedom, and discreditable citizens who didn't went bankrupt. That was all. Credicrime fines admittedly interfered with the free operation of the market, but only to protect the market itself. They were a necessary evil to prevent particular kinds of actions that infringed on personal choice, disrupted social cooperation, and impeded voluntary exchange between individuals. No other remedial measures were required; the natural, ineluctable flow of money was its own reward and punishment.

Stopping crime, therefore, was not part of the Liquidator job description. On the contrary, fines for illicit behavior were a major source of government funding to be encouraged in moderation. If it filled the public purse, said some, occasional lawbreaking was a tolerable transgression; others called it a civic duty. Either way, citizens always did right so long as they stayed solvent. Only bankrupts could do wrong. Bankruptcy itself was the only wrong, the discreditable actions that lead there odious by association. Minister Kitao's perverse ritual would have been perfectly acceptable had he not slipped irredeemably beyond financial salvation. Yet now he could never settle his loans and so long as he continued in his exorbitant doings, he was an insult to his debtors, a drain on the economy, and an affront to society. To keep his already burgeoning bad debt from growing any further, it was imperative that Amon and Rick cash crash Kitao quickly, if carefully, as his political prominence made discretion almost just as pressing.

"Rick, I found something in his readout."

"Yeah?"

"Did you notice the custom overlay he uses when he does this? He keeps it on the whole time."

"Seriously?" Rick found the entry Amon was talking about. "Shit. Well that's where all the money went."

The membership dues to use subscription overlays, like gaming environments or nostalgic, historical cityscapes, were higher than the flat hourly rate for the default, public overlay, but were nothing compared to custom overlays. Graphic artists and programmers charged ludicrous sums to build up every projected detail from scratch and usually retained their copyright, charging a second-by-second access rate.

"I found the password to get inside his overlay," said Rick.

"Hit me up."

Once Rick sent the password, Amon pasted it in, and the vista before him immediately changed.

A night sky stretched overhead, pure starless black broken only by a full moon where the sun had been. The skyscrapers still rose, billboards winking around them, but the concrete below was gone. Instead there was a rich, reddish soil atop which swathes of humanoid plants moved. Their torsos were fibrous trunks of vibrant green, their limbs thick stems, their hands blade-like leaves with five jags, and a purplish-red stalk rose from their shoulders. Pointed tendrils like elongated thorns sprouted from this neck-shaft and wrapped upwards along its length, converging and intertwining tightly together at the tip to form a bulb-shaped bud of a head.

In the middle of Hachiko Plaza, a lone human prowled. Minister Kitao, left unaltered in his world, was stalking someone. Unlike the other plants, his prey's reddish-purple bud-head was deforming, the bundled tendrils composing it uncoiling outwards like a many-fingered fist opening. When Kitao was only a few paces away, the head fully opened, blooming into a radiant white flower of sharp petals arrayed in three concentric circles, the outermost ring a mane of longer, thinner petals. Kitao grabbed the blooming person below the shoulders, lifted them up, stuck his nose into the center of the flower where delicate white strands rose, and inhaled the fluffy, yellowish pollen smeared on the tips. The moment he put the blossoming plant-person down and released them, the sky grew light, the sun rose, night turned to day, and the petals shriveled into desiccated brown refuse, falling off as his victim ran away into the crowd. Then the sun set, the moon returned and night fell again, all in an instant.

"I've never seen an overlay so detailed before," said Amon. "The design alone would cost a fortune. And I can't believe he's paying to cancel the ads." Amon gestured up at the darkness overhead. "He's got to be violating the sky estate image rights of like half the corporations on earth."

"FlexiPedia says the flower is called Fair Lady Under the Moon. AKA: orchid cactus. It blooms only at night and withers by morning. The fragrance is supposed to be sweet and intoxicating."

"What do you think he's actually smelling?" Taste and scent were crude senses limited only to the naked world.

"Maybe a bit of his own imagination to augment the overlay."

"Hallucination?"

"Woah. Sounds like fun."

"But what's with the flower obsession? And why this flower in particular?"

"You wanna go over and ask him yourself? I bet he'll give you a nice sniff."

I just want to know how one of the top officials at our organization, with prestige and a good salary, ended up like this, thought Amon, but kept his perplexity to himself as it had no bearing on the mission. Instead, he zoomed in on the holster at the minister's waist.

"Looks like a duster," said Amon, "but his shirt is covering half the handle, so I can't tell what kind."

"I'm betting nerve. His bio says he used to be a Liquidator. That was decades ago, but I wouldn't be surprised if he held on to his gear. Lots of bureaucrats do I'm told."

"Let's hope so."

Dusters were guns that fired clouds of microscopic robots called "dust," which could be programmed to perform various tasks. Cog dust did delicate repairs inside engines. Surgical dust did medical operations without scarring. Insulation dust sealed up small cracks. Others, like piranha dust, insomnia dust, and vegetable dust killed their targets or worse. Nerve dusters were standard issue for Liquidators. Both Amon and Rick were carrying one. While nerve dust was not the sort of thing anyone wanted to see unloaded on a crowd of pedestrians, it was not lethal and caused no permanent damage. If Rick's guess about what kind of weapon the minister carried was right, the chance of a bystander being seriously hurt was low. If it was wrong . . .

"We've got enough background, I think," said Amon.

Rick nodded. "Should we try to dust him from up here? He's tall so we could probably find a clean shot somewhere."

"I say no. I agree that he's an easy target, but with all those people around there's still a small chance that someone might take the spray. Let's try approaching him through the crowd. We can blend in as plants and try to get close. If possible, we'll lure him to a quiet place. Crash him privately. If he doesn't budge, we take him out right there on the street."

"Got it. Let's go."

They took the escalator down to the ground floor and exited the mall along with a draft of air-conditioning that clung to them a moment before dissipating, and abandoning them to the stagnant swelter. They crossed the scramble intersection and waded through a converging copse of Fair Ladies Under the Moon, their faceless bud-heads bobbing side to side with each step. Up close now, Amon could see small spines sticking from the joints and interstices where their body parts met, between shoulder and neck, leg and abdomen. Vines ran along the soil from the base of each plant to others close by, interconnecting them all in one great verdant web that blanketed the ground. Even as the plants moved, these organic threads never tangled, wriggling and extricating from each other in response to every adjustment in the configuration of bodies. Feeling the heat of direct sunlight on his exposed face and hands while simultaneously seeing the moon above in the dark firmament made Amon slightly queasy, as though the disjunct between sight and touch sent subtle circadian disturbances through his nervous system.

Through a brief opening in the foliage of limbs, Amon thought he caught Kitao looking right at them, but the next moment he was ogling his surrounding anthro-vegetation as before. When they reached the loam ledge of the curb at the edge of Hachiko Plaza, Amon turned to ask Rick if he'd noticed the same thing and gasped at the sight of him. Rick had become an insect, grotesque in his vivid enlargement. His nose was a sharp needle, his eyes white and lifeless, his skin pale green and translucent, with the foggy red forms of his internal organs visible through his bloated abdomen. Looking down, Amon saw that his own body was likewise transformed.

"Get low!" he hissed and pushed Rick down on the soil—which felt hard, warm, and grimy like summer concrete—and crouched with him behind a perfume kiosk. He gestured for Rick to follow as he shadowed a tight group of plants with dangling fronds like briefcases. Through intermittent gaps in the crowd, he could see Kitao darting his eyes about from his high vantage over the thicket of purplish-red bud-heads. He was searching for them, his right hand hovering next to the holster at his hip. Still stooping, they reached the streetcar stationed in the middle of the plaza and took cover with their backs up against the outer wall.

"How the hell'd he make us into . . . what are we?" Rick wondered.

Amon clicked on Rick to select his body, activated an image search engine and a FlexiPedia article popped up in the air.

"Aphids," said Rick, seeing the title of the article in their shared window.

"His software must differentiate us from everyone else."

"Uh-huh. But how?"

Amon tilted his head and grimaced quizzically.

Rick thought for a moment and answered his own question: "Maybe he's using our professional profiles. He must have configured the overlay to mark anyone whose profile he has permission to access. That way when GATA staff like us come into close range, we turn into insects."

"That sounds about right. We'd better be careful. Crazy or not, he did used to be a Liquidator."

"Yeah. Just check out those nerves of steel. He's not acting one bit like someone who knows he's bankrupt."

The visceral revulsion and shame of cash crashing was inculcated deep in every Free Citizen, so there was no telling how bankrupts might react once they saw Liquidators approaching. Amon had witnessed many get on their knees and beg for mercy. Some wet their pants, or vomited and retched, or screamed soulful terror. Others wept or sobbed silently, while a few fainted or went limp with resignation. Others still flipped into a blank-eyed stupor, as though brain dead, or smiled in a daze of inexplicable euphoria. Now and then, he had heard from his veteran colleagues, a few of them even tried to commit suicide on the spot. Amon remembered one time when a woman crumpled into a convulsive ball and pulled every strand of hair from her head. The worst was when they had tantrums, violently rampaging against anyone and anything within reach. The prevalence of such cases was the reason bankrupts were not told of their financial status until the moment of reckoning; until their cash crash was imminent and impossible to reverse.

Kitao's show of confidence, his last stand at this busy urban nexus, was an unprecedented reaction in Amon's career. Only a man who used to be a Liquidator could pull something like this off. To predict the arrival of Liquidators, he had to have the algorithm for calculating bankruptcy and be able to use it on himself. To know that being in a crowd would make them hesitate, he had to be familiar with mission protocol and the prohibitions against long-range fire around bystanders. To mark

Liquidators as enemies, he had to have access to their professional profiles. And to even consider trying to fend them off, he needed a duster
and training in marksmanship software. Using his insider know-how
and experience, the Minister of Records was trying to postpone his
own cash crash, in cleverly premeditated disobedience of a cardinal
rule he had spent his life at GATA upholding: that bankrupts were no
longer citizens.

Yet despite his apparent resolution to fight until the bitter end, the fear
seemed to get Kitao at last, for when Amon flung his perspective out of
his body and around the corner of the streetcar to scope the scene, he
saw the minister dashing off through the plaza, taking huge strides with
his long legs. Charging through the milling tangle of green figures, he
bowled over a flower that bloomed in his path, sending a cloud of white
petals and pollen fluttering in his wake, and disappeared into the dark
tunnel under a train-bridge.

Amon pulled up a cut away view of the tunnel from above, the minister's
frantically running form highlighted.

"This is getting out of hand," said Rick, his voice funnelled out of his
rod of a mouth. "We'd better call for backup."

"Forget that," Amon replied. "This guy's a bureaucrat, not an athlete.
Take a look already."

The minister had gone below street level, and Amon turned the ground
transparent and zoomed in. In the middle of a long stairwell shaft leading
to an underground mall, he was bent over with his hands on his thighs,
panting.

"Let's move in quickly while he's catching his breath," said Amon.

"No good. If he hunkers down in that stairwell, and we barge in, he's
got a good shot at one of us. We don't know for sure what kind of duster
he's packing, and we can't take the chance that someone gets hit. I'm
gonna call the ministry."

"No! He's wasted enough money already. We need to get him now,"
Amon insisted, starting off from the streetcar.

"Wait," said Rick, holding Amon back with a firm hand on his shoulder.
"We—"

"Don't worry. We can take care of it."

"But—"

"We're going in. Got it?!" Amon gave Rick a piercing look. Rick met his stare, wearing an expression of surprised indignation on his see-through bug-shroud.

In their seven years liquidating together, the two of them had always made decisions cooperatively. Rick was the details man, trawling databases for info relevant to the mission, while Amon was the strategizer, fitting plans to the situation. But their roles were fluid: Rick sometimes proposed his own strategies, and Amon uncovered useful facts. One of them seemed to always pick up on what the other missed, complementing each other perfectly. Even after his promotion to Identity Executioner, Amon had let Rick provide input as an equal, just as always. But today, something fragile had finally cracked.

After they locked eyes for a few moments, Rick's indignant look suddenly vanished. It was replaced for a flash by the brooding sadness he often wore, before he covered it up with a businesslike deadpan, turned his eyes down in submission, and released Amon's shoulder.

Kitao still stood on the stairs. His panting had subsided somewhat, his right hand close to the duster, his head tilted up to keep watch on the top of the stairs.

"I've found a route to the other side," said Rick without a hint of resentment. "How about I go around behind him and you approach from the front?"

"Okay. But first, we'd better change our privacy settings so he can't spot us," to which Rick nodded.

Amon blocked Kitao from his professional profile so that his overlay could not differentiate them from anyone else, and Rick transformed instantaneously from the translucent green insect into a Fair Lady Under the Moon, indicating that he had done the same. They set off at a brisk pace into the orchid cactus crowd and split up half-way across the plaza, Rick heading for the main gates of Shibuya station, and Amon entering the tunnel beneath the train overpass where Kitao had fled.

The walkway in the tunnel was wide enough for three or four people to walk side by side. To the right was a wall flickering with crayon ad-murals. To the left, iron railing punctuated with occasional concrete pillars cordoned off traffic whipping over a road five meters below. Across this lowered road was an identical sidewalk on the opposite wall of the tunnel. Keeping an eye on Kitao through a patch of transparency that tracked him through changes of relative angle, Amon dodged sporadic pedestrians in his path. Still jogging, he wiped the sweat gathering on his brow with his suit sleeve as he came out the other side of the tunnel.

He saw the stairwell entrance; a portal in the ground surrounded on three sides by low concrete walls. Beyond the entrance, a group of Fair Ladies stood in a circle playing some sort of ImmaGame that Amon had witnessed before but didn't know. Each player pursed their lips to blow up at a huge bubble with the words South Sea Company written on it that hovered iridescent in the moon's warm sunlight and strobing billboard promoglow.

He selected a sign reading *Do not enter!* from his hard-drive, set it to stand by the stairwell entrance, and tagged on the GATA insignia—in its jagged lavender font—to ward off any passersby.

Looking through the ground, Amon saw someone at the bottom of the stairwell in the connecting corridor, which ran perpendicular to the shaft. They stood stock still on their stems, facing Kitao with a featureless bud-face. Amon guessed they had caught sight of Kitao's duster, which was no longer covered by his shirt, apparently afraid to ascend but reluctant to take another route. The minister was facing down towards this person, and Amon could only imagine the tantalized expression his prey saw when he took a step towards them. Startled, the plant bolted frantically along the corridor out of Amon's transparency circle and out of sight. With the target alone and looking the other way, now was the time to strike.

Amon opened up Rick's perspective as a small window in the bottom left corner of his visual field. He was jogging through a basement passage lined with gift shops.

"When you arrive at the bottom of the stairs, set up a sign like mine. We've got to minimize bystanders," voiced Amon.

"Got it."

"I'm going in. Get in position to cover me," said Amon, before entering the stairwell.

Seeming to sense his approach, the minister turned around.

The ceiling was conspicuously plain concrete; the steps pasted with a churning rug of hot-spring jacuzzis; red tile walls stencilled in mother-of-pearl brand names; a metal banister recommending local decogoods boutiques in radio announcer baritone. Amon descended the stairs nonchalantly, confident of his plant disguise. Kitao stared straight at him, his blood-shot eyes open impossibly wide, slack-jawed as before. Beaming a broad, twisted smile, pooling saliva almost overflowed the corners of his lower lip.

Amon's arms hung casually at his sides, but his right-hand hovered close to his holster. Amon hated dusting bankrupts. He much preferred to cash crash them by touch, a trick only Identity Executioners could perform, but he was prepared to shoot if necessary.

With about ten stairs between them, Kitao's eyes shifted from Amon to something behind him. Amon flicked on half rear-view, his left eye looking from the back of his head. A teenager wearing Four Elements gear was in push-up position on the sidewalk at the top of the stairs. With his head arched up, he blew up at the bubble, which had sunk dangerously close to the ground, in a desperate effort to stop it from popping. He was so low to the ground that the wriggling air pockets of his shirt brushed concrete, the flaming hat almost falling off. Amon could hear the encouraging cheers of his friends.

"I'm gonna bust in and dust him," voiced Rick.

NO! texted Amon. NOT YET.

"What?"

THERE'S A KID BEHIND ME. Amon could avoid any dust fired by watching Rick's screen and sidestepping his digital aimer, but the innocent youth could get hit. I'M GONNA TRY TO TOUCH-CRASH HIM. STAY PUT!

Amon ignored Rick's grumbling and moved towards the sickly smirking bureaucrat. Only a few steps away, Amon noticed a change in Kitao's expression, his eyes revealing a cold intensity tinged with fear. Then Amon realized something strange. He was supposed to be seeing the world through the overlay Kitao was using. Yet the kid behind him had been garbed in Four Elements. This made no sense. Unless . . . Amon opened Kitao's perspective and saw himself through his target's eyes. Amon was wearing a Liquidator uniform. Kitao had second-guessed that they would adjust their privacy settings and turned off his personalized overlay. On the public overlay, there was nowhere for Amon to hide.

Returning to his own perspective, still in half rear-view, Amon reached for his nerve duster just a split second after the minister. He got the grip in his hand and tugged up as fast as he could, but the minister had the duster in his hand at the same time.

"Stop, or I'll shoot!" shouted Kitao. Amon kept his finger on the trigger and the nozzle aimed at the greenish sighter on the minister's chest, staring in terror at the weapon pointed his way. Shaped like a pistol with a black body, the squarish barrel about seven centimeters long and the grip half that length, it resembled a nerve duster, but *Arthritis Duster* popped up in flashing red letters as it was automatically identified, the nanobot cloud it fired programmed to dissolve the cartilage and tissue between joints. They froze in a tense standoff.

"You must think I'm crazy, right?" said the Minister of Records. Amon didn't respond. He just kept his duster sighted, piercingly aware of the nozzle sighted on him, waiting. If the minister fired and hit, Amon would be in decrepit agony to the end of his days, and Rick would have to finish the mission alone. If he missed or Amon dodged the shot, the kid behind him might take it, a tragedy that could end their careers.

"Let me explain," Kitao continued. "These . . . these . . . my fair ladies . . . Everyone has something they treasure, you know, and . . . I had a greenhouse; a nursery on a patch of land in the suburbs. Then I lost something . . . not the flowers . . . you see, I'm no longer whole . . . You understand?" Amon lied with a nod. "It was horrible and I couldn't stand the loneliness. But this way . . . this way I can be with my fair ladies and . . . have company too."

"But you!" he shouted suddenly, the tendons of his wrist bulging as he clenched the grip of the arthritis duster. "You! I had to disappear my ladies to take away your disguise!" A strand of drool slopped from Kitao's mouth as he bared his teeth in rage.

"I know I messed up. But I won't let you take me away. You can call me a hypocrite . . . I know it was my job for . . . yes. Responsibility, but there was no . . . would you still love anything if you lost your . . . future? Would you?"

After all his confident posturing, Kitao was sounding more and more like a typical bankrupt, desperate pleading monologue and all. But typical bankrupts didn't point guns in Amon's face. He never gave them the chance. Precarious circumstances called for quick-thinking.

"You're one of our elite executives," said Amon. "You've done a lifetime of service for GATA, so I'm certain we can make some kind of exception. If you drop the gun, I'll try to negotiate with the ministry to let you keep the overlay."

"Bullshit! You drop the gun first!"

It was bullshit. Amon and Kitao both knew GATA would agree to no such thing. But keeping hope alive—even a patently false hope—was all he could think of to stall him.

Through his left eye Amon watched the teenager blow his bubble away and walk after it out of frame.

DROP THE DUSTER SO IT LANDS NEAR HIM, texted Rick.

"Okay. I'll do it," said Amon to Kitao. "Then we'll talk." Amon tossed the duster slightly ahead. It bounced and skittered down the stairs, landing on the toe of the minister's shoe.

"Ow," said the minister, and bent over to pick it up, the nozzle of his gun pointing down.

NOW! texted Amon. The moment Rick popped out from behind the wall, Kitao, seeming to detect the ambush somehow, leapt aside to the opposite wall of the stairwell and flicked up his gun to sight Amon again, who was already leaping the way Kitao had come. Kitao swung the barrel across towards Amon, and Rick fired at the minister's back. A blur of tinkling, half-visible particulate—microscopic robots riding one another in aerodynamic formation—flew up the stairwell and evaporated on impact with his polo shirt, slipping between tiny gaps in his flesh and diverging into attack-clusters that went for each pain receptor, a trillion infinitesimal claws pinching at once.

The Minister of Records let out a horrendous high-pitched shriek, and fell unconscious.

Hearing the sound of dusted bankrupts scream was the part of being a Liquidator Amon hated most, and he winced as he rushed forward to hug the minister around the waist and stop him from toppling backwards down the stairs. His hold was strong, but the tall man's gangly limbs began to flop about limp and erratic, dragging Amon off balance. Rick dashed up three stairs at a time, putting his duster away in mid stride, and brought up his palms to support the minister's back. Once they had their footing, Amon and Rick turned Kitao around and slung him over Rick's shoulder. As Rick descended, Amon held the minister by the waist to steady the load until they reached the bottom. There they laid the inert man face-up on the floor of the corridor.

"He must have had rearview on too . . . and seen you coming," panted Amon, his heart pounding with adrenaline.

Rick shot Amon a contemptuous glare and shook his head.

Not wanting to get into a dispute while on the job, Amon ignored his partner's look and directed his gaze down to the minister.

Kitao was totally passed out, his face clenched and distorted with faint wrinkles, a residue of the excruciating pain. Amon felt guilty every time he saw this nerve dust echo. He couldn't agree with the cruel doctrine spouted by traditionalists that bankrupts needed to be penalized for their unpaid debts, but accepted nerve dust as the lesser of many evils. Only with nerve dust could bankrupts be incapacitated without permanently harming them or their BodyBank, which contained valuable information. Electric stunners could corrupt its data, biological gases could harm innocent bystanders, and pharmaceuticals had side effects. Nerve dust was agonizing but, in the final analysis, the most practical and humane weapon for liquidation.

The hardest part of the mission was complete, but many tasks still remained. Rick contacted the Ministry of Records to request a Collection Squad. The Collection Agents, men and women who had once been Kitao's subordinates, would pick him up and take him to the Archives, where all the data in his BodyBank hard drive would be seized, uploaded, and stored, before the original copy was erased. All marketable assets would be auctioned off to help cover the bad debt that GATA partially shouldered.

Next, he would be sent to the Ministry of Access where his BodyBank would be surgically removed using a non-invasive nano-procedure and discarded like snakeskin. Minister Kitao would then be taken to a pecuniary retreat—known in common parlance as a bankdeath camp—in the District of Dreams.

While Rick made these bureaucratic arrangements, Amon undertook his duties as Identity Executioner. He crouched beside Kitao and placed his palm flat on his chest. The specific location didn't matter, but he had to touch the bankrupt somewhere to access his BodyBank CPU with the interface in his hand. Once inside, he delved into the deepest, most hidden core of the embodied calculating engine. There he entered in the Death Codes.

Selected for their memory, reliability, and loyalty, Identity Executioners like Amon were required to memorize the Death Codes to make hacking them impossible. Only they were privy to this mortal secret. It was Amon's special responsibility.

Within a few minutes the execution was complete. Minister Kitao's identity signature had been completely erased without a trace. He could no longer own an account, be a part of the AT marketplace, have access to the ImmaNet, and was no longer a Free Citizen. In short, he was now officially bankdead.

When he could see that the delicate operation was finished, Rick walked over to Amon, patted him on the shoulder and said, "Off to Shinbashi for a few drinks?"

5

SHINBASHI, SELF-SERVE

A three-story high railway bridge stretched along the right side of the sidewalk ahead of Amon and Rick. It was built of chipped red bricks caked with an accreted white powder and grayscale grit, signs of decay overlaid to imitate an old piece of architecture destroyed in a massive earthquake several decades earlier. Black steel fencing edged the top where the train tracks ran, and high, rounded archways of gray stone opened from the walls at regular intervals. Each archway was embedded with a slosh-house, *izakaya*, or other dingy drinkery; their plywood frames covered in chipped, yellowing paint; their flat roofs leaving a small, rounded gap below the vaulted ceiling. Red and white paper lanterns hung on the wall beside and above the archways. They were scrawled with black calligraphic script that advertised the drinks and grilled guts on special at the establishments inside: plum wine and highballs, chicken hearts and giblets, pig intestines simmered in a murky broth. Amon could hear the muffled or distant mutter of ten-thousand inebriated conversations, the rattle of passing trains, the rhythmic beep of traffic lights, the subliminal hum of info-gabber. He could see almost invisible circles of faint lantern-light before archways and packs of drunken salarymen strolling and stumbling arm-in-arm along the length of the bridge, until its gently curving form turned in on itself and faded out of view into the sleek office tower adscape.

The InfoSun was setting. Thin beams of dying infolight slipped through cityscape cracks, suffusing the edges of the distant skyline in pinkish-red advert-radiance—ticking alphanumerics from a motley assortment of websites, service-smiles, monster truck jousting, reruns of viewer-rated Sunday sermons at branches of MegaTemple Investments—a diffuse scatter of symbols and cinematic slivers in tones of tender blood-fire that blazed around the jutting rooftop shafts.

Here and there, sunset lawsuits sprouted from the polished glass and metal of the upper stories, where viewing rights to the infolight's reflection conflicted with viewing rights to the building. Terrestrial ads violently resisted the solar ads that beamed down upon their propriety surfaces in vibrant burning hues, and writhed against them like some rabid entertisement mold. Tendrils of talking heads in *International Ten Second Academic Debate* grappling with a desert motorbike training video across the wraparound window of an investment consultancy like flaming vines competing on fast-forward. A growth of glistening, naked backs in *Diet Massage Works!* emerging horizontally from the sheer, steel wall of a law firm to obscure a real-time update stock list, like an intricately ramified mushroom exploding from a cliff-face. Images from above and below tangled and coalesced viciously into mesmerizing knots of narrative iridescence, each battle representing numerous negotiations between owners of city real estate and the owner of the sun, R-Lite. Animating the struggle over entitlements was a cooperative marketing strategy to make legal disputes visually entertaining, the medium an enthralling icing on the message.

Wearing suits tuned plain black to conceal their profession, Amon and Rick followed a blinking white navi-arrow and turned right into a cavernous archway, broader and dimmer than the others. It opened onto a long, narrow laneway cutting beneath the bridge. Bars operated out of holes in the concrete walls, the reddish glow of grills and flicker of half-dead lightbulbs providing a hazy illumination. Tiny circular tables littered with empty beer bottles, half-eaten skewers of meat, and soybean rinds sprawled into the laneway from both sides. Bottle-necked between this chaos of patios, a throng of salarymen trudged slowly along, side by side. Others sat collar to collar on knee-high stools around the cluttered tables. As though tacitly obeying an unspoken after work dress-code, they all wore their shirts with the top two buttons undone, their loosened ties hung askew at exactly the same angle, and everyone used the same low-end version of digimake that traded blemishes and asymmetries for a generically over-polished look, their hair and skin glossy like paint-it-yourself figurines. The hubbub of drunken blather, laughter, clinking glasses, and grill sizzle was almost loud enough to obliviate the overhead train rumble.

As he jostled his way through the crowd, looking at the expressions of blissful numbness all around, Amon felt nothing but regret. He wanted to be in the frugal sanctuary of his apartment. There he could have conserved money and practiced blinking and breathing while basking in relief at having just barely accomplished their mission. Instead he was bumping shoulders, brushing up chest-to-chest to the smell of sake-tinged breath, stepping on toes, squashing paper cups and the tarry remnants of unidentifiable deep-fried tidbits splat on the asphalt, saying *excuse mes* to request passage through barricades of bodies—a barrage of expensive transactions. The bargain routes recommended by Scrimp Navi were all cut off on this constricted path and the constant bodily impact made breath reduction impossible.

Once the identity execution was complete, Rick had insisted on talking in person at a place he claimed even Amon could approve, this one particular bar they used to frequent when they both started at GATA, perhaps the most affordable spot in the core of the metropolis. Comparatively cheap or not, Amon saw no point in wasting creditime around town, preferring a FacePhone meeting from home, but when Rick refused to talk anywhere else, Amon eventually conceded. To postpone resolving their problems even a few more hours was no longer thinkable, especially after the events of today. When work finished, they had left GATA together and walked to Shinbashi, the office-jockey hive of stress anaesthesia.

They turned down an even darker alley and after a few steps, hit a dead end, where their navi-beam started to blink, signaling arrival at their destination.

A sign hung aslant above a doorless entrance, dangling at a sharp angle down to the right as though attached by a single tack. It read *Self Serve* in gray bubble letters.

They entered.

Inside was a long windowless room with a bare concrete floor. Instead of walls, dozens of vending machines standing snug against each other lined the edges of the room. The salarymen patrons were sucking down cigarettes, drinking and chowing on incongruously sumptuous meals. One group picked with chopsticks at a spread of bite-size *kaiseki* appetizers artfully arrayed on small ceramic dishes: thin strips of burdock root laid crosshatched over sweetfish; tofu simmering in a delicate soy-sauce broth garnished with sesame and mustard leaf; a vibrant palette of sashimi. Another group dug with forks into a heaping spinach and arugula salad ringed by smoked seafood and prosciutto. At the head of a different table, one man in a flaccid fedora carved an entire roast duck, steaming plates of rice and a red dip on the side. The air appeared clear, but it was stuffy with the smell of cheap cooking grease and tobacco.

As Amon and Rick crossed the room towards an empty table near the back, the men burst into sputtering laughter and coughing at a comedy gameshow playing on a patch of open floor in the center of the room. A team of professional water polo players were treading water laboriously to hold an obese man who couldn't swim over their heads. The goal was to keep him above the surface of a river long enough for him to compose and read traditional poetisements. According to a competition checklist flashing on the left half of the image, the team had succeeded with a series of haikus, but were struggling to keep him up for the duration of the longer tanka, and would soon move on to epic-length haibun. On a bed of hands, the fat man said:

Cicada singing
My soul's orchestral meaning
Stirring heartful joy
Yet a thirst I still suffer
But to drink Cloud9 Nectar

Comments and evaluations from the patrons tallied in animated emoticons scrolled down the surface of the lifelike image:

Ha ha ha. So funny. 10 Smiles, 3 Frowns, 1 Thumbs-up.
  This fool can't even reader. 4 Smiles, 4 Yawns, 2 Smirks, 1 Whipping, 1 Frown.

Buy me a beer and I'll take a swim anywhere. 6 Smiles, 3 Frowns, 2 Winks.

Somebody change the station. I'm drowning in boredom. 5 Yawns, 3 Vomits, 2 Smiles, 1 Fist.

Black sunglasses appeared in Rick's hand as he plucked their image out of his desktop and set them for "publicly visible." He then placed them on top of the table to claim it and headed with Amon to the vending machines. Tall rectangles of metal and plastic in a whole spectrum of different colors filled the space between floor and ceiling perfectly, as though the building architecture had been molded around them; their hard, vibrant shells flashing with the logos and promo-glow of automated catering subsidiaries. Combined, they claimed to serve the cuisine of every region on earth, from vegan curry to haggis, and had built-in hawkers to match, who sprung to life one after the other as Amon walked along the row on his right towards the back of the room.

First a tubby black man, with a puffy afro and numerous bead necklaces hung over his white apron, popped out like a jack-in-the-box. "Ya wan steamed banana, mon," he said, bowing low. "Deep-fried dumplin. Jak chicken. Is spicy, is good." Amon walked through him without pause, whereupon a dashing tuxedoed man with a curled moustache, pen and pad in hand, appeared as a reflection on the next machine's chrome panel. "Welcome your Highness," he said, his voice inflecting at three pitches simultaneously, a barbershop trio in one larynx. "The foie gras is on special today." Next, a wild boar crawled out from an impossibly narrow space under a machine and threatened to impale Amon with tusks if he didn't try the honeyed pork steak, which began to peel from its flank in pre-roasted slices and twirl about in the air. A green-skinned Martian materialized with a poof and secreted multicolored cubes of space food from a square hole in his forehead. A Viking maiden yodeled sausage jingles. A sombreroed matador twirled enchiladas on fingertips. Ethnic stereotypes and culinary mascots made sales pitches one after another, appearing as Amon approached and vanishing as he passed.

While most vending hawkers were programs capable of a limited number of responses, some were controlled manually by staff at remote centers in deflation zones. These outsourced attendants served numerous machines spread across the globe, manifesting whenever someone neared. Dealing with a human was a service for cultured customers who felt lonely talking to a system of ones and zeros pretending personality. But whether man or software, Amon abhorred paying for communication luxuries, and kept going until he'd reached a cheaper device at the back. The machines didn't quite fit the room, and there was a small leftover space in the corner where the row following the back wall and the row following the side wall met. Inside this gap was a smaller rectangle, half-hidden in grime and gloom. It was made of yellowish-white plastic, as though molded from recycled toilet seats. Lacking even an automated attendant, its only label was the single word "order" in a font of the same toilet-seat color that floated a few centimeters above the flat top. Amon reached into the dark nook and clicked it. He could hear the muffled sound of metal scraping metal and see the faint glow of fire through its frame, the gears and wiring inside shadowy silhouettes on yellow-ish-white like a robot's innards under X-ray. Cooking smoke from the machines was generally piped out to the roof, but the exhaust seemed to be clogged on this one, as puffs escaped from cracks in the frame carrying the smell of stir-fry to Amon's nose. After less than a minute, the scraping stopped, the glow faded, and the smoke dissipated.

"Would you like the food to be digimade for an extra fee?" asked a pop-up window.

Amon clicked no. A hatch opened and ejected a styrofoam tray. On it was a dried-up portion of yakisoba noodles mixed with bits of a rubbery substance that might have been pork or tofu, a dollop of neon-red pickle strips, and several perfectly spherical meat dumplings smothered in a sweet and sour sauce.

Everything about Amon's choice machine was cost effective. Its bland appearance saved on design, lack of remote attendant on labor, lack of an automated attendant on programming. Even the food was economized—printed inside the machine itself with ingredients injected weekly by the maintenance staff. But what Amon liked best was being able to choose whether his dish came out beautified or not, which most vending machines did automatically and included in the price. Anything that allowed him to frugalize his actions gave him a sense of control and put him at ease.

Amon reached between the larger machines into the darkness, retrieved the steaming tray, and brought it to the table where Rick already sat, his golden-brown hair turned dull silver in the dim. In front of him was a golden platter of herbed meats, cheeses, fruits, and a loaf of dark bread, like a banquet for the Greek gods. Beside it were two silver decanters encrusted with rubies. One was filled with a clear liquid and the other with something thick and amber. A goblet of pure diamond was placed before him and another in the adjacent spot, where Amon put his tray and sat down. Rick removed the stopper from one decanter, picked it up, and reached across the table to pour Amon a drink.

KNO THAYNGK U. No longer on the work clock, Amon had reverted to garbled text. The default messaging style was comic book: everything he wrote appeared inside a white dialog bubble that floated fog-like above his head and pointed to his mouth. When Rick kept advancing with the decanter, Amon made a barrier with his palms to block it.

"Don't worry," said Rick, pinning Amon with his brooding brown eyes. "It's on me."

Amon refused to budge his hands and shook his head. Rick's offer made the drink more appealing, but he couldn't stop thinking about the agreement he'd consented to with his medical insurance broker that allowed them to check his AT Readout for unhealthy actions like drinking and increase premiums proportionately.

Rick frowned in disappointment, his thick eyebrows hooking down towards the bridge of his nose. "Come on. When was the last time we had a drink together?" Amon asked PennyPinch to compare the cost of making a fuss to the rise in premiums. It informed him the difference would likely be negligible, so he reluctantly withdrew his hands.

Rick poured the amber liquid into Amon's goblet, picked up the other decanter and poured in some of the clear liquid. He then took a slice of lemon from his platter and slipped it in. It was a drink called hoppy, non-alcoholic beer spiked with rice liquor.

Once Amon's goblet was brimming, Rick poured for himself in the same fashion, quasi-beer first, rice liquor next, lemon last. He then raised his glass, and, seeing no way out of this expensive social transaction, Amon brought his up with a clink.

"Cheers," said Rick.

CHEARS, texted Amon.

Rick put down his glass, picked up a massive drumstick, resembling turkey but bigger and fattier, and took a bite of the thick end.

Amon changed his BodyBank interface from gesture control to eye-dialing so he could use his hands for eating, snapped apart his chopsticks and picked up some noodles.

With the massive drumstick occupying the fingertips of both hands, Rick gestured at Amon's plate with a flick of his long, angular chin. "Why don't you add a bit of digimake to that? Make it look like gourmet pasta or something."

Amon looked around at the other tables—the kaiseki, the huge salad, the juicy duck—then back at his dry noodles and spherical meat.

EET LEWKS GEWD ENUFF FER MI, texted Amon with a few twitches of his eyes as he brought some noodles to his mouth.

"Don't joke with me. You know what I mean. I know you can stomach just about anything. Like remember the time you ate a raw eel and jam sandwich?"

Amon did, vaguely, but tilted his head to the side and frowned to show his uncertainty. Rick sent him the segment from his LifeStream, a recording of his life taken continuously by all the sensors on his body working in tandem. Amon was looking at himself through Rick's audio-visual perspective twenty years earlier.

He was in the BioPen cafeteria at the low orange tables reserved for children. A group of kids were gathered around laughing. A bigger boy was daring Amon, his kiddy nostrils flaring in mockery, promising his dessert for a month as a reward if he did it. Without hesitation, Amon spread strawberry jam on his bread, put a piece of raw eel that the big boy had stolen from the kitchen on top, covered it with another piece of bread, and stuffed the whole sandwich into his mouth. The boys groaned in disgust as Amon chewed, but were clapping by the time he swallowed. The big boy reluctantly put his sweet-bean bun on Amon's tray.

"But just because you can stomach it, that doesn't mean you should eat something that looks like *that*," Rick gestured at Amon's food with his chin again, "in front of all these people. You might as well be eating dog food. Besides, the meal is more stimulating with a bit of decoration."

AIM FAIN JAST LAIK THEES, THAYNK U. Texting this, Amon picked up a meat sphere, bit it in half, and returned the other half to his plate. Rick frowned again and put down the half-chewed giant drumstick. He then took a gulp of hoppy from his goblet and turned his attention to the marketainment in the center of the room. Drawn by his friend's gaze, Amon also turned to watch. A blank-faced male reporter, his short hair parted on the left edge of his head and slicked right, sat erect at a desk.

Shiv Birla and Chandru Birla, founders and majority shareholders of the world's highest-grossing corporation, Fertilex, both passed away today in a fluke boating accident off the North-West coast of Canada. *Footage of an aging Indian couple, their skin brown, hair white. The man wears a button-up navy blue shirt with no collar, the woman a green tunic. They stroll side by side through an expansive British garden, where curving rows of flowers in arcs and lines intermingle with stone walkways into the mountainous distance.*

On vacation in British Columbia, Shiv Birla, seventy, and Chandru Birla, sixty-seven, were aboard a rented yacht when an unspecified malfunction occurred during a squall, causing the boat to sink. *Perspective of a man clinging to an inflatable raft in tumultuous waves. Torrents of rain slapping him. Others in lifejackets scrabbling to get aboard. A white ship capsizing in the distance.*

Fertilex has withheld permission to broadcast the LifeStream segments of surviving crew-members and Birla family servants at the moment when contact was lost with the deceased, but according to their reports, the elderly couple was separated from the life-raft when it was overturned by a large wave. *A helicopter hovering above a churning ocean lowers a rope ladder to a lifeboat. Drenched, shivering passengers in lifejackets cling together for warmth while waiting for the bottom rung to come within reach, wind from the whirling propeller sending faint disturbances across the waves.*

According to reports from the local Canadian authorities, there was a slight delay dispatching the nearest rescue helicopter due to confusion surrounding a recent personnel transfer. Once in the air, the helicopter first rescued the boat's crew and then quickly tracked down the Birlas, but not before the cold had taken their lives. *The Fertilex logo appears on the screen: a hand reaching up to grasp an egg beating like a heart that is encircled by a slowly-spinning pale halo.*

Consistently rated as the two wealthiest individuals on earth for over a decade, no statements have yet been issued as to how their estate will be divided amongst their two daughters, Rashana and Anisha. Executors of the Birla estate have organized a meeting at the Fertilex home office in Mumbai to review the will, but have yet to issue a statement with specific details. *A group of suited men in a boardroom engaged in discussion.*

Some experts say that the father's estate will be transferred to the eldest daughter, Rashana, but an unnamed source speaking under conditions of anonymity has suggested that younger sister, Anisha, may inherit a significant portion. Both sisters, who like their parents have always shied away from the media, refused to comment. *Two figures descend the stairwell of a landed jet, the skin on their faces like mirrors reflecting the surrounding runway, signal officers and terminal buildings.*

Back to the reporter at his desk. Last night at a discotheque in Lisbon, new members of . . .

When Rick looked away from the news and turned back to his food, he noticed Amon staring at him, and stared back for a moment. "So . . . what do you think about that timing? The richest people in the world dying and we've got an election coming up."

KAN WI GAYT STTARTAYD? texted Amon. The question mark in the text bubble lingered for a few seconds after the sentence, spinning in circles before it disappeared.

Rick let out a sigh. "Okay, fine. You want to talk about the serious stuff. I understand. But can we take it easy for a bit first? It's been a long, crazy day and we haven't done this in ages."

AI WULD PREHFER 2 HAV AUR DISCUSHON NAUW & ENGAYGE IN CHEET-CHAYT LAYTER AWN EEF THAYR'S STTIL TAIM. AY KAN'T STEH HEER AWWL NITE.

"Engage in chit-chat? You act like talking to me is some kind of chore. Can't you just relax for two minutes?"

AI AYM RILAXED. BAWT U KNO AZ WAYL AZ MI THAYT WEEV BIIN PUUTING THEES AWF FER 2 LAWNG. AY JAYST WAWNT 2 MAYK SHUR WI SOORT THEENGS AUT BIFOR BBOTH UV USS GAYT SUKKED BAKK EENTO AUWR BUZY SKEJULES.

Rick sighed again and downed the rest of his goblet. "Alright, Amon. If you insist. But can I start?"

Amon nodded and took a sip of hoppy.

"So . . . um . . ." said Rick, cringing sourly. "I just want to start off by apologizing."

FER WUT?

"For . . . for Mayuko."

DOHNT WURRY ABAUWT EET.

"No, really, I'm sorry. I should have told you about it in the beginning when we started seeing each other. But . . . I—"

SIREUSLY, RCK. JAYST FERGET ABAUT EET. THATS NAWT WAT WUR HEER 2 DEESKUS AYNYWEH.

"No?" Rick frowned in perplexity. "So what then?"

AI AULRAYDY TEKSTED U ABAUWT EET THEES MOORNING.

"Oh, right. That. Something about being on time for an evaluation."

AIM NAWT KEEDING ARAUND HEER. DOHNT U REELAIZ THAYT MANAJING U IZ MAI RESPAUNSABILITY NAUW?

"Yeah I get it. You want me to do a little dance so you can get another raise."

THEES IZNT JJUST ABAUWT MI. EEF YER LAYT, EET HERTS MAI REZULTS JJUST AZ MMUCH AZ YORZ. & THEES IZ KNO RAYGULAR EVALUAYSHON. U WANT 2 HEER WAT SAYKIDO-SANN TOWLD MI 2DEH?

"No," said Rick sarcastically, the timing of this little jibe sending a stab of sharp irritation into Amon's chest.

HII TOWLD MII AI MAIT HAV A CHANS 2 WERK AWN AA PRAWJEKT WEETH THA EGSEKUTIVE COWNCIL.

"Great work, hero," said Rick with too much enthusiasm.

WATS RONG WEETH U? U KNO AI AWLMOST HHAD 2 GEEVE UUP THA MISHION 2DEH CUZ U WERENT EEN YAYT. WER FRAYNDS, RAIT? DUZ MAI KAREER MAATTER 2 U @ AWLL?

Rick didn't answer. He just picked up the half-eaten drumstick as though he were going to take a bite, and held it for a few seconds while he stared at the tabletop with a distant look before dropping it roughly back onto the plate.

"Look," he said, narrowing his brooding eyes to bore into Amon's. "I invited you here because I want to have a talk, man to man. I want to hear your voice and I want you to hear mine so there's no misunderstanding. This isn't us gossiping about people at work or girls we met at some club. This is important. And I know you want to be frugal, but can you please hold off on the texting just for tonight?"

AIV AGREID 2 TAWK WIITH U EEN PERSAN, texted Amon, the words appearing in his bubble. BBUT AIM STEEKING WEETH TEKST. U'VE ALRAYDY WASTTED ENUFF UV MAI MUNNIE 2DEH.

"Is that right? How'd I do that?"

I CONTAKTED U AGAYN & AGAYN THEES MORRNING 2 REMEYND U ABOUWT THA EVALUAYSHON BUUT U KAYPT EEGNORING MI, SOE AI HAAD 2 AYSK MAI DESISION NAYTWERK FER ADVAIS, & MAANIFAYST EEN YER PLAYCE. NAUW U'VE DRAYGED MI 2 THEES BAAR WAYN U KNO WI CEWLD HAV DUUN THEES MOR AFORDABLY AWNLINE.

Rick shook his head with a scornful look. "Fine, you cheap bastard, I'll accept your texting, but at least spell properly. It might save you a few yen, but you ever thought that people have to read that crap? Gives me a fucking headache." Amon flinched when he heard the profanity.

Polite language was slightly more expensive than lowbrow common phraseology, but pejoratives were some of the most expensive words of all and Rick had been using them all day.

Լ *BⲨⲨⲦ—*

"Do it or I'm leaving." Rick stared sharply at Amon, challenging him to refuse, just as Amon had done during the mission.

Sensing their talk was on the verge of flaring into something fierce and unquenchable, Amon broke eye contact and looked down at the table. After that they were silent.

Amon could hear the drunken salarymen laughing raucously and smelled the distinctive scent of *natto* in the air. Looking over, he saw a white-bearded man bringing a pinch of the tiny brown soybeans to his mouth, strands of sticky fermentation slime stretching from his chopsticks to the bowl.

Rick poured himself a fresh goblet of hoppy, topping off Amon's from the pitchers. He then made a makeshift sandwich with cheese, sliced meat, and bread. Amon continued to work away at his noodles and turned to watch a documentary special that had just come on.

The center of the room panned across a massive river. From its great width, clear waters, tall cinderblock flood barriers and skyscrapers lining each bank, Amon recognized it as the Sanzu River. It separated the District of Dreams—Tokyo's pecuniary retreat—from the rest of the metropolis. On the near bank in the foreground were stacks of bamboo crates and makeshift plastic cubicles where men and woman in suits sat at desks. A dry female voice began to narrate the scene.

This is Kindness Beyond Credit, the largest venture charity in Eastern Japan. *Cut to closeup on the stack of crates, each one pasted with a sticker reading "supply donations".*

Donations have been slim this year, but the local bankdead haven't given up hope for their children. *Women in tattered clothes lining up alongside the river in front of the crates, babies wrapped in rags held close to their bosoms. Two men in black kevlar suits flank the head of the line, cradling assault dusters, their faces hidden beneath helmet and goggles.*

Bankdead mothers gather here along the banks of the Sanzu River in hopes of better opportunities for their newborn sons and daughters. *A male reporter standing in front of the crates. He's wearing a collared T-shirt and white slacks, his hair trimmed, teeth sparkling. Beside him, a woman cradles a baby in her arms. In contrast to the digimade reporter, the woman looks rugged and hideous, her hair bristly, her chapped skin red and rough, torn clothes draped around her scrawny frame. Even the white blanket bundling the baby is stained and filled with holes.*

This is Yoshiko Matsuda. She's waiting in line to give her baby up for adoption to one of the BioPens. For mothers like Matsuda, it's a hard choice to make, but it's the only way her son, Saburo, can be eligible for a BodyBank and have a chance to participate in the AT market. *Closeup on the baby's face as Matsuda rocks him gently, his eyes closed, cheeks flushed.*

With the future of their offspring in mind, it's a sacrifice that many bankdead mothers are willing to make. *Full body shot of Matsuda, an out of focus but still recognizable heap of garbage in the background.* Her voice is dubbed over the scene. "It's been teff this yare what with the shupply shertages N' all."

When it switched to a closeup of Masuda, Amon began to feel mildly nauseous, the dusting of moles on her cheeks and her wispy patches of facial hair now blown-up vividly. He found her strange accent jarring to his ears as well. Bankdead spoke in a patois derisively nicknamed Hinkongo, or Poor-ese, a brusque, rural-sounding amalgamation of Japanese dialects, English, Korean, and Mandarin that was often the brunt of jokes in comedy routines. Amon could tell the woman was trying hard to speak standard Japanese for the interview. She was more fluent than most bankdead, but her habitual pronunciation nonetheless leaked through.

"Me n' Saburo err just gettin bay." *Cut.* "I wan Saburo ter hevv a BodyBank suz he cen get a jeb." *Cut.* "I was bern herr in the cemps. This is mer home but I'ze want him ter hev a chance fer someshing bertteh."

They finished their meals while zoning out on the news. Amon felt slightly relieved to see that nothing had been reported about Kitao's cash crash. It always reflected favorably on the assigned Liquidators if the media didn't catch on until the official GATA press release.

Amon washed down the final bite of his noodles with some hoppy while Rick gnawed off the last few strands of flesh from his drumstick.

"Can you guess what I saw on the train a few months back?" Rick asked, breaking their silence as he poured another drink for Amon and then himself.

Amon shook his head.

"A family. There was a boy and a girl and a mother and a father, and an elderly couple that must have been the grandparents. I know it could have just been digimake, but they all looked and talked so much alike—even their gestures were similar—the connection had to be hereditary. Have you ever seen that before, a whole family together?"

NO, Amon admitted, NEVER.

Fertilex had a monopoly on the actions associated with every stage of reproduction, from erotic *fondling* to umbilical cord snipping, enabling them to jack the prices up prohibitively high. As a result, almost all children were raised in BioPens where large-scale rearing facilities cut down on costs and the operators could turn a profit by selling the profiles of promising youth to corporate headhunters. Only the wealthiest one percent could afford all the *dating, chatting, foreplay, ejaculation*, and sometimes *marriage* that it took to make a traditional family; only the richest among them could do it with their own DNA, as paying someone to perform *artificial insemination* of banked eggs and sperm was much cheaper in the Fertilex payment scheme than *impregnation*; and only the richest among the rich could afford to raise their own kids rather than board them at BioPen schools. Amon sometimes saw groups of children led by SubMoms on field-trips, but the ultra affluent rarely appeared in low-luxury spaces like trains, and he had only ever seen an actual family in the InfoFlux.

"The parents were standing by the doors," continued Rick, "and the shy little girl was clinging to her mother's skirt the whole time and the boy kept bragging to his father in toddler babble about how good he was at drawing, and then he would draw these little squiggly pictures in the air, of stick people and seagulls and smiley windows and stuff and . . ."

Amon noticed a change come over Rick as he spoke. The brooding sadness always deep in his eyes had been replaced by a sparkling warmth that Amon had never seen on him. THAT'S A PRETTY RARE THING TO SEE, I GUESS, BUT WHY DO YOU BRING IT UP?

"It's connected with what I was telling you before about . . . well . . . When I was looking at those kids . . . a sort of image came to me in a flash. I was holding a baby and I felt really happy, and I could see that it was gonna be tough, but I knew that between the two of us, we'd find a way to make it work."

HOLD ON. YOU'VE LOST ME THERE. THE TWO OF WHO?

"Me and Mayuko. I could never admit it to myself, but in that moment I realized that that's what I've wanted for years."

WHAT ARE YOU TALKING ABOUT?

"A family."

"Huh?!" said Amon, so surprised that he accidentally spoke aloud, before quickly switching back to text. YOU MEAN, YOU WANT TO HAVE A BABY WITH--

"Well we haven't talked about it yet, but . . . You see, I'm planning to propose."

Amon was flabbergasted. YOU'RE SERIOUSLY . . . BUT . . . BUT EVEN THINKING ABOUT THIS IS . . . UNACCEPTABLE. Amon used the word *unacceptable*, because it was more affordable than other words of censure like *bad*, *terrible*, *ridiculous*, and *discreditable*.

"Sorry, Amon. I've been meaning to tell you for a long time. To be honest, I wanted your advice. I had to make some huge choices recently and my decision friends aren't always that helpful. But you're so busy these days. Don't give me that look. It's not like I planned for it to be Mayu—"

MAYUKO'S GOT NOTHING TO DO WITH IT.

"No? Then why do you look so pissed off?"

Amon stared at Rick for a few seconds, unsure how to respond. Now that his friend had mentioned it, Amon became aware of a painful scene stretching half-invisible across his visual field. It was too faint and blurry to make out with his eyes open, but every blink brought it into focus, and each time he could see a different tableaux painted on the inside of his eyelids for an instant. Together they depicted a series of disparate actions seen from various angles, like the frames of a film reel in the wrong order. *Rick's hand on her back. Rick's lips on her neck. Rick's skin on her skin.* Amon quickly realized that these were not admotainment segs: they were products of his imagination. And each glimpse sent a pang of some awful emotional admixture jolting down his spine, with such intensity that he wanted to reach into the fleeting darkness and crush what floated there. *But this isn't about Mayuko*, he told himself as he stuffed the feelings down some numb shaft in the underbelly of his mind. *This is about my dream. I've got to do something.* Amon took a big gulp of hoppy, put down the goblet, slapped his palms flat on the table, and sat forward in his chair, leaning across as close to Rick as he could get.

LISTEN! SEKIDO-SAN HASN'T SAID ANYTHING YET, BUT I'M SURE HE'S NOTICED YOUR LATENESS. OUR ATTENDANCE RECORDS ARE ALL THERE IN THE SYSTEM AND HE'S PROBABLY GOT IT SET UP TO WARN HIM AUTOMATICALLY WHEN SOMEONE ISN'T ON TIME. EVEN IF HE DOESN'T, ALL HE'S GOT TO DO IS CLICK. SO FORGET ABOUT MY CHANCES FOR PROMOTION FOR A SECOND. WHAT THIS MEANS IS YOU COULD GET FIRED. YOU'VE GOT THAT HUGE APARTMENT IN KIYOSUMI WITH ALL THOSE NICE FURNISHINGS, AND I KNOW THAT'S A BIT OUT OF YOUR SALARY RANGE. YOU'RE COMING TO PLACES LIKE THIS AND BLOWING CREDITIME FOR YOUR OWN LEISURE. I BET YOU'RE OUT ON DATES WITH MAYUKO AND . . . YOU'RE THINKING ABOUT HAVING A BABY?

"It's not as bad as you think. Mayuko and I are in the early stages of our relationship, and . . . I admit the apartment is kind of pricey and I'm paying a bit to take her out to nice places, get her the occasional gift, you know, but obviously I'll start saving once we're settled. Right now I can't go over to her place because she works from home and says she can't relax there. That's why I rented out my new apartment, so we'd have a place to spend time together. Plus she's been working crazy hours, seven days a week, so we can only meet at night and the only time we have to relax is in the morning before work."

At last Amon realized why Rick was late. HAVE YOU CHECKED THE AVERAGE COST FOR RAISING A BABY? IT'S #%#*ING ASTRONOMICAL. CLOSE TO THE FINE FOR MURDER. Amon scrambled the swear word to save a few yen.

"I'm not worried. Mayuko's salary is better than mine, and if we pool our resources—"

BUT YOU JUST TOLD ME THAT SHE DOESN'T EVEN KNOW THAT YOU WANT A BABY! HOW CAN YOU BANK ON HER BEING WILLING TO SHARE HER EARNINGS? BESIDES, I JUST TOLD YOU THAT YOUR JOB IS ON THE LINE. HAVE YOU FACTORED THAT INTO YOUR CALCULATIONS?

"You're not gonna understand this, but I don't give a shit. If I have to find another job, I will. This is my chance to become a father. I might never get another."

Amon felt his gut seize up with something like horror, as though his innards were being freeze-dried. He saw now that Rick's mind had been poisoned with a throwback urge, like a bear living in the tropics that insists on hibernating every winter. The instinct to reproduce might be biological, but it certainly wasn't economical. It had no place in the AT marketplace, where humankind had traded momentary carnal satisfaction for a shot at unlimited freedom. Rick was driven by dead desires. Impossible, atavistic, caveman desires. Desires beyond what he had earned.

IF HAVING A FAMILY IS REALLY THAT IMPORTANT TO YOU, THEN TAKE A LOOK AT THIS. Amon linked him a video on raising children from a blog he quickly found on the ImmaNet, entitled "Guide to Starting Your Very Own Family Creditably." A middle-aged woman appeared on the table between Amon and Rick, minimized to about ten centimeters tall. She wore a dress patterned in pink flowers on turquoise, curly brown hair hanging to her chin.

> Responsible prospective parents scrimp and save and wait and wait and wait patiently for the day when they will be able to afford their baby. In order to have your very own family, you will need to secure funding for sexual intercourse, pregnancy, pre- and post-natal medical attention, a training bank, and enough credit to pay for your child's actions until they can legally take charge

of their lives. That's why you need to make your best efforts to reduce expenses, and obtain lucrative bonuses and promotions at work, before deciding on the number of children and writing up a family initiation estimate chart as described in chapter four. Remember, the key to a healthy baby is PISC: Patience, financial Integrity, employment Stability, and Compliance with your superiors and the market. For low income parent hopefuls, mail order artificial insemination and long-distance child-rearing are highly recommended.

Amon stopped the seg and the woman vanished.

Rick crossed his arms and stared at Amon with a look of utter boredom and disgust, the warmth in his eyes extinguished.

WHAT? THIS DOESN'T INTEREST YOU? IF YOU'RE SERIOUS ABOUT HAVING A FAMILY, THIS IS EXACTLY WHAT YOU'VE GOT TO BE DOING. BUT YOU'RE NOT DOING ANY OF IT! Amon's BodyBank detected the physiological signs of anger and the text in his comic bubble automatically turned red. **YOUR LIFESTYLE IS TOTALLY INAPPROPRIATE!**

"How about saying *bad* or *dangerous* or *shitty* or something instead of inappropriate all the time. You sound totally fucking ridiculous. Cash crashing isn't inappropriate, it sucks ass." Amon flinched again at the profanity. It was as though Rick were intentionally flaunting his advice to be frugal. "I remember when you used to tell me things that were interesting, sometimes even insightful. Now you edit out so many of your words, you've got nothing worthwhile to say."

Amon couldn't completely deny what Rick was saying. Admittedly, there were a few things he was holding back on. He wanted to tell Rick how the birth rate was so low you could easily spend a whole decade's worth of creditime on sex and not get a single baby out of it; how if you were lucky and made it through pregnancy, birth, and nursing, your cherished one might slip from your hands suddenly, whether from negligence or an unavoidable calamity; how being accountable for the actions of a person too immature to grasp the dire consequences of squandering was to sacrifice your own choices, your own actions, your whole life to pay for another's, often leading to the catatonic parental budget trap; how even if you could barely scrape by, they could turn hooligan before reaching the age of majority and bankrupt you with bad behavior. In all likelihood, Rick's investment and financial risk would come to nothing but misery and regret, especially if he continued to rush ahead and gamble with his career. But to say all that would cost him a fortune. So Amon kept his typing fingers still, trying to think of easier, cheaper phrases to persuade with.

"I'm your friend, Amon. So if you're worried about me, tell me what you think instead of pasting bullshit from the ImmaNet. Speak, for fuck's sake! I know you, and I can tell you've got something to say, so just spit it out already." Rick was almost shouting, and Amon could feel the restraints against his own anger bursting like fissures in the walls of a furnace.

ALRIGHT. I'LL TELL YOU WHAT I THINK. YOU'VE GOT TO STOP SLEEP-ING IN, COME IN ON TIME EVERY DAY, MOVE OUT OF THAT EXPENSIVE APARTMENT, STOP DATING, LIVE SIMPLY, SAVE AS MUCH OF YOUR SALARY AS YOU CAN, SEEK FINANCIAL COUNSELING, AND THINK ABOUT STARTING A FAMILY IN A DECADE OR SO. IF YOU FOLLOW MY ADVICE, YOU MIGHT LOSE OUT ON A FEW LITTLE PLEASURES NOW, BUT I'LL BE HAPPY, OUR BOSS WILL BE HAPPY, AND, EVENTUALLY, YOU'LL BE HAPPY TOO. BUT IF YOU'RE NOT CAREFUL, YOU'RE GOING TO CASH CRASH.

"Cash crash? Me?" Rick pointed at his own face and then smacked his hand through the air as though brushing away the very possibility. "You don't think I know that stuff? Yeah, sure. Save. Work hard. Whatever. But there's something called timing, you know. This is my moment. If I postpone, it'll be too late for me and Mayuko, and I won't do that for GATA, or for you, or for anybody."

"You're being discreditable!" Amon snapped aloud. The rudest word there was, and an expensive one at that. He was practically shaking with rage as it slipped out.

"Discreditable! What about you? I know what you're after. It's that silly dream of yours. Do you actually think it's possible to go there? How rich do you think you can become? Can the Birlas afford your dream? You're calling me names. And maybe I'm living a little beyond my means, but at least I'm after something attainable. You're stressing out over every little thumb-twiddle and working yourself to death for something, and you don't even know if it exists."

Hearing Rick talk about his dream with such vitriol, Amon began to wish he had never confided in him about it.

The furrows on Rick's brow deepened; the brooding, tragic depth in his eyes seeming to pervade his whole face. "I'm worried about you, Amon," he said with a shake of his dull silver hair. "We could have called for backup today and got Kitao the safe way, but you wanted all the glory for yourself, even if that meant having joint pain for the rest of your life. And it's not just your own life that you're putting at risk. What if I got hit? Or that kid? You think it's okay if others take permanent damage for your promotion? What happened to your sense of responsibility? It's like you've become some kind of scrimping automaton. Like Ebenezer Scrooge gone monk. All you can think about is two things: saving money and advancing your career. You weren't always like this. I remember when we were hitting the clubs in Roppongi and Shibuya every weekend. This year you didn't even come out for Halloween. It's almost like you've forgotten how to live."

WHAT? AM I SUPPOSED TO LIVE LIKE YOU? FOOLING AROUND EVERY MORNING WITH MY FRIEND'S EX-GIRLFRIEND AND SHOWING UP LATE FOR WORK.

"Is that a little glimmer of humanity slipping through, Ol' Scrooge? If you're upset about me being with Mayuko, then why not just say it? I mean, look at all the frustration in your eyes. Well, maybe I'll cash crash some day, but maybe you'll end up raving like that flower nut we liquidated. So who's discreditable: me or you?"

Amon was about to respond with something nasty, when a female voice, icy monotone like an in-flight air bag demonstration, bleated privately in his ear. *Your vital signs show that you're angry. Please take some deep breaths. Anger is a risk factor for many medical conditions and can lead to aggressive activity. To read more, please click the link below.* MyMedic, Amon's health-watch application, had sent him an automated message.

Worried about his insurance premiums, Amon immediately pushed his styrofoam tray aside, put his elbows on the table, rested his face in his palms, and began taking deep breaths as instructed, while he considered what Rick had said. Amon knew exactly what he'd been implying. He was reminding Amon of the research paper on the psychological causes of discreditable behavior that had been required reading during Liquidator training. The most recent results showed that overtly wanton spending habits were less likely to lead to bankruptcy than an excessively ascetic lifestyle. Overaction was less dangerous because even though it required greater expense, it gave untrammeled reign to desire, clearing the mind of seeds for even deeper-rooted cravings. On the other hand, by suppressing visceral needs, underaction added discomfort and inconvenience to daily life, leading to boredom, irritation, disappointment, and anxiety. If left unchecked, these negative emotions could slowly fester and infect other areas of the mind, sometimes transforming into madness, perversion, fetishistic obsession, violence, and credicrimes of all sorts; in other words, into depravities that were far more expensive than minor daily indulgences. The research had concluded that overaction and underaction were just the twin faces of one disease: malaction. Overaction was like taking an express train that traveled the shortest possible distance from point A, a life of happy solvency, to point B, the black pit of bankruptcy. Underaction was a meandering trail that seemed to set off for the opposite shore, but through circuitous wandering and zigzag backtracking, arrived without warning at the same ruinous destination.

But Amon knew that would never happen to him. A faint sense of yearning was undeniably present now and again, but compared to his ambition, to go to the place he saw in his dreams—whether it existed or not—it was piddling and insignificant. For most, staying solvent and having a few simple luxuries was enough. For Amon, there was more to life than that. Every effort literally counted if he was going to make it there; if he was going to fill up the savings account set aside in a nether region of the ImmaNet where banks were stable and interest high. He knew that investing this money in properties might be faster. It was said that buying the rights to *procreate* at an opportune moment had kickstarted the Birla family's legendary climb to supreme opulence, and stories like this abounded, but Amon wasn't the gambling type. He preferred to earn slowly and steadily, for if there was anything he could count on in himself, it was persistence and willpower. With vigilance over every transitory impulse so constant as to rival the detection capabilities of the sensors abiding beneath his skin, he diligently calculated every step and glance, cough and sniffle, twitch and muscle tick, and saved and saved and saved, while doing everything he could to move up the ranks at GATA. Whatever the research said, Amon was always encouraged by the life of Lawrence Barrow, Chief Executive Minister of Japan, who famously rode prodigious discipline from the lowest position to the highest. It was Rick who was in real danger, consumed by a drive to spread his seed that was completely out of touch with economy. But how could Amon explain this frugally? Boiling it all down into affordable language would take too much time.

Deep breathing was expensive, so Amon tried to improvise by combining it with the guru's breath-reduction technique while still hiding his face in his palms. He allowed his breaths to extend into the range of "deepness," accepting the extra charge, but held his breath at the end of each inhalation and exhalation. Yet to his dismay, the attempt failed, and he ended up with long, truncated respiration that was neither calming nor satisfying.

"Are you doing those absurd exercises again?" Rick asked, apparently unable to contain his impatience at being ignored for several minutes. "You gotta give that up. Your face is all purple. Just fucking breathe!" Amon ignored him. He continued to focus on his diaphragm until the anger warning window closed, whereupon he lifted his head up from his palms, removed his elbows from the table, and sat up straight.

The plates before the other patrons were now empty, and the number of bottles had grown. A group of young women wearing mini-skirts and done up like ceramic masks in a thick veneer of digimake had stopped at the entrance to scan the prices squirming around the vending machines. Every man in Self Serve turned his head to stare at their smooth, bare legs.

LISTEN RICK, I'M GOING TO TRY AND EXPLAIN MYSELF ONE MORE TIME. AS LIQUIDATORS, WE'RE THE PUBLIC FACE OF EVERYTHING THE AT SYSTEM STANDS FOR. WE HAVE TO SET AN EXAMPLE, AND THAT MEANS WE CAN'T BE FINANCIALLY LOOSE. NOW YOUR LATENESS IS ENDANGERING MY PROMOTION AND YOUR JOB. I HAVEN'T REPORTED YOU BECAUSE YOU'RE MY FRIEND, BUT THIS CAN'T GO ON FOREVER. SEKIDO-SAN EITHER KNOWS ABOUT THIS AND HE'S WAITING TO TELL YOU, OR HE'LL NOTICE SOON ENOUGH. EITHER WAY, IT LOOKS BAD ON ME IF HE MAKES THE CALL FIRST, LIKE I'M PURPOSELY IGNORING THE SITUATION OR GIVING YOU SPECIAL FAVORS. I DON'T WANT TO DO THIS, YOU ARE MY FRIEND, BUT I'M GOING TO HAVE TO MAKE SOME SUGGESTIONS OF MY OWN

PRETTY SOON. SO I'M BEGGING YOU, PLEASE TAKE YOUR JOB MORE
SERIOUSLY.

"That's the way it goes, huh?" said Rick. "That's all you're gonna say.
I found something that matters to me for the first time in my life, and
you just talk about work. I don't expect you to congratulate me. I know
Mayuko used to be your girl. But the least you could do is tell me how
you feel. Instead, you push it down, and all I get is some advice on
accounting. Well I'm at a turning point. I know there are risks, and . . .
I'm sorry if my results reflect on you, but . . ."

The tragic hint in Rick's eyes grew in intensity and spread across his
face again, contorting it into a sad grimace, as though he were about to
cry. "I need someone to talk to, not just my stupid decision network.
Can't you say something, anything at all that isn't in your budget?"

Amon just stared at him, trying to think of an affordable response.

Suddenly Rick stood up, chugged the last of his hoppy, clunked the
goblet back on the table, and wiped his mouth with the back of his sleeve.
The grimace was gone, but his eyes were shaking and glazed red. "Got it.
I was stupid to think I could count on you. You've changed. You're just a
groveling, obedient little tool now, aren't you? And a pervert too—living
with those filthy nosties. You wouldn't lift a finger to save a dying friend,
or a lover, if it cost you an extra penny, all for that pathetic delusion of
yours."

Amon leapt to his feet, his teeth clenched, his shoulders flexed, his
hands bunched in fists at his hips, his vision completely consumed with
this so-called friend who could utter such precise pain. MyMedic was
bleeping, but he almost couldn't see it as the whole room disappeared.
He wanted to shout something at the top of his lungs, but he wasn't sure
what. Thoughts and feelings rose before his mind and dropped away
before he could understand them, like letters falling from the sky in a
blur too fast to make out, tantalizingly close as though he could pluck
them out of space and put together words Rick might understand, yet
impossible to grasp. Meaning wanted to fly out of him unformed and
find its own unity in the act of communication, but there was no way to
estimate the cost if he didn't know what he would say in advance, so he
groped for affordable language, eventually censoring himself into silence
while his lips trembled.

Suddenly he remembered where he was and realized that several people were staring at him. The crowd in the bar had grown, a stream of young men and office ladies dawdling hesitantly in. The seats were all taken and some elderly patrons were standing in the center of the room where the entertisements were still playing. It was some kind of fashion show, and skinny women strutted down a runway wearing aluminum tutus, clay platform shoes, and cashmere scarves tacked with tropical bird-feathers that spelled out the names of generic addiction-suppressing pharmaceuticals.

Staring at Amon, Rick nodded with a grunt, as though he'd been convinced of what he'd said. He gathered the platter, decanters, and goblets into his arms, walked over to the disposal area, and stuffed them into the garbage bin. Then he cut through the center of the room—the fashion show swallowing him for a moment like a ritzy fog—and went out the doorless exit.

6

JINBOCHO, THE TEZUKA

Walking along the sidewalk home from Jinbocho Station, Amon tried not to look directly at the InfoStars.

He remembered seeing a news story a few years back about how owners of stellar estate had finally won their decades-long lawsuit against owners of terrestrial estate for damages from flagrant light pollution that obscured the galaxy. The final ruling had stated that both parties were entitled to equal brightness and visibility in the ImmaNet night. For this reason, perhaps, the sky tonight was uncannily clear, saturated with InfoStars that glowed vividly in spite of the waves of promo-laser luminescence flowing up and along contours of the looming architectural sprawl, a wilderness of cross-sectioned beehives made into gargantuan lanterns.

Amon had trained his mind to avoid the scrambled cacophony of InfoClouds, the patchwork flux of InfoSky, the searing thrall of InfoSun, the battering compulsion of InfoTyphoon, the counterfeit hype of InfoWind. Yet InfoStars used gentler, subtler, more insidious means to get attention than these. As he walked along the sparsely-peopled sidewalk, they appeared in his upper peripheral simply as stars, a field of dense constellations shining distinctly above the strobing metropolis. This half-glimpse of unadulterated Nature promised respite from the incessant distractions surrounding him. The very instinct he had inculcated in his mind to avoid expensive sights made it unconsciously seek out such serene spaces. Usually it was a strip of blank sidewalk, a bare gutter, a pedestrian's back, an empty alley; he could almost hear his synapses gasp for air in these moments. Yet the apparent simplicity of the night sky was a lure, and the moment he glanced directly up, his line of sight was detected, he was charged for viewing, and the stars began to trace out videos, like animated connect-the-dots, imperceptibly creeping at first, fooling the mind into believing it was still on relaxation mode, but gradually coalescing into recognizable logos. *UT Corp.:* a waterfall washed over a mossy boulder and turned the exterior transparent to reveal wiring and machinery within. *No Logo Inc:* the word LOGO with an x through it torn to shreds by shotgun buckshot. TTY: a light switch flicked and electricity rippled from a sleeping man's toes to his head before sprouting into a dream bubble with a wedding inside. Try as he might to ignore them, the moving trademark images of The Twelve And One were osmotically infiltrating Amon's consciousness via his optic nerve. Twinkling, twinkling, twinkling in their pristine beauty, they seemed to offer profound connection with fate and the depths of the cosmos. They gave marketing.

Hard-soled footsteps on concrete, distant car horns, the burble of ground-ads erupting from the street—it was a quiet night. Amon passed many bookstores as he walked. These were rare sightings in Tokyo, but Jinbocho was a unique area, famous for almost a century as a town for used books, and in recent years for its many nosties.

Stalls stacked with books were lined up along the curb in front of the shops. Book dealers in jeans or cords and plaid short-sleeved shirts sat in chairs amongst the stalls while after-work salarymen stood on the sidewalk browsing. Amon caught snippets of their conversation as he passed.

"The 1984 first edition is a bit worn on the edges, but you'll never find anything like it."

"Would you consider a trade?"

"I can't say the *First Treatise* manuscript is a masterpiece, but regarding monarchy . . ."

"In the beginning all the world was America."

"I've never seen this illustration before. How much?"

These were nosties; fetishistic collectors and connoisseurs of printed books, vinyl, paintings, photographs, and all manner of *analog detritus*.

According to FlexiPedia, the phrase analog detritus—abbreviated colloquially in Japan as *anadeto* or sometimes just AD—was born in the aftershocks of the Digital Revolution when huge quantities of obsolete machinery, furniture, decorations, art, were discarded, much of it ending up in the hands of the poor (who Amon imagined to be much like the bankdead of the present). The nosties, who first appeared during the same period, were obsessed with this horrid refuse despite the ubiquity of clean and convenient digital copies. For this reason, they were seen as throwback perverts, degenerate lovers of anachronism and molder. They dedicated their lives to the acquisition, restoration, and preservation of the few remnants of anadeto still circulating around the Free World. And in Jinbocho, a subculture of book nosties had proliferated, making it into a kind of haven for the paper trash of ages gone by.

Through the glass storefronts facing the street stalls, Amon could see antique couches, vintage reading lamps, and rows of shelves filled to capacity with books. Book in gloved hand, the nosties stood beside the shelves completely still but for the occasional turning of a page, some scanning the titles while taking notes with pad and pen. There were signs of age on the furnishings that could have easily been touched up: the green velour backing on an armchair faded, a few tarnished patches on the wood of a low shelf, scratches here and there in the rubber tile flooring. Yet a certain amount of decay, if managed and controlled, seemed to add value for nosties. They reveled in the outdated, loyal consumers of the brand name called time. The books, however, were flawlessly kept without nicks or splotches, the pages still white, the spines and covers still as vibrant as the day they sprung from the press.

Amon had never set foot in these stores and had no idea how much the books cost, but guessed it was a lot. He had rarely seen anyone buy one, and even on these rare occasions, the dealers always looked reluctant to let them go. They were book nosties themselves, it seemed, and made a living mainly by overseeing the stockpiles rather than by making sales. As outcasts, nosties tended to stick together, pooling their resources to revive failing businesses and keep them in the community.

Amon approached an intersection spanned by a pedestrian overpass. It was constructed of four footbridges that stretched from each corner to the adjacent one, forming a square elevated above the traffic. He started to climb a staircase leading to the nearest footbridge, skipping stairs as needed, sometimes one, sometimes three, in accordance with Scrimp Navi's guidance, as the book chatter faded into traffic whirr and faint adfo cajolery. Standing two stories above the street, he stopped for a moment, leaned on the railing and looked out on the metropolis. A six-lane road ran between the base of massive condo thickets for a dozen blocks, where it curved left and sloped out of sight into a slot in the flickering concrete distance. Clusters of vehicles pulsed smoothly along like letters sucked through a pneumatic tube. Briskly tromping pedestrians streamed on both sides like herds of binary code incarnate. Everywhere the InfoFlux writhed hypnotic in the night, that swirling concoction of living, wriggling, desire-paint; its pigments pure extract of a million marketers' minds, essential oil of a million popularity algorithms. The cars swished sibilantly under the bridge; the crowds murmured instant chat babble; the advertainment hummed an infinite repertoire of inducements guised as stories, like a choir of sirens singing all notes at once. Amon's nostrils filled with exhaust fumes and a wayward waft of pungent pork-bone broth from a nearby ramen shop. After the exertion of climbing the stairs in the humid night, a glaze of sweat clung to his brow. Part of him ached to wipe it. A stronger part of him refused. It was unusual for him to stop until he had arrived at the affordable sanctuary of his home, but something roiled inside him, something painful and bewildering.

The head of the stairs was the corner where two footbridges met at a right angle. Amon took the left path. He walked slowly across, running his hand along the top of the railing while he tried to make sense of the strange events that day, but his thoughts refused to cohere. He was tired, and although he wasn't quite drunk, his head was still hazy with hoppy, his belly bloated with carbonation. His BodyBank had no trouble sorting the audio-video data it had collected, compiled, and categorized according to time, keyword, and visual motif. Yet Amon's measly human brain, tripped up with the added task of comprehending, was overwhelmed by his many fresh and startling experiences. His two oldest friends were now lovers. That had been the first surprise. In the same moment he'd seen his best friend's luxurious apartment and realized he was hiding dangerous habits. At the Liquidation Ministry, Sekido had praised him in his evaluation and hinted at the chance for a major promotion. Then he'd cash crashed the Minister of Records, his first mission against a GATA employee, almost getting hit with arthritis dust in the process. After work, he'd learned that Rick's relationship with Mayuko was behind his slacking and overspending, as he strove to impress her. Finally, Rick had unleashed an onslaught of words and the yawning rift between them had widened even further.

Amon and Rick had never fought before in their lives, yet somehow their talk that evening had exploded into angry confrontation. What had it all been about? On the surface, there was nothing in Rick's onslaught of criticism that Amon could accept. He had no choice but to sacrifice all trivial pleasures and fully embrace frugality. How else could he reach his dream, that tendril of shimmering silk tugging on his soul? Putting aside money for his savings was the only way, if there was a way. To make an exception and enjoy the moment—any moment—went counter to everything he lived for.

His hand hit an intervening rail, telling him he had reached the other side of the footbridge. He turned right to follow the rail and tried not to think of the amount he'd spent that day. That would only depress him. But he couldn't help it, and amidst his confusion, he let out a long sigh. Performing a discreditable action like sighing after such a discreditable day was self-destructive, he realized, and remembered Rick's warnings about the dangers of underaction. Amon knew what Rick had said was just plain wrong. Admittedly, there were many urges and feelings he pushed aside, but he wasn't going to break down. There was just no way. Yet Amon acknowledged that Rick had known him almost his whole life and could peer deeply inside him, beneath his digimade face, his naked face, even deeper, right to the bones. A part of Amon felt that there was a lesson concealed somewhere in their bitter exchange. On the train from Shinbashi to Jinbocho, he had pulled up the LifeStream of their dispute and watched it over again. Skipping past the trivial segments of hoppy-swigging and news-watching, he listened carefully to every word Rick had said. But watching the events in chronological order had taught him nothing. He needed a way to put them into the order of their significance, to connect up the circuits for an X-ray gun that he could point at himself, as if by deciphering those videos he might peer through the flesh that hid the skeletal form of his own existence. If only there was a search application that could crack the code of an individual life, automatically panning through the dust of past for the dark gold of truth.

With no recourse to his BodyBank for clarification, Amon found himself trying to sort it out with memory. Isolated fragments of their argument and other times they had spent together over the last few weeks, months, and years swirled in his mind like a snowstorm. When he tried to grasp hold of a particular memory fragment, to still it and consider its hidden meaning, it would fly from his consciousness as though carried by a gust of subliminal wind, and another fragment—an insult Rick had hurled at him, a giggle over a prank they'd played on another kid, or a silence between them on the train home from Roppongi—would appear unbidden in its place before quickly vanishing, a crystalline flake melting in a warm hand.

Then, out of nowhere, something new trickled into his awareness, and this time it stayed there: the expression of sad wonder on Mayuko's face when she'd turned away from Rick and seen him that morning. In that moment, Amon remembered being overcome with a feeling and taking it for surprise. But reflecting back more carefully, he realized that something else, a sort of bitter melancholy, had lurked beneath it. He was curious to know what had given rise to this emotion and why this memory alone had lingered when every other had fled. Yet as soon as he turned his thoughts towards such questions, the same feeling returned and he decided that no good would come from dwelling on them, so he quickly brushed the memory aside, letting it slip into the capacious black recesses of his own forgetting.

On the other side of the overpass, Amon went down the stairs to the sidewalk, walked several more blocks, and arrived at his apartment building—the Tezuka. It was a thin fifteen story high-rise that looked like a million other residential buildings in Tokyo, from the outside at least.

The doors ID'd Amon and opened automatically as he approached. He walked through the gray-tiled lobby towards the elevator, which came down to meet him and opened just as he approached. Amon stepped in, the doors closed, and the elevator began to rise. Inside, the chamber was pasted all over with small squares of paper. Each one had an individual frame from a comic book on it, depicting moments of action from various different series, most of them Japanese, some European or North American. The paper squares varied in size but had been meticulously cobbled together to cover the four walls and ceiling, leaving no spaces between.

The doors opened into a hallway lined with a similar collage of comic cut-outs. Amon stepped out, turned right down the hallway, and stared vaguely at the wall beside him as he walked. Spread throughout the building's whole interior, the frames were arranged in such a way—lined up right to left and top to bottom—as to suggest conjoinment into a single story. Reinforcing this impression, Amon had witnessed residents pacing slowly around, staring at the walls as though reading. Yet the artistic styles, inking, paper quality, dialog, and borders were all disparate, with no apparent continuity between the events captured in each square: a young schoolgirl crying alone on a fire escape high above a dark city, beside a crowned foxman sitting on a throne with a gold scepter in hand, below a gang of bike punks drive-by-clubbing pedestrians in a crowd, above a green haired woman squeezing her huge, bare breasts together and smiling seductively, next to a steam-powered train flying off into the galaxy. Amon was used to the incongruous motley of advertisement permeating life, so the lack of narrative connection between the frames didn't faze him. But he had always sensed something uniquely deficient about the individual frames, some semantic defect that was unfamiliar and unnerving. This inexplicable feeling had bothered him for years, until one day, around the time he got his promotion last year, he had figured out why. Nowhere in the drawings and text could he decipher recommendations, inducements, proposals, hints, guilt-trips, seductions, exhortations, offers, shaming, innuendo, or anything that sold him a particular action. Soliciting nothing, these dissected signs seemed to defeat their own meaning, like music without rhythm, racing without speed, cuisine without flavor.

At the end of the hallway, Amon went through a door on his left and entered a spacious room filled with rows of shelves that were lined with comics. Like the collage and the books outside, Amon knew that these were no digital projections, but palpable things of paper. Dozens of men sat in chairs before low coffee tables placed in an open area in the middle of the room, each one with several comics before him on the table. They hunched over their archaic treasures, a few peering into magnifying glasses, others into miniature monocular microscopes with one eye closed, others still with naked eyes. Some wore gloves; some used special rubber-tipped tweezers to turn the pages; some intricate gripping contraptions Amon couldn't identify; none used their bare hands. They stared at the illustrations and text before them in intense absorption, lips quivering excitedly at every new panel. One nostie even had his nose sandwiched between the pages of a pirate zombie romance, his eyes glazed and distant as though a narcotic aroma were somehow detectable in the dusty ink and pulp.

The Tezuka was a manga mansion. Like other manga mansions, it had evolved from a kind of budget hotel called manga cafes that had been widespread in the late twentieth and early twenty-first centuries of the Unfree Era. When these cafes went under one after the other during the Digital Revolution, a movement dedicated to saving the anadeto arose, later to be called the Nostie Reclamation. Composed of antiquarians, archeologists, traditionalists, luddites, historical scholars, collectors, the elderly, and other contingents of nostalgic pack rats, the Tokyo chapter's first joint venture was to buy several defunct cafes. The initial intent had been to make them into exclusive libraries for members, but the cost of actions related to the storage and use of anadeto was too great, so they were eventually converted into permanent living spaces. Thus manga mansions and similar rubbish co-ops, like art gallery condos and gaming arcade slums, were born.

While nosties were delighted to pay maintenance and storage fees for the perk of unlimited perusal, from the perspective of other Tokyo denizens, the rooms were small and drab, the common areas were pointlessly cluttered, and the idea of residing with such disreputable low lifes was just plain embarrassing, so many were reluctant to move in. To ensure there were no empty rooms, the mansion committee at the Tezuka waived the extra fees for non-nostie residents, depriving them of comic access in exchange.

The pared-down rent was very cheap—perhaps the cheapest in Tokyo aside from the capsules—and affordability had attracted a very different demographic, referred to in corporate blogspeak as comic refugees. Flat-broke salesmen starving for commission; owners of five-star restaurants struggling to cover their overhead; ashamed adulterers hiding from their wives; pale-skinned agoraphobes suicidally afraid of eye-contact. There were special miniature cubicles for such people, with just enough room to sleep on the reclining chair and live out of a bag. Comic refugees were often on the verge of critical illiquidity and Amon had crashed his share at other buildings. Most were elusive recluses, but sometimes he saw them enter late at night, perhaps from some exploitative job. They plodded straight to their rooms, rendered in such cheap resolution you could see the pixels, their faces projected without emotion to disguise whatever pained expression they surely wore underneath, an acid smell clinging to them as though their desire for a respectable home had transmuted into foul perspiration.

Taking a narrow walkway between the shelves, Amon stayed well away from the stooped figures and their garbage, as though in a quarantine zone. He was reminded of how Rick had mocked him for living with "filthy nosties," and a tight sliver of indignation bit into his gut. Rick had simply misunderstood. Just like the comic refugees, Amon thought of this manga mansion as a shameful, temporary abode. He had never mentioned to anyone at work that he lived in Jinbocho, even though there were enough normals in the neighborhood to reasonably deny he was a nostie. Amon was just as appalled by their sick hobbies as anyone. He couldn't fathom what pleasure they derived from paper when all comics could be downloaded in mint condition, complete with hand-flippable digital pages that didn't take up space. The shelves could be cleared out for a workout room or dining hall or something useful, and the silly gloves and tweezers dispensed with. But Amon had been living in Jinbocho long enough to expect this type of absurd behavior. Nosties were warped but harmless and he could tolerate just about any oddity or embarrassment so long as it boosted his frugality.

After crossing the library, Amon made his way down a hallway of more cut-outs interrupted at even intervals by white doors on each side. He reached his door on the left, opened it manually with a key, and entered.

★

Amon lived in a room with just enough floor space for a futon, a washing machine, and a small mat where he folded and piled up his clothes. The walls were made of off-white plasterboard, the floors of faux plywood. An air conditioner that resembled a smooth lego block was attached up high near the ceiling on the far wall. There was no kitchen, closet, or window, but there was a door across from the entrance leading to a bathroom and a loft suspended above the rear half of the main room that could be reached by ladder. The space between the loft and the ceiling was too small for Amon to sit up, but perfect for storage—if Amon had had anything to store, which he didn't. Aside from the futon, washing machine, and clothes, all he had was a tube of laundry soap, a fold-up table and chair, a pole attached under the loft to hang laundry, an electric carpet for the winter, two pairs of shoes, and a SpillBot.

Taking off his shoes, he stepped up the single stair into his room, undressed, hung his suit on the pole beneath the loft, and went into the bathroom. The walls, floor, ceiling, toilet, and shower were all made of an off-white plastic just like the vending machine at Self Serve. The room was so tiny he could put his palms flat on any two opposing walls without extending his arms.

After showering, brushing his teeth, and shaving (which, much like nail-trimming and other sorts of grooming, he always postponed until the hairs protruded too far from his face to edit them out affordably with digimake), he left the bathroom, put his dirty underclothes in the washing machine, and set the timer for the next morning. Next he unfolded his futon, lay down on his back in bed, and, disappointed that he had no time for the guru's lesson, gestured to activate his SpillBot. He had the most basic model, a hollow tube about twenty centimeters long with four thin, flexible legs. It scuttled over to his feet. Amon spread his legs into a V to let it closer. It stopped between his thighs, angled the tube diagonally towards his exposed crotch, and gently engaged. The inside of the tube was soft, lubricated, and warm. It began to move back and forth, first slowly, and then gradually accelerating, according to the pre-programmed rhythm Amon preferred.

SpillBots could be set to appear as anything out of the realm of fantasy, from the sublime to the twisted—the perfect mouth of a gorgeous pop idol, a disembodied hand, a robot, a peacock, a swirl of ectoplasm, a leper—and could synchronize their movements to the image. But Amon always turned off the pricey ImmaPorn features. It was just an insectile plastic tube bobbing over his sensitive region. With no soundtrack, he could hear the faint, grinding hydraulic rhythm.

Amon reflected gratefully on the advantages of SpillBots. Not only did they satiate a primal urge that might otherwise distract him from frugality, but using them actually reaped a small amount of profit. Spill-Bots operated as a repository for sperm banks operated by Fertilex. Since Amon owned the rights to his own fluids, he received a small payment for authorizing a Fertilex agent to come to his door from time to time and take away the contents of the tube, replacing the vial inside with a fresh one. This payment happened to be slightly higher than the usage fee with ImmaPorn deactivated, meaning Amon actually made money from using it and thus felt relieved in more ways than one (though he tried not to think about how many little Amons spawned by his donations might be running around out there).

While the SpillBot was going, Amon stared at a spot on the ceiling and kept his AT readout in his lower peripheral where he couldn't make it out. He did his best to limit the number of times he *checked* it in a day since this incurred a charge, but he always took a look every night before bed. This allowed him to keep track of expenses, identify his frugality weak points, and formulate strategies for future self-improvement. But that night, a feeling of dread weighed heavily on him when he finally glanced at it. His balance was much higher than the last time he looked, but that was only because he had received his salary at 9 p.m., his pay hour. He clicked *sort* to hone in on significant expenses, omitting all the breaths and blinks of the day, the pee he'd taken first thing, the subscription to his ImmaNet service provider, and the ambient meta-costs like *acting* (property of Xian Te Co.) and *transacting* (property of Yomoko Holdings) that applied to every action-transaction. (There were some regions of the world where *existing* and *living* were considered choices, and Amon was thankful he didn't live/exist there.)

His heart sank when he saw the day's total. In the morning, he had failed at blink and breath reduction; used Career Calibration, SiftAssist, and Mindfulator; opened Rick's profile; manifested across town; texted and FacePhoned numerous times; and even whispered Mayuko's name.

In the afternoon, the mission had dragged on too long, requiring all sorts of research and communication, which had brought him close to the limit of his action allowance. That evening, he had traveled to Shinbashi, bumped into all sorts of people, ordered food, texted, sent Rick links, used MyMedic and PennyPinch, and, to his horror, had somehow slipped up and said "discreditable" aloud. As he went through the list, he tagged actions that could have been avoided and saved them to his Frugality Improvement Diary for later study. Even accounting for the overall high average inflation that day, it was an unusual loss. Amon waited apprehensively for the impending sigh, but perhaps because it was hard to feel guilt simultaneously with the pleasant sensation in his loins, it never came.

After the SpillBot was finished, the machine performed a quick cleanup, retracted, and scuttled off to its place in the corner beside the foot of his futon. Amon twitched off the light.

Amon was falling headfirst from a clear, blue sky . . . or he might have been watching himself fall. He wasn't sure. The difference between watching and being watched hardly seemed to matter in this place. The wind didn't whip through his hair or flutter his clothes, as though he were drifting/watching himself drift down through a vacuum.

Below him was an expanse of forested mountains. He could hear the sound of the surf, and wanted to look where it was coming from, but his head refused to turn, the gravity seemingly intermingled with a subtle poison that paralyzed his will while dragging him inexorably downward.

At first, all he saw were blurry dabs of green and red and purple arrayed like a mosaic across the slopes, but gradually he began to make out more and more detail, the colors becoming individual shrubs and trees, faint landscape indentations becoming valleys, the flashing silver of ponds glimpsed through treetop gaps. There was something awe-inspiring about the forest; those tangled, warring canopies, those dark, hidden recesses, and the lurking presence of unseen creatures. Yet it gave him a sense of comfort; the glistening moisture on sleek bark like a succulent dew good enough to lap up, the branches holding up a bed of yielding leaves shimmering faintly in the sun, as though to cradle him when he landed. The scent of pungent lichen and wild herbs floated to his nostrils and sporadic birdsong cascaded from some hidden place, blending with the crash of the breakers. Directly below Amon, on the peak of a mountain, there was a clearing; a circular space dappled in creeping shadows and slivers of light. Around it, he could see puffs of shrubbery like green clouds embellished with bunches of tiny white wildflowers, spiked fronds jutting jaggedly upwards in rows, slender grasses bowing into shade, and pale brown trees standing on an intertwined twist of exposed roots like tentacles rising from the soil. In the middle was a depression like the fresh footprint of some giant.

The earth was close now. In a short time—a minute? an hour? a week?—he would reach the clearing. The forest was offering him a promise. Up high, the promise had linked him with an invisible fiber only half existent. Now it was disclosing itself, solidifying, becoming almost perceptible, like a physical thing. In that moment, the promise was more real than anything Amon had ever felt or touched, tasted or smelled, heard or sensed or imagined or . . . He wasn't sure, but it almost seemed more real than he was. Yet it concealed something: those shadows across the clearing a darkening veil, the light a blinding glare. The only way to understand it, for the promise itself carried clues to unravel its meaning, was to join with another and walk through that forest, to find the gateway to mystery.

Someone was standing in the clearing looking skyward. It was Amon, and he realized that he was both Amons at once.

His grounded self looked up expectantly at his falling self and down at himself, his falling self down at his grounded self and up at himself, both seeing each other and themselves, eye-contact made, the whole moment captured from a locationless elsewhere, from nowhere. They were trying to unite, one waiting, one dropping headfirst for the other.

But just as they were about to meet—whether to collide or join (the lush, fertile ground inviting his feet to sink deep and feel the warm texture between their toes together)—an inexplicable force intervened.

★

The force changed from night to night. Sometimes it was like reverse-polarity magnetism, keeping them just beyond arm's reach. Sometimes, the closer they approached, the more the earth and sky seemed to recede endlessly into some deeper horizon. Sometimes, there was a rope tying his leg to an immovable cloud high above. Sometimes—and these were the times he woke up feeling the greatest frustration and helplessness—he would get right down to his other/his other would get right down to him, their fingertips almost touching but for an infinitesimally thin space, impenetrable, like the membrane keeping apart oil and water.

Always he awoke in his room, grasping at nothing.

7

THE LIQUIDATION MINISTRY

I t was 10:30 a.m., and Rick still hadn't arrived at work.

Amon stared blankly at the office wallpaper behind the rows of chairs he faced. Under a graphical spell, it was a crystalline planet of tumultuously shifting topography. Pink and white amethyst mountains serrated with sparkling jags grew ever taller, rearing up to great heights before collapsing like slow-motion waves. The peaks poured into dark, gaping craters that twinkled intermittently from a million tiny points; the craters filling up to become glittering plains that began to ramify into hills; the hilltops coalescing and conjoining into mountains once again; this cataclysmic cycle generating ever new terrestrial patterns without repeating itself.

Amon kept glancing over at Rick's empty chair as he monitored Illiquidity Alert. Coded names shifted places up and down, dropping in and out of the Gutter like pigeons swooping just above traffic.

Another fifteen minutes passed. Still no Rick.

Amon began to wonder whether there might be a malfunction in the squad attendance diagram. He walked across the shimmering floor to the neighboring chair, stuck his arm out straight, and waved it over top of the backrest. He encountered no resistance, and concluded that Rick was corporeally absent, software okay, so he returned to his chair.

Amon remembered days when Rick had called in sick at the last minute, but even then, he had always provided notification by 9 a.m. at the latest.

He was now over two hours late. In irritated astonishment, Amon was having trouble concentrating on the Gutter and decided to contact Rick.

He opened FacePhone, selected Rick's name, and clicked *text*.

ERROR: Your text cannot be sent, said a pop up window. *Confirm who you are trying to reach and try again.* Amon clicked text a few more times but got the same message. He wondered if Rick had changed his address and decided to check his inner profile. He searched through his list of contacts, but, to his surprise, couldn't find him. He saw Eijima Ritsuko then Galinski Paul. It went straight from E to G. But Ferro Rick, there was none.

Just to be sure, he tried voice calling, but once again failed to connect. With a rush of perplexity, Amon realized what had happened: Rick must have blocked him. It was unbelievable. Amon could understand Rick being upset about their quarrel, but blocking him was beyond drastic. Their whole lives they had shared access to the most intimate parts of their digital selves; now all telecommunication links between them were completely severed. In a single night, they had gone from best friends to cold and distant coworkers, threads of meaning dangling untethered between them into an abyss of solitude.

Amon remained only vaguely aware of the scrolling text and numbers before him, staring off into the crystal depths in stunned, biting disbelief. In the wallpaper sky, another bigger planet came into view. It was covered in hazy clouds of amber dust. Through rifts in the yellowing atmosphere, Amon could see a landscape of sheer ice, jutting protrusions, flatlands and depressions polished like a mirror. He sat forward, his hands dangling over the edge of his ergonomic armrests, his breathing short and tense, his eyes wandering around the alien spectacle without really seeing it.

A giant smiling face appeared in front of this cosmic display, breaking Amon out of his stupor. It was a Caucasian man, his neck starting at the floor and his head going right to the ceiling. He had tanned skin that suggested frequent outdoor leisure and accentuated the white of his perfectly-straight, pearly front teeth. His ears were large, his eyes brown and beady, the top of his buzzcut grown in to give his head a squarish outline, his forehead a matrix of interweaving wrinkles that somehow suggested financial wisdom, like battle scars earned in a stock market war. While the man wasn't exactly handsome, he radiated a sense of seniority and authoritative ease more impressive than good looks. Amon had never seen him before in his life.

"Good morning, Kenzaki," said the face. The voice was unmistakable.

"G-good m-morning, Sekido-san," stuttered Amon, taken aback by his boss's dramatic transformation.

In addition to his tendency towards circumlocution, Sekido was notorious in the ministry for another peculiar habit: every so often, he would show up to work with a new face. It was normal to give oneself occasional esthetic tweaks that others might notice, like adjustments to skin tone, eyebrow width, nostril size, hair color, lip fullness, and jaw curvature. But Sekido was the only person Amon had met who bought whole new visual identities. Despite having a Japanese name, no one in the ministry had ever seen his Japanese face, assuming he still had one. In the seven years since Amon was hired, he had seen Sekido undergo three faceovers. When they first met he had been a brown-skinned man with Polynesian features; a few years later a wide-faced, round-cheeked, masculine Mongolian; then, last year, the blond curly-haired slavic-type Amon had grown accustomed to. Now he'd done it again. Every one of his guises was different, but they all shared one thing: rich texture and high resolution that required a team of premium designers at great expense.

According to speculative rumors circulated by his underlings in hushed, drunken slurs after the tenth drink in dark corners of dingy izakayas, he was so disfigured that digital beautification was helpless to fix him. But Amon doubted that anyone had been brave or stupid enough to actually take a naked look at his face. This would be a violation of Sekido's image and anonymity rights, and would be broadcast to him when he received legal damage compensation, making it an insulting faux pas that few could afford. In any case, this *Phantom of the Opera* theory didn't satisfy Amon. It explained why he built a new face, but not why he kept rebuilding them.

"The purpose for which I have come—or at least the primary purpose considering that there is always a support-structure of latent intentions and motives crouching beneath manifest decision-making best visualized as an unconscious pyramid of desire and planning—is to report two pieces of news to you." A pang of fear gripped Amon's gut sharply when he realized that Sekido had caught him in a workflow lull, Rick absent.

"R-really? What kind of news?"

"News of the regular kind, of course. In a word, information that will—or at least I suspect will—be fresh to your ears, that will be *new* to you; for in the interests of convenience, news can be thought of simply as the plural of new, at least in certain social circles of which I am an erstwhile member." Sekido let out a gruff open-mouthed laugh, revealing a flash of white from a red chamber cut into tan furrows. Amon tried to force himself to laugh with him, but it came out false and unenthusiastic, more like a series of faint grunts. "Like all news, what I'm going to tell you has different facets that can be considered in a number of lights. To use a convenient analogy as an illustration of my point, news of a corporate merger may be perceived in a divergent manner by shareholders in the merged companies than shareholders of the competitors' companies. There are as innumerable facets and lights as there are individuated parcels of information, perhaps more if you're willing to try counting, although not quite so many companies or shareholders as far as I can reasonably infer. As to whether this is good news or bad news, I can only let you judge this for yourself." Amon waited anxiously for him to continue, wondering in confusion which type of shareholder he was supposed to be.

"Nonetheless, I expect this news to be viewed favorably from several perspectives, including, not decisively but only probably, your own. Does that sound agreeable to you?" Sekido raised his eyebrow, compressing his forehead wrinkles into a new matrix.

Amon nodded.

"Now once you hear what I'm going to say, much will be expected of you."

"Do you have some kind of new assignment for me?" Amon asked, and then immediately regretted it. Sekido always got to the point faster when left uninterrupted.

"You haven't quite caught my meaning, Amon. When I mentioned news, I wasn't referring to anything quite so concrete as a job or a mission or an assignment, although it would be dishonest of me to say that those things are completely irrelevant to the matter at hand, when on the contrary, they are right at the heart of it. Rather, at that moment I was speaking more in the abstract, particularly about readiness. What will be expected of you above all is to be ready."

Ready for what? Amon wanted to say, but stifled his impatient thoughts and let Sekido's lecture take its course.

"*Ready for what?* you might be wondering," said Sekido, as though he had read Amon's mind. "Before I get to that, let me give you one piece of news: A meeting will be held soon. A meeting that concerns you in fact.

"Before we talk about the specifics, first please let me confirm something. Do you have any schedule impediments in the evenings: a wedding, a funeral, a date, a club activity, a reunion with your long-lost surrogate father?"

"Not particularly," Amon replied, feeling somewhat reluctant to sacrifice his frugality practice even though he knew it was well worth it for the chance this meeting represented.

"That is a positive sign, at least when seen from your perspective, once again not decisively but only probably, for you know I'm not you and can never say for certain what you see as good or bad, but am only giving an educated guess on the grounds of your behavior." There was a pause as Sekido's beady eyes drifted off somewhere and started twitching. Within a few moments his eyes returned to Amon.

"To get to specifics, there is a special task in need of completion."

"Does this have anything to do with the job we discussed yesterday?" Amon asked, his excitation escaping.

"No. The task I speak of is not the same as the assistant position with the Executive Council, although they are bound by, shall we say, threads of regard in the eyes of your superiors. Anyone who does this task will tug on these threads and might even tip the bucket of gold we call job promotion, hopefully not any less desirable buckets. Does my stab at poetic articulation conjure images vividly in your mind?"

Amon nodded hesitantly.

"Excellent. I am often delightfully surprised at the efficacy of my attempts at communication, even—or better yet, especially—when they most seem to have failed. To get back to business, I'm letting you know formally that the internal recruiter has expressed interest in you and will be meeting with you shortly."

"Is that so? I'm delighted to hear it."

"Yes, well this will be an excellent opportunity to ingratiate yourself into his world of acquaintances, elevating you from stranger to the status of someone he knows, which I would say increases your chances of success several-fold, although I want to increase your chances even more. Yes, warming up to the recruiter is an accelerating—one might even say galvanizing—force propelling you to higher positions in this organization. But the ultimately—or penultimately—deciding factor, more than anything else or almost anything else, rivaled perhaps only by faithful reliablism, is your performance, which of course has been superb—nice work with Minister Kitao yesterday by the way—yet as I always say, 'nothing is perfect except money.' IE, a little more impressive work to tack onto your curriculum vitae won't hurt, and the mission I'm going to offer you is more than impressive—I can't think of the right word, but impressive doesn't do it justice—which is why I have come personally to assign you. This mission is possibly even more important than the assistant position for the Executive Council. It will, if nothing else, stand out more vividly in memory than anything you have ever done."

"Sekido-san. I'm a little bit unclear about what you mean." Amon had gotten better at puzzling out Sekido's gist over the years, but this was too obscure even for him. "Remembered by whom?"

"I only offer guesses. The future is shrouded in the fog of unearned money. Actions and transactions yet to be performed are as unpredictable as earthquakes, more so perhaps. Yet taking into consideration the current conditions and the efficiency of your work, I would be surprised to see you completely forgotten in the demolishing onslaught of time. You see, the job involves liquidating someone of public significance, and you are the only one who I believe has the skills and professional broo-ha to do it."

"Who are we talking about? The network hasn't mentioned any new bankruptcies."

"Very observant, Kenzaki. As always I applaud you inwardly, with tiny imaginary hands. The target has been purposely omitted from the network because they would immediately be recognized by every Liquidator in the ministry, and the fine for divulging their name to the major news sites would be smaller than the payment garnered thereby. In a word, there is profit to be had in leaking this one, so we can't have anyone hear of it. If you do a good job on this assignment, I think your chances with the recruiter will be sealed." Sekido's eyes wandered off into the distance once again. Amon could see him accessing the ImmaNet with subtle twitches of his cheeks and upper lip, each finely-rendered muscle quivering under the wrinkled skin like some wriggling lizard beneath desert sand. "I must leave for a meeting, Kenzaki, so here is your mission." A telescope appeared hovering in front of Amon. "Regarding the meeting with the recruiter, the date and time will likely be decided suddenly, not at a whim nor even in a whim-like fashion but suddenly, so I trust you can keep your evenings open and remain on call in case we have to invite you out of the blue, or the red, as the latter color has always struck me as more symbolic of urgency. Other than that, I only ask that you try to forget about the promotion today since it will merely distract you from your duties here. Good luck!" Sekido's face vanished and the crystal moon came back into view.

The clouded ice world had revolved around to eclipse the sun, blotting out half of it. The sunlight slipped through its billowing vaporous atmosphere, turned pale and gray as though tainted with some obscuring hue, like optical amnesia.

Amon seized the telescope and looked inside, where a profile was burned. Lawrence Barrow, the Chief Executive Minister of GATA Japan.

PART 2
CRASH

8

GINZA NOW

"Please enter a destination . . . please enter a destination," ScrimpNavi kept pestering Amon as he walked along the foot of a train bridge that cut through the metropolis' core. To his left were shops embedded in archways cut at regular intervals into the bridge. To his right ran a two-lane street, a mall with tinted windows looming on the opposite side. Salarymen and casual shoppers criss-crossed the street from the shops to the mall and back again, like pinballs flying into jackpot holes. "Please enter a destination . . . please enter a destination." The application had detected Amon's perambulatory motion and inferred he was headed somewhere, but was helpless to guide him without a defined endpoint. As much as he wanted advice on the cheapest route, Amon couldn't satisfy its query; he had no idea where he was going.

After work every day, Amon entered Tokyo Station, got on the train to Jinbocho, and returned to his room where he could practice frugal stillness. But today, for the first time in ages, he found himself headed somewhere else. Where that was, he couldn't say. It was as if some dark spirit hibernating in his marrow had finally woken, latched onto his nerves, and jolted him with enigmatic signals, impelling him towards a destination undisclosed even to it. He'd been walking for almost twenty minutes now, sighing every time he paused to wait at a stoplight, his feelings of guilt increasing with each unbudgeted step and breath and blink.

The patchwork firmament was dotted with big, fluffy InfoClouds: billowing, misty diamonds with 3D moving pictures for facets. A black woman with braided hair thrashing about violently on a strobing stage melded vaporously with a teenage hedge fund manager vampire drama, wafting hazy about an elk mating documentary DIY package, before being absorbed into the preferred cigarettes of famous serial killers historical recap. These will-o-the-wisp segments changed shape; growing, stretching, and distorting as they folded out of sight inside and around the phantasmic promo-swirl; emerging once again moments later from another side; a cacophonous howl accompanying each InfoCloud in its slow journey across the heavens, like the internal monologue of ten thousand schizophrenics made into sound.

Amon turned left onto a wide, busy boulevard. He had arrived in Ginza.

Every one of the skyscrapers lining the sidewalks to his left and across the road had a radically different façade. Translucent concrete illuminated from the inside in marbled patterns of beige, pink, and brown like cobbled slabs of ceramic skin. A wall of cat eyes arranged in a grid that blinked in alternation like a disco floor. Huge submarine portholes with thick glass embedded in red plastic, each one displaying a product suspended in amber that changed with the angle like a hologram: wedding ring to a deck of gold cards, ostrich-leather gloves to eye-cleansing spray.

Like the buildings, the sidewalk changed every few steps. At first, it was sheets of aluminum edged in sapphire. Soon after it was bricks of red and blue, then solid gray, then yellow with coupon passwords spelled out in green. In one place Amon walked on a perfectly clear lake, each step sending out gentle ripples across the surface, bottles of Frescence perfume glittering on the bottom like sunken treasure. Then it was back to concrete, then an inferno of flames sculpted into the shape of road bikes, then pure white plaster indented with paw-marks and the tooth molds of Perma-Smile pets.

Strolling slow and aimless, past store after store and mall after mall, Amon stared blankly at the streetwalkers passing him from front and back, caught in a dull trance as the clothes and accessories they wore transformed rapidly before his eyes. A wristwatch on someone's arm transmuted from silver to wood. An earring turned to liquid metal inside a woman's lobe, wriggled up and split into divergent streams, which became three studs that pierced themselves into the flesh of her upper ear. A pearl necklace detached from another woman's neck, slithered in a spiral over her shoulder and down the right arm to link around her wrist and become a bracelet. A wallet bulging from a back pocket vanished, a small shoulder-bag appearing in its stead. A polka dot pattern on a skirt changed to plaid to tie-die back to polka-dot of a different shade, pants in fall camouflage to zigzagging stripes to computer chips. High-heels went flat-top, trainers peeled into sandals, sneakers grew into steel-toed boots. A headscarf worn by one man wrapped itself into a vest and slipped onto the torso of a different man passing by, a strip tearing off the vest and turning into a purse on a woman's arm. A fedora reformed into a bowler, a baseball cap into a beret, a cowboy hat into an olive wreath. Occasionally, Amon noticed accompanying adjustments to their features, as though matching face to outfit: irises changing color, eyes stretching thinner or growing rounder, skin tone turning lighter or darker, noses lengthening or shrinking, jaw-lines sharpening or rounding, beauty marks appearing and disappearing.

No one broke stride or strut as their look changed incrementally. Each shift came at intervals of five to thirty seconds, happening almost instantly, just slow enough for Amon to perceive—a sleeve rolling up like a compressed accordion, a manicure fading to pristine nail, a zipper sprouting into buttons—but the whole field of changes was too fast for his eyes to take in all at once. Every blink revealed a new configuration of bodies and apparel, constantly morphing, fluid, an unending fashion sleight of hand performed en masse.

For these real-time aesthetes, the transition itself was just as integral to style as the freeze frame at any given moment. They coordinated color, fabric, and design in response to location, the play of light, the time of day, the surrounding ambience, and the latest online buzz. To stay cutting edge, they were aided by aesthetic judgment apps. These compiled comments from dealers, designers, critics, models, and customers from around the world; projected brand names on the garments of others in view; gave ratings out of ten to outfits in categories like overall impact and originality; and displayed bulletins about new releases, obsolete apparel, and reemerging fads.

Knowing who and what to imitate so that others will imitate you required good taste in software, and the cultured sense to wield it with sophistication in every new context, neither of which Amon possessed. In his rookie days, he had spent several hours here, watching the crowd cycle erratically through eras of fashion from ages past and others born of the now, but today he'd turned off his app of choice—Distinction—to conserve resources. Without it, he couldn't even tell the eras apart, let alone decipher the meaning behind this complex interplay of transient garb: personality nuance and social positioning encrypted in an alien language of flickering peacock feathers.

Ginza was home to retail outlets for some of the most prestigious designers. Top brands had strict conditions of use that limited the number of copies in circulation at any given time, guaranteeing their clientele a unique, legally inimitable look. Since many exceptional items could only be bought here, Ginza was the one place this ever-wheeling dance of vogue could be consummated. (Though Harajuku was similar in some ways, but more gaudy and eccentric, less chic and refined.)

Now and again, Amon caught crystallizations of trend amidst the flux of capricious adornment. For a moment, several people were wearing silk-thin summer scarves draped over their shoulders in loose knots, frameless sunglasses of dark hazel that floated in front of their eyes, snug denim pants in earthy tones, and cotton outdoor slippers. But by the time he reached the next intersection and crossed the street, this look had dissolved into a chaos of disparate styles once again.

With Distinction on, he might have been able to at least dress respectably, but today he didn't feel like being recognized, let alone showing off, and wore a digiguise. His body was sketched erratically in pastel as if by the shaky hand of a child; his hair brown blots and scribbles; his eyes warped, uneven ovals; the red lines of his lips extending in a jagged swirl onto his right cheek; his fingers crooked streaks; the color of the blue jeans and white shirt he was wearing leaking onto his skin. He'd had it designed many years ago for just such times when he was in the mood to be alone in a crowd.

Without any breeze to purify the air, it stagnated and thickened, rife with a seeping toxic heat the city seemed to excrete, and Amon's skin was coated in a sticky sheen of sweat. As his legs carried him of their own accord over motley streets, past incongruous architecture, through the crowd of protean ostentation, his mind kept returning to work that morning. After the talk with Sekido, Rick had never showed up. No contact, no explanation, nothing. Amon had even failed to reach him using his work account, which meant Rick had blocked him with the strictest settings, automatically rejecting even professional communications that Amon initiated. Letting personal gripes interfere with their relationship as partners to this degree was just plain childish. Since when had Rick become so petty? Did Amon's attitude towards him really warrant such shunning?

Amon had warned Rick at Self Serve that he would soon have to tell Sekido about his performance, and had vacillated all day about whether to finally do it, torn by a strange mixture of sadness and anger. Part of him wanted to mend their broken friendship, another part to viciously sever it forever. To complicate matters further, protocol required that Liquidators move in pairs, and admitting his partner was missing would have meant giving up the mission. He couldn't decide whether being assigned to crash Barrow, a man he'd looked up to for his entire career, was a curse or a blessing. Yet it was surely a chance to clinch his next promotion, and that couldn't be thrown away lightly. In the end he'd remained silent, again, indecision his ultimate decision.

Now he was killing time before the biggest, most terrifying confrontation of his life. The mission start time listed in the assignment folder had been set for that evening. Amon thought this strange at first, as Liquidators were usually dispatched at the moment bankruptcy was confirmed so as to stamp out burgeoning debt with maximum haste. But he supposed Sekido and the other administrators had decided to delay it in the interests of discretion, favoring a delicate approach for this high-profile target. The Chief Executive Minister likely had conferences and roundhouse discussions all day. Not until evening might Amon catch him away from media swarms, or better yet, alone.

Coming to Ginza was a terribly discreditable move. There were no bargain sidewalk chunks or eye respites here, as every square inch was premium estate. If he could decide what he was doing, where he was going, ScrimpNavi might have helped out, but as it was, exorbitant transactions rolled non-stop down his readout. *Sigh*.

The signal at the intersection ahead turned red, and Amon stopped at the rear of the waiting crowd. A middle-aged woman in a navy blue blazer and turquoise shirt, her short ponytail skewered horizontally by chopsticks, approached him carrying a tray of paper cups filled with green tea. "Care to try some *gyokuro* from Uji?" she asked, holding out the tray. Amon ignored her. He was a bit parched, but didn't want to pay the company that owned *accept free samples*.

The signal changed and Amon moved with the crowd across the street. As he approached the other corner, he noticed a woman standing motionless by the curb with her back towards traffic. The surface of her body was squirming with a formless wash of information: a pick hacking into the wall of an iceberg middle-aged couple reclining on a heap of pillows flaming car before a raging riot and crenelated towers archive of standard operating procedure for avionics blueprints hulking brute smashing a green tornado congealing into a cartoon bat . . . As though she were a humanoid incarnation of the InfoSky, the scrambled images coating her were miniature versions of those playing above.

Becoming a living billboard was the ultimate shame. It told everyone who looked at her that she was teetering on the brink of bankruptcy. Unable to afford even digimake, she had rented out her body space. The one mercy was that the spasmodic veneer of light and color prevented anyone from recognizing her. Desperate souls like her were common sights in Ginza. With hordes of wealthy shoppers around, advertisers paid higher rates here. The side mirror of a bus came dangerously close to the back of the woman's head as it ripped past, but she didn't even notice. An attention prompter like Mindfulator ought to have been warning her of the danger, but Amon supposed she was too destitute to activate it. He couldn't grasp what was going through her head. He never turned off his Mindfulator, even though he had a perfect concentration score and could easily conserve credit this way. Until this app was released, the leading cause of death in the Free World had been absent-mindedness, with virtual tournament starvation and stumbling off train platforms occupying the largest percentage in Japan. The human mind was highly susceptible to distractions, no matter how unwavering the individual's will. The woman was risking her life for meager savings. As a Liquidator, he encountered people like this all the time, but still struggled to comprehend how anyone could give in to unmeditated urges so fully as to tempt that irreversible darkness.

Amidst a roiling ocean of noise, Amon caught sight of a meaningful signal. There was Lawrence Barrow, inside a thin sliver of video on the woman's neck. He was standing against the pillars of some grand, stone building. Built big and sturdy, his upright posture drew the square lines of his shoulders distinctly beneath his black suit. His hair was pure white of just enough length to be pulled back and tied into a tight ponytail; his nose large and commanding; his eyes a piercing blue nearly as light as a husky's. Cut to Barrow shaking hands with the CEMs of Germany and China; the three men posing for photos in a banquet hall beneath intricate chandeliers, glasses full of red wine stacked in a pyramid at the head of a long table behind them. As Amon continued to stare, the ImmaNet registered his eye-line and the scene expanded, spreading across the woman's body over the other images like a droplet of food dye through water, before encompassing the whole sky in a flash, its audio leaping into his ears.

"With the opposition mustering strength in the run-up to next month's election, Chief Executive Minister Lawrence Barrow gave a speech today at the Tonan Exhibition Hall to announce his election platform," said a female reporter. Barrow stood on the stage of a conference hall before a podium. "In his speech, CEM Barrow criticized Yoshino Sawanoi, leader of the Absolute Choice Party, for his recent pledge to privatize heartbeating, and promised to nationalize blinking."

"Absolute Choice wants to privatize one of our most crucial public assets—heartbeating," said Barrow, his husky blue eyes staring with a commanding intensity over the audience. "And yet, in proposing such policies, they are swimming upstream against the great current of facts. Our scientists agree, without a hint of doubt, that the beating of our hearts is beyond our volitional control." As always, Amon was held rapt by Barrow's masterful Japanese. The pacing was hypnotic, the pronunciation clear, the intonation liquid. His voice too was exceptional, resonating from abdominal depths with a smooth, purity of tone, yet lilting here and there for emotive emphasis.

"Think what would happen. It all starts with the privatization of the heartbeat, next it might be your digestion, then the growth of your hair and fingernails, pretty soon you'll be charged for every moment of your continued existence. As if that were a choice! If my opponent has his way, there will be no such thing as choice at all. But we can't let that happen. Government ownership of functions like heartbeating, salivation, perspiration, urination, and digestion is precisely what makes our society free. Our public infrastructure draws the line between chosen and unchosen. It is the core of the Free World." *Cut.*

"My opponent has said that blinking is a choice. But aren't the moments when you control blinking the exception rather than the rule? The majority of the time, don't the eyelids move up and down without any attention paid to them at all, just as rain falls upon the earth? That is why I promise to nationalize blinking." Applause and cheers roared up from the crowd.

Amon found himself clapping along. He was the only one on the street doing so, but no one else seemed to notice, the oncoming stream of real-time aesthetes parting indifferently around him. The news segued seamlessly into an adfoshow about a knight questing to save the kingdom from a warlock's spell of gloom by wresting a potent antidepressant treasure from a dragon (newly developed by the TTY Corporation and only ¥56,896,542 per bottle!). Amon found a blank wall to rest his eyes, but it immediately divided into slats and opened like venetian blinds, revealing clear plastic pedestals, each one topped with a miniature mannequin woman reclining on a posture-healing bed. He looked away and started along the sidewalk again into the midst of the streetwalkers, many of whose cheeks were adorned with gold dust patterned like the rings of a tree.

A heavy feeling of foreboding fell over Amon now that he was reminded of his mission. How had it come about that he would liquidate Lawrence Barrow, a man whose career he had taken as the blueprint for his own? Just like Amon, Barrow's flawless concentration score had earned him the title Liquidator. Rising up the ranks on sheer effort and skill, he too had become an Identity Executioner, then Minister of Liquidation, before getting shifted to the Executive Council, where he first confronted the ongoing debate over physiological functions. For decades the ruling Absolute Choice Party had maintained the orthodox line that blinking, breathing, urination, and defecation were volitional actions, eligible to be bought and sold. Admittedly, these borderline processes operated automatically in sleep and when the mind was busy with other tasks. But since they could be manipulated consciously at any moment, postponed or hastened depending on present needs, they were different from say temperature regulation, digestion, salivation, and perspiration, which completely refused to bend to the will. Being potential volitional movements, they deserved to be defined as action-properties, just like eating, copulating, somersaulting, and all the rest.

Once chosen as leader of the Moderate Choice Party, Barrow had spearheaded the controversial bill to nationalize urination and defecation, arguing the flip-side of the Absolute Choice doctrine. While such voiding might be put off temporarily, it could not be deferred indefinitely. The need to perform these actions was thrust upon the individual without their consent, and like a "ticking time bomb," as his famous catch phrase went, had to be satisfied within a certain duration. Otherwise, they would execute themselves, with dire and embarrassing social consequences; and in some cases, refraining from them could even be fatal. This was more like biological duress than a choice. Therefore, these urges only gave the illusion of volition and ought to be public property unavailable on the open market.

Expressed eloquently, this platform won him the election on the back of overwhelming support. Despite deep-rooted political apathy, with 90 percent of citizens ignoring or blocking pop-up voting windows, almost a quarter of the populace had participated in the previous election, setting a new record in Free Era Japan. (GATA was a direct democracy in principle but quorum had never once been reached on any legislation so it was a representative democracy in practice.) Amon had been amongst them, in spite of his reluctance to pay the prohibitive cost of *voting* (property of LYS Dynamics).

But once in office, Barrow's plan for following through on these pledges encountered resistance. Nationalization required more funding, which meant credicrime fines needed to be raised. When a credicrime was committed, part of the fine paid by the perpetrator went to the victim as compensation for damages and a small cut went to the Judicial Broker in charge of the case, but a full half of the total amount filled GATA's coffers, making up the largest portion of government revenue. When Barrow tried to jack up fines across the board, there was dissent from a rival faction of fiscal conservatives within his own party, sparking concern amongst the electorate that they would bear the financial burden. But Barrow was not shaken. He calmly emphasized that only criminals would pay, convincing the conservatives with promise of stricter retribution for deviance, and law-abiding citizens—like Amon—with their overall savings on number one and number two.

During his single term in office, Barrow had even managed to bring about economic reform. Under the reign of Absolute Choice, the markets had crashed unpredictably an average of five times per day, but after implementing a new regimen of regulation and stimulus, Barrow had brought this down to three, and ensured the crashes occurred at vaguely predictable times, usually twice in the early morning and once around 3 p.m.

Now he was fighting for nationalization of blinking, a wise and just objective on Amon's view; anything but the polices of Absolute Choice, which set his skin burning with indignation. If they were re-elected, he would have to return to the guru's urination and defecation reduction lessons, and had no idea what to do about his heartbeat. In truth, Amon thought that breathing and swallowing ought to be nationalized as well, but this was considered radically left wing, so he generally kept his political opinions to himself. Yet from watching Barrow's strategic maneuvers thus far, Amon felt he could sense his convictions, believing, in some indeterminate hopeful sort of way, that Barrow just might concur.

What made Barrow's achievements particularly remarkable, thought Amon, was his being the first non-ethnic Japanese to rule the country. Although born and raised in Japan, only Barrow's mother was Japanese, his name coming from his New Zealander father. As an island nation that had closed itself off to the world for centuries, this would have been unimaginable at any other time in Japan's history, but there were far more foreigners in the archipelago than ever before. According to FlexiPedia, the first and largest influx came in the aftermath of the so-called "Bubble Rewind," when the economy had imploded, prices had fallen rapidly, and skilled workers were desperately needed to replace the ever-shrinking, aging population. Then, after the "Tokyo Roundtable," numerous foreign bureaucrats had arrived—along with the construction of GATA tower. And soon after, the staff of numerous foreign corporations started taking advantage of the Free Era's amped-up market liberalization. Further waves of immigration followed, as the new system made all Free Citizens equal irrespective of borders, and international agreements had finally forced Japan to grant non-native residents suffrage (in spite of fierce protests from entrenched traditionalists who preferred economic ruin to acknowledging the rights of outsiders). So, while Barrow's main support base had been voters of Japanese ethnicity, it was a surge in turnout amongst the numerous ex-pats and second or third generation migrants that had turned the tide, his message of fairness speaking to the minorities. Perhaps because he was half-Persian, half-Japanese himself, Amon had also been touched by this message.

From a purely professional perspective, Amon knew he ought to feel pride at being entrusted with the job of cash crashing such an important figure. The recognition garnered would surely dwarf all his other achievements combined. Yet he still felt a seething, painful apprehension of what was to come. To liquidate Barrow, this articulate leader of unprecedented vision and tact; to apprehend him and strip his BodyBank, cut short all his projects and annihilate his potential—these were his duties and Amon could never neglect them. But he didn't look forward to success—no, he dreaded success—feeling that any rewards earned this way would be cheap and undeserved.

"Please enter a destination . . . please enter a destination." Lost in thought, Amon had wandered onto a side street. There were fewer pedestrians here, most of them dressed in plain business attire. The buildings too were simpler, made of metal and glass with a few of brick. Each one had a black, rectangular sign hanging lengthwise from the first story to the fourth. They were segmented into boxes containing neon text that advertised the name of the businesses on each floor: Spring Aroma, g&g, Hid-Ing, Coco Crescendo, Enya 999, Night Mist, Sparkle, Club Star Blossom, Club Bubble Burst. This area of Ginza was where all the most renowned *kurabu* operated, classy lounges where wealthy businessmen dropped the amount of an average monthly salary just to sit for an hour beside a chatty, primped-up hostess. Amon had no idea why he'd come here. Pretty soon he realized that he'd stopped walking.

He was standing next to a familiar building, a place he had visited once long ago. It was a ten-story rectangle of impenetrable black, as though a block of the metropolis adscape had been wiped from existence. Grafted onto its left side was a sheer cylinder of chrome; the silver light reflecting off its surface unable to penetrate the void beside it. On the right side of the ground floor, a doorless hallway led inside. It was lit by small lights shining from circular holes that ran in three parallel rows along the length of the ceiling. Unlike every other building on the street, there was no sign. Instead, in gold cursive script about three stories up on the face of the blotting absence, there was a single word: *Eroyuki*.

Being next to this venue, this fragile crystal of his past, a flurry of memories arose, memories of childhood and adolescence, and, for the first time in years, the old days with Mayuko. Standing beside Eroyuki, the last place they had been together, Amon began to wonder how she was making out in the world. His encounter with her the previous morning had aroused thoughts of her that had lay dormant in his mind for ages, but only now did he pay them heed. He tried to imagine what she might have been doing with her life, whether she was still working for Capsize Solutions, still living in the company dorm, still treasuring her spare time, when he suddenly realized the obvious: if he was going to find Rick, it would have to be through her.

With mission time fast approaching, Amon was assaulted by a barrage of worries. Rick was like the other lobe of Amon's brain; his information-gathering talents an integral component of Amon's strategizing. Without him, the mission in Shibuya would have ended in disaster, and this time Amon was expecting far trickier complications. What if he couldn't overcome them by himself? What if he was caught breaking the GATA bylaw against liquidating solo? Would he succeed in completing the mission, only to be reprimanded later on? Or worse yet, not complete the mission at all? All slacking aside, Rick's presence would be invaluable if there was some way to track him down and persuade him to join. Yet Amon didn't want to waste credit on contacting Mayuko, especially not after all these years of silence between them.

Gazing vaguely at the black building with its faintly gleaming cylinder, Amon opened Career Calibration and typed out a description of his situation for his decision network. As always, he was hit instantly with a deluge of messages. *You're obviously stressed, go on vacation . . . Maybe you can get her in bed, here's how . . . Screw that bastard, I'd just . . . It's not your responsibility but I'd call her . . .* Before he'd finished reading through the options, his hands began to move seemingly of their own accord, as though possessed by the same occult impulse that had driven his legs to this place. He was dialing up one of his contacts. FacePhone was connecting. Amon swallowed nervously. After three rings, Mayuko appeared and half Amon's perspective shifted to her location.

She was in a white room running full tilt on a treadmill. Wearing a red and black striped t-shirt with tight blue short-shorts, she wrapped the treadmill handles with petite fingers, her slender frame surging forward without advancing, cheeks flushed, beads of sweat clinging to her forehead like pearls suspended in time. Unlike the previous day, Amon could no longer see part of her naked face, he had been denied access to her incisive eyes. Instead, her whites, irises, and pupils formed three swirling, concentric circles of white, dark brown and black, like whirlpools of milk and darkening chocolate gradations. These whirlpool eyes looked up and beyond him into some distance that Amon couldn't see.

Hesitant to interrupt, Amon froze and watched her dynamic form. Her joints were fluid, the coordination of her legs and upper body graceful, her slim yet powerful muscles sculpting her perfect physique with each contraction and release. He had watched her run countless times before—she had been athletic ever since they were kids—and he picked up on subtle kinetic minutiae unique to her. Like the specific offset rhythm at which her shapely breasts and loose comet hair bounced, sent dancing by a syncopation of forces reverberating from her toes with each powerful stride. *How beautiful to see her move again*, whispered a voice inside him. Along with it, he felt a bittersweet ache, as though a breeze were playing dissonant notes on wind chimes in his chest, but he ignored them both. There was no sense attending to thoughts and emotions from a lost era. He had made his choice after all, had made the right choice. Fretting over the irreversible was just masochism, and superfluous pain—self-inflicted or otherwise—only spawned compensatory desires that would one day lead to discreditable behavior. Financing had to come first. The forest was everything.

"Mayuko," he said aloud, unable to bear watching her in silence any longer.

Her whirlpool eyes came down, focused on him and went wide with surprise, as though she had been roused from a daydream.

"Amon?"

HAI. AIM SORY 2 INTERUPT. DU U HAV AA MINUT? THAIRZ SOMTHANG ID LAIK 2 AYSK U.

"Oh . . . yes . . . but I'm almost . . . up to a thousand calories," she panted. "What . . . is it?"

R U WEETH RCK RAIT NAUW?

"Rick? Just . . . hold on . . . a second." Her pace suddenly quickened until soon she was sprinting. Amon could see tension increase in her face as she pushed herself to the limit, brow muscles tightening, forehead veins popping, the V-shaped wrinkle between her eyebrows deepening, whirlpools looking off into that hidden distance again. *Gee-shaw, gee-shaw, gee-shaw,* the pitch of the treadmill rose, and it began to wheeze as though struggling to keep up with her. Just when the exertion around her brow looked so great that Amon thought her brain might bloom like a flower from her skull, her pace began to slacken incrementally and the pitch of the treadmill dropped. After a minute or so she was at a cool down pace. Panting like mad, she took a towel from a plastic loop on the side of the handles, wiped the sweat off her face, neck, and forearms, before draping it around her shoulders. As her breath slowly settled and the tension in her face eased, she took a swig of water from a holder on the right side of the panel.

"So . . . you were . . . asking about Rick," she said between pants, continuing to walk.

Amon nodded. *TROOLY SAWRY 2 EENTERUPT.*

"Oh . . . that's . . . okay. It's very strange to . . . Is something . . . wrong?"

AIM CAWLING AWN AAN EEMPORTANT PROFESHIONAL MATERR THAYT CANCERNS RCK & EETS KRUSHAL AI SPEIK 2 HEEM. IZ HHE THAYR?

"No . . . not yet. I mean . . . he was supposed to be . . . here actually . . . about an . . . hour ago. But I . . . guess he's running late."

Not surprising, thought Amon. AI SII. EEN THAYT CAYS, AID LAIK 2 ASSK U AA FAVER.

"Oh. Okay. What's . . . that?"

CULD U CAWL HEEM RAIT NAUW & SAYT UUPP A 3-WEGH COMYUNI-CATION?

"Why can't you just call him yourself?"

CUZ HEEZ BLAWKED MII.

"What?" she said, frowning and jolting her head back slightly. "He. . . but why?"

AI DONT KNO. AI TRAID OPAYNING HEEZ PROFAIL BUUT AI KANT AKSESS EET AYT AULL. NAWT EVVEN THA PAUBLIC VERRSION.

"Could this have anything to do with your talk at the bar?" Apparently, she'd heard about that.

MEHBI . . . Words failed him as he was drawn hypnotically into her steadily swirling eyes. He looked away at the wall behind her to regain his control.

He could see her fingers twitching for a moment before she frowned.

WATS RAWNG?

"I'm trying to call him up like you asked, but there's nothing there."

WAT DU U MEEN?

"I mean, just like you, I can't find his profile."

???!!! DED SUMTHEENG HAPEN?

"No, not really . . . He should be here. He's never late, and . . ."

Rick is always late for work, but never to meet his girlfriend, the bastard, thought Amon.

SOE YUR TAYLING MI HI BLAWKED U 2?

"I don't know. His name just isn't in my contact list anymore, and . . ." Still wearing a look of perplexity, she tilted her head slightly to the side for a few seconds as if in thought. "Did you guys have something important at work today?"

AZ AIM SHUR RCK HAZ TOWLD U, LIKWUIDASHON MEENISTRY AFAIRZ R KAWNFIDENTIAL, SSO AIM NAWT @ LEEBERTY 2 SEH.

"Confidential?" she said in exasperation and broke out into a short burst of laughter, a laugh that he remembered well. "I've caught you now. You're not Amon, but just some stiff imposter, aren't you?"

WAT R U--

"Don't tell me you haven't realized for yourself. The Amon I grew up with would never have brushed me off with 'confidential.'" Amon couldn't think how to respond while looking into those whirlpool eyes, as though they were drawing his thoughts whirling into the depths of her.

AVERYWUN CHAYNGZ.

"Don't patronize *me*, Mon-chan." When he heard her nickname for him, Amon felt memories and emotions rise up almost to consciousness, sensed rather than directly experienced, like the vague shape of abandoned toys wrapped tightly in a black garbage bag. "Just tell me what's going on."

RCK & AI WER ASIGNED AAN EEMPORTANT MISHON 2DAY, BUUT HII NAYVER SHOWD AYT THA AWFICE.

"Oh. So he was working in another department or something?"

NAUGH. HI NAYVER KAYM IN 2 GATA AYT AUL & AI HAV NNO AIDEA WHER HII IZ.

"But that's . . . I thought he was late to meet me because of work."

WAYL AI THAWT HII WAZ ABSAYNT FRUM WERK BECAUZ UV . . . Amon left the sentence unfinished. In the silence between them that followed, he could hear the inescapable infohum, passersby talking to themselves, and the slow, steady rub of the treadmill as she continued to walk on it.

Suddenly Mayuko's whirlpool eyes narrowed and looked behind Amon, as though noticing his location for the first time. "Where are you?" she asked. Amon realized that he had forgotten to edit the background out of the feed and felt the warmth of blood rushing to his cheeks. "Is that where you're going these days, to the *kurabus*?" She spat out the word kurabu with such vitriol that Amon flinched.

NNO. AIM JAST PASING THROO. He knew that wasn't going to convince her, but there wasn't much else to say. For a few moments, they went silent again. Mayuko's walking gradually began to slow until she eventually stopped and turned off the machine. Looking at her standing there in her striped shirt and short-shorts with the towel draped around her shoulders, he noticed again, as he had the previous morning, that she looked much thinner than he remembered, and wondered why she was working out so hard.

AI HAV 2 GAYT GOEENG. EEF U HIER FRUM RCK PLEEZ LAYT MI KNAUGH. AIM SORRIE AGAYN FUR EENTERUPTING.

"Sure. And feel free to call anytime, even if you don't really want to talk to me." He could hear thinly-veiled anger in her voice. "Maybe next time you can actually speak instead of writing gibberish in that bubble." Amon wondered whether she had thought to say that herself or was purposely echoing what Rick had told him at the bar.

GEWD8IE, texted Amon, but she had already hung up.

The apartment view faded back into Ginza clubland streets, but a faint afterimage of her ocular whirlpools lingered for a few moments, as though Mayuko and her whole world had been sucked, round and round and round, into the deep, dark abysmal waters of Tokyo twilight.

9

GINZA THEN

Needing a place to clear his head, Amon asked ScrimpNavi for the cheapest cafe within a kilometer radius. The app guided him down the street to an intersection with another club-lined avenue. On the ground floor of one corner was a small cafe with gold wallpaper and royal-red carpeting. There was seating for about twenty, but at that moment, the place was empty.

He entered and walked to a brown acrylic counter at the back. Some kind of music was playing, but it was too low for him to make out (a trick that added atmosphere without racking up listening fees). The clack of his soles on the floor sounded at odds with the carpeted look. Atop the counter was a silver espresso maker and a row of several glass tubes filled with coffee beans roasted to different shades; from green, to dark brown, to almost black. Behind it stood a young woman in a blue silk headscarf, icons with the names of snacks and beverages floating in front of her.

He clicked Americano with one milk and no sugar (less expensive at that moment than having it black, or gods and buddhas forbid, double-double). The woman took out a half-full pot of coffee and steel shot-glass of milk from under the counter. He could hear a mechanical gurgling noise as she did this; a sure giveaway that the girl and counter were just graphical decorations over a vending machine—a low quality one without any audio masking. She poured the two liquids into a ceramic mug, where they mixed immediately into a pale brown of even consistency without need of any stirring. She then gently slid the mug across the counter with an inviting smile and bowed as Amon took it.

Warmth felt through styrofoam in hand and the smell of stale coffee in his nose, Amon took a stool at the counter running along the front window. Outside, twilight had deprived the city of its full vibrance. The concrete and tarmac before him seemed duller than usual, having reverted to some nethercolor more lifeless than gray. A hazy promo-glow from the sky drifted in marbled patterns over this figment of a street like the play of light on an ocean-floor gone sepia. These phantom images were too faint and distorted for Amon to recognize, but he felt something inside him respond to their dim flicker, as though they transmitted in a subtle visual code intelligible only to his shadow.

Amon sipped his coffee, the milk taking the edge off its bitterness. Every minute or so, he saw lone women wearing gaudy kimonos and *geta* pass by the window. They carried at least one purse and one brand name shopping bag, sometimes several strung over their shoulders at once, loose strands dangling elegantly from their pinned-back hair. These were the *mamas*, owners of the kurabus who managed the stables of young girls. Their after-work clientele would soon arrive in droves, and the mamas were headed to their respective establishments early in preparation. Strutting gracefully, backs straight, they held their heads high, a look of almost haughty dignity on their plain, all-business faces.

After a long day's work and a long walk, Amon was tired, thirsty, and hot. The impending mission had him anxious and Rick's inexplicable absence had him stressed. He needed to relax; that's why he was paying to be in this air-conditioned space. It was unavoidable. But however he spun these excuses, none of them were convincing. He couldn't remember doing anything so wasteful as visiting a cafe in years, not to mention the preceding stroll, and he was overcome with guilt for his lapses in budgeting. Memories overwhelmed him too; moments from his past revived by his talk with Mayuko.

Before he could sigh, Amon opened up the app SelfCapture, through which he accessed his LifeStream. SelfCapture promised to make LifeStream segments better than memory. It sifted out boring moments like sleep and waiting for the bus and pimple popping, honing in on actions of dramatic importance, just as memory did. Yet it retained vividness no matter how much time passed, was never blotted out by the capricious ink of forgetting. And whereas memories arose sporadically in response to some obscure, unconscious trigger, LifeStream segs were fully searchable by date, time, keyword, image, sound, and could be conjured instantly at a whim. Yet for Amon, the application could never be a complete substitute, and as he pulled up scenes from his digitally remastered youth, his mind was a partner in the remembering, layering in the scents, tastes, sensations, thoughts, and emotions that his embodied hard-drive could never replicate.

Early that spring morning, Amon arrived at the clinic on foot. The ImmaTainment that writhed in the sky above was rendered in vibrant hues that seemed to match the warm air, but the trees surrounding the skin-beige walls of the clinic were bursting with cherry blossoms colored a strange blood red.

He passed through the glass doorway into a skin-beige waiting room with reddish-pink rubber flooring, where a nurse in a matching beige uniform greeted him. The auto check-in downloaded his medical background as she guided him down the corridor to the examination room. There he was introduced to the Identity Giver, a man in a lab-coat of the same beige. He had a thin moustache and busy eyes that seemed to look through rather than at him. Amon undressed and stood in the middle of the room as the nurse directed. A pattern of evenly-spaced silver splotches interlinked by snaking, thread-like silver lines was spread across his skin, glittering faintly under the bright, sterile light, like a many-forking network of streams and lakes seen catching the sun from high altitude. Combined with contacts and ear-clip speakers, this constituted his training bank, a system of smart clothing all minors wore. Usually it was invisible, edited out of the ImmaNet, but today was a special day. Today was Amon's Identity Birth Day.

The nurse brought over a gray, plastic probe with a metallic roller on the end. As he stood there naked, she ran the roller over his skin and the points fell away like sparkling dandruff, the snaking lines peeling away with them.

Just then, the segment stopped; the circuit connecting his sensors had been severed, disabling his recording capabilities. It was frustrating to be denied the photorealism of data playback for such a significant event, but all that existed was the inferior copy kept by his brain. Thankfully, he hadn't forgotten; it was probably the only unrecorded moment of his life that he did remember. He would have to make do.

Within a few minutes, his training bank was just a dusting of glitter at his feet. He lay down on the hard hospital bed and stared up at the ceiling, where a steel cylinder sprouting various robotic limbs was attached. The arms began to move, strange prongs bathing him in beams of light; some visible, some sensed only vaguely. At some point the nurse instructed him to roll onto his front, and the process continued as before, now out of sight.

Eventually the arms came to a rest and the Identity Giver approached. He carefully examined Amon's eyes and ears without tools, the measuring devices and analytical applications built into the lenses of his eyes. When the examination was done, the nurse gave Amon contacts to wear. Now he could see the life-sized 3D blueprint that the Identity Giver had conjured. It floated a half meter off the floor in the center of the room, a gray outline of his body sketched in fibrous branches of biological chips.

Implants were unstable in rapidly growing youth, but being twenty, he was ready to receive a grown-up BodyBank at last. With a training bank, he'd always had to obey the parental restrictions imposed by his SubMom, uncomfortably aware of her surveilling eye whenever he flossed or masturbated, winked or cleared his throat. Now at last he'd be an adult with anonymity rights guaranteed; now at last he'd be the master of his own account; now at last he'd be free.

Amon had always looked forward to identity birth—as every youth should—but his heart pounded like mad when the nurse brought over a needle and gave an injection into his arm. After that he dropped into darkness, rising intermittently from the dreamless depths to skim the surface of consciousness: a sharp, sweet smell like warm rubber; the chatter of half-glimpsed labcoats hovering about him; the soft, hydraulic swish of mechanical appendages. And common to all of these dim moments of waking, he always felt a faint tingling sensation that fizzled across different patches of his skin and organs. The surgical dust was spreading inside him, inducing his cells to build the computer system on spec, molecule by molecule; his physical structure reorganizing itself; the emergent parts bonding with fat, muscle, and tendons; his flesh integrating with the other flesh.

At some point Amon awoke suddenly, his mind perfectly clear as though his sleep had been the deepest imaginable. The Identity Giver was waiting for him. Turning his head to the side on the pillow, Amon watched him approach, his white slippers silent on the hospital tiles. He felt his blood go cold with anticipation, accompanied simultaneously by a strange gratitude as he imagined the bounty of possibility that would soon be his. He sat up on the bed, dangling his legs over the edge. The Identity Giver leaned over and put a hand on his forehead, entering in the Birth Code like a blessing. After a few seconds, it was done. Endowed now with a signature and an account, Amon had entered a world of infinite opportunity and danger, for now he could earn all the freedom imaginable—or lose the freedom to earn altogether.

A subtle vibration in his hand awoke Amon from his reverie. Mindfulator had detected that he hadn't sipped his coffee for several minutes, and was reminding him to pick up his cup. What Mindfulator hadn't detected was that Amon had *finished* the coffee. He was loathe to order another, but the store policy flashing in a lime green box before him indicated that if he didn't order something within ten minutes, he would incur a seat charge three times the price of a drink. He clicked the order icon, retrieved his coffee from the machine/girl behind the counter, and returned to his seat at the window.

Twilight was beginning to edge towards night outside the cafe. The InfoSky reflection on the street had taken on a pale brightness. Half-formed faces, silhouetted landscapes, and indistinct bundles of color now flitted fluidly about like glimpses of a dream montage through a silk veil. The kimonoed mamas were gone; in their place were the hostesses who worked for them. Like the mamas, they carried multiple purses and shopping bags, but their hair was done up in a heap of curls resembling an intricate hedge of lustrous gift ribbons. They wore stilettos, and dresses with slits that exposed fishnetted thighs and shapely breasts, their chalk-white skin and blush-red cheeks floating in the Tokyo night like molten moons approaching the end of time.

When the nurse escorted Amon back out the front entrance of the hospital and departed inside with a deep bow, a man was waiting for him. The man stood on the edge of the curb with his hands in the pockets of his pinstripe suit. He was skinny; his below-average height diminished further by a slouch; his afro-textured hair rising one centimeter from his head; his nose wide and flat; his brown skin richly textured in streaks like a Zen garden graft. Watching the segment now, the realer-than-life resolution was unmistakable, but at the time Amon had been surprised when the man introduced himself with the name Yoshiyuki Sekido, as his features had seemed more Polynesian than typically Japanese.

Back then, Sekido hadn't yet been appointed as Liquidation Minister. He was a high-ranking Identity Executioner and had come to sign Amon up for the GATA payroll. Identity birth and a job always went hand in hand, for all Free Citizens started out in debt from purchasing their BodyBank and registering their identity, and immediately had to pay their own way. After the nerve-wracking experience of his first independent action—walking down the hospital corridor without any money to pay for it—Amon was grateful for this gesture.

Sekido drove him in a blue sports car to an izakaya in Shinbashi. They switched their shoes for slippers at the entrance and walked down a dim hallway. The gray slate walls and dark wooden flooring looked like half-existent abstractions under the steel-blue lighting. Men and women in suits of concrete gray crowded around an L-shaped bar, two dozen occupying the seats and a dozen more hovering around them with glasses of beer in hand, everyone laughing and gabbering loudly. As he approached, Amon glimpsed Rick and Mayuko through the crowd at the far end of the longer counter, both of them wearing nervous smiles.

Rick, Mayuko, and Amon had grown up together in a BioPen called Green Ladybug. Like many BioPens in the world, it was run by the life-property

MegaGlom Fertilex. Vague images of the compound came to Amon in the cafe: a long rectangular dormitory lined with tight rows of futons; the haloed-heart and grasping hand of the Fertilex logo pulsating on the walls of endless stucco corridors; enchanting foxes and other cute characters appearing unbidden to teach lessons on using the ImmaNet, dressing, hygiene, reading, programming, mathematics, fitness, following rules, being frugal; announcements on the unsurpassed quality of all things Fertilex playing on endless repeat; and the stomping feet of their vicious SubMom, the only person Amon ever knew who could make pacing sound like an effort to kick through the floor.

When they were teenagers, Mayuko had told Amon that she could remember the day he arrived at Green Ladybug, but Amon had no memory of this. The event in question would have happened before they reached four, when their recollections were still unformed, and Fertilex retained exclusive ownership over their LifeStreams, denying access without payment. As far back as he could remember, Amon had always been at Green Ladybug and Mayuko had always been with him. At the very least, they had been together for their whole digital lives, and that was all that seemed to matter.

Rick, on the other hand, hadn't moved in until they were around ten. He was the only one of them who knew his own origin; his parents had lost the capacity to pay for his actions, for reasons Rick had been too young to understand. The majority of BioPen kids were said to be either abandoned by free couples—like Rick—or were the orphans of bankdead, although there were a few test tube babies that the SubMoms carried. Whatever the truth, no child was ever told anything about where they came from, so as to protect donor anonymity and mitigate clone discrimination. According to the ambiguous hints of their SubMom, Mayuko was of Japanese ancestry, while Amon was half-Persian and half-Japanese. Neither of them ever put much trust into anything she said, but this was the only story they had, so they tentatively stuck with it.

When Rick was assigned to be Amon's bedmate, they had become instant friends. The two boys were inseparable from morning till night; sitting side-by-side in the classroom and cafeteria, playing on the same teams during recess, incurring the wrath of the SubMom for chatting past lights out; the kind of friends who studied together for tests, allied against bullies, and forgave each other quickly after childish quarrels.

Mayuko embraced Rick too, but he was a latecomer to their group, stepping into a circle whose boundaries were etched in some oblivious dawn. The connection between Amon and Mayuko went back to their primal, half-conscious infancy. Familiarity had soaked into their cores, into layers of self deeper than emotion and thought. Although the boys' and girls' dorms were separated, and there were many daily activities in which Amon and Mayuko had to be apart, Amon always held an unconscious place for Mayuko in his mind and could sense that Mayuko did the same, distant in space but somehow jointly partaking of the moment. They were not merely compatible; were much more than just two matching profiles. An ineffable *something* had always drawn them together, like the roots of different trees reaching together for the same underground stream. They had known the depths of each other—if not completely then as much as anyone could know another—perhaps more than they had known themselves. Unable to lie or conceal anything, yet always beyond the other's comprehension, they encountered one surprise after another amidst their intimacy, inspiring curiosity and fascination that was never exhausted. That was how it seemed. And yet, Amon realized now, as he made a bitter face upon sipping his second cup of coffee (now black, because adding milk had gone up in price), maybe he had misunderstood something. Maybe what had existed between them was much more flimsy and tenuous. Maybe there had never been anything there at all.

When the time came to move out on their own, the three of them had applied for the same jobs, hoping to keep together the closest thing they had to a family. Their top choice had been Fertilex—the wisest and most innovative company on earth they knew well from their adverteducation—but they also sent out applications to other MegaGloms, and to GATA as well. The primary screen for young applicants was their score on standardized concentration tests. With information permeating every nook and cranny of existence, there was no rationale for testing memorization of facts and figures; what mattered was how long a potential employee could stick to a task while inundated with distractions, stay afloat on a raft of signal through a torrent of noise. And while the tendency to constantly flit about from one thing to the next was said to benefit the economy by encouraging impulsivity, it was the very antithesis of frugality, perhaps even a sign of cash crash to come. That is to say, it was a discreditable liability and was therefore generally looked down upon. Amon remembered when they got their results back and spent the night laughing together in the dim of the boys dorm (Mayuko having snuck in), feeling certain Fertilex would take them. Their scores had all been in the top ten percentile, Amon's perfect.

But none of them were even offered an interview. Amon and Rick were accepted together into the Liquidation Ministry, and Mayuko into Capsize Solutions, a promising startup. Flunking the Fertilex application and being separated from Mayuko had been a shocking disappointment for them all, but with starting salaries as high as fresh BioPen grads could hope for, they could hardly complain.

On the night of their initiation into GATA, Rick and Amon wore the concrete gray suits of their newfound profession for the first time. Mayuko had picked a sparkly, black evening gown; two silver bracelets on her right wrist, and earrings made of three green crystals hanging from a horizontal silver bar in each ear. She had been initiated into her company the day before and had received her BodyBank already, but since the three of them wanted to celebrate together, Rick and Amon had got special permission from Sekido to let her attend the GATA event.

After each attendee had stood up one by one and given their mandatory self introductions, the three of them sat together at the edge of the bar downing glasses of beer and trading stories about their ID birthdays. Soon everyone was roaring drunk, and Sekido proposed moving on to the next venue. None of the penniless recruits were about to turn down another treat on their first day of adulthood, but the other ministry staff traded knowing smiles, and gave their congratulations before heading off to catch the last train of the night. That left only Rick, Amon, Mayuko, Sekido, two other senior staff members, and half a dozen recruits (including Tororo and Freg).

Together they stumbled raucously through the glowing streets to Ginza and arrived in front of the cylinder of chrome and block of pure darkness with the golden word *Eroyuki*. They went two-by-two down the hallway beneath rows of lights led by Sekido, who opened the door at the end. Upon entering, Amon immediately shielded his eyes from a blinding glare. As fully the façade was black, so the interior was white. The counter, the barstools, the bottle-lined shelf behind the bar, the two chandeliers, the table cloths hanging over round tables, even the outfits of the voluptuous hostesses waiting in a row to greet them were all made of powder snow. As a hostess with curly red hair wearing a tutu led them to their private booth in the back, Amon heard a crunch under his shoes with each step and remembered the feeling of the conditioned air, not nearly cold enough to match the frigid decor. Seated before the snowy tabletop, he watched flakes drift from the ceiling and swirl around the room on unfelt drafts, before striking the floor or a piece of furniture or a hostess's white garment and being absorbed without a trace. Amon had never seen such a complex overlay, as though assembled with delicate hands, fragile flake by fragile flake.

Four girls wrapped scantily in snow brought bottles of sparkling wine and sugary cocktails in primary colors. The dozen remaining attendees raised an ecstatic *cheers*, and began downing glass after glass. With looser tongues, they slipped into uproarious banter, now accompanied by the girls, who found every joke funny and were experts at flattery. Amon held Mayuko's hand beneath the table. There was a resplendent glitter of joy in her incisive dark eyes, and by the way she stared back at him, he guessed there was something similar in his own, as they laughed mirthfully with everyone and poured each other small cups of fine sake.

Chest tight with feelings he couldn't name, Amon paused the seg to reminisce over that moment. Although Mayuko and Amon had hardly ever had a chance to be alone in the crowded BioPen, the kids had been calling them boyfriend and girlfriend for years. They had denied this embarrassing taunt in childhood, but had grown mature enough to accept it after traversing adolescence; thinking of themselves as a couple seemed the inevitable next stage in the evolution of their relationship. With every gesture tabulated by their SubMom, and the occasional furtive kiss incurring a lecture, sex had been impossible. Yet that night, at last, they were finally ready.

Amon remembered the warmth of her hidden hand, but there was also a second warmth: a warmth emerging from the intimacy between them, a warmth that belied the illusion of winter, a warmth they might have cherished together for a lifetime.

Amon felt no regret for the creditable life he had chosen, but knowing what would come next, he wanted to tell something to his younger, happier, oblivious self, if not a warning then at least a few words of consolation to take on the lonely road ahead.

After Amon had finished his fourth cup of sake, Sekido put a big hand on his shoulder and shuffled him out of the booth. They walked across the room to the wall opposite the entrance and went through a door. It led to a spiral staircase built of snowy cinder blocks, which Amon guessed to be the inside of the cylinder he had seen outside. They wound their way up the white tunnel for half a minute and went through another door into a spacious, lofty chamber, built of the same white blocks in the style of a gothic castle. Four armchairs of snow were placed around a low table of white with slivers of gray and black bleeding through, as though composed of winter mountaintop. Sekido sat down in an armchair and gestured for Amon to take the opposite seat.

"Now, the moment present, the current time between future and past, is an occasion for you to partake, to savor, to relish if the mood takes you, in an old—though not quite ancient and certainly not mythological—tradition. A certain modicum of surprise inevitably penetrates the hearts of our recruits upon transmission of information regarding this tradition, but emotion arising in the face of the unexpected is not an altogether unhealthy phenomenon according to hearsay and anecdotes, no less scientific evidence and the conclusions of renowned pedagogues. Moreover, this is a gift I bestow upon every one of the Liquidators under my tutelage, and it makes me very proud—as one beholden to my mentors and to their mentors and to those who came before them and to those who came before the ones who came before my mentors' mentors and on and on and on and on and on—to offer this same choice to you. Are you ready?"

Before Amon could answer, Sekido pulled up full body shots of two girls, neither of whom had been in the bar. The one on the left beamed a broad bleached smile, her blond-streaked pigtails bobbing up from the back of her head, her skin richly-tanned. She wore a lace bra revealing perky breasts, below which her belly was bare. A low mini-skirt of snow flared outwards above her sleek, toned legs. The other girl had raven black hair that hung loose to her shoulders in the front and tapered shorter and shorter as it approached the back of her head; her skin creamy white; her lips tilted up at one side in an alluring half-smile. She wore a long-sleeved gown of snow that exposed only her ample breasts and delicate ankles, her black eyes and hair vivid in contrast to her attire, her complexion, and the surround. They both appeared to be around Amon's age, give or take a few years.

"What is this? I don't understand?"

"The gist is that you are being asked to examine their profiles with due care, considering the pluses and minuses, and divisions and multipliers, and square roots and pies, calculating lasciviously to your heart's content. After this you will make a choice."

"What kind of choice?"

"We've arranged for you to spend private time with one of them."

Amon was stunned and confused. He'd heard that some old companies had weird hazing rituals, but never expected such treatment from GATA. There was nothing morally wrong about it, so long as GATA could afford it on their budget. And yet . . .

"I-I'm not sure—"

"Not sure about what exactly? This is a great chance to learn what having a BodyBank is all about. All the freedom you can earn and you've earned it by proving yourself qualified to be with us. We're giving you a present, a token of welcome, an advance reward for your services to come. You—"

"But-but Ma-Mayuko is here," interrupted Amon. "I can't just—"

"You're looking at a funhouse mirror through the wrong end of the telescope, so allow me to reorient you to the correct facet. This is about being part of a great tradition at the doorway to a great organization in this great Free World of ours. We're talking greatness here. Now we're all hesitant sometimes about the choices we have to make and think first before we act—that's the key to creditability after all—as it's only bankrupts who act on every impulse that comes their way, like automatic doors with survival instincts, if you'll forgive me this less than poetic comparison. But hesitation in the face of an opportunity offered, of a chance for ascent, a chance to earn freedom beyond anything you conjured speculatively in that dim little BioPen of yours; well that's not any kind of creditability. At best that's fear, at worst ingratitude. I won't make any accusations, Kenzaki. From your profile and your remarkable concentration scores, I see great potential. You might even be a prodigious leader like Lawrence Barrow someday, and I certainly wouldn't say that to just anyone—no one ever said that to me so you can count yourself privileged already if that stimulates your jollies in a nice ticklish sort of way. So to be blunt, now is the time for you to take a free action, and not just freely chosen, but a complimentary action—all charges on us. If you're still feeling a bit nervous, just remember: I'll be proud of you, GATA will be proud of you, even your girlfriend will be proud of you when you get a promotion, and you can be proud of yourself. Now which one would you like?"

Sekido sunk into the armchair with his fingers outspread on the rests. Under his boss's urging stare, Amon began scrolling through the profiles of the girls. The one with the pigtails was called Akane Kozue. She liked bubblegum, mountain climbing, and wanted to marry an astronaut. The one with the tapered hairstyle was called Aoi Tsubomi. Favorite drink: White Russian. Hobby: reading mystery novels. Favorite way to relax: roasting marshmallows in a fireplace.

Nothing about them was even remotely interesting to Amon. They seemed more like two-dimensional cut-outs from a men's webzine than human beings. He could think only of Mayuko back in the bar, smiling politely at the drunken antics of the other recruits and wondering where he'd gone. He wanted to be back there with her, but Sekido's words reverberated in his head. Could he really say no to his boss on the first day? Could he refuse a gift just because it wasn't to his liking and enter the ministry on the wrong foot? The BioPen had taken care of everything before, but now he had become responsible for his own transactions. He had to be professional or he might end up unemployed, destitute, bankrupt. He wanted to ask his decision network for help, but could see in Sekido's eyes that he would tolerate no dillydallying. Amon had to decide alone. When he thought about Mayuko, he wanted to scream at the top of his lungs, but when he thought about the career possibilities ahead of him, he could almost convince himself that the sacrifice would be insignificant in comparison to the payoff in freedom over the long term. Surely nothing too serious would happen with these girls. Surely Mayuko would forgive him once he explained.

Amon noticed that Akane was about half the price of Aoi. They both seemed equally attractive in their own ways, more or less, and he wondered what determined the difference. Perhaps Aoi showed her patrons a wilder time. Perhaps Akane was lacking experience. Amon didn't really care. He just wanted to fulfill his duty and get it over with, so he could enjoy the remnants of the night with Mayuko. And he figured that by choosing the cheaper girl, he could show his modesty and restraint—that is, his creditability. He clicked the purchase button for Akane.

"Good choice my boy," said Sekido, getting up from the chair, clapping his hand on Amon's shoulder, and guiding him down the hall to another door of snow. "You've got thirty minutes of creditime, Kenzaki, so make it last." The door opened.

And there, standing in front of him, was Akane. Exactly identical to her picture, with the pigtails; the short, flared skirt of snow; and the long legs. There were no walls or ceiling in this room, just a blizzard of thick snowflakes blowing in all directions. Her hips swayed as she prowled over to him, her symmetrical smile and skimpy outfit blending in with the blizzard as though she were one with the snow; an arctic chameleon. Amon realized there was a bed in the middle of the room, not of snow, but pure white silk, almost invisible at first glance. After a brief greeting and a wet kiss on his neck, Akane wasted no time in undressing and laying him down in bed.

Before Amon knew it, something unstoppable had been put into motion, a biological avalanche. Rising and falling amidst the snow above him, her flesh was a hearth in the polar frost; her breasts throbbing with a superhuman liquidity despite their perfect tautness, like ripples spreading on a pond of lava; the surface of her skin quivering with each panting breath and moan; her whole body a beating heart of fire that wrapped and consumed him with pulsing pleasure. There was nothing about her touch that belied this miraculous sensuality, he remembered, her undulating form hot from the inside, each crystalline snowflake melting on impact, adorning her with a tantalizing steam and filling his nostrils with the twin aromas of lust and winter (the latter arising from where he knew not).

Amon was nearing climax when something happened.

Since this was his first day with a BodyBank, he hadn't fully adjusted to using it, and meaning to dim the brightness of this blinding snow just a little, he accidentally opened the wrong program and, without reading the warning message that popped up, clicked "accept." Next thing he knew, he was in a room with yellowing, checkered wallpaper and navy blue carpeting, as though he'd been transported to a worn-out business hotel. He was joined with a middle-aged lady who looked rather plain. She was in good shape and obviously took excellent care of herself, but there was no denying the wrinkles around her eyes and mouth. She still looked somewhat like Akane, but she also could have been Aoi. Her features were somewhere in between the two, so that with a cheap, simple digimake she could become either one. Realizing he had mistakenly shut off the overlay and stripped the projections off the naked room, he turned it back on. Immediately the blizzard returned, and the Akane/Aoi prototype, the woman who could play two roles, was in her prime once again.

The revealing had only lasted a split second, but it was enough to set a chill in his gut and render him limp, as though the cold of the phantom snow had seeped into his viscera.

When Amon returned to the private booth, the men were cheering, but Rick kept his eyes averted with his usual tragic look and sipped his sake, while Mayuko stared at the straw on the tip of her green bubbly cocktail. She remained deathly still, like a single blade of grass in a field that refuses to stir in the wind. At some point while they were having their last few drinks of the night, Mayuko slipped out to use the makeup room and never returned.

A crew of salarymen in dark suits were starting to gather with the hostesses directly in front of the window. They milled about from sidewalk to street having jerky, muttered conversations on FacePhone, apparently trying to decide which kurabu to visit. One hostess in a crimson dress carried a silvery red purse shaped like a lamborghini and two paper shopping bags with brand-names Amon couldn't see. She chatted with another hostess in a dress of plain, violet lace with thick slits in the skirt and sleeves. They showed each other the new products in their bags, and cast alluring glances at the salarymen. Amon reflected that, unlike Aoi/Akane, these women he saw on the street were not prostitutes. They were just hostesses hired to look good and chat up the patrons. Only a select few of the kurabus here offered services like Eroyuki. He remembered other initiation events he'd attended over the years. Like the senior staff, he always left after the first bar. Many of his colleagues declined because they were married and had signed prenuptial agreements that automatically transferred astronomical sums to their wives if they cheated. But for Amon, avoiding Eroyuki wasn't just about the money. Painful emotions were endemic to frugality, so he avoided even thinking about Ginza, let alone visiting. Until, that is, he'd wandered over there earlier in the evening and contacted Mayuko . . .

That night, after everyone said *adieu* at the train station, Amon staggered alone to the residence GATA had prepared for him; a bachelor apartment in Kanda only slightly larger than the place he lived now. Once in bed, he tossed and turned and thrashed about, gritting his teeth, punching his pillow, and swearing at himself, overwhelmed with a stabbing combination of regret, guilt, and disappointment, like ten-thousand knives trying to rip their way out from under his skin. Eventually these feelings overflowed from his flesh in the form of tears and he wept himself to sleep.

That night, he had his forest dream for the first time. Until then, Amon had rarely remembered his dreams. And if he did remember them, they were usually about a SpillBot upgrade, a concentration-enhancing gene-booster, or some other enticement that had filtered into his mind from gods knew where. But this dream was different. It was more vivid, more compelling, more *real*. He didn't know what it meant, and it would take him many months to risk a guess, but even on that first morning, he knew immediately upon waking that nothing would ever be the same.

After that, the dream came to Amon every night. Actually he wasn't absolutely certain it really came every night, but it seemed prudent to guess so. Either he remembered his dreams, in which case it was invariably the dream, or he didn't, in which case he felt its lingering resonance. Remembered or not, awake or asleep, the dream spoke ever-present. His thoughts seemed to arise from the dream, his feelings to find shelter in it. His sensations reached out to the dream, his memories whirling it away. It cycled in his consciousness like a boomerang trapped within an elastic membrane, rebounding endlessly off the transparent walls. It had no beginning, nor end. Its exhaustion only triggered its replenishment, the way exhalations and inhalations follow each other to the grave. He never lost it, nor could he escape it. And only from this pervasive mystery that followed and abided within him like the daemon that spoke wisdom to Socrates, only from this could he find the will to live truly alone.

In the ensuing weeks, Amon and Mayuko continued to talk on Face-Phone for a while. He never mentioned what had happened, and Mayuko never asked. But a rift had undeniably opened up between them. There had been no final confrontation, no decisive end, just a slow extinguishment of interest suffused with a glow of melancholy.

It must have been around this point, thought Amon, *that my path began to diverge from Rick's too*. Two single men with big salaries, they reveled in the Tokyo nights. Sure, in their rookie days, there were thrills and stories to tell, but nothing ever felt quite right for Amon, for at some point, although he couldn't say precisely when, he realized that the dream was calling him, and he would need plenty of money to heed it.

After he'd eventually paid off the debt from his Identity Birth and the fine for accidentally violating the images rights of the woman and room in Eroyuki, Amon created his savings account and allowed frugality to pervade his life. He was partying less and less, ignoring messages more and more, and assuming foolishly that his friendship with Rick would stay strong when all the while, nothing remained but lingering inertia from childhood kept going by their interaction as co-workers. Now that Rick had blocked him, Amon could see that their relationship had been declining for years, as though he'd noticed a tiny hole in the bottom of a ship only as it capsized.

Downing the dredges of his coffee, with his ears to the faint notes and beats of the half-audible music that played in the cafe, Amon wondered at what point, as he drifted from his friends, they had drifted together. He supposed that Mayuko had found other lovers in between, but nonetheless felt a sharp pang of jealousy when he imagined that it might have been Rick who had been the first in his place.

Aimlessness, loss of purpose, lethargy, sadness, a list of symptoms popped up one after the other. MyMedic had checked his physiological data and given its diagnosis: he was depressed. "If left untreated," the application warned, "depression can result in compulsive behavior and irresponsible accounting." Amon clicked a link to more detailed medical-financial advice that pulsated before him. A freckled cartoon physician wearing a white lab coat and huge glasses appeared and said: "Analysis of the latest data shows that aerobic exercise, particularly jump rope, is the most effective treatment for your particular type of depression." The doctor stuck his hand out, and a three centimeter tall man holding a jump rope materialized on his palm. The man, who was middle-aged and pudgy, wore a gray track suit stained with sweat patches around the armpits, his face twisted in a scowl. When he began to skip, the stress seemed to drain out of him, for his expression relaxed, the stains vanished, and by the time he was going at a good pace, he began to smile. Amon considered the doctor's prescription and did a quick search through the online action-property registry. He discovered that *skipping* was owned by a certain company A, buying skip ropes by company B, and the programming studio that developed MyMedic by company C, all of which were subsidiaries of the health MegaGlom, H&H Kenko. With all the collusion involved, Amon began to doubt that skipping was actually as effective as demonstrated with the little man, and decided it wasn't worth the investment, even if his depression might make him a bit more spendthrift.

He was about to pick up his styrofoam cup and take it to the trash bin under the far side of the counter when he noticed a man staring at him. Sitting along the window three stools away, the man looked to be about forty, with intense, dark eyes, his eyelashes long and elegant, almost feminine, yet piercing as though sharpened at the tips. His nose was long and slightly hooked, his skin milky brown and smooth, suggesting a cultivated upbringing. His clean-shaven chin and jaw were small and delicate; his shoulders and waist slim; his posture proud but relaxed. He wore a thin vest of gray wool over a white dress shirt, on both of which the same pattern of black vines grew; the shadow branches and leaves extended upwards across the two garments, sprouting new offshoots, reaching beyond the boundaries of his body where they vanished, a slow, inexorable process of burgeoning and vanishing, burgeoning and vanishing.

Meeting Amon's gaze, the man began to speak: "There's no need to introduce yourself, Amon Kenzaki." His voice was quiet and clear, his Japanese distinctly Indian accented. "I'm here to discuss a job opportunity with you. The talk and the dinner are on me."

A window popped up, asking Amon if he would consent to being leashed. In stunned amazement, Amon sat there gazing vacantly into the man's eyes. He couldn't believe that this man, whoever he was, was making such a generous offer, although he was reluctant to click yes. While leashed, the man would pay for each of Amon's transactions, but he would need to see what he was paying for, which meant Amon's AT readout would be disclosed. He would see every action Amon was performing, including his *subscribing* to various apps and services, as well as anything he might want to do privately online. Amon didn't want to provide such personal information, however unimportant it might be, to someone he'd never met before. He tried to click his profile but the public one was blank and no premium version was available. The man just kept staring at him, as if he hadn't noticed the prying clicks.

Amon was reminded that his own profile was blank and that he was wearing a digiguise of pastel scribbles. No one should have been able to recognize him, not least this total stranger. He was starting to get suspicious when he realized with excitement who the man was: the internal recruiter! Only someone from GATA could have accessed his professional profile to identify him, and Sekido had told Amon to expect a surprise call from the recruiter on an evening in the near future. Apparently that evening had arrived.

Amon clicked accept and texted AI WULD BII DELITED 2 SPIIK WIITH U, before remembering with embarrassment that this man was covering his expenses and misspelling would only make him look like a cheapskate.

10

TSUKIJI, SUSHI MIGRATION

A strange vehicle, like a giant F1 race car combined with an armored van pulled up in front of them with a screech. With six wheels on long axles jutting out to the sides, its body was narrow in the front but became incrementally wider as it approached the rear, expanding from a hammerhead nose to a single driver's seat to a bloated chamber for six passengers. Painted navy blue with two red stripes and one of white running from nose to rear, the vehicle opened its passenger doors upwards. The driver faced straight ahead, expressionless, wearing a gray conductor's cap and white gloves. The recruiter got in the passenger chamber and Amon went around to join him through the opposite door. They each took a spot by the window on either side, leaving a long, empty space between them. The seating looked like leather, smelled like leather, and Amon felt a sleek texture like leather on the skin of his forearms as he sat back, guessing it was probably leather. The doors floated down silently to a close.

"Tsukiji," said the recruiter. The driver nodded and the car started forward with a lurch, flattening Amon's head against his seat. The race-car design had to be more than digital deep, for they ripped down the club-lined street, the neon signs turning to hazy streaks of light as though time itself had been stretched, the milling clusters of salarymen and seductive hostesses rendered faceless in the passing blur. Intimidating the other vehicles with both speed and size, the racing van barged through narrow rents in traffic and careened left around the following intersection, cutting off a tow-truck. Amon could hear a steady, musical hum that increased in pitch as they accelerated. Like harmonizing notes plucked on harp strings that never stop reverberating, this engine sound was beautiful and soothing, and almost took the edge off his fear. Noticing that the recruiter had not buckled his seatbelt Amon followed his lead, despite the continuous thumping of his heart. The recruiter's hands were constantly twitching and he muttered the occasional bit of gibberish, apparently busy online. Through the rearview mirror, Amon could see the driver's face; narrow and sleek, with not a trace of hair—even eyebrows—as though he were born to be aerodynamic like the car he drove; his eyes beady, almost furtive, so that it was difficult to tell where he was looking. The city went by so fast, Amon almost couldn't see it. Crowded patios sprawling across bar-lined alleyways that cut into the red brick train bridge flashed by, Shinbashi gone in a gasp. Soon the poles of the fence enclosing the old Tsukiji fish market were whipping past like vertical stripes of steel and absence.

Then the market was behind them, and the car began to slow. As the engine song dropped in volume and pitch, Amon could make out a strip of sushi bars in low five-story buildings outside the recruiter's window. Gently the driver brought the car to a stop on the side of the road and the doors flipped slowly and smoothly open. Still gesturing and muttering to himself, the recruiter got out and Amon, wanting to avoid the traffic on his side, scooted across the long seat to follow him out. By the time he stepped onto the sidewalk, the recruiter had already opened a heavy black door in a brick wall and was crossing the threshold. Amon paused for a second to watch as the car doors shut without a sound and the car evaporated with a roar around the next bend like a mirage in reverse.

The words "Sushi Migration" were written in black calligraphy directly on the brick over the black door. Amon entered.

Gasping with a rush of vertigo, Amon stepped into an indigo sky. Profound blue surrounded him in all directions—even down—as though the entire world had been erased but for a sphere of darkening atmosphere. Although the encompassing sky was radiant with rich silver light, there was no sun anywhere to be seen. Just an endless shade of winter melancholy.

For a moment Amon thought he had somehow stumbled into his dream, but nowhere could he see a forest or hear the surf and something strange flitted above his head. Little white flecks stood out against the indigo. A flock of origami cranes spread through space forming the double loop of the infinity sign. The paper birds bobbed up and down within a field extending about five to twenty meters above his head, snapping back into line whenever they began to drift out of formation, as though magnetically positioned. Straight ahead of Amon were two parallel rows of four-seater booths split by an aisle two metres wide. The aisle ran to a square bar surrounded by stools. The tables, seats, and counter were all made of a dark gray marble. A window rose from the bar counter, behind which vibrant cuts of seafood rested on chipped ice and grated daikon. The glass curved at the top towards the center of the square to form a second, higher counter about chest high. Atop it, small sheets of white paper were stacked every half meter. Sushi chefs wearing *tenugui* bandanas and *jinbe* robes—both in indigo-flecked white—were hard at work behind the bar. They were slicing fish, squeezing it into place on clods of rice, and putting the finished product onto sheets of paper, whereupon the paper would automatically fold itself into a crane and tuck the piece of sushi into some hidden recess inside, before immediately taking flight and ascending to join the looping flock above. A handful of patrons sat on stools around the bar and a dozen or so were scattered amongst the tables.

Amon fought off waves of exhilarating nausea as he took another step out into this high altitude. He had never felt this way in his dream, but apparently his waking fears were different. He was grateful to feel solidity beneath his shoes and hesitantly, step by step, followed the recruiter down the aisle to a table halfway to the bar. A complex rhythmic soundscape of whispering bird cries—structured around a beat that wasn't quite jazz, wasn't quite African polyrhythm—emanated from nowhere in particular, the pointed white beaks of the origami cranes mouthless and unmoving. The cranes dive-bombed from their place in the sky and swooped evasively around the two men as they walked, alighting on tables before customers and then unfolding into a sheet of uncreased white paper with a piece of sushi resting on it.

They took aisle-side seats across from each other, the recruiter with his back to the bar, Amon's to the door. On top of the table was a wooden box containing yellow pickled ginger; a glass jar of soy sauce with a thin cylindrical metal spout; a tin of powdered green tea; four small, gray ceramic dishes for soy sauce; four cups of the same material stacked lip down; and four pairs of chopsticks laid horizontally in front of each of the seats with their tips resting on a flat, circular white stone.

Without wasting a moment, the recruiter began flipping through a stack of still images like index cards that floated a few centimeters above the table and depicted the dishes served. Amon began to do the same and clicked sweet rolled egg, skipjack tuna, and pickled mackerel. One after the other, four cranes alighted in front of the recruiter and three in front of Amon, unfolding their hidden morsels in sequence. Amon glanced at the recruiter's order: octopus suckers; sea urchin; scallops; and the finest cut of tuna, its flesh reddish-pink with a haze of fat.

Amon began to wonder how the cranes worked. He had once watched a show about a sushi bar where plates of sushi rotated around on a conveyer belt and were placed in front of customers by robotic arms, while the whole process was digimade to look like the plates were bouncing through a pinball machine to the table. Yet the aisle in this restaurant was empty and Amon couldn't imagine where such mechanical rigging might fit.

He then noticed a faucet sticking out of thin air to his right, the spout overhanging the edge of the table. Glancing around, he saw that the tables ahead and across the aisle to his left were equipped with the same. He guessed that the faucets were fastened to walls running beside each row of tables that had been rendered invisible against the all-subsuming indigo. This meant they were probably in a rectangular room, with the entrance at one end and the bar at the other.

Amon picked up two cups from the stack, brought them up one by one to the faucet, and pulled its lever to fill them with hot water. He then opened the lid of the tea tin, took out the tiny spoon inside, scooped two small pinches of green powder into the cups, stirred the hot water to mix in the powder, and put one cup of the resulting thick green liquid on the tabletop in front of the recruiter, one in front of himself. The recruiter didn't say a word of gratitude or even nod his head, as though the gesture were too obvious to be worth acknowledging.

"Let's get started," he said, taking a sip of his tea, the shadow vines growing up his vest and shirt seeming to grasp for the indigo sky. Amon nodded and poured some soy sauce into one of the flat dishes. "I've done a lot of research, Amon, and I know a lot about you already."

Amon felt odd having a stranger address him by his given name. The only people on Earth who did that were Mayuko, Rick, Freg, and Tororo (though truth be told, these latter workmates made him a bit uncomfortable when they failed to call him "Kenzaki-san," like the other ministry staff, as their relationship wasn't all that intimate). But he wasn't about to cut the recruiter off just as he was getting going and quickly forgot all about it.

"Your perfect concentration score, your excellence as a Liquidator, and so on. I probably know things about you that you don't even know yourself, so we can skip the introductory chit chat. To assess your suitability for the job, I'll need to ask you some questions about areas that appear nowhere in your records. These questions might seem surprising to you, but I want to get to know who you are on the inside, so the key here is to try and answer them as honestly as you can. Do you think you can manage that?"

"Absolutely," said Amon. "I'd be happy to."

"Good. But first let's begin our dinner, shall we?"

The recruiter brought his palms together above the table with his chopsticks resting perpendicular to his hands in the nook between thumb and pointer finger, and closed his eyes as if in prayer. Amon imitated this ritual to show gratitude for the food, but kept his eyes open, waiting until the recruiter opened his, whereupon they broke the pose and reached for their sushi. Amon dipped his piece of skipjack tuna in the soy sauce and ate it. He found it exquisitely delicious. The chemically-harvested seafood found at most conveyer sushi bars was printed one-slice at a time and usually had a mild scent, neither pleasing nor off-putting. The aroma of this fish was sweet, nothing he'd experienced before. It almost seemed . . . He struggled for the proper archaism—wild caught, or . . . organic? With such high-quality ingredients and the impeccable decor, this restaurant was clearly in a category all its own.

"My first question," said the recruiter, after taking another sip of tea, "is about your job."

"Yes, what would you like to know?"

"Do you believe in it?"

"Believe in it?" said Amon, frowning with confusion.

"Sure. Do you believe in what you're doing? Do you think it serves some meaningful purpose?" The recruiter blinked and his sharp, elegant eyelashes tore silently and gracefully through the air, beautiful yet somehow threatening.

"Liquidating is the only job I've ever done and I approach my duties with a sense of their great importance every day. This brings me a feeling of . . . satisfaction." Amon wanted to go on, but he couldn't think what else to say. Now that he was leashed, he could speak freely, but had become so used to censoring himself and misspelling his texts that the words wouldn't come. He considered turning on VentriloQuick, an app that predicted what you were trying to say as you spoke and made suggestions on how to phrase it. Supplementing the user's knowledge with information from the FlexiPedia database, VentriloQuick displayed recommended sentences and auto-corrected them rapidly in tune with the intended message. Many people left it on constantly and set it to audio mode, so they could parrot whatever it whispered in their ears and come off as eloquent with hardly any mental effort. But Amon generally kept it off for frugal reasons, and since the recruiter could see all his transactions now that he was leashed, he would likely notice if Amon turned it on and take him for a blathering fool that relied on a communication crutch.

"Why? What makes being a Liquidator satisfying?"

After a brief pause, Amon found his answer. "GATA upholds the principles of the AT market. As a Liquidator, I can help to defend these principles by apprehending those who drain the economy. The informational assets we seize from bankdead hard-drives also provides GATA with an indispensable source of funding."

"So you're proud of your role in capturing bankrupts."

"Yes. Very much so."

"You don't feel sorry for the people you cash crash? You believe it's right to banish them into the camps just for running out of money, and never give them another chance? Keep in mind that I want you to take your time in answering, not just so we can enjoy this food as we talk, but to make sure you give the issues careful consideration."

Amon wracked his brain to figure out what any of this had to due with assisting the Executive Council. The recruiter was inquiring about something so self-evident, it had caught Amon off guard and tangled his tongue. It was as though someone were asking him what he breathed: *air of course,* he wanted to say. The justice and magnanimity of GATA were standard lessons given during Liquidator training, and any half-witted ministry employee could have answered adequately. Yet the Executive Council position would clearly require something more than mediocre aptitude. This told Amon that the recruiter's questions couldn't be aimed at testing his knowledge. But if it wasn't knowledge then . . . perhaps it was something else like . . . loyalty. Yes! Sekido was often talking about the importance of what he called "faithful reliablism," which seemed to mean something like loyalty. That had to be it. And since these questions were too obvious to even ask, it clearly wasn't so much what Amon said, but the way he said it that was under scrutiny. Any stutter or falter in his speech would be interpreted as a sign of his doubt in the organization. Clearly, he had to demonstrate his faith by the fluidity of his communication, and although he wasn't used to speaking aloud, he resolved to be as articulate as he could. Once Amon realized what was expected, words suddenly came pouring out in a great torrent that surprised him.

"I admit that some aspects of bankruptcy are sad, but it's far more humane than any punitive system thought up before. In the past, we had many ways to punish people for the crimes they committed: prison, penal labor, execution, torture. However it was done, public funds were wasted on paying the salaries of workers like guards, judges, lawyers, and hangmen. This meant that the earnings, and therefore the freedom, of creditable people were used to cause physical and psychological pain to the discreditable. But this is a lose-lose situation. Overall freedom is lost and nothing is gained.

"With GATA, for the first time in history we've found a way to bring deviants to justice without taking freedom from the working person or the deviants themselves. Free Citizens are not deprived of freedom since deviants pay for their own justice. You see, the Tokyo Roundtable unanimously agreed, correctly I believe, that the sole purpose of government is to ensure that everyone follows the rules that make the market possible. And in a society where everyone always lawfully and voluntarily paid the correct amount for their actions, the various institutions of GATA would be superfluous. Therefore, blinding, monitoring, judging, and so on are merely public services for deviants who break rules, so only they should bear the costs. Taxing lawful citizens for the system of law and order without their consent would amount to theft of their hard-earned assets, which is basically a form of enslavement. That's why the committee eliminated taxes and made credicrime fines into the main source of public funding. Prisons, healthcare, schools, and other pernicious welfare institutions used to require taxation, but there's no longer a need for such frivolousness. Now we can truly earn as much freedom as possible.

"Bankrupts, on the other hand, have demonstrated that they cannot function in the Free World without racking up bad debt and thereby undermining the market, so they have to be removed from society. But cash crashing only takes away their Freedom, with a capital f. Even after bankdeath, they're still completely free and no one is ever forced to enter a pecuniary retreat. GATA only transports them to the nearest site as a courtesy. This complimentary trip is the last remaining social program, and bankdead voluntarily choose to stay because that's where they can find the most comfortable livelihood available without a BodyBank. Admittedly, life in pecuniary retreats is tough. But with all the generous donations and charity infrastructure and freedom, even the most radical critics agree that they are 'the best of all possible slums.' Complaining about the conditions there, however bad they might seem to be, is simply arrogant because the Free Market operates according to a logic that even financial specialists can never fully understand, but always provides more freedom for the world's poorest than in any other arrangement we could hope to realize in practice."

While Amon was speaking, the recruiter sat across the table, staring intently at him, his eyelashes like slender razors raking straight into his consciousness with every blink. By about halfway through Amon's speech, he had started to frown and now looked almost bored. As soon as Amon finished, the recruiter clicked the image for scallops and octopus, which quickly brought two cranes flying over to unfold on the table. Amon picked up a piece of rolled egg, dipped it in soy sauce, and was lifting it to his mouth when the recruiter began to speak.

"I'm going to remind you that I want honest responses—from your heart. No more of this nonsense. I know exactly what the mass media drills into you right from the cradle at the BioPens. Or did you learn that at your GATA training? It doesn't matter. I want to know what you, Amon, truly believe."

Amon wasn't sure what to make of the lackluster expression on the man's face, but he was nonetheless feeling encouraged. As he'd expected, the recruiter was not looking for banal truisms that any old Yoshi could regurgitate. He sought something deeper, something subtler—perhaps in the tone of Amon's voice or the pacing of his speech—that could bring his convictions to the surface, turn his soul inside out.

"Now I'm going to ask you another question. You said that your job as a Liquidator is to protect the AT market. But is it really worth protecting?"

"Of course."

"Why? What makes it so important?"

After the previous speech, Amon's tongue felt looser and this time he found the words he needed immediately without needing to think at all, as though some person or app had personally arranged them in his mind.

"The AT market is important because it gives us unlimited freedom. In our Free Era, each citizen can pursue their own unique vision of happiness—no matter how abnormal—just so long as they're willing to work hard enough to pay for it. For a typical lifestyle, an average salary and a bit of financial common sense will do. For special desires," Amon thought of Minister Kitao and Rick, "hard work and frugality is a must. Sure, credilaw fines put a premium on some desires, but these serve as a necessary disincentive on actions that disrupt the market and take away freedom from others. The beauty of the AT market is that even these barriers can be overcome with enough talent and effort, since credilaws carry no consequences other than their price. Everything that can be paid for is permitted. Therefore, we are as free as free can be.

"At the same time, the marketplace creates a mutually beneficial economic cycle where fulfilling our desires helps our fellow citizens fulfill theirs. Credicrimes support the government and legal actions profit companies so that all actions in pursuit of our own happiness—all actions that keep us above the bankruptcy line for that matter—fuel the economy. A bigger economy means more money and jobs, which means more opportunities for citizens to earn and pursue what makes them happy. Indirectly, the bankdead benefit too, as more charitable donations trickle down to the pecuniary retreats. In this way, serving yourself is the ultimate form of altruism.

"My job is to get rid of those who are too lazy or weak-willed to bring their actions in line with their earnings and drain the freedom of others by building up bad debt. If this task weren't performed and people could act without earning, the whole circle would come apart.

"By protecting the AT market, we Liquidators also help to uphold the policies of *Pax Economica*. In the past, world peace was just a faint hope, but in the battle against terrorism the side of freedom won once and for all. Now not just terrorists and their ism, but terror itself has been vanquished, and with huge fines for credicrimes against humanity like genocide and . . ."

Part way through his speech, Amon began to notice that the recruiter's lips were moving. He was feeling so proud of how well he was articulating these grand truths that he couldn't even hear the sounds coming from the man's mouth. But eventually they began to penetrate into his awareness. "Enough. Enough. Enough. Enough. Enough." When he heard this, Amon shut his mouth mid-sentence. He realized then that he'd been so absorbed in speaking, he was still holding the uneaten piece of egg above the table and a few drops of the soy sauce had dribbled off, leaving a brown smear on the origami paper. He put the egg in his mouth and began to chew.

"Let me guess what's coming next. 'GATA is the only road to freedom, happiness, reciprocity and peace,'" said the recruiter, mock bombastically. "I think we learned that little platitude in elementary schooling. Or did I just see it on GATA's website? Anyways. You know. Very, um, inspiring stuff. Thought I might shed a tear."

Amon was perplexed by his response. Why had the recruiter interrupted? And why the mocking sarcasm? Amon had been expressing what GATA stood for perfectly. He had finished eating the egg now, but was so focused on the terrifying words of disapproval that he couldn't remember what it had tasted like. Only a pale sweetness remained, the echo of an unrecordable olfactory moment lost forever.

"I suppose I'll move on with a few more questions," the recruiter said with a sigh. As though emulating his mood, the growth of the dark vines had slowed to a barely perceptible creeping. "This time, I want to know your thoughts more specifically about GATA itself. You praised the AT market for its beauty, freedom blah, blah, blah. But it's not as simple as you make it out to be. Some people are born into this world with investments in various lucrative properties and enough credit coming in every moment to never have to worry about their actions. Others scrimp and save just to take a stroll. If the rules of GATA let things turn out like this, are they really fair?"

"Yes," Amon replied without hesitation. "Most definitely. Because of history. Because every bit of property possessed by anyone today was acquired since the Free Era began in accordance with fair rules. You see, in the Age of Acquisition that followed the Great Cyberwar, all entitlements to assets were erased and—"

"Enough! Don't patronize me with this trite history lesson. Everyone learns about the Age of Acquisition by the time they're eight. You haven't answered my question. I asked you whether GATA is fair, and you were trying to say yes because everyone started off in the same original position and the rules ensured that they all had a fair chance to get ahead. But this assumes from the start that the rules are fair."

"Well I—"

"Forget about that anyway. You've said more than enough." The recruiter wore a fed-up look that seemed to border on disgust. "Even if your little story were true and the rules were fair they might not be applied correctly, have you considered what would happen if the system were abused?"

"Impossible."

"Is that so?"

"Yes, of course. The House of Blinding was established to prevent the government from having access to information about our bodily movements, which is the rightful property of each individual. But in addition to this, it guarantees that there is no way for GATA officials to give preferential treatment to anyone. Monitors can't charge their enemies more than they deserve for an action; Judicial Brokers can't let their friends off for credicrimes they have actually committed; Executive Ministers can't eliminate protesters because the identity of every individual is hidden, so there's no way to identify a friend or an enemy or a protester.

"Since all workers at GATA are forced to do their jobs without knowledge of details like skin color, gender, or political affiliation, they cannot discriminate in any way. There can be no racism, nepotism, favoritism, sexism, ageism, intellectual or religious oppression; no escaping the rules or using them for personal advantage. All actions are charged at their correct rate; all rules are applied without any exceptions; and the benefits of the Free Market are available equally to everyone, just as the sun at its zenith shines evenly upon the plains."

"Stop right there," said the recruiter. "That last bit was a quote from Barrow's inauguration speech, wasn't it?"

Amon nodded proudly, feeling pleased with himself for slipping it in at the end of such a clear explanation.

"I ask you for your own personal thoughts, and you plagiarize the soundbites of a famous politician! Let me remind you for the last time, I don't give a shit what information you've got jammed in that skull of yours. You claim to know about history and fact, but anyone can find the same thing on a bronze search engine. Are you absolutely sure you're not missing something crucial? Have you ever tried a premium search engine: platinum, gold, or even silver?"

Amon wasn't about to admit it to the recruiter, but whatever information he didn't get from the InfoFlux came from bronze websites and mostly from FlexiPedia in particular. In principle, anyone could edit this encyclopedia, but *accessing* it was owned by No Logo Inc., and actions like *revising, referencing, sourcing, researching, debating* were owned by Xian Te. These MegaGloms charged high licensing fees, which made contributing too expensive for most, but provided action subsidies to their PR teams and paid team members a full-time salary to contribute anonymously while swearing no joint affiliation. This allowed them to form invisible cliques that dominated the forums and ensured that changing even a single punctuation mark was a vicious struggle. As a result, many articles remained the same for years or even decades. Experts seemed to agree that the stability of the content across time demonstrated that it had withstood sustained criticism and was therefore maximally true. But Amon could remember when reports of a particular agricultural chemical causing liver problems in infants had been in the news for weeks while the FlexiPedia article continued to display its impeccable safety record. He also occasionally spotted product placements slipped into lists of purported facts. This suggested to him that FlexiPedia lacked diversity in perspective and might even contain a certain amount of bias. Other bronze sites certainly weren't any better. He had only taken momentary peeks at silver websites and couldn't hope to afford gold for even a second, let alone platinum. The cost of research was one of the biggest barriers to getting the information he needed to realize his dream. It was the bane of his existence, and it hurt—almost physically—to be reminded of it.

Unsure how to respond, Amon simply shook his head.

"Then just shut up with all these fairy tales. You think I give a shit? I'm a very busy man you know. How many times must I tell you? I want to hear what you sincerely believe in your gut, what you've learned by living, not by memorizing. But I'm starting to think you've learned nothing; that you're just a swollen sack of marketing and lies. I want to believe in you. Something tells me there's more to you than that. But my patience only goes so far. This is your last chance. *Got it?*" he shouted, opening his eyes wide with intensity as though daring Amon to say no, the razor lashes poised ready to strike. Amon nodded apprehensively. "What is your purpose in life?"

Taking this as a typical human resources question, Amon leaped right in with the answer: "I want to dispose of my collection duties with efficiency. Hopefully in a few years I can move up to a higher management position or—"

"Fuck! You're not understanding my question. I don't want to know what your short term goals are or how hard you work. They have templates for designing the professional you everywhere!" In his anger, the recruiter was a frightening spectacle to behold. His milky-brown cheeks had turned red and his eyelashes shuddered rapidly, reaping scythes over lakes of fire. The shadow vines on his shirt were growing ever more furiously, nascent sprouts multiplying and expanding at such an intense pace as to almost completely swallow the few remaining specks of white on his shirt and gray on his vest.

Then suddenly the recruiter seemed to become aware of himself and, regaining his composure, took a deep breath and smoothed out his shirtsleeves. Soon the growth began to slow to its original pace and, in a much calmer tone, he said: "How's the sushi?"

"F-fantastic."

"Good. Please eat as much as you like." Resting the tip of his chopsticks on the white stone atop the table, the recruiter began to rise from his seat.

"W-wait? But I was just . . . This is . . ." *Could he be leaving just like that?* It was unimaginable. There had to be some way to salvage the interview. "Please give me one more chance. I promise I'll answer honestly the way you asked. Please just one more chance," Amon begged, getting to his feet and bowing so low his nose was almost in his soy sauce.

Amon could feel the recruiter's eyes boring into the back of his lowered head, smelling the salty soy sauce and wasabi, seeing the marbled texture of the gray tabletop for what felt like several minutes, until at last the man's reply reached his ears.

"Alright then. One more question."

Amon thanked him with another bow and they both got back in their seats. "It's the same one as before, but I'll try to make it simpler for you. Tell me, without any bullshit, why you're working hard at all? What is everything you're doing for in the end?"

Amon knew the answer to this one, but was embarrassed to utter it aloud. The only person he'd ever told about his dream was Rick and even he, his closest friend, hadn't understood, so he couldn't expect a complete stranger to get it. He considered fibbing a few socially respectable objectives like *to play ImmaNet games*, *to travel the world*, or *to start a family*. But the "right answer" had failed him every time, and this was his last chance. Perhaps he needed to try giving the wrong answer.

"I often have this dream . . ." a few words splurted out before apprehensive shame paralyzed his tongue.

"A dream?" Suddenly the recruiter was rapt with interest. "What kind of dream?"

"About a forest . . ."

"A forest?" For just a moment, the recruiter smiled with his whole face, joyful wrinkles radiating from his eyes, and the shadowy foliage on his shirt seemed to glow with a faint hue of early spring green. Then he blinked with razor lashes and the smile was gone, the pattern of vines black as black once again. "Tell me more."

"I'm watching myself fall through the sky towards another me waiting in a lush clearing . . ."

The recruiter took a sip of his tea and waited patiently for Amon to continue.

"I want to get to the other me and join with him, but something always keeps us apart and before I can reach the forest, the dream ends. When I wake up, what I want to do more than anything is to go there: not a simulation, but the pristine place itself."

"Why?"

Unprepared for this question, Amon stared off blankly into the horizonless indigo, white avian forms drifting like flower petals in a slow twister, and noticed again the hypnotic syncopation of sibilant birdsong that permeated the air. It seemed to Amon that he could grow old watching these cranes, their graceful cycling unending even when he was a bleached skeleton gazing eyelessly upon them. He knew going to the forest was important to him, but he didn't know why, at least not consciously. From the beginning, his desire to seek it out had been more of an intuition than a decision, and the more he thought about it, the less he was sure of his reason. When he looked back at the table, he saw that the recruiter had ordered several more papers of sushi and wondered how long he had been lost in the distance. Bright red salmon eggs glistened a few centimeters from the recruiter's lips as he held a piece of maki aloft on chopsticks.

"So have you figured it out?" he asked.

"Well . . ." Amon paused, desperate now to say anything. "The dream leaves a kind of a vague something or other that follows me around through waking life. I feel like this lingering resonance, or whatever it is, sort of separates me from the bustle of the metropolis. After the first time I had the dream, the delights of Tokyo I had always longed for as a youth in the BioPen—like ImmaGaming and experimental digimakes and designer pharmaceuticals and cool cars and all that kind of stuff—they all began to lose their pull. The only things that mattered to me were actions that might help me meet that forest. I thought about hiring a team of designers to build that green landscape and overlay it across the city so I could inhabit my dream twenty-four-seven." Amon thought of Kitao when he said this. "But something about this idea never seemed right. Maybe for the scents and smells that the ImmaNet can't bring—I still don't know why—but for some reason I wanted to actually be there in the flesh."

Afraid that the recruiter would take him for some kind of religious wacko or twisted nature nostie, Amon stopped. But to his surprise, that fleeting smile he'd seen before returned momentarily to the man's face.

"Go on, Amon. Don't stop there when you're on a roll. I knew my instincts were right. There is something powerful driving you after all. No one produces results like yours for nothing. How about digging a bit deeper?"

"Well, it's not like frugality brings me joy. It's more like . . . like . . ." feeling more confident after the recruiter's encouragement, Amon held nothing back, "like I'm a nameless creature in a sea of night and up above, just beneath the surface, are ten-thousand hooks floating on the end of ten-thousand lines. Some hooks have worms, others have pellets, others have hunks of processed meat. Only one has nothing . . . except it's not really nothing, just that the bait is invisible, and that's what I'm swimming for at full speed. Every time I hold my breath or refrain from scratching an itch, I'm beating my fins to lunge for that hook, knowing full well that it's going to lodge itself into the roof of my mouth and yank me hurtling out of the abyss, yet sensing somehow that it will provide the greatest nourishment.

"I've got no proof that forests exist anymore. I've bought up all the info I can afford on the bronze search engines and I can't find a definitive answer anywhere, but I believe there must be at least one out there somewhere. Whatever the websites say, I'll keep on believing until I see the severed stumps before my eyes. The research is expensive, so I guess that any forests still remaining on earth must be scarce, luxury destinations. That's why I want to be successful in my career and save as much money as I can, so that one day, if there's a chance, I can go visit for myself."

When Amon was finished, the recruiter picked up a shrimp nigiri, ate it, and sipped his tea. Amon realized that he had been so immersed in talking that he had only eaten two pieces of sushi since arriving in the restaurant, and picked up a piece of pickled mackerel.

"I might have a job for you, Amon. But it's not the kind of job you've probably considered before."

"Really? What sort of job?" Amon was so excited he felt his hand shaking as he brought the sushi to his mouth.

"I've met lots of people like you, who feel out of place, who want some kind of calm or relief, sometimes just escape, at least a respite from this." The recruiter gestured around with his hand and a rift about two meters wide opened in the digital overlay. Inside this gap, the sushi bar was just as it was, but the indigo sky had been replaced by walls covered in yellowing white paint that was peeling in places, a ceiling hung with rotary fans not spinning, and graying white floors stained with splotches of grime. The meandering origami cranes had vanished. Instead there were men with dark bags under their eyes walking around with trays of sushi on pieces of white paper. The crisp suits of the other customers were faded, their faces lined with wrinkles, speckled with moles, unplucked hairs protruding from nostrils, potbellies bulging, their crooked teeth flashing as they opened their mouths to let sushi in. "This bargainstore illusion," continued the recruiter and lowered his arm. In a flash the rift closed, and the indigo sky, origami, and groomed salarymen flooded back in, this glimpse into the naked world so brief it was as though it never happened.

Amon was astonished by this display of wealth. The recruiter's own peek beneath the overlay was costly enough, including as it did fines for violating the image and anonymity rights of the restaurant and patrons, but he had also paid fines to hack into Amon's eyes (taking advantage of the access privileges granted by the leash) and force him to see through without his consent. And what Amon had witnessed gave him a new appreciation for the quality of this sushi eatery. The cheapest joints digimade conveyer belts carrying the sushi as waiters. Medium-range ones had human serving staff that looked like serving staff, but fancy restaurants paid the labor costs for people yet disguised them as something else: in this case the waiters had been edited out and the transfer of sushi from tray to table rendered as a dive-bombing crane. It would have made no difference if the recruiter had conducted the interview at a more affordable venue. So why had he chosen to leash Amon at a nice place like this, to order the best dishes on the menu, to rip through the overlay and hack part of his body? GATA surely didn't have a budget for such waste? Could he be paying for this on his own? Who was this man?

"I'm interested in change," said the recruiter. "I want to create a place where people like you, like us, anyone—regardless of their financial status—can be happy. Isn't it twisted the way this *Free World* operates? People work and work for more and more freedom, but everyone is trapped. Every bit of freedom we earn has a cost. So we strive and labor and sweat to remain in this world of figments, this world of phantoms, this world of finance." He waved his arm about the room, and once again the overlay ripped open, revealing the yellowing interior, tired waiters, and slovenly patrons. Then in a gasp, the origami cranes and blue skies were back. "But we don't need all this. Do we, Amon?"

"Well, I'm not sure—"

"You have that forest dream," interrupted the recruiter, "so I know you understand exactly what I mean. With a bit of effort in the right direction, we can live more simply. With your cooperation and leadership, we can go beyond GATA to start a new life closer to the raw, naked, reality of our bodies and nature."

"What do you mean beyond GATA? That's no way to speak about your employer."

"*My* employer? How ridiculous! Do you seriously think I'd work for such an absurd bureaucracy?"

Amon was so surprised by this response he jolted back in his chair, scuffing the front legs off the floor with a clack that drew the eyes of a few nearby patrons.

"If you don't work for GATA, then how did you know it was me wearing the digiguise?"

"If I'm interested in someone, I have ways of tracking them down, that's all."

"Who are you?"

"I'm just a concerned citizen who wants everyone to have a chance for fulfillment, whether bankdead or free."

"So what, you're some kind of activist?"

"Not exactly. Think of me more as an entrepreneur. I'm planning to start a new venture independent of the stifling charges and injustices of the AT marketplace. And I want you to be the manager. You're exactly right for the position. What you told me just now has only confirmed what I already knew from studying your records."

Amon was getting increasingly disappointed and annoyed with the conversation. He was already shook up from everything that had happened with Rick, the conversation with Mayuko, and his impending mission. Now some strange man was asking him to quit his job at the most prestigious organization on earth in order to work at the grassroots level? Amon knew that activists and charity workers of all kinds were compensated poorly even by the most successful NGOs. To join one would be to take a pay cut, to sacrifice his amount of freedom, and this meant taking steps away from his dream.

Amon had thought it odd that the man hadn't introduced himself in the cafe, assuming he would get it over with once they were settled at the restaurant. Dragged along helplessly through the course of the interview, he'd never found the right moment to ask for his name, but now he no longer cared. This rich activist, whoever he was, was offering a measly salary to join at best a crackpot project, at worst a cult. Amon was somewhat tempted to sit out this pointless interview, eat complimentary sushi, enjoy the spectacular décor, and let the leash subsidize all his actions for the duration. But if the talk wasn't about his promotion within GATA, he wasn't interested. He had an unprecedented mission to take care of, and dispatch time was fast approaching. If he stalled now, he would have no time to prepare and his evaluation might suffer; which was unthinkable now that he would soon meet the recruiter—the actual recruiter. The man was saying something about transformative ideas and new paradigms, but Amon wasn't listening.

"Thank you for this wonderful meal, sir, but I've got to be off," he cut in and stood up. "I have some work to take care of."

"What?! But I haven't finished explaining the position." The man's eyes flashed with indignance, and the vines thrashed about violently like snakes in their death throes.

"I think you've explained enough already. I don't have time for this now." Dropping these words, Amon turned around and began to walk down the aisle.

"Amon!" The man called with urgency across the restaurant. Amon stopped for a moment and looked back over his shoulder. The man was standing before his seat. Paleness on his cheeks and lines around his eyes had bled through his digimake, and the vines were drooping motionless like wilting shadows. He looked tired and forlorn. No one had made an order for several minutes, so the cranes around him had begun to drift into a scattered, random formation, as though lost in a desert of indigo.

"I'm not just offering you a job but a chance to extricate yourself from a tangled mess. Nothing can be taken for granted anymore, especially not our safety. You'll never find the way to that forest without my help. I promise you that."

"Thanks for the sushi," said Amon, unimpressed by the man's bloated sense of self-importance, and turned around again to walk towards the exit. As he was stepping out the door, a business card appeared before him. A baseball-sized 3D version of the man's head floated above the card, the name *Makesh Adani* written below it.

THE OFFER STAYS OPEN, said a text.

Walking along the empty street, past the locked gates of the Tsukiji fish market and the rows of sushi bars, Amon briefly considered the business card before flicking it into his digital dumpster.

11

TSUKUDA

A grayish-green tongue with swollen, pus-oozing taste buds—the before image for a mouth-sanitizing tonic—drifted along the surface of the Sumida River with the gentle current. Twinkling streaks of promotainment wavered and warped on its black waters wherever the lights of surrounding buildings struck: instant abs bloopers and sherry tastings, officials bowing deeply in public apology and reality TV behind the scenes of reality TV.

The InfoRiver flowed ten meters below Amon, over the side of the black steel railing edging the Chuo-Ohashi Bridge. The top of the bridge consisted of two narrow sidewalks split by a two-lane road. In the centre of the bridge, a pair of suspension pillars curved up overhead to form a sort of archway shaped like downward-pointing, open scissors with the handle sawed off. Black cables were strung taut from the point where the pillars criss-crossed, gripping the bridge at regular intervals down its length. With the rank fumes of water pollution rising to his nostrils, Amon walked along the right sidewalk towards Tsukuda on the opposite bank, towards the home of Lawrence Barrow.

Tsukuda was located on a small island where the Sumida met a sky-scraper-ringed pocket of sea—one of the few remaining slivers of Tokyo Bay not paved over. It was a residential district that juxtaposed luxury condos with the traditional craftsman's town. Terraced vines climbed hills that rose steeply from the river to a flat bank lined with cherry trees. Edging this lush riverside, skyscrapers of yellow, aquamarine, and magenta rose up like gargantuan blocks hewn from concrete rainbow, low wooden houses with sloping *kawara* clay tile roofs clustered about their base.

It was a dim, cloudy night. A pale membrane of InfoClouds hazed the sky, not so thickly as to completely block the InfoStars, but not so thinly as to reveal them either, turning the firmament into an indistinct splatter of grayscale tie-dye that fluctuated rapidly, as though ten-thousand layered scenes were doing cinematic fade-outs into each other. Yet a single patch of sky was clear, just large enough to reveal the full InfoMoon, a round island of signal floating amidst the ever-shifting pattern of visual noise. Suspended inside the glowing circle, Amon was horrified to see himself. He was sitting back on a beach chair as two voluptuous, bikinied girls leaned over him on each side and stroked the hair on his bare, tanned chest. A single word was written on each one of his eyes, together reading "Instant Get" from left to right. The two girls smiled seductively and gazed down on the metropolis, where another Amon was crossing the Chuo-Ohashi Bridge and reproaching himself for giving away the copyrights to his image all those years ago. In unison, the girls said: "Find hotties like us in your area. Anonymous one kilometer personality match half-price for a limited time. Try Instant Get now before someone gets her first." Amon's doppelganger winked slyly with his right eye, "Bargain Love" now written in his open left.

Cringing at the sight, Amon remembered with regret the chain of websites he'd looked at when he was a teenager back in the BioPen. Full of videos and documents and passionate web forums, they had purported to be campaigning for universal open access to all property. And inspired by this message in his youthful idealism, he had consented to a contract allowing every Free Citizen unconditional use of his likeness. Little did he know at that young age how economic stimulus law forbade anything from remaining in the public domain for more than six months. He'd discovered later that the site was created by XXXTrust, a MegaGlom specialized in porn, sex toys, perversion, gambling, and when the copyrights to his appearance were put up for auction six months later, it bought them immediately, bidding far higher than he could ever hope to convince his SubMom to front. Amon wasn't alone in being duped like this. Unknowing youth signed away various aspects of their personal estate all the time. The practice was normal and something about this struck a chord of indignation inside him, although he refused to entertain the possibility that it was unfair. In the grand scheme of things, the AT system was always fair, and he was grateful that, even though he was no longer allowed to copy his image, the conditions of use he'd signed at least allowed him to continue looking like himself. Others had not been so lucky. Still, he always felt idiotic when, like tonight, his mistake came back to haunt him, and he hated to imagine what debauchery XXXTrust had his image doing in their more tawdry wankomercials.

The disturbing scene slipped from sight as the InfoClouds closed up on the gap and smothered the glowing InfoMoon. Soon Amon reached the end of the bridge. The neon red navi-beam guided him to the right through a long, narrow walkway of beige bricks that ran in a straight line between two golden skyscrapers. Vines hung thick around him from a latticed archway of burnished bronze poles that spanned the walkway. The verdant path came to an end at a small street, and he crossed to follow another brick walkway two metres wide that continued in its stead, winding its way through the curving rows of wood and clay houses he'd seen from the bridge. They were two-stories high, with sliding paper front doors facing him on both sides and thin second floor balconies for hanging laundry. Potted aloe vera, tangerine trees, cactus, and bonsai stood grouped together around the doorways, further constricting the narrow path. He passed other intersecting laneways with the same layout and dimensions, traversing a labyrinthine streetscape that had survived from a time before automobiles.

A middle-aged couple was walking their tiny white dog, and a young lady carried groceries in the basket of her bike. Aside from this, the streets were empty. There was no advertisement here, except in the sky, which told Amon how wealthy the local inhabitants were: some well-to-do neighborhoods like this one pooled their resources to buy a diminished atmosphere of quaint tranquility.

Soon he came out into a courtyard with brick sidewalks running in a square around a trim lawn. A brick-embanked artificial pond opened up dark and still in the center, surrounded by tall ginkgo trees and thick vines winding along the ground. A semicircular bridge made of thin planks arced over the water. It was painted white, highlighted pale in the light from nearby windows and the half-peeking moon.

Even without the navi-beam pointing it out, Amon immediately identified Barrow's residence at the end of the courtyard. Like a cross between a Buddhist temple and a skyscraper, this tower of deep brown wood rose forty stories, vying for visual prominence with the vibrant condos as it loomed over the craftsman's town. It had been built without nails or screws in the ancient way by tightly interlocking thick wooden beams—horizontal shafts slotted into support pillars at various heights and angles, their tips jutting out slightly from the wall every few meters—an intricate puzzle of carpentry held together by its own counterweight and tension. Sliding windows of glass on each floor poured golden-red light into the night, illumination dyed by the wooden interior. Every ten stories, a pagoda-style roof tiled with grayish-blue clay sloped gently down and outwards from the tower before curving upward ever so slightly at the edge; this culminated at the top with a fourth roof longer than the rest.

Amon knew that wood was an incredibly scarce and expensive commodity; even digimaking it wasn't cheap. Only the likes of Tsukuda denizens could afford to decorate their homes in this way, and Barrow had clearly invested far more than most. Not only was it an unbelievably massive building for one person to own in Tokyo, where real estate had always been premium, it was also one of the most impressive works of digitecture Amon had ever seen, tastefully synthesizing cutting-edge urban design with time-tested forms to unite the two faces of Tsukuda. According to Barrow's profile, his official residence was in Shinjuku on the other side of the downtown core. *If this is just his getaway*, thought Amon, *I wonder what his home looks like?*

After the veil of blinding was removed, Amon always thoroughly studied the AT readout of his targets to prepare for the mission, but this time he had only taken a brief glance on his walk over from Tsukiji. He felt like he knew everything about Barrow already and didn't need to do any further research, although it was gradually beginning to sink in that his impressions of the man might be mistaken. The Barrow Amon knew would never have come to an end like this, getting involved with an underage girl and . . . He was a wealthy man, and the fines withdrawn from his account for the string of credicrimes he'd committed was a big boost to GATA. This grand building, his LifeStream data, and every other asset he now possessed would soon be seized. However profitable for GATA, Amon usually pursued bankrupts with a numb, businesslike impartiality, acknowledging their end as sad but inevitable. Yet this time he felt different. An admirable leader was about to be cut short in his prime, and although protocol dictated that the deed must be done, that Amon must fulfill his duty to the market, his every breath felt heavy, as though the humid air were ripe with tragedy.

Barrow's life had served as an example of how ascetic budgeting could bring great success, and knowing that such success was possible had always given Amon reassurance in his moments of doubt. Like the other night at Self Serve when Rick had warned him that underaction was dangerous. Yet now this exemplar of frugality had taken a dire plunge. And perhaps, despite appearances to the contrary, he had been heading in that direction all along. Perhaps there was only one direction, the very fabric of market-space bending in upon itself to redirect all striving—whether for immediate pleasure or long-term fulfillment—towards cash crash, like some law of financial entropy. Amon could have made his way more quickly by going straight across the lawn, but absent-mindedly found himself crossing the bridge over the pond. At the halfway point where the arc was highest, he looked to the side at the fan-shaped ginkgo leaves hanging over the water and suddenly felt Rick's absence. Every mission he'd ever done had been with Rick. Other Liquidators like Freg and Tororo had occasionally helped out, but Rick had been there no matter what. To his own surprise, Amon no longer felt anger, just a hollow sadness weighing him down, like a cold, metallic anchor in his gut.

Stepping off the bridge onto the other side of the lawn, he could see a turnaround driveway at the foot of the wooden tower with a garden of purple ferns in the center. A group of about twenty burly men wearing black kimonos and wooden sandals milled about, chatting around the loop of road. These were Barrow's bodyguards; or rather they had been his bodyguards until about an hour ago. With their boss now bankrupt, they were no longer being paid for their services and had lost their authorization to remain inside the building, which was now technically GATA's even if Barrow hadn't yet been informed of this fact. In keeping with protocol, the guards had been given a few minutes to vacate the premises as a grace period before GATA would charge them for trespassing.

When Amon crossed the lawn and stepped out from the shadow of the ginkgoes onto the brightly-lit tarmac ring, the guards all went silent. Now that his mission had begun, Amon had traded in his pastel disguise for his gray uniform. The presence of a Liquidator was always an omen of someone's impending doom, and this time the guards knew exactly who.

Ignoring their stares, he slipped between their muscled forms to the entrance. Two wide doors of glass rectangles set in a wooden frame faced him. He opened the door on the left and entered.

Inside was a four meter by four meter square of gray stone flooring that was edged on three sides by a small ledge as high as a single stair. A red, velvet screen stretching along the front and right sides of the ledge obscured the interior. Three black shoehorns with gilded edges rested inside black stands near the open left side. Without taking his shoes off, Amon stepped up the ledge.

Behind the screen was a long room with *tatami* flooring and walls of a dark wood, dimly lit by paper lanterns hanging intermittently about fifty centimetres below the ceiling. On the left side, a dozen low tables rose every few meters from square pits set in the floor. On the right side along the wall, a carpet of the same red velvet ran down to the end of the room, intersecting several others that went down halls to the left and right. A sweet, pungent smell he couldn't pinpoint permeated the space. Amon walked across the room to the carpet and followed it to the first hallway where he turned right.

Five doors made of paper squares stretched across a grid of wood were set in the wall on each side. The navi-beam pointed to the door on the left at the end of the hall. Amon walked over and the door slid open automatically, revealing a chamber with paper walls identical to the door with a bare wooden floor big enough for about ten people to stand. Amon stepped inside and saw four buttons of the same dark wood numbered "36" to "40." It was a paper elevator. He searched around his visual field for clickable links that corresponded to the floors, but couldn't find any. After a few seconds of confusion, he hesitantly put his index finger on a button on the wall marked "40" and pressed. Immediately the paper elevator began to ascend slowly with a swishing rattle like branches in bluster. He found it strange that the buttons were analog and, just out of curiosity, he gently prodded one of the paper squares. To his surprise, it was delicate and taut. Stroking it with the tip of his finger, he felt the unmistakeable grainy texture of Japanese paper. His finger bumped into the frame and he found it was smooth like treated wood. *Why isn't it made of more affordable materials than wood and paper?* he wondered, when the elevator stopped with a loud click and the doors rattled open.

Before him was another room of *tatami* flooring and dark wood, this time full of various Japanese relics. In the center of the room, sitting-pillows patterned in white and gray were arranged around a small wooden stand. On top of the stand was a Buddhist altar, the delicately carved black cabinet engraved and painted in intricate patterns of gold, scarlet, and orange. On the wall behind the altar was a mannequin wearing samurai chain mail. Above that, a five-stringed *biwa* and a sheathed katana rested high upon pegs. Along the right wall was a series of shelves lined with clay vessels of various shapes and sizes depicting obscure gods and symbols and beasts. Above that were several paintings: an ukiyoe of an Edo-era actor with a sickly smile holding up an umbrella to ward off falling snow, an ink sketch of a long-goateed man leading an ox through winding valleys. On the left wall were a series of glass cabinets arrayed with yet more artifacts: a crane carved into a bronze plate, a gold amulet with a blue imprint of a momiji leaf, a wooden mechanical doll, an abacus. There were so many different things crammed together in one place, it took time for Amon to absorb it all, his eyes wandering about in awe as he stood stock-still in the elevator.

In any other situation, he would have immediately dismissed the room as a quirky projection and passed through it without a second thought. But after touching the interior of the elevator, he could not ignore its appearance so easily. A suspicion arose in him that the objects might not be digital. It seemed impossible to have such thoughts about possessions of the great Lawrence Barrow, but he had become the bankrupt Lawrence Barrow; now anything was possible, and Amon had lived with nosties long enough to know how they took care of their trash. The meticulous arrangement here was undeniably similar to that of books in the stores of Jinbocho, manga in the library of the Tezuka, and the various knick-knacks he had glimpsed through doors left open in the hallway leading to his apartment. But these things couldn't be anadeto. Not Barrow. No way.

Amon had been standing stupefied in the elevator so long that the door began to close. He stuck his arm out to stop it, and it spasmed with a swish before retracting. Seized by an impulse, he rushed over to the stand in the middle and gripped the door of the altar. Sure enough, it felt solid, and the hinge creaked slightly as he opened it. Could Barrow, the man he had looked up to for his whole adult life, actually collect rubbish? Amon scrambled his brain for explanations. Perhaps he was just storing it temporarily for a friend, or these were decorations to please a mistress. Yet Amon knew that Barrow would never take such a careless political risk as to harbor shameful garbage when it could be easily exposed to the media, unless that is, he had a true passion; unless he was a bone-deep nostie. And when Amon cast his perspective down, divebombing headfirst from floor to floor, he saw rooms fly by him in a blur, all furnished and equipped in a similar way, with items from different places and eras: renaissance Italy, Han China, twentieth century America, pre-historic Egypt.

No! This is like a museum, he thought, a word with connotations worse than slaughterhouse, dump, or quarantine. Overcome with a skeptical horror, Amon began to rush about the room, picking up and fondling anything he could get his hands on. From the glass cabinets, he pulled out trinkets and jewels and turtle shells bearing inscriptions; scrolls with text and pictures like rolled-up comics, and stone-carved maps with north pointing down. Staggering across the room to the shelves on the left side, he picked up clay pieces one after another, feeling their smooth, chalky surfaces and tracing the engraved patterns with his finger; he stroked the canvas of the paintings; and put his hand close to a lantern on the wall, feeling the heat of the flame inside. Every time he was disappointed to find that nothing deceived him. The appearances always matched the weight, texture, and solidity of the things. Yet he refused to believe it; for that would mean he had nothing left to believe in. If Barrow was a nostie, Amon's frugality might very well be what Rick had said it was: madness. Therefore, Barrow was not a nostie. The absence of deception had to be an illusion.

When the room had fallen into disarray with motley antiques scattered across the floor, Amon stepped onto the stand in the center, driven by an obscure urge. *What are you doing? These actions are expensive and the commotion will draw the target,* shrieked a voice of warning muffled inside him like a banshee in a bottle. But in his frenzy, Amon couldn't hear or didn't care. He had to be sure, absolutely sure, and took the five-stringed biwa off its pegs on the wall below the katana. It was a beautiful lute-like instrument, with mother of pearl and gold inlay depicting a minstrel astride a camel on the Silk Road. It felt light and fragile in his hands, the surface sleek and glossy. He plucked a string, and a low eerie note hummed out across the room, penetrating his turmoiled mind. Its resonance perfectly followed the vibration of the hollow body in his fingertips, the way the sound of footsteps follows the impact of the foot on the ground, an inextricable link between sensations. He dropped the biwa clattering on the tabletop and reached for the katana. Drawing it from its sheath, he held it tip upwards in his right hand. He had never held a katana before, but immediately sensed the delicate balance of the blade as it gleamed surgical-sharp in the lantern-light. Bringing it out slowly, he gently touched the edge to the pinky of his left hand. Immediately he felt a sting and saw a red drop sprout from his finger, slip off the side, and fall to the floor. At last his disbelief was sated. He could doubt his eyes and ears, but there was no doubting the pain. Returning the katana to its sheath, he stepped off the stand and collapsed down onto his knees atop one of the pillows.

He saw a red smudge on the wall where he'd touched it without noticing, and a small blot on the *tatami* floor. *That's what the smell is,* he realized, *it was the straw of the* tatami. He wrapped his finger in the sleeve of his suit, counting on digimake to hide the stain, and squeezed his tiny wound. Sitting on the floor amongst the clutter he had made, Amon was suddenly overcome with self-loathing, partly for his inexcusable breakdown in budgeting and professionalism, partly for the realization of who the man he had looked up to really was. He tried to put Barrow's choice of decor into the most charitable light he could muster. *At least,* he tried to convince himself feebly, *Barrow was not the worst kind of nostie.* The residents of the Tezuka were grime nosties, the lowest of the low; collecting not just garbage, but kitsch garbage. Barrow on the other hand was a dandy nostie, a slightly more respectable breed because his trash was the high culture of the past. But however he spun it, the truth didn't change. Without a doubt, Barrow was a nostie. A dandy nostie, perhaps, but a nostie all the same.

Amon let out a sigh, followed by another . . . and then another. *Has the sigh spiral finally caught me?* he wondered, and was on the verge of slipping into despair when he remembered his mission. *There's no time for this.* He leapt to his feet, running after the navi-beam where it pointed down a corridor. A fourth sigh never came, as though his guilt were a dust clinging to the room he'd fled.

The corridor continued straight to a dead end where a red rope hung down from a loop attached to the ceiling. The loop was in the center of a circular door cut into the wood. Amon pulled the rope, the circle came down, and a spiral stairwell rotated down to the floor. Keeping his still-bleeding pinky wrapped in his sleeve, he stepped onto the first stair.

Drawing his duster, he began to ascend.

When Amon opened the door at the top of the stairwell and stepped across the threshold, his body was swallowed in a waft of warm, moist air. Sheltered by the sloping beams of the top-floor roof was a lofty, spacious spa. There were three baths: one bubbling on the left, one steaming in the middle, and one remaining still (which Amon supposed was cold) on the right. The floor and baths were made of cedar beams attached almost seamlessly together. A square in the center of the roof was open, revealing the flickering, hazy layers of the clouded InfoSky. There were no walls, but the roof sloped down to just above the floor, leaving a crack of about half a meter through which a refreshing breeze entered. In the left corner beyond the baths was a fogged-up glass door leading to a steam sauna; in the far wall beside it, a clear glass door leading to a dry sauna; and in the far right corner, a sit-down showering area with little stools and washing basins.

Barrow was leaning against the rim of the steaming middle bath with his elbows resting on the edge, his back to Amon, naked, a folded white hand-towel resting on his head. Amidst the sweet aroma of cedar, Amon could faintly smell sulfur and wondered if these baths were fed by hot springs. He clicked on the middle bath and learned that, sure enough, the water was pumped from nearly a kilometer below the ground through a shaft drilled especially for this building. This particular spring water was reputed to have skin-healing properties, especially effective for acne and allergic rashes. It seemed like the perfect way to relax at the end of a long day, soaking up minerals in soothing warmth beneath the open sky. It certainly beat lying on a futon being serviced by a SpillBot. Amon didn't know why he was entertaining such irrelevant thoughts when he ought to be focused on the task at hand. He wasn't stable. He had to stop wasting money in stupid ways, and pointed his duster at the green crosshairs appearing on the crown of Barrow's head.

This was the ideal situation to crash him: there wasn't a soul around. Barrow's AT readout showed that he was in deep irreversible debt, the interest compounded further by *relaxing* and *soaking* in this luxurious spa, in this luxurious building, in this luxurious neighborhood. If Amon pulled the trigger, he would undoubtedly clinch the meeting with the recruiter—not that counterfeit activist, but the one who could get him a job near the Executive Council. The simple contraction of his finger would propel him closer to his dream than any other single action in his entire life, as though going from baby steps to a rocket launch.

But something was wrong. Seeing Barrow relaxed and oblivious, his breath deep and slow, Amon hesitated. He was still trying to process the unbelievable revelations about Barrow's affair with a minor and his nostie habits. At the same time, many doubts assailed him. *Was this really the right thing to do for Japan, for an electorate who had finally found a leader of real substance? Why is it me that has to make this choice? Sekido could have assigned a Liquidator who was indifferent to politics and the greatness of this man.* Somewhere in his heart he hoped that something miraculous might intervene. At the very least, he wanted Barrow to confront him face to face, to know about his own bankruptcy and be prepared for liquidation, whether guilty or afraid, desperately violent or resigned to his fate.

As if to make Amon's wish come true, there was a splash. Barrow had drawn his arms suddenly off the edge of the bath into the water. Amon noticed a vague reflection of the room on the the glass door of the dry sauna, and in it he saw Barrow's surprised face, his white hair tinged brown with wetness, the bangs slicked back behind his ears.

"What are you doing here? Where are my guards?" Barrow stood up in the bath and turned around to look at Amon. The bottom half of his body was still submerged, steam wafting about him, but water dripped down from his hefty torso, the bulging muscles of his arms and chest covered in a layer of fat, a build that suggested both training and leisure.

"My name is Amon Kenzaki."

"You haven't answered my question. What are you doing here?"

"I'm here to liquidate you."

"Liquidate *me*?" Barrow shook his head in stupefaction, tipping the towel into the water with a faint plop. "You must have lost your mind. I'm perfectly liquid."

"I'm afraid not. You went bankrupt at 10:57 a.m. this morning, but the liquidation was delayed until now to avoid political disturbances."

"That's a bunch of rubbish! The Blinders should have given you access to my account by now. Why don't you check for yourself?" When Barrow said *rubbish*, Amon couldn't help thinking of his collection.

"I'm looking at it right now. It says you're bankrupt."

"Nonsense! How?"

"Your AT Readout says you sexually assaulted a twelve year old girl last night."

"That's disgusting. Did you come up with that yourself? I've done no such thing."

"It says right here that you have."

"Is that a fact?"

"I'm afraid so."

"THEN WHY HAVEN'T YOU FINISHED ME OFF!?" Barrow shouted, raising his right fist threateningly and giving Amon a penetrating look. The nerve duster shook ever so slightly in Amon's hand, but the rest of his body remained still, including his trigger finger. They faced-off in this way for nearly a minute, the silence broken only by the bubbles of the jacuzzi and the gradually slowing *drip*, *drip*, *drip* of water from Barrow's body. Eventually, Barrow scrunched his right brow slightly in an inquisitive manner as though something perplexing had just become clear. He then relaxed his fist, letting his arm drop to his side, and the look in his husky blue eyes softened.

"In regular circumstances," Barrow began, his crystalline voice echoing musically like churchbells in the winter, "if a Liquidator stalled like you are now, I would demand an inquiry. But in this case, I can see you're following your intuition. Something is telling you that I don't deserve this. Isn't that right?"

Hesitantly, Amon nodded.

"Well let me assure you, your intuition is right. A mistake has been made, for I am indeed innocent."

"I want to believe you, Chief Minister Barrow, I really do. I've admired your work for a long time, but . . . this is my job and—"

"I completely understand how you feel, but please allow me to assuage your worries."

Barrow's fingers began to twitch. Seeing on his readout that Barrow had opened a window to send a text, Amon shouted "Close the window immediately or I'll shoot!"

"I'm just trying to show you my bank account records. They prove that my assets are still fully intact."

"I can't let you do that. My mission is to liquidate you, not judge you."

"Is that so? Well, if you're not willing to hear me out, then what are you waiting for?"

Not sure of the answer himself, Amon shook his head and stood there with his duster sighted. In his peripheral, he noticed a strange object behind Barrow that hung from the wall by the glass door to the steam sauna, and allowed his eyes to wander towards it. It was some sort of contraption with two wooden handles protruding from a leather sac. He wondered what it could be for and frowned in confusion.

Seeing what Amon was looking at, Barrow said: "That is a bellows. You must be wondering what it's for. Well, I use it for my sauna. The design of the sauna is ancient, Roman in fact. There are two floors inside; the one we stand on is grated and the second floor underneath has water in it. The bellows is used to stoke the flames underneath, which turns the water to steam. Usually one of my guards assists, but I suppose since you're here they've all been dismissed. Having fire in a wooden building like this might seem dangerous, but there's a fool-proof system of extinguishers in place. And I assure you it's worth it. There's nothing like the experience of sitting in a sauna operated by hand. Nothing like it at all. It really is qualitatively different from the regular electronic kind. Once you try it, you'll see what I mean right away. The heat, the smell, the density of the steam."

"I know what they teach you in the BioPen—to revile anadeto and despise nosties. The rise of digitization freed us from space-wasting, dusty, unecological, cumbersome, rotting analog filth. This is one of our central myths instilled in each of us at a young age by the marketing ether that surrounds us. I'm sorry you had to visit my private abode without any warning. I guess after what you saw, you've reconsidered your opinion of me. Maybe you even think I'm some kind of degenerate, is that right?"

Amon remained silent with his duster sighted on Barrow, entranced by the subtle lilt of his voice, a mysteriously attractive tonality hidden almost imperceptibly beneath each mellifluous syllable, like the hum of a rubbed wine glass synched to the notes of a cello.

"That you feel disgusted by my hobby is understandable and natural. I don't blame you for it, but I think it's important to understand what the pejorative 'nostie' means. Have you ever thought about the origin of the word?"

Amon shook his head.

"How about 'cash crash?' That certainly is a piece of terminology central to your profession. Do you know the etymology of that?"

Again Amon shook his head.

"Well, it's connected to the meaning of nostie, so allow me to explain. The phrase 'cash crash' itself is an anachronism. Originally cash referred to a box for keeping goods and then coins, before becoming the notes redeemable at a bank. Yet 'cash,'" Barrow made the quotation sign with his fingers, an odd gesture that struck Amon as distinctly American, "in the form of paper money with any significant market value, no longer exists in the Free World. And crash, well that's just an onomatopoeic verb signifying the collision of two physical objects that make a particular sort of sound upon impact. *Cash crash* entered our lexicon in the early days after the Great Cyber War when the BodyBank system had already been established but paper money was still being phased out. It has a nice consonant ring to it, don't you think? It certainly slips off the tongue easily."

"'Bank' too, have you ever thought about the meaning of that? It meant 'bench,' which was where the early bankers in Italy sat. And 'bankrupt'— that just means to rupture or break the bench—which is what someone did to your bench if you were too far in debt. So you see, the meaning of everything important to your work—cash and banking and so on—they all derive their meaning from things of the naked world, like benches and paper bills, or actions like crash and rupture that only make sense in relation to such things. They all signify what you call 'anadeto,' but when you think of etymology isn't it really something more profound than that? The original meaning of everything that forms the basis of your profession can't truly be garbage, or what does that make you?"

Amon just continued to stare at Barrow, entranced by his speech, by a voice that seemed to hook his soul with penetrating music, yet kept his duster sighted on his head.

"The Japanese language today has become so bastardized and discontinuous with its prior forms, it has lost connection with the essence of things. It continues to incorporate English words by the thousands without any understanding of their semantic pedigree. Now we have dozens of terms for narratives told in visual mediums: promotisement, adshow, commercitainment, infomarketing, ImmaStory. Each one is either a direct transliteration or translation of an English word, and each one has a different nuance that expresses a particular genre of marketainment. We Free Citizens understand the difference immediately, but good luck explaining it to one of the bankdead or someone from an earlier era who grew up without the ImmaNet. It would be like trying to teach a fish the difference between amble, strut, saunter, stroll, or any other expression for walking. The digital has become so important to us; it's all we can communicate about anymore. The ImmaNet itself is no different. You must know the meaning of that, don't you?"

Amon shook his head.

"Do you remember that thing from BioPen History 101 that they called the Internet?"

Amon nodded.

"Well, unlike the Internet, which we could only view on screens, the ImmaNet is thoroughly pervasive, right in our face and close to hand all the time. That is to say, it is the immanent Internet, hence ImmaNet. And where does 'immanent' come from? It is Latin from the word *immanere*, which means 'to dwell in.' The net we dwell in. So if the ImmaNet is so important to you, then you have to ask: Where is it dwelling? Where does it find its home? Most people hate to admit it, but the answer must be in the naked world; the world that shelters, gives abode to the digital. Only there can we find true information, from the Latin verb *infomare*, 'the forming of the mind.' So are you starting to see where I'm coming from?"

Amon wasn't sure, but he nodded his head anyway.

"Good. So to get back to the meaning of nostie, you've probably heard what everyone says, that the slang 'nostie' came from noxious, derived from *noxa* meaning 'harm or damage.' But in fact, it comes from nostalgia, *nostos* for homecoming and *algos* for pain. Nostalgia is to return home—that is to the past—in pain. It is painful for us you know, us nosties, to dedicate all our spare actions to the past—what with the censure of society—but all the while what we're really doing is going home, to the birthplace of humanity, the origin of everything, the naked world. This is the primary act—this homecoming—and it underlies everything we do. It is the grounds of the AT market and thus the whole Free World."

If any other person had uttered the same speech, Amon would have dismissed it as a ludicrous rant. But there was a soothing glow surrounding Barrow's face, especially around his husky-blue eyes, that worked together with his silver tongue to soften the obfuscating fallacies and transgressions of logic, so that everything he said made perfect sense.

"So please, Amon. I'm not lying to you. If you'll just let me send you my AT readout, I can prove to you that there's been a mistake. I'm asking you, as the Chief Executive Minister, as someone who has the future of Japan always in his heart, to please just give me this chance."

Amon was taken aback by Barrow's plea. Nowhere could he sense the terror and resignation that most bankrupts displayed when confronted with Liquidators like himself. The lack of terror he could understand. Kitao too had faced them with confidence. A political prodigy like Barrow was adept at turning confrontations to his favor, and this had to lend him a certain optimism that fortified him against fear. But the lack of resignation was something else. Even Kitao had known he deserved to be liquidated and was only delaying the inevitable. Barrow, on the other hand, displayed not a hint of guilt or shame, remaining collected and articulate in the face of his predetermined end. Could this mean he was in fact innocent as he said?

"Alright," said Amon. "I'll let you send me the AT readout, but if you try to contact someone or do anything else, you're finished. This discussion has to stay private, between you and me."

"Thank you very much young man—what did you say your name was?"

"Amon Kenzaki."

"Amon Kenzaki. Once this mistake is all settled, I'll see to it that you get a fine promotion for giving me your trust." While he said this, Barrow was flicking his fingers through the ImmaNet. "Here you are," and flung a folder to Amon, which he clicked open.

According to the file inside, Barrow's bank account was brimming with credit—more credit in fact than Amon had ever seen—and it was growing rapidly. He was so rich that Amon even wondered where he could have gotten all the money. His profile had said nothing about an inheritance and while the CEM salary was good, it wasn't *that* good. But that hardly mattered now. The file was obviously fake.

"Why are you wasting my time with this?" said Amon. "It's clearly a forgery."

"Is it? Try looking at the authentication tab."

Amon clicked through a few menus and did as instructed. To his amazement, he found it had a seal of authenticity. These were transmitted in real time by the Ministry of Records and removed immediately if any data tampering was detected. The file was as authentic as it gets.

"It-it says you're . . . but . . ." Amon was flabbergasted.

"That's what I was trying to explain to you," said Barrow, his fingers still moving as he executed another command. "Where is your partner by the way? Is it not a violation of protocol to be alone?"

Amon didn't answer. He was staring in disbelief at the AT readout in his assignment folder. It too was verified by the Ministry of Records. *How could both AT readouts be authentic?*

He pulled up both and compared them side by side. The same actions and transactions scrolled by, but one account was going deeper and deeper down the debt hole every second, and the other, full of more credit than Amon had ever seen, was accruing interest at a similarly steady rate. Both checked out on authenticity, but one of them had to be wrong and, until he figured out which, it was impossible to make a decision about Barrow. He was caught in a contradiction, for if he dusted the CEM now and it turned out there was an error, he would be committing a credicrime. But if he didn't dust Barrow and he actually *was* bankrupt, he would fail his mission and maybe even lose his job.

"What's going on?" said Amon, putting his hands to his head in consternation, the duster pointing to the ceiling "Something is very wrong here. I don't know what to do. How can I trust you?"

"You can trust me because you've read about me and you know what I'm all about. You know I'm not the type to give into carnal impulses, especially not with minors," said Barrow getting out of the bath. He walked naked towards a towel cabinet built into the wall, his bulwark torso glistening with a sheen of hot spring water and sweat, his legs and buttocks dripping.

"What you say makes sense. I couldn't believe you would do that to a young girl, not after all your years of discipline. But if you're lying, I could lose my job."

"Don't worry about that. I assure you I'll sort everything out. There may have been some kind of glitch, for which a programmer is responsible. More likely, someone is out to ruin due political process, and there are many who might take me as a target—they've been making me all sorts of scandalous offers you know. Either way, I'll make you my personal assistant in the investigation."

"Your assistant?" From out of the confusion, Amon's heart fluttered into his throat.

"Yes. I can see already that you're very capable," said Barrow, standing in front of the towel cabinet and partially obscuring it from view with his bulky chest as he reached inside.

"There's one more word that I forgot to tell you about," he said turning to face Amon, now with a large towel draped over both hands so that they were hidden. "Do you know the original meaning of the word credit?"
"No."

"From the latin *credere*, to trust, to believe. Do you believe me?"
"Yes."

There was a thwap of some tensed mechanism being released and a glinting blur leapt towards Amon's face. He toppled himself sideways—the floor slamming against his shoulder—whipped up the barrel of his duster towards the crosshairs and fired. There was a great shriek, as the power of Barrow's voice was unleashed through the spa in an agony of manifold frequencies, like a singing crystal being tortured. Barrow flopped heavily to the floor with a thud, his flesh rippling with the impact, and something metallic flew out of his hands, skidding over the cracks between the floorboards before slipping into the cold bath with a plop and a small splash. Amon got to his feet. When the sloshing water had settled and cleared, he saw at the bottom of the tub a crossbow. Behind him, lodged in the wall at the level of his eyes, was a bolt.

12

JINBOCHO, THE TEZUKA

A thin layer of ad-vapor still flickered across the sky as Amon walked home to the Tezuka. Tiny rents had opened up here and there in this shifting sheen of grayscale tie-die, offering jagged glimpses of InfoStars twinkling their logo-hypnosis, and of the InfoMoon, this glowing peephole into other worlds and times slivered into unidentifiable video shards. The bookstores he passed were closed, the shelves indistinct shadows under the streetlight dim that crept through storefront windows. The nosties too were gone, back home to masturbate over their new artifacts or whatever it was they did alone after nightfall. The streets were almost bare, with only a few people going in and out of convenience stores and the occasional passing car.

As Amon climbed the stairs to the pedestrian overpass, his exhausted body seemed distant and unfamiliar. The only sensations he felt were his left hand gliding along the railing, the faint sting of the cut on his pinky from the katana and the dull ache in his shoulder where he'd landed hard on the spa floor. Since lunch nearly twelve hours earlier, he'd eaten nothing but two pieces of sushi and his hunger had long since transformed into a dull lethargy that gnawed away his energy from the inside out. Dreary thoughts murmured in his head like half-nonsensical realizations seeming to promise great wisdom that would bring him salvation, before collapsing into mental gibberish whenever he paid them attention. Yet a single thought remained clear; a picture that had congealed over his mind's eye, standing out in contrast to the vague numbness of his consciousness.

Making his way along the bridge above the quiet street, he could see it vividly, like a freeze frame etched on his retina. There Barrow had been, insensate on his back atop the wet, cedar floorboards, his legs sprawled out in a V, his right arm stretched out above his head and his chin nestled into his left shoulder. Water slowly trickled from his unconscious form along the wooden floor into the baths. Still trembling with adrenaline from evading the shot, Amon was bent over Barrow with his hand on his chest: hot, moist, hairy, and pulsating with respiration. He entered in the Death Codes and, just like that, executed the identity of Japan's Chief Executive Minister. After descending the stairs to the sidewalk, Amon walked slowly along the edge of the curb and opened up the LifeStream moments that followed.

He had waited in that steamy room, his uniform sticking to his skin, the combined scent of sulphur and pine filling his nose. All day he had worried about how he would perform on this most important of missions. In the end he had pulled it off discretely, but not as fast as he could have, and the ministry was unlikely to view his performance favorably if they saw how he had done it. Barrow's building was now GATA's property, and it would be simple for someone in the Ministry of Access, where seized assets were handled, to open the interior sensors and watch everything that had transpired. They would see Amon go in alone against regulations; they would see him make a mess of Barrow's things and cut himself with the sword; they would hear everything Barrow and Amon had discussed; they would witness Amon's dangerous hesitation. Decisiveness was not listed in the ministry evaluation criteria, but it was no doubt included implicitly, and in this case it was bound to be weighted heavily as Amon's stalling had almost gotten him killed.

Compounding the anxiety about his performance, Amon felt a strange regret. He knew he ought to be proud of himself for crashing Barrow. Though the mission had not gone perfectly, he'd at least pulled it off, and Barrow had proven himself to be a nostie and a liar in the end. His forged AT readouts and ludicrous speech, Amon decided, were merely smokescreens to buy him enough time to wiggle out of his fate. There was nothing left to admire and no reason for regret. All the same, flipping from reverence to contempt for the man required a revolution in his being that Amon could not complete so quickly, and the cash crash occupied an ambivalent place in his memory.

He could still hear Barrow's scream echoing inside his head, the agony ringing out from his throat in a beautifully lilting pitch, his voice somehow maintaining its charismatic overtones so that Amon almost wanted to join in that pain. Amon hated bankrupt screams more than anything, but this time was the worst; for the sound seemed to have vibrated into his spine and gotten trapped there, reverberating shudders of revulsion down his back and outwards beneath his skin to his extremities. For some reason, this awful feeling conjured up the faces of other targets whose screams he had heard. They had not all been criminal perverts like Kitao. Some had been patients no longer able to pay their medical bills. Some were students overwhelmed by the interest on their tuition loans or unemployed technicians whose jobs had been outsourced. Others had been senior citizens whose spent pensions had not adjusted with inflation. Others still mentally or physically handicapped. He saw them all lying there on the wet wooden floor in place of Barrow, unconscious, cringing from the nerve dust echo, and remembered all the things he'd said at Sushi Migration about the necessity of his work. Could the recruiter or activist or whoever he was have been right? Was there something unjust about exiling citizens forever to the best of all possible slums merely for losing control of their finances?

Amon knew these questions were silly, but he was in too much shock to brush them aside, and they mumbled incessantly in his mind until a pair of Collection Agents he didn't recognize arrived. Skinny, middle-aged men wearing gray work jackets with numerous pockets. Bowing perfunctorily to Amon, they rolled a folded-up stretcher along the wooden floor towards the bankdead, and relieved him of his duty.

"You're hungry and low on electrolytes," MyMedic informed Amon, popping out and expanding on top of the LifeStream segment. A few seconds later, the cartoon doctor appeared: "I recommend eating a meal rich in starches. Include a banana." Amon flicked off the seg as he entered the elevator of the Tezuka. He suspected that Lys Inc. (the company that owned MyMedic) owned the right to grow and distribute bananas, but couldn't deny that he was indeed hungry. He'd been hoping to take the guru's lesson and go straight to bed, but on the advice of his health application, he decided to get a bite to eat and clicked the link for the fourth floor.

The comic-plastered chamber shot up briefly, stopped and the door opened. Stepping out, Amon turned right down a collage-pasted hallway and left at the end, into what would have been the library on his floor. Instead of manga-lined shelves, the spacious room was crowded with vending machines lined up like dominoes in a half-dozen rows. The mansion committee had acquired antique machines with slots for coins, little flashing lights, buttons, and clear plastic windows into cubbies containing soft drinks and snacks. None of them actually served the food and drinks they displayed, since most of the companies that made them no longer existed or those that did had long since redesigned their products. Amon couldn't use most of the machines since he didn't want to waste money acquiring coins from the nosties (who paid for the luxury of owning cash and the extra charge for trading it). Thankfully, there was one in the corner that accepted credit.

Amon walked along one of the aisles over a carpet of jade green streaked white. Being surrounded by vending machines, he was reminded of Self Serve, which reminded him of his conversation with Rick the previous night, which reminded him that Rick was missing. The sadness he had felt as he approached Barrow's residence returned and he wondered whether Mayuko had heard anything from Rick. He wanted to call her right then and there, but didn't think he could face her in his tired and unstable state. *Better to do it after a good night's sleep*, he told himself and did his best to sweep his worries aside.

As he passed the vending machines, their lights blinked on and off in various rhythmic patterns, strobing from right to left, flickering every other bulb, or blinking one at a time at erratic intervals. Guilt, confusion, hunger, revulsion, pain, sadness, exhaustion: Amon was just thinking what a mess he was when he reached the vending machine in the corner. Molded from the same toilet-seat plastic as the model he used at Self Serve, it stood in the shadow of one of the flashing antiques. Amon clicked the "order" link.

Then out of the corner of his eye, he caught sight of someone familiar lurking across the aisle and turned quickly on his heels to face them. It was Mayuko.

She was standing beside the adjacent machine wearing a blush red overcoat, a cord tied around her waist to accentuate its narrow delicacy, and a dark blue skirt, the layered contours of its lace frills flaring and drooping like an overturned tulip. Beneath her skirt she wore stockings of the same red covered in a pattern of transparent lips; kissing portals through a veil of blood to the flesh of her long, toned legs.

Amon was speechless.

"Amon, I'm so sorry to startle you like this," said Mayuko, her voice choked as if from crying, "but I really need someone to talk to."

"Mayuko? I was just thinking about . . . w-what's. . . ?"

"Rick still hasn't come back yet. I don't know why, but he never showed."

"Really? But . . ." Words failed him in his broken state. *Still hasn't come back? But where could he be?*

"Are you okay, Amon? You look awful."

"To be honest, I could use someone to talk with."

"Oh, what's wrong?"

"I . . . It's been a long day."

"Did something happen at work?"

"Well, um . . ." Amon paused. "The mission today was a bit . . . challenging, that's all."

"You don't mean—I saw it on the news tonight. Were you the one who liquidated Barrow?"

Amon grimaced and let his head hang in shame. The green carpet strobed a sickly yellow tinge under the flashing bulbs. It seemed too soon for the story of Barrow's end to have reached the media, although there was no reason to be surprised. He was the CEM after all, and it was only a matter of time before word got out.

"I was happy when you called me today, Amon. It's been so long since we talked."

Amon looked up at Mayuko. Her left hand, as though absentminded, was slowly caressing the spot just below her navel. Amon felt waves of heat roll across his skin as though his memories of her were wildfire spreading across his body hair.

"Why don't you tell me what happened?"

"Well . . . it's kind of difficult to explain, and . . . I could really use some sleep . . ."

The way she was looking at him with her light brown eyes, glittering with vending bulb flicker, he felt all vestiges of clarity in his chaotic thoughtstream drift from his grasp, the password to his own mind wrenched into oblivion.

"Oh. Well if you're too tired to explain, why don't you send me the seg? That way I can watch it now and we can talk about it together in your room." She licked her lips slowly and sensually and Amon thought he could sense a subtle hunger reaching out to him. *Here she is, all alone in my apartment building and Rick is nowhere to be found*, he thought and felt himself getting hard. Part of him wondered whether he could afford to spend quality time with her, but this reluctance vanished when he thought how wonderful it would be to have someone in his arms to share his sorrows, to have Mayuko in his arms . . .

"Y-yes. That sounds great." Amon sliced the seg from his LifeStream and saved it as a golden locket on a white-beaded necklace, a fitting icon for a fine woman. She outstretched her hand expectantly and locked eyes with him. He was grateful that she had turned off the whirlpools, feeling the undertow of those deep, sad eyes pull him in with more strength than ever.

He was reaching out to give her the locket when he noticed something odd and paused his hand halfway across the gap between them.

"Your hair. Did you digimake it?"

"No-o," she said with rising intonation, keeping her eyes fixed on the locket. "You don't remember my natural color?"

It *was* her natural color, but somehow, that special luster, mahogany laced with hot mercury, was missing.

Suddenly her hand whipped out to snatch at the locket. Amon leapt away, his back thwacking into a machine, and dissipated the locket back into his hard-drive.

"Amon, please. What are you doing?"

He stared in shock at her pleading eyes.

"Why do you . . ." stopping his words short, he tried clicking her, but no profile appeared, so he opened her entry in his contact list and saw that Mayuko was at home in her apartment in Tonan Ward, on the other side of the city. "Who the hell are you?"

Immediately Mayuko melted away to be replaced by a twisted apparition of a man. His body was composed entirely of translucent strands like rubbery plastic colored white, aquamarine and a pale reddish-orange best described as morbid peach. The strands were woven together along the regular course of tendons and muscles, forming a man's outline, except he had no skin, and through his translucent flesh Amon could see that he had no bones or organs either. His toothless fish mouth gaped below two holes of a nose, and his empty eyesockets emitted a pale glow. It was as though some demented biological seamstress had patched together a man out of ten thousand jellyfish.

"I asked who you are. Answer me!"

The man said nothing and stared at Amon with his glowing sockets, his strange flesh swaying as if in a breeze, though the air was still.

A teenage memory came back to Amon: Mayuko had sold the copyrights to her likeness around the same time as him, swindled by the same website. This thing—whatever it was—must have acquired permission to look like her. Amon traced an outline around the creature with his finger to copy its image into his search engine. The result appeared, attached to a name he immediately recognized.

"Kai Monju," said Amon. This was a digiguise often used by the famous Phisher, Kai Monju. Phishers were blackmarket information dealers, and Monju was the most renowned Phisher of all, a Phisher-King, some said.

"I almost caught you," said Monju. "I'm impressed that you didn't take my bait." His voice was muffled, sibilant, and bubbly, like the rustling of sea anemone in a deep ocean current.

"You sneaky piece of shit, how dare you!" Amon's anger at the deceptive intrusion had lifted him out of his confusion. He wanted to whip out his duster and blast him right there, but was wary of the fine for violent assault.

"I've got an offer for you, Kenzaki-san."

"Fuck off out of my home or I'll throw you out!" Amon growled with a shake of his fist. The swearing was expensive, but it couldn't be helped. He was more incensed than he'd ever been in his life.

"How much will you take for the LifeStream segment of your encounter with Barrow?" Monju's sickly-glowing sockets stayed fix on Amon.

"I'm not negotiating. Get the fuck out now!"

"I can provide you with heaps of credit for exclusive access."

"I'm a Liquidator. Do you think I'll deal with worms like you? Huh Phisher!"

"I'm not a worm, although I do use them for phishing from time to time. Unfortunately, they're not much good for catching bottomfeeders."

"The hell's that supposed to mean?"

"Nothing, Mr. Liquidator. You didn't take my first bit of bait, so here's some information for you, completely free of charge: lots of people are interested in that segment. If you deal with them, you may find yourself in a compromised position. But if you do business with me, I promise to give you information that you can use to protect yourself."

"For the last fucking time, I don't do business in the shadows. How did you get in here anyway?"

"I'm *not* here."

Amon blinked and the creature was gone. Monju had merely been present as a digital figment. "I can see you're not ready to negotiate. Contact me if you change your mind. Everyone knows where to find me."

Amon knew alright: Akihabara. But there was no way he'd be going to that perverted carnival of a district.

He noticed a steady beeping sound and realized that the vending machine was telling him something. A styrofoam plate of sesame-spinach, grilled anchovy, and rice jutted from a slat in the plastic. His food was ready.

13

AMON'S APARTMENT

mon sat hunched over a small fold-up table on a fold-up chair and devoured his food. With his left elbow propped on the tabletop, he used the chopsticks in his right hand to scoop up morsels of fish and spinach alternately with pinches of rice. He hardly paid attention to the taste as he ate. It wasn't that it was bad, only that he could save creditime by packing it in without savoring. When he was finished, he tied the styrofoam plate and chopsticks in a plastic bag, put the bag on the floor near the door, and sat back down at the table to surf the net.

Making gesture commands with his fingers, he checked through all the major media sites for news about Barrow's cash crash, but found nothing. Clearly Monju had been lying. The story wasn't out yet, meaning he must have learned about it elsewhere. Where or from whom Amon couldn't guess, but there was no point worrying about that, for Monju surely had a diverse network of sources privy to all manner of secrets. He was the PhisherKing after all.

Somewhere amidst the mindless flow of link-clicking, a 3D representation of the earth appeared before him. Unconsciously or by mistake, he had opened the website God's Eye. Amon knew this site well. He could zoom out far enough to make the earth an infinitesimal dot in black, starry space or zoom in close on a section of land to watch ants crawl out of their colony in real time. The map was meticulously detailed, but certain regions were blotted out. As he twitched his fingers to rotate the globe from satellite perspective, he saw irregular black patches here and there on the surface of the blue and gray, like oceans of petroleum darker than the darkest night. The Southern Gobi Desert, Central America, parts of Bangladesh, the coast of British Columbia, islands in the Pacific, half the Arctic—numerous places were hidden from view—and it was these that interested him most. Amon had invested an enormous portion of his salary scouring the globe in search of his dream forest—looking from all different altitudes and angles—but had found it nowhere. The best clues were the sound of the surf and the green mountains. He had traced every shoreline looking for those mountains, from the vastest oceans to any lake big enough to make waves. The only places left were the ones he couldn't see.

Of course it was possible to make them visible—in the Free World, anything was possible if you earned it—but the viewing rights were more than he could afford. Amon was only subscribed to a bronze search engine. It wasn't clear to him exactly which areas of the ImmaNet were off limits for bronze users, but presumably silver, gold and platinum provided a wider range of access. For if the premium engines didn't yield more hits and more content, why the difference in price? All else being equal, a higher-priced sports car usually had better handling; a higher-priced house a better location than a cheaper one. A higher-priced search, therefore, following the same line of thought, ought to guarantee more knowledge. It was elementary reasoning. Amon had once used silver for a few minutes at great expense and tried opening God's Eye, but to his disappointment, the black patches on the globe had remained. He wanted to open the site using gold and platinum, but a single gold search was more than his monthly salary, and the cost of platinum wasn't even searchable via bronze and silver. Getting information about getting information was immensely difficult.

In the bronze man's world, there were no forests anywhere. Sparse groves of GMO trees that secreted chemicals mortally toxic to insects and rodents could be found here and there, but Amon hesitated to think of these heavily-maintained, symmetrical gardens as forests. The wild place everpresent in the private theatre behind his eyelids seemed essentially different. A fear sometimes arose in him that info of the kind he sought was hard to find for a reason: because nothing resembling a wilderness existed anymore. But he believed otherwise. Surely he would find his destination somewhere. The first step was saving enough to use a platinum engine to his heart's content. Then, like an origami letter unfolding, the map would reveal itself fully, and he would fly in over the hidden areas, searching them from root to shore as he had done with the rest of the world, until he found the right angle and recognized the vista he pursued, no matter how long it took. In the meantime, he could only look at the black patches with yearning and wonder. Playing around with God's Eye was a waste of credit, but he was tired and distraught and needed a distraction from his woes; the apparent proximity of his dream providing hope, as though all he had to do was reach out and draw aside a curtain. These were merely excuses for his discreditability, he knew—dangerous excuses—but in his weakened state they ruled over him, deluding torches that cast even bigger shadows.

As Amon spun the globe slowly, watching the oceans and continents cycle out of sight and return, he wondered, *What lies concealed in the dark spaces that only the world's richest can see?* At moments like these, Amon wished he knew more about economics. Then he might have understood why some information was so expensive and why its price seemed to go up the more controversial it was, although he sometimes wondered whether anyone knew how the market worked. Now that Barrow's policies had reduced the total number of boom-bust cycles to an average of three per day, it was reasonable to expect two busts in the morning and one in the afternoon, but there could sometimes be as many as ten boom-busts in a single day (not to mention the occasional recession that could last days) and no one could ever say at what time precisely they would occur. Even with the help of sophisticated AI designed for monetary prognostication, financial specialists consistently failed to make accurate predictions.

With billions of transactions occurring every second, the market was immensely complex and resisted simplification, for its basis was choice, and choice remained a mystery. Every transaction was an action, and behind every action lay a choice. Choice was inextricably bound to the economy, for a choice was a promise to one day act, and each act had a financial effect that changed the price of transactions. This new pattern of prices, in turn, influenced the choices people made. In principle, the interaction between choice and price could be predicted. Yet in practice, it was always guided by unknown factors; unlike movements that could be detected by the BodyBank, choices were unobservable, arising as they did in the dark cave of consciousness, and deeper, more obscure cavities of the mind. Private resolutions were made and abandoned constantly, the ever-shifting configuration of hidden wills and whims influencing the totality of actions that shaped the economy, like the new moon turning tides. The most eminent experts could compile statistical likelihoods, but there were always a few wildcards whose influence created ripples in the price scheme, leading others to make unexpected choices, which created unexpected prices and more unexpected choices, nudging the economy further and further off course until seconds later it had completely diverged from any abstract picture meant to capture it (barring the occasional lucky guess). With confident posturing, specialists spouted intricate rationalizations, citing the fleeting peeps into the inner workings of the market that their domain of expertise afforded, but in the end their guesses were as good as anyone's. So while confidence in the evanescent flow of money could be maintained on the basis of a shared belief in the same tendencies and trends and half-baked theories—a consensual hallucination that maintained tenuous stability—the cause of price fluctuations seemed to defy human understanding.

Amon, like most others he knew, took this as a positive. The very inscrutability of the AT market was thought to be its strength. For if the market could be understood, it could be manipulated. If it could be manipulated, it could be subdued and controlled. If it could be subdued and controlled it would no longer be free. But the market had to be free in order to determine the price of choices fairly. Otherwise Free Citizens would be unable to earn as much freedom as they could. And without maximal freedom, charity donations would not trickle down in sufficient quantities to turn pecuniary retreats into the best of all possible slums. Therefore, only if the market were incomprehensible could anyone, citizen or bankdead, truly be free. At least that's what the talking heads and techbloggers always said, and Amon believed them more or less, though he occasionally had his doubts about such esoteric liberalism, especially when the information he wanted was prohibitively exorbitant (acknowledging full well he didn't have enough qualifications to form opinions that mattered).

Although the present state of the world's forests was off limits, Amon had been able to find FlexiPedia pages describing their history using only a bronze search. On such sites, he had learned about Japan's total deforestation. Its territory had always been covered in densely-treed mountains, even throughout the twentieth and early twenty-first centuries, as it was cheaper to import lumber than to harvest it from the steep slopes. But after the nuclear meltdowns, earthquakes, three lost decades, and the ensuing Bubble Rewind, the economy imploded. At around this time, Japanese scientists were making major break-throughs in nano-clear-cutting technology. To get desperately-needed funding, the newly invented lumberjack dust was put to use, and the main islands were stripped bare within weeks. This was at the peak of global deforestation, when demand for lumber was rapidly outstrip-ping supply, and a sale to several global trading partners gave Japan a quick financial boost. After this, the clear-cut mountains became the new frontier. Theme parks, power generators, resorts, and immigrant housing projects went up rapidly, turning the surface of the archipelago into an undulating landscape of industrial vacation wonderlands and teetering slums.

Now that they were gone, forests had become almost legendary, fantastic, as unreal as the seven spheres of hell or the eight million gods. No one took any serious interest in them (excepting natural historians—a particularly pedantic species of nostie clinging to tenure at obscure universities), and Amon could never figure out why he was any different. Forests hadn't ever come up in his BioPen education, and although they'd appeared at certain times through-out his childhood and adolescence as the setting for some fantasy game (or as wallpaper at the Liquidation Ministry), these were just imaginary overlays like any other. He wasn't fascinated by the pocked surface of the moon or the inside of a DNA strand, so why a forest? Yet for some reason, ever since that night in Ginza, what had never drawn him in the slightest had become something he wanted to know everything about.

★

Amon was beginning to get tired and closed God's Eye. He stood up from his chair, went into the bathroom, brushed his teeth, had a shower, unfolded his futon, and lay down in bed. Drowsily, he began his routine of scrolling through his action-transactions of the day. There were no surprises here: his performance had been terrible. He tried to tag some of the actions for his Frugality Improvement Diary, but there were too many and he quickly gave up. He had wandered over to Ginza, called Mayuko, paid for two cups of coffee in a cafe, used Self-Capture for almost an hour, trashed Barrow's home, wasted words with him, agreed to go to his room with Mayuko, swore out loud at the PhisherKing, and, after all that, browsed mindlessly on the net when he could have taken lessons with the guru. His overall expenses were slightly lower than yesterday because the activist had covered a whole hour of his creditime, a whole 1/24 of the day, and he'd been compensated when the activist had illegally forced him to see through the overlay. But this was just a bit of luck. Every opportunity within his control had been squandered, and he couldn't blame his lapses on Rick this time. Whatever the haphazard result, he deserved to be ashamed for failing in his responsibility to himself. *This is not a taste of the madness Rick warned me about,* he told himself. *I'm just under a lot of stress right now. Then again, if Barrow can crash, anything is possible,* and even his own willpower, which had never failed him before, came into doubt.

Amon's breath stopped mid-sigh when he noticed something odd on his readout. His bank account balance was low . . . unbelievably low. Far lower than it should have been, even after two consecutive days of discreditability. A jolt of panic gripped his bowels. His dream savings account was untouched, but over half of his regular account was gone. He scrolled through his charges for the day. His balance had increased significantly at 9 p.m. sharp—pay hour—before gradually decreasing over the next several hours. Then, just after midnight, it plunged. There it was. Somehow he'd missed an action that he'd performed while eating. Its licensing fee was immensely high. It was so high in fact that it didn't fit on his readout and he clicked it to see the full amount:

¥66,009,724,686,219,550,843,768,321,818,371,771,650,147,004,059, 278,069,406,814,190,436,565,131,829,325,062,449

It had to be the most expensive action Amon had ever undertaken in his life, more than a year of paydays gone just like that. But he didn't even know what kind of action it was.

The name of the action was jubilee:

Property	Fee	Time	Licensor
...	...	...	...
Chew	¥9,630	00:15:49	No Logo Inc.
Swallow	¥157	00:15:50	UT Ltd.
Nasal exhalation	¥1,834	00:15:51	LYS Dynamics
Sitting	¥404	00:16:56	Latoni Sedo
Blink	¥7,575	00:17:01	Xian Te
Use chopsticks	¥222	00:17:02	Latoni Sedo
Eat fish	¥749	00:17:05	Latoni Sedo
Use chopsticks	¥222	00:17:12	Xian Te
Eat rice	¥10,001	00:17:16	Yomoko Holdings
Nasal inhalation	¥2,345	00:17:18	LYS Dynamics
Chew	¥7,890	00:17:19	TTY Group
Jubilee	¥66,009 . . .	00:17:23	Fertilex
Nasal exhalation	¥1,722	00:17:24	R-Light
Chew	¥7,090	00:17:25	TTY Group
Chew	¥6,998	00:17:26	LYS Dynamics
Blink	¥7,943	00:17:27	LVR
...	...	...	...

Amon lay on his futon staring at the ceiling. All his muscles were in a state of arousal, as though preparing him to pounce from bed suddenly at the slightest provocation. This tension culminated in his eyes with an almost electric intensity, making them so wide and sensitive as to take in every detail on the ceiling, like searchlights. Drowned somewhere underneath this nauseating insomnia, he could sense his exhaustion and despondency, rendered faint and futile against stronger, more insistent mental currents. He felt angry, shocked, stupefied, betrayed; there were so many words he could use to try and pinpoint his emotions after the events of the last few days, but every one of them seemed to leave some aspect unnamed, some nascent hue emergent from a cataclysm of stars. For several hours now, inexorable thoughts had swarmed and swirled violently in his head. *Something has to be done*, he admitted at last and allowed himself to sit up in bed.

Cross-legged on the mattress with his back against the wall, Amon cleaned up his hard-drive, ran a system diagnostic, and checked that his virus guardian was operating, as if that would recharge his account balance . . . but of course it didn't. His BodyBank was working fine. Next he opened up the LifeStream seg from the moment he got the charge. There he was in his room, eating the same vending machine fare as every Tuesday evening, sitting on the same fold-up chair, at the same fold-up table, in the same hunched over posture, with the same kind of disposable chopsticks, shoveling in food at the same rapid pace. Admittedly, he was eating dinner much later than most nights, but that shouldn't have mattered. *Left elbow resting on table and torso hunched over plate. Chopsticks held in right hand. Chopsticks go in, pick up piece of fish, scoop rice, arm brings chopsticks up to mouth. Fish and rice inserted. Chewing. Inhale. Chewing.* **Jubilee.** *Exhale through nose. Chewing. Chewing. Blink.* No matter how many times he re-watched the sequence of actions and compared them to the sequence of transactions on his readout, he just couldn't see anything between chewing and exhaling that would warrant an extra charge of any kind, let alone such an enormous one.

He took his perspective outside his body, did a close up on his face, and replayed the seg in slow motion at the crucial instant. His mouth opened as the fish and rice approached on the tip of his chopsticks, revealing his white teeth and pale, red tongue in the dark orifice. The chopsticks entered his mouth, shrouding the food in shadow. His lips closed around the chopsticks. The chopsticks withdrew from between his lips devoid of food. Chewing began, his jaw muscles tensing and relaxing, his cheeks stretching and puffing. Then he spotted something. After his first chew at exactly 00:17:23, Amon's lips squeezed together ever so slightly. Doing an extreme closeup on his mouth, he replayed that moment and discovered an infinitesimal speck of fish on his lower lip. It was nestled in the crease of a wrinkle on the dark red flesh just outside the border between inner and outer where the lips come together. His lips flexed together slightly and brought the measly speck inside his mouth. *Is that jubilee?* he wondered. *That* can't *be jubilee.*

After watching the few milliseconds that immediately preceded and followed that moment—in first person and then third person view, in slow motion, fast-forward, reverse, ultra close-up, from a distance, from every angle possible, flying around his body to see if any other parts were moving—Amon couldn't find anything else that could be responsible. Yet the movement in question was barely visible at all. He would never have been able to pick it out without slow motion. GATA ought to have dismissed it as a negligible twitch. It was outrageous to call it an action. It was more like an autonomic reflex, one of those cases where the nervous system unconsciously detects the slightest sensation of discomfort and automatically makes a remedying adjustment. In Amon's case, the inappropriateness of a small morsel on the lip had been detected and the response was the faintest activation of his lip muscles. It was inevitable and automatic. If Amon had stuck his tongue out all the way to lick his lips, or fully pursed his lips to bring them inside his mouth and clean them with his tongue, that would be understandable. That would justify a licensing fee for *lick lips, purse lips, stick out tongue,* but there was no way what he had done should count. Sure, Moderate Choice and Absolute Choice had their debate about the proprietary status of physiological functions like blinking and heartbeating. Whether these borderline cases counted as actions was debatable, but they were clearly one or the other, and not the side-effect of some other action. Charging for the slight flexing of the lips was like charging for the swinging of the arms in addition to running, or the movement of the blood in addition to heartbeating. Amon's lip movement had merely co-occurred along with the proper action of chewing. It was certainly not its own action, and it certainly shouldn't have costed what it did. *O what madness! I've been charged for an action that isn't really an action at all!*

But Amon quickly realized that there was another possibility: he might have been charged for a legitimate action he had not performed. If this were true, the lip twitch was irrelevant. He would have been charged for jubilee whatever he had happened to be doing at that moment, because the transaction had nothing to do with his movements.

But upon further consideration, this seemed unlikely. Knowing how GATA operated, such a major blunder was inconceivable. As he'd tried to explain to the fake recruiter earlier that day, blinding prevented GATA officials from identifying particular individuals and thereby giving them special benefits or harms. This still left open the possibility to wreak random mischief upon strangers. For example, a Monitor could raise the price of an action arbitrarily, or a Judicial Broker assign a fine to a legal action, not knowing in either case who would pay for it. But a system of internal oversight prevented even this by requiring officials to process each other's actions. Monitors monitored Monitors, Judicial Brokers judged Judicial Brokers, Blinders blinded Blinders. And with blinding in effect, they were forced to match the actions and transactions of their colleagues with as much fairness and objectivity as for anyone else. As a further safeguard, random spot checks were carried out on the actions of officials when they processed the actions of other officials. Never knowing when their blinding, monitoring, or judging of their colleagues was being blinded, monitored, and judged, officials were constantly afraid to fail in their duties, especially since the fines for violations of protocol were extremely high. And since the House of Blinding was the lynchpin for the whole system, credilaw assigned Blinders the worst sentence of all—bankdeath—for even the slightest infraction. Finally, there was no chance for anyone to evade the law as Judicial Brokers took a commission for every conviction, but had the same amount deducted from their salary if their rulings were overturned by juries in a court of appeal. This made them intensely vigilant to catch all crimes, while giving them strong incentive to get sentences right the first time.

Admittedly, small errors did occur now and again with sub-prime actions like walking and enunciating. But in the vast majority of cases, even these were rectified within minutes by the Ministry of Monitoring's sensitive action-detection software. When GATA was first established before the Year of Acquisition, mistakes sometimes occurred, but the AI had been patched and adjusted over the decades to respond correctly in a wide range of tricky situations. Any instance the computers were unsure about was transferred to an appropriate technician and abnormally large transfers were always double-checked. The GATA system ran according to the ideal combination of artificial and human judgment: unbiased, neutral, completely free of error and abuse. The programs were too well-written, too frequently updated, the technicians too well-trained, too closely monitored for errors to persist uncorrected more than a few seconds.

So then if it wasn't GATA's fault, the only other possible culprit was the company that owned the action: Fertilex. Amon gripped the top of his head with both hands and pressed his thumbs to his temples as he tried to work out how this might have happened. Since Amon's identity signature was blinded, Fertilex didn't know who he was and couldn't have pinpointed his account. Therefore, it was hard to see how they could have mistakenly charged him. Unless, thought Amon, due to some kind of typo the company had hit upon the code for his signature by accident. He tried to imagine the chain of events that might have led to this.

The House of Blinding created a new blinded signature for each individual every time they acted. Someone else in the world with a blinded signature very similar to Amon's at that moment must have performed jubilee (whatever the hell it was). Then an accountant or accounting program at Fertilex must have somehow incorrectly entered the code for that's person's signature, hitting upon an erroneous code that just happened to match Amon's, before making a withdrawal request to the House of Blinding. It was a one-in-a-gazillion chance, but there were billions of transactions occurring every second so something like this was bound to happen eventually. And since GATA was beyond reproach, there was no other reasonable explanation.

If Amon was right, Fertilex had committed a credicrime. He wasn't sure what kind, maybe fraud, maybe negligence, but either way it had to be illegal. Amon knew that the standard fine for such offenses was much higher than the cost of jubilee. This was to be expected, as GATA specifically fixed the penalty for credicrimes at a level that would make them unprofitable to commit. As a result, illicit behavior like embezzlement and insider trading no longer existed in the Free World. Why the Judicial Brokers hadn't forced Fertilex to pay him legal damages Amon wasn't sure, nor could he guess who had authorized the withdrawal; whether it was an irresponsible clerk or a computer glitch. A specific explanation eluded him, but of one thing he was convinced: whether he had been charged for an action that was not an action or for an action he had not performed, Fertilex owed him big for the damages. But what to do about it?

Amon briefly described his situation to Career Calibration and sorted the influx of suggestions with SiftAssist:

1. GATA probably made a mistake so you should report it immediately 95%
2. Other (go on vacation to Hawaii, eat less cabbage, donate all your money to charity, etc.) 5%

To his surprise, there was only one piece of advice that had recurred often enough for SiftAssist to pick it out. This was the first time he had ever seen such concurrence across his decision network. He couldn't believe how ignorant his so-called decision friends were about the infallibility of GATA's monitoring system, and blocked the one's who'd agreed, cutting his network down to half.

Amon began to scroll through the leftover advice grouped under *other*, most of which was utter nonsense, until he eventually found something useful, and added it manually to his list of suggestions:

3. Fertilex may have made a mistake, so you should try calling them 0.02%

Amon was delighted to find that at least one of his decision friends was thinking clearly and changed his settings to make their advice worth ten times the others. He quickly settled on option 3.

While Amon grappled with these thoughts, the night slipped steadily towards morning. In just a few hours, he had to get up for pre-work frugality training. All these activities were expensive and tiring, and for the sake of his budgeting and job performance at work the next day, it was prudent to get some rest. But sleep wasn't going to happen. He wanted to—no!—he had to call Fertilex right then and there. With his account balance depleted, he would accumulate proportionately less interest on his savings. Losing that source of funding was unthinkable, as piddling as it was. To think that half of his balance had been stolen! Amon was a hard-working man. He had saved and pinched and scrimped and saved for years to build up that amount. It was admittedly only his spending account, not his savings account, which was thankfully unscathed, but that wasn't the point. Amon could feel his face flush with heat and indignation. MyMedic warned him to take deep breaths, but he shut it off. Some forgotten part of him was flaring up, as though a torch had been dropped into an abandoned oil well. The very idea that someone would rob him for an action he had never undertaken was unjust, deranged, evil. He could never forgive his own complacence and weakness if he let it pass even for a few hours.

Fertilex was a respectable MegaGlom, the largest in the world. Amon had contacted their customer service once several years earlier when there was a malfunction in his SpillBot. The agent had been helpful and had sent him a replacement immediately with no fuss. Compared to a product malfunction, this situation was far more serious, so Amon was confident Fertilex would quickly own up, return the pilfered money, compensate him for lost interest, and offer their sincere apologies. They might even give him a bit extra to build bonds of trust (he had been a loyal customer since childhood after all).

After a quick search through their homepage, Amon was happy to find that the customer service was open twenty-four hours. There were email, live text, and FacePhone contact options. He decided on FacePhone. It was relatively more expensive, but he wanted an agent he could hold accountable in case something went awry, and Fertilex would surely reimburse him for the wasted creditime. Immediately, a siren went off in his ear. PennyPinch was reminding him he should be lying motionless in bed. It warned him that he was behaving discreditably and should hang up immediately. Amon put PennyPinch to sleep and stayed on the line. As it began to ring, he reflected gratefully on how rare round-the-clock service was for a MegaGlom. It was a sign of just how much Fertilex valued their customers.

The line connected. Amon was greeted by an automated answering woman sitting at a mahogany desk. She was middle-aged with chestnut brown hair highlighted red and an attentive but reserved expression. She was wearing a pomegranate red button-up jacket with the Fertilex logo on her left breast, her hands stacked neatly left over right on the desk, her back uncannily straight.

"Good morning valued patron, you have reached the automated messaging system for Fertilex. Please listen to the following options before making your selection. We ask you to keep in mind that the directory will not respond to your selection until all the choices have been listed. Press one for answers to frequently asked questions, press two for the names of our subsidiaries, press three for branch locations, press four for hours of operation, press five for information about our products, press six to leave a message . . ." As the list went on and on, the monotonous drone of her voice began to lull Amon to sleep. "Press thirty-six for special saver rewards." Amon pressed zero, hoping to hear the options he had missed again. "You chose 'hang up.' Thank you for calling," the woman said, before vanishing along with her desk into blank silence.

Amon paid to grit his teeth.

Even more wide awake now, he sat on his pillow to get more comfortable and called back. He got the same automated woman with the same message and patiently waited through the whole list. "Press twenty-five for birth control. Press thirty-six for special saver rewards. Press thirty-seven for the song of the day. Press thirty-eight for a message from our sponsor. Press thirty-nine for a list of the latest product releases from Biolove. Press fifty-four for the baby of mine contest entry rules. Press fifty-five to go back to the beginning of this message. Press . . ." By about option seventy-three, Amon found his attention waning again. He might have scored perfect on his concentration tests, but this relentless string of irrelevant information recited in a dull tone after midnight seemed to draw up his suppressed exhaustion. "Press eighty-nine to proceed in reverse order through the menu. Please make your selection now." Amon pressed "89" for the options he had spaced out on.

"Press eighty-nine to proceed in reverse order through the menu. Press eighty-eight for our latest product manuals read by American actor Wallace Rush. Press seventy-nine for Personalized Assistance." *Could "Personalized Assistance" mean "speak to a customer service agent,* thought Amon. He pressed "79."

The woman stopped reading the list. "You chose 'Personalized Assistance.' We will put you through to the next available customer service agent."

Amon breathed a sigh of relief (which cost him ¥10,984, but accompanied no feeling of guilt, and so didn't induce his spiral).

After a brief pause during which the woman was disturbingly still, she continued: "We're sorry, our agents are currently not answering your call. Please wait on hold for an indefinite amount of time. This is a recording." The woman disappeared and was replaced by the on-hold pacipromofication.

It was the Nebari Taste-Enhancing Gumball Family. The antics of the Nebaris were famous: eating nothing but gum for breakfast, lunch and supper; brushing their teeth with gum; mumbling to each other from mouths sealed shut with gum; blowing giant bubbles and floating around; spitting gum wads at each other when they were angry; sticking to each other when they hugged. The show was for kids, and Amon was irritated that they would force adult customers to watch it in the middle of the night. This episode centered around the pudgy pigtailed daughter, Momo Nebari, who was made of turquoise gum. She was getting ready for her first date but various gum-related accidents were interfering. First she got stuck to the shower; then when she was all made up into beautiful shape, some human picked her up and chewed her into a mutilated blob. At first, Amon stared at the video in disgusted contempt, but as five minutes turned into ten and ten minutes to half an hour, the cheap slapstick gags started to affect him in his tired state, and he began to laugh. It had been so long since he'd actually paid attention to promoadvertaintion, the humor was abnormally potent. A feeling of guilt began to creep its way through the hilarity when Amon noticed the price of "waiting on hold" and "watching Nebari" tally up on his AT readout. But he reminded himself that Fertilex would reimburse him for everything, and gave himself up fully to the laughter wracking his torso. His fun was cut short when the automated answering agent reappeared and repeated the same message: "We're sorry, our agents are currently not answering your call. Please wait on hold for an indefinite amount of time. This is a recording." Then the show came back on for a few seconds before suddenly turning off. Amon was no longer on hold. The connection had been lost.

What? Those fucking bastards! In a fit of rage, Amon punched down between his thighs to pound his pillow, squeezing a few buckwheat beads out onto the futon. Less than three hours remained until he had to get up for frugality practice and he desperately wanted to sleep, but couldn't bear to think of giving up now. The more time and credit he wasted, the more urgent it became to find a resolution and get reimbursed. He called back, waited for the automated woman to read through his options, and immediately pressed "79." Once he was on hold again, he got up, left his apartment, and began to walk through the halls of the Tezuka, trying to take his mind off the maddening situation. The Nebaris came back on and without thinking, he found himself in the elevator headed for the fourth floor. He got off and walked towards the vending machine zone. Passing rows of blinking bulbs, he reached a machine at the back that didn't require coins. There he bought a pack of Taste-Enhancing Gum. *This is my revenge for being hung up on*, he told himself, without any doubt that Fertilex would be forced to make it complimentary.

Sitting in bed with his back against the wall, Amon chewed his gum and watched the Nebaris. The flavor he had chosen was pickled plum. It tasted salty, sour, and sweet, and felt rubbery smooth on his tongue. He wondered if it would really regenerate his taste buds as promised. Somehow the advershow was even funnier now that he was chewing. Soon he was rolling around in bed gripping his belly in paroxysms of joy that made his chest hurt, stuffing more and more gum into his mouth until the wad was so large, his jaw muscles began to tire and he feared he might choke.

Suddenly the image vanished and a slim man appeared against a white background. He wore a black suit, his hair buzzed, a silver ring in each earlobe.

"Hello valued customer. My name is Tuesday, representing Fertilex for the FacePhone assistance department. What can I help you with today?"

Amon was startled out of his gum chewing, laughing, reverie, *Tuesday?*

"Erm. Hewrlo," he said his mouth full of gum.

"Is your mouth full, sir? I see also that you're dressed for bed." Amon slept naked, not wanting to invest in pajamas, but he was digimade automatically in a nightgown. "Your attitude shows that you are unable to take this customer service meeting with commensurate seriousness. I would like you to remember that there are other customers waiting on the line for whom speaking to a representative like myself is very important. We ask you to kindly show more respectful and solemn formality to Fertilex and its representatives in the future if you wish for us to hear your complaint. Thank you for choosing Fertilex." Before Amon could pry his mouth open again, the man hung up.

When it sunk in that the man was actually gone, Amon clenched his hand into a fist and held it hovering out in front of him, gritting his teeth and drawing deep, quivering breaths as he stared off blankly into the darkness of his room. He was wondering when MyMedic would pipe up, until he remembered he had already turned it off. When his breathing had returned to an almost normal pace, it was just past 5 a.m. He wasn't tired any more, just muddled with rage.

This wasn't the Fertilex customer service he remembered when his SpillBot had malfunctioned. This wasn't customer service at all, but some kind of torturous prank. There was no way they treated all their customers like this. They'd be boycotted in droves. If Amon didn't know any better, he might have even thought he was blacklisted. But of course there was no reason for Fertilex to do this to him. It had to be a fluke dysfunction in their system. If he was persistent and followed through to the end, everything was bound to get resolved.

Amon digimade himself with a decent shirt, and called customer service again. Immediately a man with a gruff voice picked up and greeted him in a language he didn't understand.

"Hello. Is this Fertilex customer service?"

A rapid chain of incomprehensible sounds followed.

"Hello," said Amon. "I don't understand." After letting out a jarring, guttural shout, the man hung up.

Amon checked his call history and saw that the number he had just dialed was the same one he called earlier for the customer service. But when he opened Fertilex's contact page, he realized that the numbers listed there didn't match. He had dialed 672-4635, but on the page it was 672-4653. The last two digits were switched. Wondering how he'd been able to connect with the wrong number earlier, he dialed the new listed number.

Again he was greeted by the man with the gruff voice. Amidst his barrage of alien syllables, Amon, who knew a bit of English, caught the phrase "wrong number douchebag."

"Sorry," said Amon in English, but the man had already hung up.

Knitting his brow in befuddlement, Amon checked the number against the website again. The two final digits had been switched back to "35" but the third last digit had been changed from a six to a seven. Amon turned on his translation app, InterrPet, and tried dialing the number again. This time he was greeted with an inarticulate howl, almost beast-like, but unmistakably originating from the voicebox of the same man, before it was cut off and replaced by the unnervingly calm and cheerful voice on InterrPet's audio playback: "Stop making them call me. I never did anything to you. Leave me alo—" The vowel extended, transforming back into another awful howl that the app couldn't translate. This continued for a dozen seconds at ear-splitting volume until the man hung up again.

Amon went back to the website. He saw that the third last digit was a six again but the fourth last was now an eight. Assuming that some mischievous hacker had broken into the Fertilex website, he tried to punch in the original number he had been successful with.

To his relief, the automated woman appeared again. He waited through the options to press "79" for the fourth time, and was put on hold yet again. A different episode of the Nebaris was playing but he paid the fee to dim the visuals and tried his best to ignore the spastic audio. After exactly one hour, someone finally picked up.

"Hello, valued customer." It was the same man with earrings and a buzz cut, except the voice was different. "My name is Tuesday, representing Fertilex for the FacePhone assistance department. What can I help you with today?"

"Hello. My name is Amon Kenzaki. I have been billed for the use of something called a 'jubilee' at 00:17:23. I believe there has been a mistake." *At last I've said it and someone is listening,* he thought with relief.

"Can you send me your blinded signature for that moment? I'm just going to check it against our records."

Amon sent him the signature and, while the man was performing some operation online said: "By the way . . ."

"Yes?"

"I called about an hour ago and you hung up on me."

"Is that so? Are you sure it wasn't someone else? I just started my shift five minutes ago."

"No, it was you. I remember the name was Tuesday."

"That's not my real name, sir. That's my customer service alias. Everyone in my department uses it on Tuesday."

"Okay . . . but I called you after midnight, so it's Wednesday now."

"Technically, sir, you are correct. In any case, if you'd like to track down the previous agent, I'll need his name."

"Well I don't have it. He hung up on me before I had a chance to speak. In fact I was hung up on twice, once by . . . the other Tuesday, and once while I was on hold."

"My apologies, sir. There's nothing I can do about that. It's company policy." Amon was about to ask what he meant by that when the man's hand stopped twitching. "Yes, I see it right here. One jubilee today at 00:17:23. What exactly is the problem, sir?"

"I never did a jubilee, so I would like be refunded for the charge and receive compensation for damages."

"I can't do that, sir. It's been more than six hours since the time of purchase." Amon saw that the clock now said 6:18.24. "Company policy is no refunds or exchanges after six hours."

"But it's only a minute over and I called as soon as I noticed the problem. As I told you, I was put on hold and hung up on, which made it impossible to file a complaint any sooner."

"We're very sorry for the inconvenience, but I'm afraid it's company policy."

"Company policy? That has to be a joke."

"No sir. Not as far as I am aware. I can send you a full explanation if you would like." At that moment a thousand-page document typed in tiny font with no option to enlarge appeared on Amon's screen. The title, which Amon could barely make out, was "Fertilex Customer Service: Standard Operating Procedures for Receiving Complaints."

"As part of our 'See the Heart of Fertilex' transparency strategy, we have made our protocol public." Amon clicked the reject button.

"No, I'm not interested in your policies. I've been unjustly billed and an entire night's worth of my creditime has been wasted as a result. I insist on a refund. What the hell is a jubilee anyways?"

"Would you like me to check for you?"

"I would like to speak to the manager."

"I am the manager."

"Then connect me with your supervisor?"

"Unfortunately, that is a bit difficult."

"What's that? Why?"

"We are supervised anonymously from an undisclosed location. Sometimes we receive automated messages condemning or praising us for the quality of our work. Other than that, we really do not have contact with upper management. But if you'd like, sir, I can patch you through to the Policy Complaints Department."

"Yes, right away!"

"Certainly, sir. Thank you for choosing Fertilex." With that the man hung up.

The answering woman reappeared and repeated her message: "We're sorry, but our agents are currently not answering your call. Please wait on hold for an indefinite amount of time. This is a recording." A repeat of the first episode of the Nebaris came back on. Amon sat through it in numb silence for close to thirty minutes, his head groggy, completely incapable of any thoughts other than *How could they? Those bastards! How could they?* until the answering woman reappeared. "We're sorry, but none of our agents are available to take calls at this time. Please leave a message after the tone and someone will respond as quickly as specified by company policy. Thank you . . ." *Beep.*

"Hello. My name is Amon Kenzaki. I received a charge from Fertilex for something called a jubilee at 00:17:23 today. I did no such thing as a jubilee. I would like to have the charge removed from my AT record and be reimbursed the amount of the charge. I would also like to be compensated for this mistake, which I have reason to believe is ILLEGAL, and for all the creditime I have spent dealing with your customer service system. My contact info is included as a link in this message and I can be reached by mail, text, or FacePhone at any time. I hope to have this difficulty remedied quickly and would appreciate your prompt response. Thank you."

14

THE LIQUIDATION MINISTRY

The narrow hallway on the ground floor of GATA Tower was packed with officials lining up for elevators. Doors slid open, uniformed bodies filed in, doors closed, more bodies arrived with a buzz of greetings and chit-chat, repeat.

Above the gathering of heads, Amon spotted the hulking forms of Freg and Tororo. Not in the mood to chat, he slouched low behind the crowd with his back against the wall, hoping they wouldn't notice him. As always, Tororo was blathering on and Freg was rumbling out laughter in response. The two giants looked cheerful and refreshed, just the opposite of how Amon felt, the heavy anchors of sleepiness and resentment dragging at his every movement and thought.

He hadn't caught a wink of sleep the previous night. Ever since he'd left that message on the policy complaints answering machine, emails had begun to arrive in his inbox one after the other. The first came only a minute after he'd hung up, with the subject line, "Important Information." When Amon saw that the sender was Fertilex Policy Complaints Department, he'd been delighted, expecting an apology from a responsible agent who would sort it all out. But when he opened it, a toothbrush wearing a little bowler hat did a jig while spurting toothpaste luminescent like fireworks. *Self-pasting with hand-massaging vibrations.* Amon had quickly closed it. After that, emails from the same sender purporting to contain "Important Information" began to arrive every ten seconds. The second one was the ghost of a famous actor playing new Mindfulator alarm rings on a xylophone; the third a raccoon emitting from its nostrils the soothing mist of dust-repelling sinus decongestant; the fourth a granny able to play ping-pong thanks to her two-second rice-cooker, all of them sold by a Fertilex subsidiary. Amon stopped checking after that.

In general, he kept SpamFortress on a strict setting to subdue the pop-ups that lurked all over the city and prevent spammers from appearing to pester him in person. But the application charged for every item blocked, and if he rejected the "Important Information," his spam intake would more than double, likewise doubling the fee. So for the time being, he allowed the messages into his inbox.

What does Fertilex have against me? he wondered. Respectable corporations didn't send spam directly, but instead hired spam agencies to do their dirty work. He could only think that someone had maliciously added him to a spam list as retribution for making a complaint. The very idea set his teeth grinding.

Amon looked around at all the people in the hallway chatting eagerly in their crisp suits, the Liquidators before him in gray, the GATA staff in other lines wearing brown, baby blue, and lavender. It seemed that they lived in a different world, a world where the price of actions was fair and customer service agents were helpful. Every cheerful eye and attentive nod seemed to taunt him. When the elevator door opened, he hung back, hoping to avoid the obligatory conversation with Freg and Tororo. But once everyone in front of him had squeezed on, Freg noticed Amon dithering alone in the hallway.

"Good morning, Amon!" he said and clicked the 'hold door' link. Tororo, who was standing closer to the front, spread his thick, muscular arms out to the sides and pushed backwards, compressing the passengers further into the corners. Now there was just enough space for one person to squeeze on. With no excuse to wait for the next elevator, Amon grudgingly boarded.

"Mernen," said Amon, uttering the mandatory greeting with the minimum enunciation possible.

"How you doin'?" said Tororo, stroking his goatee. The huge man was always stroking his goatee. It was a compulsive habit, and Amon sometimes wondered how much it ran him each month.

"Not bad," lied Amon.

"Amazing news about Barrow, isn't it?" said Tororo. "Did you hear?" Amon nodded.

"Such a shock," said Freg, shaking his head, his mohawk spikes gyrating. Amon said nothing. It had been only a matter of time before GATA issued the press release or the story was leaked. It hardly mattered which at this point. Either way, the incident would be on everyone's lips for months to come, and he dreaded the thought of having to listen.

"I'm glad they didn't assign that job to me. Who wants to get in a bath with a wet, naked nostie?" said Tororo with a wink, and Freg laughed right on cue.

As always, Amon was amazed by Tororo's lack of discretion, discussing a sensitive matter so profanely in the middle of an elevator that might even be carrying Barrow's associates. But he was also relieved that they didn't know it had been Amon's doing. Thus far, confidentiality of the Liquidator had been maintained, protecting him from dangerous political forces and media eyes that could infiltrate his life.

He was savoring this merciful glimmer of relief amidst his troubles when Freg said, "Real shame what happened to Rick though."

"Yes, real shame," said Tororo with uncharacteristic seriousness, adding "and sad too."

"Rick? What about Rick?"

Tororo and Freg gave each other a sidelong glance as if to say, *Oh shit, he hasn't heard.*

The elevator reached the ministry and the doors opened. Today the office was a close-up on an ocean dense with microscopic creatures, their jagged blob-like bodies and half-formed appendages squirming frantically through an over-enlarged blur of greenish-blue. The three men got out with a stream of other Liquidators and stood to the side of the doors.

"So what was that about?" asked Amon. "Did something happen to Rick?"

"Well . . . um," Freg stalled. "Since you're his good friend, and uh . . . you're looking kind of down today, you know, I just sort of assumed you'd already heard."

"What? Heard what?"

"I hate to be the one to . . . but . . ."

"Yes?"

"Rick is gone."

"What do you mean gone? Where?"

"To the District of Dreams."

"The retreat? You mean he's gone to work for the Charity Brigade?"

"No, he's been cash crashed," interjected Tororo, apparently unable to stand Freg's inability to get to the point.

"Cash crashed . . ." mumbled Amon as he stared at Tororo in disbelief and waited for the cheap punchline that never came. The two giants both looked back at him with sympathetic eyes. "Rick is bankdead?"

It was hard for Amon to believe, but if Rick's frivolous spending at the bar the other night were representative of his lifestyle, it almost seemed possible. He'd ordered from a premium vending machine, decorated his food with appealing digimake, and spouted lots of foul language; he was living in a luxurious apartment, buying gifts for Mayuko, and sacrificing his bonus to be late for work. And it also explained why Rick's profile had been inaccessible. After their fight, Rick had reason enough to cut off Amon, but it had been hard to imagine his motive for doing the same to Mayuko, if it was indeed true as she'd said that they were getting along fine. Now it was clear. Rick hadn't blocked them from digital communications: his digital presence no longer existed at all.

"W-when . . . How did this happen?"

"I don't know the details," said Freg. "All I heard is it wasn't a credicrime or anything like that. He was just sort of living beyond his means and went a bit too far."

Amon took a few steps back, reeling from the news. From the sounds of it, the story was all over the ministry; and he wasn't surprised, just overwhelmed. Someone involved in Rick's liquidation—whether Liquidator, Blinder, Collection Agent, or Archivist—was bound to gossip about such a rarity as the downfall of a GATA man.

"Who was it that—"

"I heard it was one of the veterans in another squad," said Tororo. "But that might've just been a rumor."

Amon leaned on the teeming liquid wall with both hands and hung his head, suddenly overcome by the weight of everything.

"You alright, Amon?" asked Freg.

Saying nothing, Amon clenched his jaw and took deep breaths to keep his emotions from spilling to the surface. MyMedic gave him a green checkmark of approval.

"I lost a cousin like that once," said Tororo, sympathetically. "Can't help wondering how he's making out in the camps even now, five years later." Amon kept his head down, unable to meet their eyes.

"Come on, friend," said Freg putting his arm around Amon's shoulder. "Let's try to keep our minds off this. It's time to get to work."

He was right. Amon couldn't let personal issues interfere with his duties, and allowed Freg to guide him by his shoulder along the wall to their squad, smelling the acid fragrance of the man's cheap cologne and generic laundry detergent. When they reached the aisle to their seats, Tororo started to tell Amon about an erotic movie he'd watched the other night.

"Hey Amon. You ever seen *Memento of Flesh*?"

"No," he said, adding, "not yet," to feign interest.

"It wasn't one of them fluff films. It was hot but like the ending was deep man."

"Heard they've nominated that one for a Splurt Award," said Freg.

"Is that right?" said Amon.

Amon arrived at his seat. The two giants stood in front of theirs for a moment and bowed their heads consecutively to Amon, first Freg and then Tororo, before sitting down and vanishing.

Molding into his seat, Amon logged in and accessed Illiquidity Alert. He scrolled up and down through the list of coded names in the Gutter, but his mind was elsewhere. How could he focus after everything that had happened over the last two days? The Kitao mission, the fight with Rick and then his disappearance, the talk with Mayuko, the false recruiter, the cash crash of Barrow, the PhisherKing's visit, jubilee, and now Rick's bankdeath. With each event coming one after the other, he'd had no time to make sense of any of them.

Thoughts of his lost friend filled him with regret as he wondered whether his cash crash might have been averted. Could their bitter parting have been connected in some way? Perhaps Amon's advice about Rick's path towards bankruptcy, which had floated unspoken in his mind at Self Serve, could have saved him. Uttering it would have meant wasting money on someone who had been selfishly putting Amon's job at risk, but were his money and his job so important that he could neglect a friend; even an ungrateful, irresponsible friend? He knew his savings account was the road to his dream destination. He knew that he would sacrifice this for nothing in the world. He also knew that Rick had gotten the amount of freedom he'd earned. *This was inevitable. This was fair. This was justice.* These truisms came easily to his mind, but he wasn't yet able to accept that his friend was actually gone. All he felt was confusion and a vague apprehension about facing his colleagues over the coming months. Close relatives of bankrupts were known to shut themselves away for days or weeks after a cash crash, sometimes triggering their own fall, and although he didn't think he would go that far, being a Liquidator—the public face of cash crash enforcement—he couldn't deny feeling a certain amount of shame. He wondered how long it would be before Sekido heard the news and learned that Amon had hidden Rick's absence to complete the Barrow mission solo. Then his career would be in jeopardy.

Yet despite these worries, the fact that he would never see Rick again still seemed to Amon like an abstract and nebulous idea rather than a truth close at hand. Jubilee felt more immediate; jubilee felt more threatening; for if his money could be arbitrarily taken away, then everything he did became meaningless. There was no point in working, in earning money, in scrimping and saving . . . no point in even dreaming. Try as he might to fulfill his Gutter duties, he could think of nothing but restoring balance to his account. The gash severing him and his friend was too deep and tender to face now. First he had to get his life back on the rails. First he had to sort out jubilee.

The *Important Information* from Fertilex just kept on coming. He really wasn't supposed to check his private emails at work and usually set his inbox to hide it from view, but today he couldn't help himself and had turned up its opacity so that a white mailbox icon was pegged to the center of his visual field. The numerous envelopes that kept flying into it were like little teases reminding him of his predicament. Every time a new one appeared, he thought *perhaps Fertilex has realized its mistake at last and I'm saved*. Then he would open his junk folder to check it, only to find an ad and swear to himself that he would never check another. But a nagging thought always said, *it could be the next one*, and when he opened the next one to find another ad, he thought, *it could be the next one*, and the next one, and the next one.

Gradually, he began to believe that his initial suspicion was right. Fertilex had put him on a blacklist. For what reason he couldn't guess, but it meant that nothing would get resolved by waiting around for policy complaints to contact him. If he were going to find a solution, he would need to take a more active approach. Calling Fertilex again obviously wasn't going to work, so he had to think of another way. The responsible course of action would have been to wait until his shift was over to investigate. Already he'd gone on the Barrow mission alone, trashed his apartment and hesitated to liquidate him, so if Sekido found out about this and then saw him slacking off, Amon might lose the trust of his superiors at this critical turning point in his career. It was better to figure things out on his own time, especially since Fertilex would surely reimburse him. But he couldn't bear to wait any longer. With this issue unresolved, he was useless. As productive as a pylon. *For the sake of my efficiency*, he told himself, *I must take care of this right away*. So long as he got it done quick, Sekido probably wouldn't even notice.

Despite what most of his decision friends had foolishly suggested, Amon knew that the Ministry of Monitoring couldn't be responsible for what had happened. All the same, there was one issue he wanted to inquire about. Clearly, he had never performed any such action as jubilee, whatever it was, which meant he was the victim of an unauthorized and illegitimate withdrawal. This was obviously a credicrime, meaning that the Fiscal Judiciary was supposed to force Fertilex to pay him legal compensation for the damages. The fact this hadn't happened suggested to him that there had been some sort of credicrime detection mix-up. Even if the fault didn't lie with the Ministry of Monitoring, he decided it was best to at least call them and report the situation. This was the only way forward.

It might have been a big rigmarole for a regular citizen to call up GATA and make a complaint (*although surely it couldn't be as difficult as it was for me to contact Fertilex,* thought Amon, *that would be plain sinister*), but since Amon was on the inside he just looked through the staff directory and immediately found the number he sought. He dialed it into FacePhone and a man immediately picked up. He had short brown hair greased neatly to one side, narrow, bony shoulders that poked slightly forward and cheeks with oddly-defined musculature, like a facial six pack.

"Ministry of Monitoring, Ryuta Hashimoto speaking, how may I help you Liquidator Kenzaki?" He was sitting at a chair just like Amon's, the squirming ocean behind him.

"Can you put me in touch with the Monitor who oversaw my bank account at 12:17:23 this morning?"

"*Whose* bank account?" He tilted his head to the side inquisitively. "Would you mind repeating that?"

"Mine. I'm making an official request for a transaction review."

"Pardon me?" said the man.

"I'd like to have my transactions at that moment double-checked," said Amon. "Seriously."

"Certainly, Liquidator Kenzaki," he said, smiling and compliant, but with a hint of resentment in his eyes. Clearly Liquidators rarely made such requests about their own accounts, if ever. "I need your consent to allow the House of Blinding to open your identity signature for the action in question. This is required to disclose the identity of the Monitor in charge of your account at that moment."

"Of course." Amon clicked *agree* on the window that popped up.

"One moment please." The man twitched his cheek muscles to scroll through the database. "Liquidator Kenzaki."

"Yes?"

"I regret to inform you," said the man frowning apologetically, "that I will be unable to process your request."

"Why not?"

"Because you didn't perform any action at that moment."

"What? But I have it in my AT readout. It says I performed an action, a very expensive one."

"Well I'm afraid, sir, that that is not the case. At that moment, our records say you did nothing."

"Well, yes. You're totally correct. I didn't do anything. That's why I want a review."

"I see. Well sir, if you didn't perform the action, and the records concur that you didn't, would you mind explaining what exactly the trouble is?"

"The trouble is that the records don't agree in fact."

"I'm afraid sir that I'm not quite following you."

"Alright, look. I'm telling you, my AT readout says I did it and money was withdrawn from my account even though I didn't do it. This is a credicrime but I was never compensated. Here, you can see for yourself." Amon sent his AT readout and action-data, but the man declined.

"That won't be necessary, sir. I have the same information right here."

"Is that so? Could you tell me what the hell jubilee is then?" Amon immediately regretted wasting money on profanity, but he was getting extremely irritated.

"Well sir," he said, the same hint of resentment returning for a split second, "like any other property, I presume that jubilee describes a pattern of bodily movement attached to nervous system activity indicating volition and—"

"I know that! What I want to know is what kind of movement is it?!" Amon was almost shouting.

"If you would like more specific details about the definition of the property, I recommend getting in touch with the Ministry of Access and asking for the Property Section. You could also try contacting the Fiscal Judiciary about their crime definitions."

Realizing that he wouldn't get any further with this technocrat, Amon hung up.

Amon contacted the Property Section as the monitor had advised and requested the file that defined jubilee. Property definitions were publicly available, so the access fee was minimal. The file provided a description of muscle motions and physiological processes. It was expressed in technical language in which Amon was not versed, although he knew enough to get the basic idea. If he was reading it correctly, jubilee was the simultaneous combination of a rotational pelvic thrust, foot tap, slight lowering of one shoulder, glottal moan, and arm wave in standing position that was accompanied by accelerated pulse, narrowing of the pupils, increased afferent signals from the fingertips, and various other physiological signs Amon wasn't familiar with. As far as he could tell, it seemed like an incredibly complicated dance move.

But I've done no such thing! he thought, and immediately felt a deja vu chill go down his spine. The thought had spoken inside his mind in Barrow's voice. Just yesterday, the CEM had said *exactly* the same thing when Amon told him about his relations with the underage girl. Amon had thought it pathetic and deceitful at the time, but now he could almost sympathize. Something inside him had changed, the unknown now staring him defiantly in the face with merciless eyes. A feeling somewhere between excitement and terror rose in him as a question formed. *Could there be some connection between jubilee and Barrow's cash crash?*

It was an unbelievable question, based on so many absurd propositions that Amon almost laughed when he thought of it. But he didn't laugh, and the excited terror kept bubbling away in his gut like acid champagne. *Alright,* he told himself, *I'm just looking too closely at a bunch of coincidences. I'm being superstitious. Time to get back to work.* But instead of working, he found himself opening the copy of Barrow's AT readout stored in his hard-drive. He'd only taken a brief look at it the other day, not seeing the need to study up on a man he already knew so much about. Now he began to read it closely, scrutinizing the finer details of daily, even hourly routines.

After an hour or so, he began to notice something strange. Although Amon's many years as a Liquidator had honed his insight into AT patterns, something about this one baffled him. From his experience, there were only four personality types that ended up bankrupt. There were chronics like Z98 (a subject he'd seen in the Gutter two days ago) who indulged in pleasures until they were on the verge of bankruptcy and then turned cheapskate until they had built up some savings, repeating this cycle until one wrong move sent them over the edge. There were bingers like Minister Kitao whose prodigal spending gradually escalated, growing more intense and frequent until the momentum of debt and desire was unstoppable. There were sliders who ate away their assets slowly but steadily, unwilling to adjust their standard of living after a drop in income or rise in expenses that resulted from some unexpected event (such as being fired or getting ill). There was also a fourth type that Amon had encountered only a handful of times over the course of his career, the diver, who began with a stable financial base before suddenly frittering it all away. Yet even for divers, there were always events that foreshadowed this descent; a crime or a foolish gamble or a clumsy investment somewhere in their past.

But Barrow's readout showed no such hints. It was all hard work and saving, from Identity Birth to Death. He did make regular purchases of nostie knick-knacks, like paintings and swords, but these were all well within his means. Then all of a sudden there was the incident with the young girl—which had nothing to do with his anachronistic hobby—and bang. Within a few short hours, he was finished. This pattern was unique. It was the first time Amon had seen such an abrupt collapse without any warning whatsoever. It was also the first time he'd been assigned to liquidate such a great man, and he knew what was often said about the private bedrooms of great men: perhaps this result was to be expected. Yet something didn't seem right. A man like Barrow wouldn't discard a lifetime of frugality and discipline for lowly, animal urges. Barrow had said that Amon's copy of his AT readout was a forgery. After he'd tried to shoot him with a crossbow, Amon had dismissed this as a crafty diversion, but Barrow's copy had had all the marks of authenticity. Could Barrow have been telling the truth? Could his copy have been the correct one?

Amon didn't know, but now that he was entertaining the possibility, some slumbering part of his mind awoke and began making wild associations between disparate memories, like an octopus frantically trying to reassemble a wrecked ship from bits of flotsam. Only two days ago he had liquidated Minister Kitao. Neither Amon nor Rick had noticed anything strange about his AT readout; Kitao was the epitome of a pervert gone haywire. And what about Rick? He had cash crashed the day before yesterday. From what Amon knew about Rick's spending habits and unprofessional attitude, this wasn't particularly surprising either, yet three GATA employees—Kitao, Rick, and Barrow—all cash crashing in the same week was unprecedented, not to mention that two were upper executives, and all of them had interacted with Amon in some capacity.

Amon wondered for a moment whether this whole chain of events was not just some paranoid hallucination spawned by the frustration of his action deprivation, as Rick had warned him at Self Serve; mad thoughts leading him like will-o-the-wisps into a black fate. To confirm his own sanity, he would need more information. He had Kitao's and Barrow's AT readouts, as well as the forged readout Barrow had sent him. If he could get a copy of Rick's readout and the LifeStreams of all three men, he could corroborate whether their transactions matched their actions, just as he had done with jubilee. Amon felt strange thinking about transactions and actions as distinct categories, attached as they were by unbreakable bonds of bureaucracy. It was like imagining a difference between O_2 and oxygen, epidermis and skin, the universe and the cosmos. The contours of existence seemed to be warping, individual things losing their unity, splitting into duplicate, like reflections that don't match the reflected, a third eye suddenly visible in the mirror, and his mind was struggling to adjust. If the LifeStreams matched up with the readouts, he could rest assured that he was just paranoid. This was no problem. There were pharmaceuticals for all that ailed the psyche. If they didn't match—they did match. They had to match.

Amon contacted the Ministry of Records to see about licensing out their LifeStreams. All seized LifeStreams were strictly protected, and the penalty for making alterations to archived data was bankdeath, but copies could be licensed out to the public for a fee. Next to fines, this was the second largest source of funding for GATA.

Amon was disappointed to find that the LifeStream of all three had already been licensed out. The Archivist explained that the buyers had secured exclusive rights for ten years, and Amon thanked him for his help.

At first Amon didn't think much of this. It was normal for documentary filmmakers, historians, journalists, pornographers, voyeurs, lovers, admirers, stalkers, and family members to license out the LifeStreams of recent bankrupts. But a few moments after he hung up, he realized that something peculiar was going on. First was the fact that Rick's LifeStream had been borrowed. Barrow was famous and Kitao, at the very least, was a newsworthy politician, but Rick was a nobody. The tabloids might have spun some tantalizing rubbish about the disgraceful end of a low-ranking Liquidator, but the immense costs of exclusive rights for ten years was hardly worth it. The second part that struck him was that all three LifeStreams had been licensed out for the same duration under the same conditions of use. Even if Amon had thought to ask, the Archivist would have been unable to disclose the identity of the buyer, but this similarity suggested to Amon that a single person or entity was responsible.

Brushing these worries aside, Amon considered another way he might get their LifeStreams: he could request an official inquiry from the Executive Council. But he was wary about this. If anyone even took his request seriously, seeking confirmation of AT readouts would insinuate corruption and suggest his lack of faith in the organization. Also, the inquiry process might meet resistance, earning him many new enemies and dragging his good name through the mud. It might even get blown up by the media. Initiating such a struggle right before the meeting with the recruiter was too risky; requesting an AT review and the jubilee property file had been risky enough. If he were to have any chance for promotion, he would have to find another way to get the information he needed. But how?

On an impulse, he began doing a websearch for jubilee. Before he'd noticed it on his readout, Amon had never seen the word before in his life and could tell right away that it wasn't of Japanese origin. It looked like it came from some European language and he'd been able to guess its pronunciation, but had seen no point in spending money to look it up until now.

The first thing that came up online was a dictionary entry: "a time of celebration and rejoicing." Checking FlexiPedia, Amon found a section explaining the meaning for Christian people, a periodic celebration in which sins were universally pardoned.

Nothing Amon found described any kind of action. It all seemed unrelated to his inquiry until he clicked a link about the more ancient Jewish jubilee. At the top was a quote from Leviticus 25:10:

> And ye shall set aside the fiftieth year, and proclaim liberty upon all inhabitants throughout the land: it shall be a jubilee for you; and ye shall all return to thy ancestral property, and ye shall all return to thy family.

The encyclopedia went on to explain the quote: "The jubilee signified a year of emancipation for the Ancient Jewish peoples. Every seven years was a designated rest year called a Sabbath year in which crops were not planted and a break was taken from toil. Every seven cycles of Sabbath years, that is every forty-nine years, was a special year called the jubilee. In this year, slaves were freed to rejoin their families, property returned to their original owners, and all debts forgiven."

Amon wondered what this could mean, "all debts forgiven," but his thoughts were cut off by FacePhone ringing. It was an incoming call from the policy complaints department at Fertilex. *At last! This call will set the world right and I'll laugh later at my far-fetched delusions.* He knew he shouldn't pick up personal calls at work, but this one was too important to miss. He clicked accept.

The same slim, buzzcut man with the silver earrings appeared against the same white background.

"Hello valued customer," once again, the voice sounded different. "My name is Wednesday representing Fertilex for the Policy Complaints Department. Is this the Mr. K. who left a message with our answering service?"

By "Mr. K." Amon supposed he must mean "Kenzaki" and said:"Yes it is. I've been waiting for your call."

"Mr. K., we are disappointed," the man said, "with your business manner."

"Huh?! My what?"

"You were supposed to call us by 10:37 this morning."

"Supposed to call? I've been waiting for you to contact me all day!" he was almost shouting again.

"Well if you had bothered to read the message we sent you, you'd know what I'm talking about."

"What message? I've been getting nothing but spam."

"According to our records, the transmission succeeded at 11:03:34."

Amon began to scroll through his inbox and, sure enough, a message had arrived from the Fertilex Policy Complaints Department at 11:03:34 entitled, just like all the others, *Important Information.*

"Shall I read the message for you?" the man asked, beginning to read before Amon answered. "Dear Amon, We apologize for the delay and have prepared the information you requested. We hope to dispense with this matter promptly and ask for you to call us at 10:37 a.m. by clicking the link below. If you have any que—"

"Just stop alright," Amon interjected, having already read his own copy of the message. "I got the message, but it was mixed up with so much spam that YOU sent me, I didn't even notice it. And the time you requested I contact you is before the time you sent the message, is it not? I can't exactly travel back in time you know. Anyways, I'm at work now and I couldn't have made a phone call then."

"You don't seem to be having any problems talking to us now."

"Well . . . I . . . but—"

"The point is, you didn't read a message which I very clearly labeled as 'Important Information.' If you can accept this call, you could have at least made an effort to call us at the specified time. This is very unprofessional."

"Unprofessional? I thought this was customer service?"

"I'm sorry, Mr. K., but I'm going to have to terminate your complaint."

"What!?"

"I recommend re-starting your request through the usual customer-service channels if it's really as urgent as you say."

"Wait!" Amon shrieked, but the man was gone.

Holding back tears, he returned his gaze to the Gutter. Still, work was impossible.

PART 3
JUBILEE?

15

AKIHABARA

Outside Akihabara Station, the InfoSun had sunken far out of sight. In that last breath before twilight, its infobeams coated the skyscrapers and streets with a silvery glaze of advermation that seemed to darken by the second. A shadowy undertone crept over the high-fidelity vistas swirling across windows and walls and asphalt—a fluorescent bulb shaped like a grinning cat swinging on a wire from a chipped plaster ceiling, a baby reading the news of the day as it tumbled in sitting position through a spiral nebula—all color draining away with the death of the day. Up above, across the sky slivers visible between rooftops, five granular streaks of InfoCloud ran in parallel—giant mahjong pieces flipped by teams of bodybuilders, alongside Siamese toddlers walking on hot coals, next to rental origami friends chatting in your bedroom—milky imagery finger-painted in the patchwork firmament by the invisible hand of the market.

Amon was in the middle of a four-lane road strangely devoid of cars. Instead it was packed curb to curb with idol fan clubs and hordes of passing salarymen: ornate, silken hair, and vibrant gowns interspersed amongst trim comb overs and black suits. Glass towers a dozen stories high lined the sidewalks, their windows coated in a lacquer of tropical hues. Text of a different shade blinked across the opaque surface, advertising the motley assortment of shops on each floor. There were dealers in anadeto collectibles like camera lenses, laptops, figurines, cards, Geiger counters, light bulbs, and board games. There were coin-operated arcades, karaoke hotels, and cafes served by blonde yodel-girls. Sex-doll flea markets neighbored anime brothels, adjacent to maid reflexology parlors, below medieval jousting dojos that edged breakfast-in-water-bed butler bars.

He made his way through the crowd in the direction of his navi-arrow. It pointed to a dead end several hundred meters away where the row of skyscrapers was interrupted by a gap. *Why is ScrimpNavi directing me to an empty lot?* he wondered, but his mind went blank when he entered a pocket in the crowd and found himself surrounded by a circle of teen girls who all looked nearly identical. With four dozen pairs of eyes all fixed on him, Amon's step faltered and he rotated his gaze slowly, warily.

They were masterpieces of physiognomic stylization; erotic cartoon exaggerations of the female form with the same face, the same attire, the same posture. Wearing frilly black miniskirts and blue bodices decorated in intricate patterns of purple and orange lace, their figures were impossibly proportioned: waists with no more circumference than a croissant somehow supporting double G breasts; outward-curving crescent-shaped legs so slender they almost seemed two-dimensional. They had lavender eyes wide enough to extend beyond the sides of their faces and whiskers of long, golden pins. Lips of molten cherry from which steaming droplets fell to the tarmac and cherry-colored curls down to the waist. Their skin sparkling and crystalline; their expressions of perfect serenity disturbed now and then by slight bodily trembles as though suppressed ecstasy were erupting to the surface.

Their mutual resemblance seemed perfect at first, until Amon realized that each one possessed a different graphical flaw. Some had spots of glare or blurriness on their clothes where light was reflected all wrong; others had patches of skin discolored metallic and grainy like some low-res leprosy; others still had missing chunks of breast or leg or skirt where the image had been left blank.

As he gaped at them for a moment, they covered their mouths with delicate, child-like fingers, and *tee-heed* in unison. Then they joined hands to keep him in the circle and sent him shy smiles from all directions. It was an unnerving sight, for despite projecting themselves with hyperbolic femininity, Amon knew that many were probably full-grown men. The majority of most teen idol fan clubs were men, and he doubted this one was any exception. Although fans chose to believe otherwise, idols were merely a collection of images, voices, songs, catch-phrases, gestures, designed and owned by MegaGlom lobby groups. And whether male or female, they had all paid membership dues for the right to resemble their chosen superstar, although never perfectly. Restrictions on the conditions of use for the likeness legally obligated fans to mar their appearance in some way, this very unattainability what created the ideal that attracted them in the first place.

A cloud of myriad, clashing perfumes wafted its acid fragrance about him, tickling his nostrils and stinging his eyes, as Amon wondered how he might bust out of the circle without bowling someone over. Then suddenly, music blasted out from nowhere, and the fans broke into a synchronized dance routine. To pulsing base, low-fi synth, and chipmunk vocals, they did flamboyant hand-waves, elbow-flaps, pouts, finger-points, twirls, and poses. While moving, they sang along together and Amon recognized the lyrics of the chorus:

E-e-everything is up to you-hoo-hoo! The universe is yo-ours to doooooo!

It was Absolute Choice's most recent slogan. Showing political support for the party preferred by one's idol was a way of expressing devotion, and the MegaGlom lobby that owned them reciprocated with reduced membership dues. This sort of sponsored activism strengthened both the economy and democracy—Amon had heard some talking heads say—since growth in the celebrity worship industry was tied to increases in the voting rate, which was higher among fans than any other population segment.

Now that the chain of hands was unlinked, Amon seized his chance and twisted his torso sideways to charge between two girls, dodging their swinging limbs and giant breasts. Once out of the circle, he continued to trail his navi-beam, cutting through lines of salarymen that stretched from the doorway of ground-floor ramen shops out onto the street. Porky fumes piped out ventilators mingled with the still-lingering perfume alloy, permeating his nose with an unctuous but fruity pungency. He could see packs of feral children in tattered fur rags prowling furtively

about him. Taking cover behind suited bodies, they breathed gouts of
white flame at each other, their hair dreadlocks of blue light, their rough
tanned skin smeared with soot. Elsewhere, men with a single monster
wheel for legs and totem pole animal faces—eagles, turtles, and caribou
carved of wood—left a trail of mountain landscape panoramas behind
them as they looped around each other at high speed, fleeting patterns
of alpine imagery interweaving in their wake.

Little had changed since the last time Amon visited Akihabara.
Little ever seemed to change here except for the fads. It was timeless:
the inevitable point of convergence for electro nosties, cosoplayers,
gamers, and all sorts of maladapts who could find friendship nowhere
else. Although this was his first visit alone, Amon had gone on missions with Rick here many times, and a tender sadness nipped at his
chest when he realized they would never go on another. His friend
was gone. Jubilee, Barrow, and Kitao seemed to be connected to his
disappearance in some way, but Amon still couldn't see how. He continued to hold out hope that it was all just a bureaucratic error, but
the more time passed, the more his anxieties began to coalesce and
his doubt to grow. In order to restore his own trust in the system—or
else to get the ear of those who could rectify the damages done—he
would need evidence. But after GATA and Fertilex brushed him off,
his avenues of investigation had appeared to be closed. That is, until,
at the end of the work day—the most unproductive, worthless work
day of his entire career—he'd come up with an idea, at first odious and
impossible, but, after more thought, crucial and inevitable. He would
contact the PhisherKing, Kai Monju.

According to blog rumors Amon had read, Monju was a GATA Blinder
gone renegade. Using his insider knowledge of government security systems and his expertise in cryptography, he had seized enough clandestine
information to build a database of such immensity it was rivaled only by
the GATA Archives. He was the bane of many a politician and tycoon, but
his castle walls of incriminating leaks kept enemies at bay and allowed
him to build a semi-independent kingdom in Akihabara. There, hackers,
cryptanalysists, and rats of all shades had gathered around his banner.
The PhisherKing was now thought to be one of the most powerful men
in Japan, certainly the most powerful black market businessman.

Amon hated Phishers. They preyed on poor souls desperate for hard-to-get information, and other poor souls desperate enough to sell it. The fact that Monju was top Phisher only made him top scumbag in Amon's reckoning, and he would never have imagined dealing with him, especially not after his trick at the Tezuka last night. But the only way he could hope to obtain the info he needed without kicking up a nasty fuss at GATA that could ruin his career (and might not work anyway) was from a master data-peddler like Monju. And since Monju had expressed interest in the segs of Barrow's cash crash, Amon expected to have leverage in the negotiations.

After reluctantly deciding on this plan, he'd researched the PhisherKing on the darker portals of hackspace. The only listing he could find, echoed again and again on various sites that kept going offline the moment he opened them, was for an address in Akihabara. Every step he took deeper into this fetishistic carnival filled Amon with a nauseating dread, but he'd thought it all through and had determined that there was no other way.

The perfume and bass thumps gradually began to fade as he neared the empty lot. The crowd too was thinning. In its place, clouds of mechanical parts hovered here and there above the street. Hydraulic limbs, cables, metal plates, circuits, batteries, sensors, kept folding, rotating, connecting, and reorganizing into new configurations in the air. Amon watched as a tin sheet floating amongst a particular cloud of parts began to peel into strips and curve around on itself, forming into a metallic flower. A long steel probe floating in another cloud spun its long shaft rapidly like an axle and tried to insert its bulbous tip into the center of the flower where a glass bud was attached. Meanwhile, a sleek, sharply-angled, humanoid robot worked to prevent them from making contact. It fired magnetic blasts from a long cannon propped on its shoulder, changing the orientation of the flower and trajectory of the probe. Several triads of part clouds and robots were engaged in the same type of conflict at various points ahead.

Otaku, thought Amon with disgust and picked up his pace, wondering, *Has the OtaPlay actually spread this far?* ImmaGames were staged constantly throughout the city, the overlay of each game world hidden from those who didn't subscribe. Gamers played as they shopped, worked, exercised, their escape from living in the moment integrated invisibly into every moment of living. But the OtaPlay, short for Otaku Playground, was where all games came to completion. It was the stronghold of the last boss, the last Tetris slot, the epicenter of the Armageddon, and the gateway to paradise all at once. It had evolved over the years from a car-free pedestrian-heaven Sunday event to a twenty-four-hour-seven-days-a-week society, gradually enlarging its territory each year, block by block. Soon, Amon supposed, it would reach the station, and who knew how much of the city it might one day consume. Otaku, the permanent denizens of Akihabara and its offshoot communities, were generally well respected. Always running about in interaction with gaming environments, they got lots of exercise, which was healthy, and did lots of strategizing, which showed they were clever—somewhere between say a sportsman and a chess master. They certainly had a better reputation than nosties, since their obsessions were at least for digital things rather than filthy analog detritus. Yet for some reason, otaku had always creeped Amon out in a way that nosties didn't. And remembering Barrow's speech from the previous night, he began to think that there might be something to his knee-jerk reaction, that learning about old relics might have more value than such escapism.

One of the robots stepped absentmindedly backwards and bumped Amon's shoulder, sending him a whiff of rank BO. With the gun knocked off target for a moment, the probe of the robot's opponent was able to reach its targeted flower successfully. The tin blossom closed tightly around the metal pole and the pole quivered, ejaculating black oil that spilled between the sharp petals onto the street. The two sets of parts then began to coalesce and interlock rapidly, self-organizing into some sort of giant machine. Amon zigzagged along the street as necessary so as to keep his distance from the players, but their movements were erratic and unpredictable, reacting to stimuli perceived as mortal dangers that he couldn't even see.

The reek of the otaku told Amon just how close he was to bankruptcy. All the targets he had executed in Akihabara had smelled much the same, their sweat gone stale with stress, overexertion, and insomnia. Many deprived themselves of sleep and food for days, putting every ounce of their waking attention into living off gaming, but only the most exceptional players could stay afloat for long. Prestige, that is, position in a game, was directly connected to income. The percentage each player paid to join a game was proportionate to their standing, with low-scorers paying the most and high-scorers paying little or nothing at all. Assets like virtual property, level, tools, and points could be converted into one of the gaming currencies, which could be spent on the open market or used to buy items in other games. Yet their value fluctuated depending on demand to play that game, which varied in response to new releases and trends. To make matters more complex, otaku were usually immersed in a dozen worlds at once, switching rapidly from overlay to overlay. The robots might also be knights, the metallic flowers damsels, the floating machines dragons, and perhaps ten other characters simultaneously. In one world, two players might be on the same team, in another enemies, competing and cooperating in the same instant, losing and gaining points for the same move. Given the ambiguous cost of individual actions, the prestige-based price system and the fluctuating value of assets, it was easy to miscalculate, to get drawn too deeply into a campaign, and forget how much one was spending.

To Amon's relief, when he got within a few meters of the empty lot, the otaku kept back, as though warded off by some unseen line. Before him was a gaping pit bored down through the city. It was shaped like a clean-cut rectangle, as though a building that once stood there had simply evaporated. At the edge of the pit, a chrome door stood. Divided top to bottom into two equal halves, it looked like it ought to lead to an elevator. It even had up-down buttons and an arcing band of steel above the doorway with ten holes in it that might have indicated the floors, except they were unlabeled.

Stepping up to the brink, Amon looked warily down into the pit. Like a cutaway of the city's underground, the top layer was sidewalk, then there was piping and dangling shreds of severed wires, then open ducts, then some kind of maintenance tunnel, then soil marbled with exposed metal and concrete. Nowhere was there an elevator, nor a shaft for an elevator, nor even cables that might have carried one. Behind the doors, all he could see was the hole, reaching deep into the bowels of the metropolis and fading into an utterly black abyss.

Blowing softly from below, Amon felt a cool draft tinged with the scent of mildew, as though it originated in a cave. Without any hesitation, he approached the doors and pressed the "up" button. He could have just as well pressed "down," but somehow up seemed like the more promising option. Immediately the ten holes above the door lit up simultaneously from an indeterminate source. A few dozen seconds passed and nothing seemed to happen, when suddenly the doors slid open to reveal an elevator across the threshold, like a box from behind a magician's handkerchief.

Slowly, Amon edged towards the open doorway. Inside, the elevator had walls of the same chrome but no ceiling whatsoever. Standing with the toes of one foot right up to the threshold, he carefully stuck out the other foot and probed the floor of the elevator with the ball. To his relief, he felt solidity. The navi-arrow was pointing straight into the chamber and Amon glanced around to double check that there wasn't an alternate route he had missed; there was nothing around but the office buildings and their inverted kin—the hole. Rallying his courage, he stepped in with his outstretched foot and gradually shifted his weight over. When the floor continued to hold, he brought over his other foot.

He was in.

On the front wall of the elevator, there was a panel with clear plastic buttons that were unnumbered and unlit. The address had not specified a floor and Amon paused with his hand hovering indecisively before the buttons, when suddenly the elevator began to plunge, the door still open.

His body felt like it was being stretched upwards, and he moved into the corner to lean on the two walls for support, but his hands went right through, disappearing behind the insubstantial graphic. Wind whipped around him as air rushed in and was sucked out the open ceiling, his clothes *thwapping* hard against his skin. He felt as though he had become weightless and would be sucked out the ceiling like a wisp of dandelion fluff. Struggling to stand upright, his heart thundering, he looked up through the square of open roof and watched in horror as the rectangle of city slipped away. He fell beneath the sidewalk, beneath the sewers, beneath the maintenance tunnels, beneath the soil and the bedrock, until all he saw was a rectangular glow in the distance, which kept shrinking and shrinking, turning into a point of light that grew ever more distant as though he were reentering the womb; soon he could no longer keep his eyes open against the harsh wind, and it too disappeared.

Then, at the very moment he found himself in total darkness, the elevator drew to a smooth stop, and immediately he heard a deep, husky voice. "State your business."

"My name i—"

"We know who you are. State your business." The voice seemed to create subtle disturbances in the space around him, as though it resonated within the very darkness. A cold sweat had broken out all over his head, neck, armpits, and crotch and he felt the blood throb violently in the veins of his forehead and chest. At that moment he saw an incoming call from a number he didn't recognize. Too afraid to even move, and guessing it was from Fertilex customer service, he ignored its ringing and said: "I-I'm here to see Kai Monju, the PhisherKing." Barely fighting down the quavering of his voice he added, "I have a trade I'd like to propose."

"Look down," said the voice. Amon looked down and saw a skeleton key made of pure white light that somehow failed to illuminate, leaving the darkness total and untouched. Picking it up, he looked around and found a small hole in the wall opposite the doors he had entered, letting in a faint, dusty glow. He put the key in and turned.

The door opened with a blinding rush of sunlight. Amon shielded his eyes, and stood there squinting until they adjusted.

The elevator was hovering over an ocean of mercury, the floor just above the peak of the glittering waves. This grayish, liquid silver tossed and turned to the horizon where it met a scarlet sky. In place of clouds, the heavens were ribbed with streaks of metal contraption like bulges of robotic flesh, tendon, and muscle. The sun appeared the same size as always, but Amon could make out its texture, suggesting it was smaller and closer than the one that rises on Earth. It was a golden circle of sand flecked with gray pebbles. Hanging just above the ocean, it seemed to signal early morning or the immanent onset of night, there was no telling.

The sunlight it gave off was thick and radiant as though a rare mineral had sedimented in the air.

A large rowboat of a smooth, white substance resembling mother of pearl was headed straight for the elevator. Six hooded men in billowing robes of midnight green sat on each side facing backwards. They rowed through the quicksilver with white oars, sticking out through holes in the gunwale like bone threaded through bone. The heads of the men were hidden beneath their hoods, but Amon could see their hands, transparent strands of a sickly reddish color: that morbid peach.

At the bow of the boat stood a man with shoulder-length, sleek-brown hair bleached blond from eye-level down. He had a dark five-o'clock shadow on his sharp, defined jaw line. His ears were pierced with numerous studs and rings, the color of tarnished lead, and he wore a black cloak with a large hood. Beneath his skin, the original silicon BodyBank, now obsolete, was visible. Wires linked to tiny computer chip nodes, to more wires, to circuitry, to sensors, to other nodes, appeared as a dark presence all over the visible parts of his body—his face and hands—like a meticulously detailed blueprint sketch of a machine beneath tracing paper. The man stared at Amon with eyes that caught the sunlight in a strange way, as the twelve rowers heaved and heaved to bring the boat straight towards the elevator.

The air smelled like carpet cleaner and disinfectant and Amon felt a cold draft from above on his sweaty skin that might have been air-conditioning. He could hear a hiss like the sea, but there was a strange clinking sound accompanying it that he couldn't identify. He was terrified by this outlandish scene and the ineluctable approach of the boat, but knew he had nowhere to run. His only way out might have been the elevator, but he had no clue which button to press or whether the buttons even worked. With no choice but to face them, he kept focused on his right hand, which hung down to just below the holster at his hip, and intently watched the crew's approach.

When the prow was just below the elevator, the two men at the front of the lines stopped rowing, drew the paddle of their oars out of the silver water, wedged the handle beneath their seats to keep them upright, and left the dripping shafts to jut out over the sea. They then stood up and turned around, their faces still hidden in the darkness of their hoods.

Going to the fore of the deck, they bent over and Amon could see them pulling on something hidden by the bow. After a few heaves, they drew out a boulder-sized sphere of bronze from some recess, and rolled it out behind them to the two men now at the front of the lines. Somehow spotting it with their backs turned, they took one hand off the oars while still seated and gave the ball a little push in the direction it was going. The four pairs of men ahead of them did the same in turn, guiding it to the stern where it rolled to a stop against the back lip. The weight made the rear sink slightly, raising the prow up just to the level of the elevator floor. The seated men then stopped rowing, stood to face Amon, and all twelve threw back their hoods at once, revealing the transparent white, aquamarine, and morbid peach of their fibrous faces, just like the apparition sewn of jellyfish Amon had met by the vending machine at the Tezuka. All of them were staring at him, the crew with empty eye sockets, somehow glowing despite the sunlight, and the man at the front with his strange eyes, which Amon could make out now that he was close. His pupils were mercury like the sea, his irises pebble-flecked golden sand like the sun, the outer ring scarlet like the sky ribbed with a miniature version of the same metallic pattern.

The boat remained angled up towards Amon, bobbing only slightly with the waves. The front oarsman on the left gestured for Amon to advance, and he hesitantly stepped aboard. Immediately, the two oarsmen at the back bent over and began to plough the bronze ball forward up the sloping deck. When it rolled past the midway point, Amon felt the deck drop under his feet as the boat began to right itself, whereupon the oarsmen released the ball, letting it roll to a stop at the bow just beside him. *If the boat can move*, realized Amon, *then it's no mere projection*, and his terror increased as he lost all sense of where he was. The oarsmen put their hoods back on and sat down, letting their oars lie still. The boat rocked gently in the waves, slowly drifting away from the elevator, a chrome portal floating against the scarlet sky.

"Welcome Kenzaki-san," said the man in front with a smile, revealing teeth of glass. Amon wasn't pleased that Monju had recognized him in his pastel digiguise, but for an information dealer it was hardly surprising.

"We spoke briefly last night, but allow me to introduce myself. I'm Kai Monju." Reminded of how the PhisherKing had impersonated Mayuko to fool him, Amon felt rage seething in the bottom of his gut, but it was submerged deep beneath the cold fear that filled his abdomen. When the man bowed, Amon gave only a slight nod, not wanting to let his guard down. Still poised to draw his duster at the first sign of danger, his skin tingled with an electric readiness. A moment of tense silence followed, as Amon stared into the PhisherKing's multicolored eyes. The only sound was the strange clinking he'd noticed, the boat bobbing gently on the waves. The PhisherKing spoke again. "So you've come to make a trade."

"Yes. But first, I want reassurance that you are who you say you are. I won't deal with anyone but Kai Monju, the PhisherKing."

"I told you who I am, did I not?"

"And last night you told me you were Mayuko. I won't be fooled again."

"Then check my profile if you wish." He held his arms out to the sides, inviting Amon to click his torso. Amon clicked. *Name: Kai Monju. Date of birth: July 1, 1971.* Amon stopped reading there.

"This is nonsense. No one born in 1971 could still be healthy and walking around."

"Are you certain? Longevity science has come a long way."

"More likely your profile is a forgery."

"That's quite an accusation to make of a man who prides himself on the quality of his information. I'm afraid my profile is the only identification I have. Do you have any other suggestions on how I might convince you, or should I have my men carry you back out through that door?"

Not wanting a fight, Amon abandoned his line of inquiry and asked, "What do you know about jubilee?"

"Joo-beh-lee? That sounds Indo-European. Latinate perhaps. What does it mean?"

"Come on, you Phishers know everything. You know my name, where I live, where I work, who my friends are, what model gun I carry. Don't pretend you don't know about jubilee!"

"But I truly have no idea."

"Bullshit!" said Amon, his anger radiating from his belly to his fingertips. "You came to my apartment right before jubilee arrived. That was no coincidence."

"I have many nets, but there's no net so large that it can catch all fish."

"Is that right? Then why did you try to trick me last night? What do you know about Barrow?"

"Usually I would charge for the answer to such questions, but I can see that we'll never get down to business at this rate," said Monju. "We acquired some news about Barrow through certain sources and learned that you were the lone Liquidator assigned. Your LifeStream will certainly be worth something if we can secure exclusive rights, so I sent one of my disciples to bait you."

"Do you expect me to believe that?"

"I swear that's all I know."

"Hah. A promise from a Phisher. Do you have any proof to back up your words?"

"Well, if you've already decided you don't trust me, will you be satisfied with anything I show you? Any proof I give you will be data, but data has nothing to guarantee its truth other than itself. Maybe you'll ask to see the sources and the official stamps that certify the data as authentic and true, but these too will inevitably be data. Then you'll want to see proof of the truth of the proof until, in the end, you'll have to look through my whole database, but what would there be to verify that? Perhaps you'll think that I have other data stashed up my sleeve or that the whole thing is forged and we'd be right back where we started. Whoever I claim to be, at some stage you'll just have to take my word for it. I have a reputation to maintain and I promise to give you the most trustworthy information you can afford. If you can't accept that, then I'm afraid I can't help you."

Amon stared into Monju's red, gold, and silver eyes, searching for signs that he was lying, but his intuition uncovered nothing, the windows to the man's soul hidden behind digital curtains. Breaking their gaze, he looked off into the ocean. After a moment, he realized where the clinking sound he had heard originated: when waves rose, the mercury divided into silver balls that collided with each other, as though momentarily transmuted into solid things, before melting back into the undulations of the current. Watching this rhythmic process, Amon felt his fear and rage begin to dissipate. As the PhisherKing had said, was there any choice but to trust him?

As though sensing Amon's change of feelings, the PhisherKing continued. "So you want information about Barrow, Kitao, your partner, and now this jubilee . . . is that right?"

"How did you *know* that?" said Amon, meeting his gaze again.

"Just a guess," Monju winked his right eye, the silhouette of the multicolored rings visible through his eyelids, which seemed abnormally thin. "Now tell me exactly what you're searching for. Information is my trade, but my guesses only go so far."

"As you say, I'm looking for four pieces of information."

Monju nodded and waited for Amon to continue.

"First, I want a chunk of Barrow's LifeStream."

"At the moment he was said to be sleeping with the minor I presume."

Amon nodded, trying not to let the exasperation at being read so easily show on his face.

"Okay," said Monju. "What else?"

"I want Kitao's LifeStream at these time points." Amon sent Monju the parts of Kitao's readout from when he had entered his orchid cactus world. "Next, the AT readout and LifeStream of my partner, Rick Ferro. The segs showing his cash crash."

Monju nodded. "And the last?"

"The last one is jubilee."

"As I already explained, I don't know what you're referring to. The dictionary lists it as some kind of celebration or religious event. Is that what you're after?"

"No. Not that. It's . . . well, I don't know what it is. I got this charge last night from Fertilex. The property was called jubilee but I just don't get it. I . . . I never performed the action and . . . I need every bit of information you can find on it."

"Please send all the information you've collected about jubilee so far. With vague requests like this, I'll need some sort of lead."

Amon copied the section of his AT readout and LifeStream from the time the charge occurred, as well as the segs of his talk with the Fertilex agents and GATA officials, pasted them all in one glass orb and tossed it to Monju. Each of the PhisherKing's eyelids then began to flutter in alternation, right and left switching places rapidly between half-open and closed, as though he were having a waking dream. This continued for a dozen seconds until his eyes opened normally and he said: "Is that everything?"

Amon was overwhelmed with the urge to ask about forests. He desperately wanted to know whether they existed. And if anyone could breach the information divides, it was Monju. But now was not the time. Without funding to go there, such hints would do nothing but tease him. First and foremost he had to restore balance to his account.

"Yes, that's all."

"Alright. Well, before we begin negotiations, I have a question: Why do you need this information?"

"Is that important?"

"It could be. Sometimes the exact information my clients request isn't available, but I can procure related information that performs the same function. Since some of what you seek is licensed exclusively, it may be necessary to phish out such replacements. But to make sure you're satisfied with what I catch, I need to know what you're aiming for."

"Fertilex charged me for an action called jubilee that I'm sure I never performed. This is a crime, but I've received no compensation and am getting nowhere with them or with GATA. In the same week, three people at GATA went bankrupt for the first time in history. One of them was my best friend. I want to know if there are any connections. I want to check whether Barrow and Kitao's LifeStreams match their AT readouts. I want to know what happened to Rick. I want to be reimbursed for the money taken from my account and all my other expenses. Ultimately, I want to know the truth."

"Right. Thank you Kenzaki-san. Your goal has been well-noted," said Monju, smiling again with those glass teeth. "Now let's discuss the price."

"I'm offering the Barrow segment in exchange for your services."

"That one bit of info? It will hardly cover everything."

"Huh? You're joking, right?"

"Of course not. You've requested politically sensitive information that's not going to be easy to come by. Selling the LifeStream of Barrow's demise will barely cover the fines for the credilaws I'll need to break just to get the job done."

"I came here to make a trade, not waste money."

"Then let's make a trade. But you'll have to pick which bit of info you requested is most important. I can't get the others without fair incentive."

"That's ridiculous! I'm not paying you—you bastard!—not after what you did last night." Amon was starting to get worked up again and felt an impulse in his hand to reach for the duster.

"Why don't you at least take a look at my estimate? You can always refuse if it's too much. There's no harm in checking, is there?"

Amon reluctantly nodded in agreement. After a few breaths, Monju sent the estimate. Amon took one glance at it and said: "Forget it. This is outrageous."

"Is that right? Even with all the scrimping you do on that government salary?"

"Do you have any idea how hard I've worked to build up my savings?!" Amon shouted, his annoyance with how much Monju seemed to know about him compounding on his anger. "Can't you give some sort of discount?"

"After the way you accused me of lying about my name and then called me a bastard?"

"But I gave you a bunch of information about what I'm investigating. How about at least subtracting the value of that from the bill?"

Monju let out a wide-mouthed laugh, his teeth glittering crystals in the radiant light. "In business, Kenzaki-san, you ought to discuss that sort of thing in advance."

"In that case, this negotiation is finished. Let me back in the elevator." Amon stepped onto the prow. He felt the chill of despair creep through his gut, as though his organs had turned to stone. He couldn't give up on getting back all the credit he'd been robbed of, but this was his one opportunity forward. If he left, he'd have to swallow jubilee and the other mysteries, holding them inside him to the grave. If he agreed, he'd be allowing the PhisherKing to exploit him, and he wasn't going to be a chump, no matter how desperate he was. "Roll that ball back to the other side. I'm getting out."

The two oarsmen at the front of the lines stood up, moved towards the ball where it rested at the bow, and looked to Monju for permission, but he chopped his hand down to signal "stop," and the men froze where they were. The PhisherKing stared at Amon with eyes like the alien sun and sea and sky, seeming to beckon him into a realm of whispered truths.

"I can see you're in a tough spot," said Monju, "and I'd like to help if I can. I'm also grateful for the info you gave me, and appreciate that you seek truth and justice, even if it's clear your motives are purely selfish. But I'm running a business here and I've got expenses. As I mentioned, phishing often requires breaking the law, so the sale price of the information I receive has to be more than the fine for the crimes I commit. Otherwise it becomes a loss. If I kept on like that I'd go bankrupt. This means I certainly cannot provide complimentary services. Not for you, not for anybody. But I'll consider giving you a discount under one condition."

"What's that?"

"Promise me you'll never stop asking questions until you've found all the answers you seek."

"Huh? What does that have to do with anything?"

"Usually I'd charge for such a tale, but you explained your goal, so I'll explain mine in kind. The black market may be my way of life, but I'm not a purely calculating being, you know." As he talked, the white pebbles in his gold iris glinted in the sun and his half-bleached hair swayed in an unfelt breeze. "Before I begin, I'll need you to agree to relinquish all rights to the recording of our conversation and to never disclose anything I say to anyone else. I doubt anyone would believe you anyway, but I want this to be legally binding just in case."

Amon nodded.

"Good. So, you've probably heard what they say about me, that I used to be a Blinder?" Amon nodded again. "Well that's not exactly true. I never worked as a Blinder, though I did build the system architecture for the House of Blinding.

"You built—"

"Yes. It was my design and I oversaw the team that realized it."

But that means he must be at least in his seventies, thought Amon, and remembered his date of birth. 1971. Could it be true?

"The details of the project were confidential, so there are very few people who know about my involvement. You won't find anything about it on a bronze search, you'll have to search gold, and even that version is fragmentary and full of errors. The only accurate record left is memory." Monju tapped the side of his head with his fingers. "So take my story as you will.

"Due to my involvement in the project, I ended up with an extremely rare neurological disease that affects a very particular aspect of my cognitive function. I can't write new programs."

"You can't—but you're a Phisher!"

"I can still hack. And if someone gives me a routine operation I can still code. But whenever I think I have a new idea, it floats all vague and formless around the edges of my consciousness. Then, if I try to reach out and grasp it in my awareness, the thought liquefies and slips away. Whatever I do, the products of my creativity refuse to stay solid, so there's no way to put them into computer language. In other words, I've lost my ability to conceive."

At that moment, the tips of the front oars that were jutting out from each side of the boat began to bleed. Globules of red liquid dripped out and fell to the surface of the mercury. There they painted flower-like patterns that stretched, warped, and dispersed as the waves rolled.

"What does this disease have to do with the project?" asked Amon.

"One day I went into a clinic for a customized BodyBank upgrade. I wanted to switch to the biological version," he said, gesturing to the wired skin of his face and hands. "They did some scans and tests and sent me home. The next morning I couldn't do my job. Within a week, GATA fired me.

"The researchers they hired to examine me said it's a side effect of the psychological strains of my profession. I put my heart and soul into designing the blinding and was thoroughly exhausted. They insisted that something must have snapped inside me." A new intensity came into his eyes when he said this, the force of his gaze so strong that Amon felt like the colors might leap across the space between them and stamp themselves onto his own eyes.

"So I guess you have your doubts about their explanation."

"I have no evidence, but I believe it was intentional. The brain function I lost is too specific and the timing of the onset too convenient. I was the only one who understood the blinding architecture top to bottom. Even with my knowledge, the encryption of the system is impenetrable. But in theory, I could have created my own blinding that even Blinders can't penetrate. Then I could become anonymous even to GATA and perform all sorts of actions they couldn't detect."

"But as you said it's a very specific function. If someone did this on purpose, how could they have damaged only that part?"

"With conception dust. It's a subtle neurological weapon that takes out the brain's ability to realize concepts it has invented as linguistic thoughts, and you can set it for any language, from Swahili to mathematics. In my case it was all computer languages and their formal equivalents. The technology is banned by international law, but apparently it was worth the investment to disable me."

"You must have looked into some kind of treatment."

"Of course. But no matter what kind of offers I made, the MegaGlom that owns the patent refused to license it out. Incidentally, it's the same MegaGlom that markets Conception Dust. It's also the same MegaGlom that gave you jubilee."

"Okay. So that stuff you said about asking questions, I mean, you're hoping my investigation into Fertilex will lead you to the cure, and—"

"No. I have long since come to terms with who I am after the accident and have no interest in restoring my former self. I am the PhisherKing now and I will die the PhisherKing."

"So what then?"

Suddenly Monju's eyes went distant, as though watching the horizon of a landscape inside Amon's eyes. "The ImmaNet binds the naked world to itself. To us Phishers, it is a Treasure Matrix interreflecting everything in existence and non-existence, every one and zero. Peering into the deepest reaches of the mysterious DataGod, I sometimes see hints of events to come." His voice was liquid calm now, as though his mind were resting in a cool mist.

"After I built the House of Blinding, I wasn't the only one who lost the power to conceive. Now that Fertilex charges us for every drop of sperm we excrete, for every ovum fertilized, for sensual touch, for romance, and for birth, hardly anyone can afford to conceive and even fewer to reproduce. The richest one percent can have children. But for them, kids are just a way to show off their wealth, no different than buying the best brands or performing expensive actions like whistling. The family has been outsourced to BioPens where we're treated like electronic components, personality modules to be sold to corporations who assemble us into optimally efficient teams. And the bankdeath camps . . . well, that's another story . . . Wherever you look, we balance the cost of future generations against their benefits. The only thing that keeps our kind barely clinging to existence is some perverse industrial inertia.

"I don't know how or why, but something tells me your search is leading you towards our rejuvenation. It's no coincidence that you, an Identity Executioner, one who delivers souls from the Free World to the next, have become tangled up with the owners of life. Working in the threshold between digital life and death, you're in the perfect position to cultivate a rare and powerful sort of wisdom if only you can keep your eyes open and not let the shadows lead you astray.

"So do we have a deal? Can you swear to keep asking questions until no doubts remain in your mind?"

"Alright. I'm not sure about everything you said, but I've got no intention of giving up, at least not until things get a bit clearer. Before I make any promises though, tell me: how much of a discount are you offering?"

The PhisherKing sent the offer back to Amon, with the estimate dramatically lowered. It would still take a big chunk out of Amon's checking account, but his dream savings would remain untouched, and it was still measly compared to jubilee.

"Deal," said Amon, and shook Monju's hand. His skin felt dry and chapped. "But why do you trust me?"

"Just a premonition," said Monju releasing Amon's hand. "Now send me my payment."

A window popped up asking for Amon's consent to the transfer. When he clicked "agree," another window popped up asking for a password, as he had his BodyBank set so that exorbitant online transactions required his approval. He entered in the password but hesitated a moment before finally clicking "accept." It seemed like the right choice, but a feeling of defeat slammed him hard as the majority of what remained in his account was sucked out. He thought of his blink and breath reduction, his dialog text box and bargain vending food. In comparison to what he'd just willingly spent, all the days he'd chastised himself for being wasteful seemed so trivial. He could only hope that this investment would help return things to how they were, when a small amount of money was still worth fretting over.

Now that he'd been paid, Monju morphed before Amon's eyes into one of those jellyfish men, and the oarsman at the front of the right row turned into Monju. The jellyfish man put on his hood and stepped back to take his place at the front of the line, while the new Monju stepped forward to stand in front of Amon. *The profile had been fake after all*, thought Amon, but realized that it no longer mattered. The deal had been done.

The PhisherKing immediately set to work.

Putting his fingertips to his forehead, he began to pull on the wires beneath his own scalp, drawing the mesh of computer chips out of his skin. There was no tearing of flesh or blood, but when he was finished, the outline of where the electronics had been remained as a matrix of transparent channels. The BodyBank sparkled in the sunlight and Amon could see that it was woven into the shape of a fishing net. At each point where the wires of the net criss-crossed, there was a diamond. As Monju flung the net into the air over the side of the boat, each diamond refracted the color of the sky, the sun, the ocean, and the boat, into all the other diamonds, reflections of reflections overlapping and magnifying each other again and again, until a ghostly radiance floated about the net's unfurling form like a fog containing myriad universes. Then the net submerged in the quicksilver ocean and the misty dimensional kaleidoscope blinked out suddenly.

After a brief pause, Monju began to haul in the great net. It looked as though he were merely pulling something heavy towards himself, but each subtle motion—a slight tug to the right or left, or the easing off of a bit of slack—was triggering complex programming. Amon couldn't see the ImmaNet space Monju was navigating, but could tell from the flickering of his eyes that he was rapidly processing an immense amount of information. The PhisherKing ripped smoothly through encryption, blackmailing connections and cutting deals with every flick of his wrist.

To make a profit, Phishers had to get the juiciest leaks with the least number of costly actions. Amon was watching a trade secret unfold before his eyes; these fine movements the curriculum for his guild of hackers like magic spells to be concealed from laymen at all costs.

The net seemed to catch on something and Monju jerked hard; all the muscles from his wrists to the tendons on his neck clenched, and the net tore out of the silver water, sending up a spray of spherical droplets that clinked against each other like a wind chime. The ten-thousand radiant universes re-emerged from the diamonds, encompassing the spray and the net, which was now full of wriggling sea creatures.

With one last pull, the PhisherKing swung the teeming net into the air and landed it on the deck, the boat rocking with the impact. His crew immediately reached their hands inside the net and began to sift through the contents, tossing octopus, manta ray, sharks, jellyfish, lobsters, and countless stranger catch Amon couldn't recognize back into the ocean. When they were finished, there was only one fish left on the bone-white deck, flipping and gasping for air. Monju whipped the empty net over his head and slipped it down over his body, where it threaded itself back through his skin. He then picked up the fish and handed it to Amon, whereupon it became deathly still. It was black and small enough to fit in his palm. Monju looked at Amon and smiled his glassy business smile. The concentric circles of his eyes began to spin, the pupil clockwise, the iris counter clockwise, the outer ring rotating back and forth like an automated steering wheel.

Then Monju walked out over the waves, stepping from crest to crest.

"Wait!" called out Amon. "There's only one file here."

A cyclone was twisting up all about him as he said: "Check inside its mouth. There you'll find your treasure . . . and a complimentary gift from me to you."

The PhisherKing kept walking across the ocean until his black-robed form and shroud of swirling mercury dissipated into the scarlet-silver haze glowing along the horizon.

16

KANDA

From the open doors of pachinko parlors lining the sidewalk, a cacophonous roar blasted onto the street. It combined the jangle of pinballs pouring in streams through jackpot holes and the bleep of score-keeping sound effects. The noise was accompanied by wafts of rank tobacco smoke and the flash of fluorescent bulbs blinking away the night. Through the front glass, Amon could see grubby men and women hunched before flickering consoles. Their hands rested on dials and buttons, long ashes clinging to the end of the half-lit cigarettes that dangled from their lips. Tall girls in skimpy glam-rock garb flanked the doorways. They shot Amon alluring glances from slits down the middle of popsicle red or purple bangs; the metal studs on their leather corset dresses rapidly scattering and reorganizing to spell out "BONUS TIME," "SPECIAL LUCKY HOUR," "WIN IT ALL NOW OR NEVER," in silver lettering, as if to say that by gambling on pinball and slots they would all be his. Perhaps heeding these solicitations, a few of the salarymen crowding the sidewalk would step through the doors now and again.

The heavens were black with ominous InfoClouds, fluffy blots of promohorror that smothered the stars; monstrous snarling maw dripping with blood; Chinese cleaver amputating a gangrenous arm; disemboweled young lovers lying in embrace on parking lot tarmac. The void overhead strobed with dark, vaporous swirls of violence and gore, as piercing shrieks and weeping punctuated the pachinko racket. Then from out of nowhere, Amon would spot amidst the carnage a mangoberry candy in soothing yellows and pinks, or a warm smiling face in a park discussing architectural blueprint stock options, his eye drawn unconsciously to this oasis of serenity.

He was usually immune to such contrast marketing, the crafty psychological trick of bringing attention to one image by making everything else intolerably revolting. But tonight, in his state of distress, he felt a powerful aversion to anything with negative content, as though his nerves were full to capacity with stress and could take in no more. *Sigh. Sigh.* He counted two in a row this time. The spiral wasn't far off now. He could feel the guilt rising in his throat like bile.

After the meeting with Monju, Amon had decided to walk home and avoid touching costs on the crammed rush hour trains. Jinbocho wasn't far, and if he followed ScrimpNavi's recommended route, he would have just enough in his checking account to get there. It was impossible for him to believe that he had fallen this far. First jubilee, then his talk with Fertilex and GATA, and now his deal with Monju. Action after transaction, his funds were dissipating at a mad pace. Now, a few false moves would force him to dip into his savings, and pay hour wasn't until nine o'clock that evening. He almost expected to wake up on his bed in a cold sweat, but apparently the only nightmare in his life was the one playing itself out in the InfoSky. *Have all dreams forsaken me?* he wanted to scream, but told himself the answer was no. There was still one dream left. That could never be doubted. So long as he lived, the forest would always be waiting for him.

For the first time in ages, Amon could feel a breeze. Somehow cutting its way through the narrow byways and airways of the concrete maze, a warm bluster penetrated the stagnant humidity. It came straight at him, fluttering the fabric of his suit and tugging him backwards. As Amon fought his way ahead through the crowd, he could hear snippets of the conversations around him.

"Have you heard of Alice Garden Estate?" said a man.

"You mean the new luxury condo close to Ueno Zoo?" a woman replied. Amon couldn't spot the speakers in the crowd, but thought they sounded middle-aged.

Then just as their voices faded from hearing, a younger woman began to speak. "I just moved into a new place."

"You don't mean that luxury condo near Ueno Zoo do you?" replied a different woman.

"Yes! How did you know?"

"I hear the facilities are just fantastic," said a young man.

"They are. You should see the billiard room," said another.

It was the InfoWind, trying to mask the audio it carried as street hype on the lips of passersby. *And doing a poor job of it*, thought Amon, for anyone with half a brain could tell the repetition of that one topic was no coincidence.

Craving for answers, he took out the fish from his jacket pocket. On first glance it had looked black, but under the flash of pachinko and the dim streetlights its scales gleamed greenish-blue. Pinching jaw between thumb and index finger, Amon opened its mouth and dumped out four silver coins onto his palm. All of different sizes, they were marked with faded and illegible scrawls, like the currency denominations of a dead civilization in a dead language. He now had five files: the fish and four coins. The second largest coin was wrapped in a scarlet bow, and Amon guessed that this was Monju's gift. With the writing unreadable, there was no telling which was which, so he decided to watch them from smallest to largest and the fish last.

He flipped the smallest coin and it expanded in mid-air, morphing into a vista that covered his visual field like a translucent membrane. The streets became a faint background sheen along which he continued to walk, the rest of his perspective shifting over to that of a woman's.

Wearing a revealing white dress, she lay inside the blossom of a white flower. She could see the face of a tall, lanky man bent over sniffing her. It was Minister Kitao, an expression of analytic appreciation on his face like a sommelier tasting a fine wine. Cut to another seg in a Japanese-style room, the date a few years later. In the same outfit, she knelt on a *tatami* floor in line with a dozen other young women, their arms flower stems, a mane of white petals ringing their heads. Kitao bowed low to take sniffs of each head in turn, a slight hint of delirium creeping onto his sommelier façade. Cut to the following year. A salaryman stood alone with Kitao in an elevator. Without warning, Kitao put his hands under the man's armpits and lifted him off the floor, his eyes bloodshot, his lips smiling slanted. The salaryman struggled to no avail as Kitao took repeated sniffs, all the way from floor ten to the ground level. Just before the doors opened, Kitao put him down and, while others began to board, sauntered casually away through the lobby as though nothing had happened.

Amon fast-forwarded through the following segs, of which there were about twenty more. Each one showed someone being assaulted by Minister Kitao. At first there was only about one seg per year and his flowers were paid, willing participants, but gradually the frequency increased from bi-annually to monthly to weekly. And from there he began to molest strangers in more and more obvious places, until one day, multiple recordings were taken by different victims on a single busy street.

Amon now understood why Monju had asked what he needed the information for. The exclusive license on Kitao's LifeStream made it unavailable, so Monju had acquired segs from the minister's victims instead. And for Amon's purposes, these were just as good, for they showed the escalation of Kitao's perversion that he'd wanted to confirm.

Leaving the LifeStream playing, Amon opened Kitao's AT readout and compared its transactions with the actions he'd just watched. Apparently, the PhisherKing had not managed to get footage of every instance Kitao entered his Fair Lady world. But there was enough there to convince Amon of his original suspicion: the ex-minister's bankruptcy had indeed resulted from his own choices, not the secret meddling of others.

Immersed in peering into the lives of strangers, Amon had made his way further along the pachinko stretch. The glam-rock girls had been replaced by mermaid broads who beckoned inside with their tails, the soundtrack of misery shrieking from the heavens louder and more urgent.

Amon flipped the second smallest coin.

★

A woman wearing a maid's outfit of black frilly lace was dusting items placed atop a granite mantelpiece. Using a brush with a cylindrical wooden handle, she began with a Russian-style wooden statue of a ballerina posed in pirouette. A housework app guided her along the maximally efficient task-path, appearing as a faint-outline of her hand holding the same brush. The ghost hand dusted the statue first, and the maid's hand shadowed its movements, starting from the toes up to the tutu and ending with the statue's upraised fingertips. Watching her work, Amon decided his first impression had been wrong: the maid was not a woman, but a young girl. When her visual field glanced downwards now and then, Amon could see that her breasts were small and undeveloped, her shoulders scrawny, her fingers smooth and unblemished by time. And her motions had that clumsy awkwardness often seen in adolescents. When finished with the ballerina, the ghost hand jumped to the neighboring kalimba. But the maid had fallen behind by half a second and was still working on the ballerina, so it froze and began to pulsate, urging her to hurry along. Once the girl's hand had caught up, it took her through dusting the other objects in turn: a turquoise music box topped with a model city; an avacado-green accordion with immaculate, varnished keys; before finishing with the surface of the mantelpiece itself.

Behind her, there was a low moan. The young maid glanced back, panning quickly across a room cluttered with antique furniture. Her eyes stopped on a large, topless man who was lying face down on a waist-high bed getting a massage from another man. The broad, naked back and white hair dangling off the side of the mattress, not to mention the ana-deto-crammed room, were unmistakable. The girl turned around, moved on to a wall adjacent to the mantelpiece, and began dusting a dresser.

The seg ended suddenly.

Amon opened the two versions of Barrow's readout: the one GATA had given him before the mission and the one Barrow had given him in his spa. He then compared them to the seg. At the moment Barrow moaned in the seg, the readout from GATA said he had begun to molest the minor. Yet according to the other readout, Barrow was *lying down, moaning, relaxing, breathing deeply*: that is, it matched the recording perfectly. This suggested that Barrow's version was the correct one, unless the seg was fake, which Amon knew was unlikely. It was an expensive credicrime to *tamper* with LifeStreams through *editing, erasing, altering,* so it was difficult to see how the PhisherKing would have profited by doing so.

Yet when Amon double checked the authenticity tab of the two readouts, he found, just as the night before, that they both had seals. Apparently, the Ministry of Records continued to vouch for the accuracy of two contradictory records. *But if the version from Barrow is correct,* Amon wondered, *how has this error come about? And why hasn't the contradiction been rectified?*

There was something else that puzzled him as well. The cash crashes of two GATA officials in a single week seemed bound to be connected in some way, but if they were, why did Barrow's bankruptcy seem like a setup while Kitao's didn't?

The pachinko parlors had faded into pharmacies, convenience stores, kitchenware dealers, and on the corner of the approaching intersection, a pet shop. ScrimpNavi guided Amon around the corner and he turned off the main road onto a residential street. As he passed the pet shop, beasts lying in clear plastic boxes stacked behind the display window—chimera, gremlins, baby raptors—tracked him intently with their inscrutable eyes, perhaps hoping for him to adopt them, perhaps for the chance to devour him alive.

The present from Monju—his second-largest coin—rested in Amon's palm. When he pulled a strand to unravel the scarlet bow, it flipped itself.

An AT readout opened. Scrolling through, Amon quickly realized who it belonged to: himself, Amon Kenzaki. The readout began last night around the time he'd headed for Tsukuda and ended after he'd crashed Barrow. Amon was impressed that Monju had been able to acquire such a confidential document as a Liquidator's readout during a sensitive mission. Yet he was confused about why Monju had given it to him. Amon already had his own readout; nothing was gained by having a copy. *Then again,* he thought, *perhaps this is a different version,* and began to compare the two files, transaction by transaction. On a quick skim, they looked pretty much identical. All the transactions at the beginning of the mission matched: *walk, cross bridge, walk, blink, breath, walk . . .* But when he switched the display settings to show shorter time spans, he discovered an odd discrepancy. The times listed for each transaction differed by several nanoseconds. The ones on Monju's version came slightly earlier than the ones on Amon's. Scrolling ahead, he came across something even more perplexing: when he'd gone over the threshold of Barrow's front entrance, his readout said *entering residence*, while the copy from Monju said *trespassing*.

But why? Barrow was already bankrupt at that point, which meant he no longer owned the building—or any property for that matter—so trespassing made no sense. Yet according to the readout copy from Monju, as Amon walked through the building, he was sentenced for the credicrime repeatedly every second. While Amon's original readout listed *walking, breathing, entering elevator, ascending . . .* the copy listed *walking, trespassing, breathing, trespassing, entering elevator, trespassing, ascending, trespassing . . .* Then, when he trashed Barrow's room, he was convicted of *vandalism* instead of *making a mess*; when he drew his duster, for *violent intimidation* and *verbal threats*; and when he shot Barrow, his readout said *disable bankrupt* as always, while the copy said *unprovoked assault* and *unauthorized use of a government weapon*. Last, and most disturbing, at the moment he input the Death Codes, his readout said *identity execution*, while the copy said *identity murder*.

At first Amon decided that Monju's version had to be a forgery because he hadn't been charged for any of the credicrimes he supposedly committed. If he'd really been trespassing, he would have noticed his balance drop as soon as he entered and immediately aborted the mission. Moreover, such sustained illicit behavior was enough to sap most of his savings, and identity murder alone would have cleared him out a thousand times over. Yet he hadn't been fined a single yen. His original readout was consistent with his bank account activity and balance. Therefore, it had to be right.

It was then that Amon realized he'd been looking only at his expenditures and decided to try opening the incoming deposits column in the copy from Monju. There he saw the strangest thing of all: he'd been compensated for his losses. That is, every time he committed a credicrime, the exact amount of the fine had been simultaneously deposited into his account. This explained why he might not have noticed the drop in his balance—every depletion of funds had been replenished faster than he could blink.

So am I an identity murderer or not? The answer was yes if he trusted this new version of his readout Monju had given him, the version of Barrow's readout Barrow had sent him, and the maid's LifeStream, all of which agreed that Barrow was never bankrupt to begin with. The answer was no if he trusted the version of Barrow's readout from GATA and Amon's version of his own readout, both of which said Barrow was a bankrupt pedophile. One group of records had to be false, either the files from Barrow and Monju or the files from GATA. If the records from Barrow/Monju were false, Amon had been ripped off and was back where he started with no clues about jubilee. If the records from GATA were false, he was a criminal and a fool, for it meant that someone had tricked him into cash crashing an innocent man, an admirable man, a man Amon had respected and revered more than any other.

Just to be sure, he checked the authenticity tab of the readouts for his mission against Barrow, but found that they were sealed like the other two. This seemed to indicate that the Archivists had sealed the wrong readouts. But there was an even more horrifying possibility: maybe all of the readouts were forged. If authentication could be misused in one instance, couldn't it be misused in all instances? No! He wouldn't believe it. There were measures in place to prevent this: blinding, monitoring, credilaw. It was clearly an isolated breakdown. One record of transactions had to be authentically authentic, had to match the actions that had actually been performed. But if it was the files from Barrow and Monju, a string of credicrimes had been committed; at the very least, Amon's readout and Barrow's readout had been forged continuously over the course of several hours from the time he was dispatched on the mission until the time it was concluded, and erroneously authenticated from then until the present moment. Moreover, Amon remembered how Barrow's bodyguards had been milling about in front of the building. The Ministry of Records would have had to send them a forged message saying that Barrow had gone bankrupt so as to get them to vacate. Last, when the Archivists checked Barrow's LifeStream, as they did for all fresh bankrupts in order to ensure that their action-data matched their readout, they would have had to turn a blind eye to its inconsistencies. Amon knew that laws to prevent governmental corruption set fines for such violations high enough to ensure that perpetrating officials went bankrupt before any serious harm could be done to the system. There was no way an Archivist could hope to afford this on their limited salaries, and it was unclear why they would do it in the first place. What was the incentive? Had someone put them up to it and paid the fines? If so, then who?

Looking again at the version of his readout from Monju, Amon spotted the company that had paid off his fines. It was called Atupio. He couldn't find any listing for it on a bronze engine, so he used the remainder of his checking account to do a silver search and quickly found its owner—Fertilex. Amon felt an eerie ping of foreboding chill his gut. If this information was accurate, then a subsidiary of Fertilex had covered the expense of Amon's credicrimes, which included the enormous fine for identity murder, and most likely the Archivists' crimes as well. Yet to sway the Archivists into violating protocol in this way, merely compensating their losses would not be enough: they would surely need to be bribed in addition. The funding required was enormous, even for the largest MegaGlom on earth. Why would Fertilex invest so much into deceiving him? What purpose did crashing Barrow serve? And what did this have to do with jubilee? The more Amon tried to untangle the meaning, the tighter his knot of confusion became, as though there were an invisible layer wrapping his consciousness that thought could not penetrate.

He had wandered his way deep into a quiet neighborhood, eight-story houses lining both sides of the narrow road. Between the sidewalk and curb to his right was a thin ditch containing a stream that ran a meter or so below the concrete. Under the faint glow of streetlights, he saw tall grass growing out of the riverbed, and the shadowy form of large carp swimming beneath the water's surface. As the InfoWind blew across the grass, it parted neatly to form the silhouette of triangular lips, the well-known trademark of Fortune7 cigarettes.

Amon flipped the largest coin.

He looked through the eyes of a man waiting for an elevator on the ground floor of GATA Tower. The hallway was empty but for a small group of officials in GATA uniforms standing in a circle and chatting several meters away. The man's eye level was several centimeters over their heads, showing that he was nearly as tall as Amon. He was looking at someone's AT readout overlaid on the elevator doors dead ahead. Between typical actions like *click, blink, breathe, scratch nose, open window*, were many Amon had never seen: *blind identity, unblind identity, withdraw funds, transfer funds*. These were actions only performed by a Blinder. But Amon began to suspect that this wasn't a Blinder's LifeStream he was watching when he noticed a green border around the readout indicating that it belonged to someone other than the user. Also, the way the man scanned it, honing in on big losses and patterns of spending, was very familiar. Amon's suspicions were confirmed when the man glanced down, revealing his suit of concrete gray, and Amon spotted the outline of the man's partner in the corner of his eye. He was watching the LifeStream of a Liquidator preparing for a cash crash.

But it didn't make sense for them to be waiting around inside GATA Tower. They ought to be reviewing the readout while pursuing their target. The account balance rolled up into view and Amon saw that it was deep, deep in the red and rapidly accruing interest. The owner of the readout was most definitely bankrupt. But that meant . . . It was unheard of for a Blinder to go over the edge. They were the most carefully screened, reliable profession in all of GATA, perhaps on Earth. Amon doubted that a Blinder had ever gone bankrupt in all forty-nine years of Free History. So why now? What had brought this unprecedented occurrence about?

The Liquidator scrolled up to more recent actions and Amon spotted the clincher: *exposing subject* and *transmitting forged action-data* at exactly the same moment; then a few seconds later, *erase cipher for blinded signature*. These three transactions were heinous infractions. In particular, exposing a subject was the very antithesis of blinding and warranted the bankdeath penalty. Then Amon saw the time these credicrimes were committed and gasped: 00:17:23, the exact moment of jubilee. The Liquidator was about to click on *transmit forged action-data* to look more closely at the details of the action, when the down arrow on the elevator lit up. *Check it! Click the action please. I need to see it!* Amon found himself shouting aloud, indifferent to whether he *disturbed the peace* on this quiet residential street, as though his words could alter this pale glimmer of the past. The Liquidator closed the readout, drew his duster, and pointed it at the elevator doors. The down arrow turned off. The doors began to slide open. The seg ended.

Between two houses up ahead, Amon saw a miniature Shinto shrine fronted by a fence of rectangular stone pillars, the names of corporations inscribed vertically down each shaft in bright red. The shrine, which looked like a red cabinet with a sloping roof, rested atop a stone block. Through the open doors he could see a bottle of Cloud9 Nectar and several coins that had been placed as offerings on a wooden ledge inside. Passing by the open gate, Amon allowed his wailing maelstrom of thoughts to consume his mind.

The seg had been brief, but its significance was clear enough. Jubilee had not been a fluke mix-up of his signature with someone else's or a mistake made by one of the Monitors as he'd once supposed. It had been intentional, and Amon could now make a pretty good guess about what had happened.

First, a Blinder had exposed his identity in order to locate his account on the system. Then, after identifying him, they had attached forged action-data to his blinded signature and sent them to the Ministry of Monitoring. Amon supposed that this data must have fit the property description for jubilee, and the Monitor had correctly matched the two as was their duty. Once the matched action-transaction was sent back to the House of Blinding, a different Blinder (or the AI drone that represented them) had withdrawn the amount of jubilee's licensing fee from Amon's account and transferred it to Fertilex (also in accordance with their duty). After this transfer was complete, the first Blinder—the criminal Blinder—had erased the cypher needed to decrypt the blinding that protected Amon's privacy. Without the cypher, the key required to open his blinded signature and unlock the identity signature behind it was gone. As a result, Amon's identity at that moment became irretrievably anonymous on the GATA system.

This explained why he hadn't been compensated for damages from jubilee. There was no way for the Judicial Broker who'd overseen the Blinder's case to identify the victim of the credicrime. So while the Blinder had been sentenced to bankdeath, Amon could not be given his due. This also explained why the Monitor he'd contacted at work that morning had denied that Amon performed any action whatsoever. According to GATA's records, performance of jubilee was attached to Amon's blinded signature at the time in question, but there was no longer any cypher to link this signature with him. This meant that searching for any action at 00:17:23 using Amon's identity signature would yield nothing; the only action-data recorded was the forgery, which was attached to a blinded signature connected to no one.

Amon was starting to get a headache. It was all so complicated, but he felt a faint stirring of hope now that he had some understanding of what was going on, however incomplete it might be. If he could prove in court that the jubilee transaction in his AT readout matched the action-data forged by the Blinder and show that the action-data in his LifeStream didn't match the jubilee property, he might convince a Judicial Broker to rule in his favor and order full compensation for all expenses associated with the mishap. Of course the situation was far from resolved. He had no idea how far-reaching the corruption might have spread, nor who best to approach about the matter. He had to be careful who he trusted. But now he could at least see how to go about bringing his account back to balance. The crisis had changed from an incomprehensible mess to a political one.

Almost. One implication of the seg still troubled him greatly. The mandatory sentence for intentionally distorting blinding was the bankdeath penalty, a fine larger than the world economy. This meant that not even Fertilex could have afforded to compensate the Blinder, let alone provide them with worthwhile incentive. And that was the unbelievable part: by exposing Amon's identity and erasing his cypher, the Blinder had willingly chosen to go bankrupt. Amon could understand how the Archivists might have been enticed to forge readouts and authenticity seals if given generous bribes, but how could any amount of money motivate someone to sacrifice the very possibility to have money, to give up their BodyBank and their job, to lose everything?

There was only one file left to review: the fish. Pinching the tail between his thumb and index finger, Amon let it dangle headfirst and scraped the nails of his other hand along its flank, scales falling to the sidewalk like dead leaves. When the last scale detached from its flesh, the fish opened its mouth and spat out a seg that bounced up off the sidewalk and expanded across Amon's visual field.

As far as his eyes could see, balls of glass colored in rainbow swirls orbited around each other like celestial bodies. Amon was a man sitting in a chair, his arms stretched out forwards on ergonomic rests. Overlaid on this vibrant wallpaper was someone's AT readout: at the top, the name Rick Ferro. At first Amon thought it might be a Liquidator looking at Rick's readout as in the last segment, but then he saw that the man's sleeves were the brown color of the GATA uniform, rather than Liquidator gray, and that the border around the readout window was red, indicating that the subject was already bankdead. This meant it had to be an Archivist doing a final comparison of Rick's AT readout and action-data after his liquidation before storing them both away in the Archives.

The Archivist clicked "filter" to edit out minor actions and leave only major expenses on the list. The readout began at 8:59:00 two nights ago. At that time point, Rick had just enough money to stay above the debt line. But within a few minutes, his transactions came to an abrupt end. Rick's last moments went like this:

Ride train. Exit train. Walk. Bump stranger. Descend stairwell. Receive FacePhone. Running. Talk on FacePhone. Running. Check real-time map. Running. Bump stranger. Run up stairs. Running. Slide down escalator banister. Running. Talk on FacePhone. Bump stranger. Running. Jump. Train suicide.

When the seg ended, Amon found himself standing on the corner of a small intersection, rows of houses stretching in four directions. He could hear his own heartbeat and realized that a strange quiet had settled over the neighborhood; not a single person or car on the street. Amon couldn't remember ever experiencing such a lull in the city, but he was in no mood to appreciate it: a ball of sad disbelief clenching in his gut like a spiked iron fist.

Train suicide was one of the leading causes of death in the Free World, topped only by cancer and absentmindedness. It was common for borderline bankrupts to off themselves this way, either out of shame for their financial failure or fear of the bankdeath camps. Looking at Rick's spending pattern with the trained eye of a Liquidator, his suicide was predictable. He had been chasing after an impossible dream—a family—but refused to give up simple pleasures and fulfill his professional duties. Some of Amon's targets had ended their lives before he could get to them. Why not Rick too? Imagining him as another faceless bankrupt, there was nothing to be surprised about.

But thinking about Rick as a unique individual, as the friend that Amon knew intimately, it just didn't make sense. While Amon might have one day been able to accept the fact of Rick's bankruptcy, he could never believe that he'd willingly jump in front of a train for any reason. Rick had too much to keep him going—Mayuko, his job, his dream of family, and maybe even Amon if their friendship had meant anything to him in the end—and since he had only just slipped into debt when he supposedly made the leap, he was well above the bankruptcy line and still had a chance to hold onto these treasures. Ever optimistic in the face of adversity—maybe a bit too optimistic—Rick was never the sort to give up until the very last, having a passion for the little joys in life, a passion to create life. Perhaps he had tripped and fallen onto the tracks by mistake? But Amon knew that Rick used the same brand of Mindfulator as him, which should have prevented such a fatal accident. Besides, Amon had heard no news of his death. Freg and Tororo had said he'd cash crashed, not killed himself. The rumors they were relying on could have been misleading, but Amon doubted this. In his experience, ministry gossip had the power to distort, but not so much as to blur the line between bankdeath and death. The other possibility was that this seg had been fabricated, but if the Archivist's seal could be faked, anything could be faked. And without reason to believe otherwise, it was just as trustworthy as any other file he possessed.

Amon was feeling disoriented, almost dizzy. He wanted to find somewhere to sit down and think, but with the deluge of emotion rushing through him, even walking around felt like too much. He remained standing alone at the corner, at this vacant crossroads. Somehow even the InfoSky had gone quiet, as the loss of his friend struck him at last, rendering him immobile. He knew he had to do something. He had to get his segs to someone at GATA so that an inquiry could be conducted into jubilee, Kitao, Barrow, Rick . . . but who to contact? Should he instigate a lawsuit at the Fiscal Judiciary? Would anyone trust segs obtained from a disgraced politician and a Phisher? What if Monju's files were fraudulent? The media would feast on that. He could see the headline now: "Liquidator Suing GATA with Forged Files Forced to Resign." He wanted to ask his decision network what to do, but couldn't think how to phrase his query in a way that would enable his friends to help without including confidential or incriminating information. Who knew what ravenous journalist might be waiting amongst them for a juicy leak? Normally, he would have called Rick in a situation like this, but now he was . . .

Then Amon remembered that he hadn't told Mayuko about Rick yet. Caught up in one thing and the next, he'd totally forgotten. Admittedly, breaking the news was a daunting prospect, especially now that he was lost in a labyrinth of bureaucratic trick-mirrors. But talking to her might help him clear his head, he realized, and either way, he had to do it. Surely she was worried sick by now and had a right to know that her lover and childhood friend would never return.

He opened her profile and clicked call.

Once again, Mayuko was running on the treadmill in her apartment. She was wearing the same outfit: blue short-shorts below a red and black striped t-shirt, her comet ponytail bouncing, her whirlpools gazing off above Amon into that same hidden horizon, sweat glistening on her flushed forehead and neck. The worry line cutting down between her eyebrows seemed deeper than yesterday, her feet thudding harder on the treadmill as though she were trying to stomp out tension.

MAYUKO, texted Amon. A few days ago, he might have insisted on his bad spelling in any and all circumstances. But remembering how Mayuko had complained about it last night, Amon couldn't bring himself to go that far, not knowing what he had to tell her.

Her eyes came down and stopped on him. "Oh. Hi . . . Amon . . . A call from you . . . twice in one week. How . . . wonderful," she said and gave a forced smile. He couldn't tell whether that was a hint of sarcasm in her voice, broken as it was by the panting. "Have you . . . heard anything from Rick?"

WELL, NOT EXACTLY BUT YEAH.

"So you have . . . news?"

YES. THERE'S SOMETHING I NEED TO TELL YOU.

"What is it? Do you . . . know where he is?"

NO. I DON'T. BECAUSE YOU SEE, RICK IS GONE.

"Gone? Where?" she said, the vertical furrow deepening further with her frown.

Amon was reminded of the similar question he had asked Freg that morning. He remembered how much Freg's efforts to convey the grim tidings delicately had irritated him at the time, but could now appreciate how difficult it was. And Amon's task was made even harder now that new, more disturbing facts had come to light . . .

HE HASN'T GONE ANYWHERE. HE'S GONE FOREVER.

"Forever?! You-you mean bankrupt?"

THAT'S WHAT I THOUGHT AT FIRST TOO, BUT NO.

"So what then?"

HE'S PASSED AWAY.

"WHAT!?" Mayuko was so shocked her legs just stopped going as the treadmill kept whipping on, forcing her to step backwards off the edge. Regaining her balance on the floor, she tapped her finger in the air, sending the machine gliding to a stop.

"What . . . did you say?" She stared at him with a look of utter horror, her chest rising and falling rapidly.

I HATE TO SAY THIS, BUT RICK IS DEAD. HE JUMPED IN FRONT OF A TRAIN LAST NIGHT.

"Are you fucking serious?"

It was so rare to hear Mayuko swear, Amon was stunned into silence. As she stared at him, her whirlpools began to swirl faster and stretch outwards as though from centrifugal force, almost swallowing the upper half of her face.

"That's crazy. I know he's been hard to reach, but . . . We . . ."

I'M SORRY I COULDN'T TELL YOU EARLIER. I'M AS SHOCKED AS YOU ARE. BUT I'VE BEEN CAUGHT UP IN A DIFFICULT SITUATION. VERY STRANGE THINGS ARE HAPPENING.

As quickly and as simply as he could, Amon told her about all the events of the last few days, beginning with the Kitao mission and ending with the segs he'd just watched (leaving out Monju's personal tale, as he was forbidden from disclosing it). Mayuko listened while standing for the first while, but eventually wiped herself off with a towel, sat down at her dinner table, and sipped at a glass of milky sports drink. She remained silent for the most part, only humming in surprise at certain points, like when he told her about his decision to do business with Monju. When he was done, Amon sent her the important sections of his LifeStream and told her to watch them later.

SO WHAT DO YOU THINK I SHOULD DO?

"I don't know. It's way too much to take in all at once. All those things happening behind closed doors and . . . and then Rick . . . I mean, are those files accurate?"

I HAVE NO IDEA. BUT MAYBE YOU CAN HELP ME FIGURE IT OUT.

"You think so. . . ? How?"

WELL I'M PRETTY SURE YOU WERE THE LAST PERSON WHO TALKED WITH RICK, RIGHT? DID HE SAY ANYTHING BEFORE HE DISAPPEARED THAT MIGHT MAKE THINGS CLEARER?

"Not that I can think of. We were supposed to meet, but he called that night to cancel. He talked about your fight with him at Self Serve. And then . . . I guess there was one thing."

Amon nodded for her to continue.

"As you know, Rick is the type of guy who likes to keep his private and professional lives separate. Once work is over, it's over and he takes it easy. But that night he told me about some kind of job he had to do."

REALLY? I NEVER HEARD ANYTHING ABOUT THAT FROM ANYONE AT THE MINISTRY. DID HE MENTION WHAT KIND OF JOB?

"No. All he told me was that it was a big deal and that once he got the bonus, he was going to take me out for a night on the town. Then he said there was something important he wanted to tell me in person. He was kind of building it up, like it was some big secret. He always does this when he's about to give me a gift, like a new car or tickets for a trip or something. Do you know what he might have been on about?"

Amon remembered what Rick had said at Self Serve about wanting to propose, but decided that now was not the right time to bring it up, and simply shook his head.

"This is too much," she said, hanging her head and cringing sadly. "What are we supposed to do now?"

Amon was trying to think how he might comfort her when a window popped up indicating an incoming FacePhone. It was Sekido. Amon hesitated, flipping his eyes back and forth between his friend in distress and his boss's call, until a text arrived: "I would like to receive an explanation from you regarding certain behavioral initiatives during your scheduled work hours today and request that you pick up immediately."

MAYUKO. LISTEN. I'VE GOT AN URGENT CALL COMING IN.

"You're leaving?" She lifted her head and glared at him. Her whirlpools glowed red in patches as though sunken ships were burning beneath the surface of her milk and chocolate eyes. It wouldn't be right to leave Mayuko in this state, he knew, and an image of himself comforting her in his arms arose unbidden, as if she would ever let him touch her like that. The least he could do, anyways, was stay on the phone and lend her his ear. But he couldn't very well ignore his irate boss, not with a promotion on the line. *You must go now*, he told himself, *for your dream!* But another part of him didn't agree, and acutely painful emotions surged down the middle of his abdomen, as though he were being ripped in half, as though horses were drawing and quartering his very being.

IT'S SEKIDO-SAN. I REALLY NEED TO TALK TO HIM NOW. I PROMISE I'LL BE RIGHT BACK. As she continued to glare at him, the spiral motion of her eyes slowed and the patches of red glow were replaced by a hazy gray, as though extinguished and smoking. *Click.* Mayuko and her apartment were replaced by the silhouette of a giant face, the features veiled in darkness. In the background was an indistinct black mound against a sky of red stars, shadowy figures holding hands and dancing around a fire atop it.

"Kenzaki," said Sekido, his silhouetted jaw moving, the faintly visible whites of his eyes dyed red with starlight. "This telephone conversation was initiated by me on the basis of my feeling that it is incumbent upon me to present the outline of a situation whose many facets refuse to take determinate shape, not least of which among them is my own, lest I resort to conveying to you my disappointment, dismay, and incontitude with certain aspects of your behavioral undertakings."

Amon had adjusted to Sekido's circumlocutions over the years, but this was too convoluted even for him, and he stared fearfully into the faint red outline of his boss's eyes for a few moments before he was able to muster a response: "Y-yes, Sekido-san. What would you like to discuss?"

"I'm not entirely sure that providing you with such information is the best course of action at this time. Rather, I would prefer to have you inform me."

"Of course. I will happily tell you whatever is required."

"That will have to wait, I believe, as this is a most inauspicious time. Not merely for myself and the organization, but for you as well. At least I can say for certain that the facets of this situation visible from the viewpoint most appropriately characterized as yours are sure to lean more towards the negative than the positive by a significant margin. Do you cognize the meaning of my utterances?"

"Yes. Of course," lied Amon.

"I thought you would, Kenzaki. You always do. I can at least count on you for that. But not to be on time it seems."

"On time? For wh—"

"For the meeting with the recruiter of course! How could you be LATE?" Sekido shouted, the red stars vibrating violently behind him as though on the verge of going supernova.

"L-l-late?" stuttered Amon, thrown off by Sekido's directness. "But . . . when was I late?"

"As I mentioned to you yesterday morning, a meeting will be coming up on an evening in the near future. Well, that near future has come, or to be more precise, the near future of yesterday morning has become now."

"Now? You mean the interview is—"

"Well interview might not be the best word for it at this juncture. You see, if you'll remember, I mentioned the inauspicious timing, for this was supposed to be a meeting where we discuss the Executive Council position, including the various intersecting objects of inquiry by which we can seek a reduction of the obfuscation surrounding your eligibility. However, given our recruiter's busy schedule it is not entirely clear we will have creditime for that particular topic. Instead, matters will be discussed in the order of their urgency, as they ought, don't you agree?"

Amon was too astonished to speak and simply nodded. Of all the moments in his life, this was the worst he could possibly imagine to have a job interview. His thoughts were in such disarray, he doubted he would have the presence of mind for a casual chat, let alone to be grilled about his qualifications for a job that all his aspirations depended on.

"The points I wish to touch upon concern areas of your performance, not only on the mission but also in the office—that were less than perfect—which is quite readily apparent since nothing but money is perfect and your performance hardly counts as money, so on second thought I probably shouldn't have mentioned perfection to begin with. First of all, what I would like to know, and I'm sure the recruiter will be equally curious, is why you didn't pick up the phone when I called you today, even though I expressly suggested that you keep your weekday evenings open for the foreseeable future."

"Phone call? I didn't—"

"Don't pretend oblivity! I called to arrange the interview at 7:20 and you neglected to answer or return my call. Furthermore, I didn't get a single reply to any of the emails I sent."

"But I didn't . . ." then Amon remembered the call he'd received in the elevator just after arriving in Monju's realm. Afraid for his life, he'd ignored it and then let it slip his mind. Searching through his inbox, he found several emails that had arrived soon after with the subject "Meeting Invitation." They had gotten lost amidst the Important Information that had flooded his account all day. "Sekido-san, I-I—"

"Most disappointing of all is the way my model Liquidator, the most faithfully reliable in the ministry, who is an exemplary example of excellent performance and superb performance excellence, has been wasting work time to make inquiries into the Ministry of Monitoring about so-called MISTAKES in his records. You even had the nerve to follow this up with requests to the Property Section and Archives, and then took calls from an external organization. What slacking is this? What laziness? And the mission with Barrow. A historic mission such as this should be approached with historic care, and as you know protocol is unequivocal about the requirement that all Liquidators travel in pairs irrespective of historicity, but you hid Rick's absence to go on the mission alone and thereby flew in the face of our internal regulations in a manner that is hardly to be appropriately classified as a minor infraction."

"But Sekido-san. You must have heard about—"

"Yes, yes, yes, yes, yes, yes, yes. Of course. I must, am most behest to my duty to, express my sympathy for the recent events which I suspect attend great pain for you. But the best I can do, as far as I can see here and now from my limited place in space and time, is to offer my condolences. It's a real shame about Rick's bankruptcy and we're all extremely sad to lose him here, as he was a talented Liquidator if a bit lacking in punctuality."

Sekido's silhouette grinned sadly, the lurid hue imbued to his teeth matching his eye whites. Amon was searching for words to tell him about Rick's suicide, when Sekido took a breath and began again.

"Thus, apropos, my first instinct when I heard about your deceitful little solo endeavor was to forgive you, given your long and flawless track record. But now I see that you vandalized Barrow's apartment. What happened to you? Did you derive some sort of demented thrill out of breaking and disordering all of those ancient artifacts? The motive of a pre-schooler having a jealous temper tantrum on a playmate's toy collection has greater perspicuity than yours, for what reason could there be to destroy valuable property on your salaried work time? Yes they were bizarre items of nostie paraphernalia and, no, I'm not defending his twisted tastes, but there is a market for such oddities and they were all to be auctioned off to raise lucre to reimburse his creditors. As a result of the damage you did to some of them, the value is much lower and that is a great disservice to this organization and a demerit to our public image and a detraction from our wealth of successes, none of which we should be proud of for obvious reasons that I'm sure you're already aware of. You *should* be aware! This lapse is a splash of soy sauce on your records that it is up to you to clean away, to find the stain remover for your negligence as it were."

"Sekido-san, I'm so sorry about—"

"Now is not the occasion for apologetic excuses. Now is the occasion to join us for a meeting. Check my email for the address. I expect you to be there in twenty minutes. No lateness will be tolerated this time." Sekido disappeared.

Mayuko was back, but Amon was already running down the street full tilt towards Kanda Station. "Amon! What's going on?"

"I've got to go," said Amon, forgetting to text in his haste.

"What? Where?"

"To an important meeting with Sekido-san. I'm running late"

"But we're still—"

"I can't talk now. I'll call you later. I'm sorry."

With that, he hung up.

17

KABUKICHO, SHUFFLE BOOM

Rushing out of Shinjuku Station, Amon dashed around a flagstone square filled with milling hipsters in Four Elements garb and deked his way across a scramble crosswalk through the converging throng. He came to a pedestrian road fronted by an archway of latticed black steel wrapped in blue Christmas lights. The arc at the top was hung with lanterns of brown and yellow stained glass, *Kabukicho* written across it in black lacquered script. He passed beneath it and continued running along the road.

Around the perimeter of his peripheral vision—up, down, and sideways—a restless tangle of febrile light and shadow squirmed. The Neon Void it was called, a marketainment spectacle unique to Kabukicho. The sidewalk, the street, and the walls of all the skyscrapers were composed of an ever-shifting fabric woven from alternating strands of luminous neon and strands of pure darkness. Fine threads of dazzling color and liquid pitch had been braided together into ropes as thick as a man's thumb. These threads rapidly intertwined, untwined, and retwined into new patterns, functioning like pixel pinworms to animate the ropes into long snaking advertisements that promoted the local businesses: half-naked girls brawling on a bed of satin, champagne bottles spurting foam into eager upturned mouths. In turn, these video-ropes knitted the warp and woof of moving trompe l'oeil tapestries that danced atop the surfaces—a syringe sticking into an arm played on the road, a cat-o-nine-tails striking a naked back appeared on a building's façade—the whole streetscape adorned in a textile of intricately textured polychrome and squid-ink images within images. "Slum Theatre," "Karaoke Underskirt," "Gasmask Girls," "Talent in Pub," flashed the bright white text of storefront signs embedded in this phantasmagoria, and the strobing clouds of promo-horror still looming high above cast their lurid glow over all.

Amon hardly saw any of it as he dodged his way past drunkards, johns, dropouts, part-time models, his every nerve focused on getting to the interview. He followed the navi-beam when he could, but speed was of the essence: saving a few bucks now would mean nothing if he was passed up for promotion. Every few meters, sex hawkers stood at the curb, men with slicked-back hair wearing nylon jackets with the names of rub-and-tugs, pleasure dungeons, narcotic lounges, and whorehouses emblazoned on the back. They shouted out to Amon as he passed, but in his hurry their words carried no meaning. The sounds of the city—from these curbside enticements to the relentless infohum—had melted into a sonic goo of jibber-jabber that seeped nonsensically into his ears. His heart beat wildly as he shouldered through a crowd clogging the corner of a small intersection; leather on his skin; the smell of tobacco, booze, and dandruff wafting from a head too close.

He launched out across the Neon Void fabric of the street but heard a roar like a jet engine and stumbled to a halt just short of a passing luxury sedan. Through its tinted windows Amon could see the spectral gray outlines of strait-jacketed women bending forward to snort lines of red hot cinders off of mirrors in their laps, before the car ripped away and he dashed to the other side. A line of hosts posed along the sidewalk, thin and effeminate figures in tight blazers with jewels dangling from the sleeves. And Amon felt enervated gazes on him as he charged by, the outrageous sculptures of their bleach-highlighted hairdos passing in a blur; a towering samurai castle surrounded by a moat, a lightning bolt standing vertical on its tip, a banana-shaped spaceship.

For a fleeting second the crowd opened up and he sprinted through at full break, galloping to the left around the next corner. Just ahead he saw his destination at last, highlighted in white by ScrimpNavi. Untouched by the Neon Void, it was a tall building of sparkly gray marble with ramp-like balconies rising diagonally over the street. Amon turned left through the glass doors of the entrance, went across the lobby to an elevator crammed with rowdy salarymen, and squeezed himself in just as the doors closed.

His panting chest pressed against the shoulders of those around him upon expansion, and sweat dribbled down his forehead as the elevator rose. When it stopped at the seventh floor, Amon stumbled out the doors and bent over with his hands on his knees. While his lungs heaved rapidly, a nauseating current of stress and anxiety pulsed through his body, as though it had replaced the blood in his veins. *You only have two minutes, the meeting's just down the hall, get inside, GET!* urged a voice rising from within, somewhere between a thought and a raw impulse.

When he'd almost caught his breath, he raised his head. He was in a dark corridor with a solid white door at the end. Staggering over to it, he saw a sign nailed on the upper part of the door. It was a wooden board spray-painted black and carved into bubble letters that read "Shuffle Boom." Amon could hear muffled singing, bass, and percussion through the walls.

Switching from pastel scribbles to regular digimade Amon, he configured his settings to conceal the sweat, emotion, and exhaustion on his face as a business smile, and tuned the color of his suit black. He then took a moment to collect himself before opening the door.

Tight rows of round tables bathed in a steel blue light covered the black room, men in double-breasted suits and fedoras sitting or standing around them. They smoked cigars and played mahjong, some with their arms around the back of a woman's chair. These dames leaned into the men with the shoulder of their glittering gowns; one leg invariably folded over the other; long cigarillos and the stems of cocktail glasses held between slender fingers. A circular cloud of smoke floated above the heads of the crowd. It seemed to dye the light coming from some hidden source in the ceiling, giving the room its metallic tinge. Everyone faced the far wall, which Amon could not make out in the thick haze, but he heard a slick beat like bossa nova except with grimy, distorted bass blasts and guessed there was a stage. He stepped across the threshold.

The only way across the room was by one of two aisles cutting between the tables on the left and right sides. Waitresses paced these aisles with trays of martinis held at shoulder-height on their palms, the structure of their bodies wavering and destabilizing in time with the music. For a split second, their black dresses clung tight to perfect hourglass figures, a slit up to the waist revealing slim legs. The next moment their contours went through a flash transformation, the shape of torsos and limbs warping and bending fluidly to the beat, holes straight through them forming and closing, like stop-motion inkblot tests. Then they condensed back into sexy form again with every musical rest, the trays of drinks staying unperturbed above them all the while. There were four waitresses undergoing this rhythmic metamorphosis: one changing to the voice, one the high hats, one the bass, and one erratically distorting to the flute solo.

Along the right side was a black bar. Men lined up beside their cocktails on the counter with arms crossed and fedoras tipped low over their faces, striking pugnacious poses. Along the left side was a row of four-seater booths, each with a small window covered by Venetian blinds. From the booth closest to the far wall Amon noticed a hand waving in his direction. Looking over, he saw a black man in a whitish-beige suit sitting at the edge of the seat. Noting the stooped shoulders, Amon guessed it was Sekido and clicked him to find that he was right.

As he approached the aisle, Amon could see another man who sat beside Sekido, the back of his head peaking above the booth. He guessed it to be the recruiter and gulped nervously, a frosty wave propagating down his spinal cord.

Passing the second booth from the entrance, Amon's eyes caught on two odd patrons seated across from one another; a pair of huge demons with blackish-red leather for skin. Wearing tattered, billowing gray trenchcoats, they sipped ink-black cocktails, perfectly-shaped droplets of what looked like blood floating inside; their deformed fingers clutching with spiked claws around the glass stems; their gaping eyes bloodshot in mold-like green; their mouths tilted diagonally with a half-dozen piss-yellow fangs of different sizes curving between and through their swollen lips; their large ears crumpled and pierced with bite marks. One had several gnarly horns twisting up from its bald head, the other hair like rusted steel wool and a small spike of hard flesh jutting from its chin.

Once halfway down the aisle, the tobacco haze opened up and Amon could see the stage. Four figures of condensed smoke sat on stools, one holding a mic, one a stand-up bass, one a flute, and one sitting before a drum set. Tendrils of smoke from the cloud below the ceiling dangled down to touch them, as though sustaining their beings. Stepping around one of the corporeally unstable waitresses, who was placing drinks from her tray on a table to the right of the aisle, Amon reached the far booth, whereupon Sekido stood up to greet him.

With skin of deep brown that verged on pitch, the Liquidation Minister had large, handsome eyes and a flat nose, his hair in neat cornrows. He smiled, his ivory white teeth and beige suit looking sharp in contrast with his complexion. "Glad you could make it on time," he said and patted Amon on the back. Not used to such gestures of intimacy from his boss, the touch made Amon uncomfortable and he flinched slightly. "This is the headhunter I've been telling you about." Sekido gestured to the man in the booth with his upraised palm.

When Amon looked at the recruiter, he was glad he'd set his digimake to hide his emotions, for his eyes went wide and his jaw literally dropped. It was the same man who'd taken him to Sushi Migration. This time he was wearing a thin silk jacket that shimmered from burgundy to dark brown like a hologram. The long collar was flipped up and drooping outwards at the top in an elegant curve. He also wore a black shirt of obsidian fabric that held a rippling reflection of the room between the jacket lapels, like a river at night.

"Good evening," said Amon bowing. The man didn't stand up to return his bow. He didn't even nod. He just kept his eyes fixed on Amon watchfully, his razor-lashes slitting space itself. "I do believe we've met."

"Have we?" replied the recruiter in his Indian accent.

"Yes. Just the other day at that cafe in Ginza. We . . ." The recruiter and Sekido exchanged glances. The ensuing silence was filled by the grimy jazz and the blather of the audience.

"I do believe you're mistaken," said the recruiter.

"Oh. How rude of me," said Amon. "I could have sworn we met, but . . . perhaps I've confused you with . . . someone else."

The resemblance between the man across the table and the one who'd called himself Makesh Adani was uncanny. They had the same milky brown skin; the same intense eyes; the same sharp, feminine lashes; the same accented voice; the same slim, but sturdy build; the same upright posture; even the same taste for subdued but exquisitely-tailored apparel. Admittedly, there were differences too: this man's shoulders looked thicker and more muscular; the curve of his jaw ever-so-slightly more gentle, his nose smaller, his ears bigger. Yet these differences were subtle enough to be mere digimake adjustments, and Amon had to fight off the intuition that this was indeed Makesh. The recruiter had insisted he'd never met Amon, so there was no choice but to accept it for now.

Feeling embarrassed, awkward, and perplexed, Amon took out his business card. He held it between the thumb and pointer finger of both hands, raised it level with his heart, and extended it to the recruiter with a bow, saying: "I'm Amon Kenzaki. A pleasure to meet you."

The card was a compact version of his professional profile, with a 3D picture of his face popping up from it. The recruiter plucked it casually from Amon's hands and put it in the inner pocket of his jacket without even taking a glance. Amon waited a moment for the recruiter to draw his business card and return the introduction, but he simply put his hand on the table and continued to stare silently, his razors shearing. *Slice. Slice.* It was then that Amon noticed he couldn't smell any smoke.

In the wall over the center of the table was one of the covered windows. Beside the wall sat the recruiter. On the table before him was a small gray turntable with a 45 millimeter record on top and, to the left of it, a thin glass of something amber that looked like sherry. To the left of that, a blue cocktail stood before the aisle-side seat from which Sekido had risen. Amon was wondering why the turntable was there when Sekido said, "Please take a seat," and gestured to the spot across from the recruiter. Amon sat down and Sekido took his seat before the cocktail. Facing the two men, Amon felt a strange itching warmth begin to radiate across his back. He wanted to scratch it, but had long ago overcome such urges for frugality's sake, and certainly wouldn't break decorum in front of the recruiter. Within a few seconds, the sensation had subsided.

"As I already explained to you in summary form by FacePhone, before conducting an interview in the traditional sense of the word, there are certain preliminary matters we must venture to confront together, preferably through discussion, although we ought not completely discard the possibility of coming to a resolution by other communicatory means, say the drawing of a meaningful diagram for—"

Suddenly the recruiter put the fingers of his left hand on the edge of the round turntable plate atop which the record rested and spun it counterclockwise, causing Sekido's words to go backwards: "rof margaid lufgnineam a fo gniward . . ." Sekido immediately shut his mouth and turned to look at the recruiter wearing an expression of forlorn confusion Amon had never seen on him before. But the speech he had just uttered continued to reverse itself eerily atop the laughter of mahjong players and the music like some satanic spell: "eht ro refsnart. . ." Then the plate began to gradually lose momentum and the rotation of the record slowed, the syllables stretching and deepening in pitch, until finally it came to a halt with a drawn-out vocal groan that was consumed by the background noises.

"Get to the point," said the recruiter, but Sekido said nothing in response.

"Could we perhaps discuss these issues another time?" Amon said to Sekido, taking advantage of the pause, and stared pleadingly into his eyes as if to say, *You do realize the recruiter is here, don't you?*

"Absolutely not. For you see a crucial intersection of concerns has come into the spotlight this evening and in the interests of satisfying the interests—if you'll excuse this unwieldy turn of phrase—of all parties involved, namely mine, yours, and our headhunter here, not to mention the various institutional apparati of which we are serving as a crucial component, an exchange of information must take place, although when we consider the direction of information transfer, primarily from you to us, we might rethink use of the word 'exchange,' and consider instead—"

"Deatsni redisnoc dna . . ."

The recruiter spun back the record again and glanced sharply at Sekido with narrowed eyes, as if challenging him to speak, but once again the minister was silent. When the rotation began to slow and the reverse speech to stretch out, the recruiter turned his gaze to Amon and said:

"Sekido here has told me many good things about you, and after assessing your track record, I decided that you might be the right person for a position I'm confident you'd be eager to fill. But after hearing about your behavior over the past few days, I now have some doubts. So in order to ensure that you're still eligible, I need to ask you some questions. Now don't worry too much. I understand that this interview must be very nerve-racking for you, but if you haven't done anything wrong, there's nothing to fear. That's why it's of the utmost importance for you to be as honest as you can. Are you ready?"

Amon was feeling déjà vu. Here was the recruiter, the *real* recruiter, saying something so much like what Makesh Adani, the impostor, had said last night, targeting him with razor lashes that seemed to carry the very same menace. Amon remembered how Monju had impersonated Mayuko. That performance had been superficially convincing, but the PhisherKing had messed up on a few crucial details, whereas this copy before him was meticulously fidelitous. The more time he searched, the more similarities he seemed to find, even in areas digimakers had trouble capturing, like mannerisms, bearing, and posture. Yet Amon could do nothing but play his part, for his job was on the line and said: "Understood. I'll do my best."

"Why did you contact the Ministry of Monitoring, the Ministry of Access, the Ministry of Records, and then take a personal call during work time today?"

"Well . . . I . . ." Amon faltered. He was trying to come up with an explanation that wouldn't make him sound irresponsible, but the recruiter's blinks seemed to dissect the river of his consciousness into its component droplets of thought so that meaning refused to flow coherently. In his mad rush to arrive on time, Amon had no time to think of what to say. He'd been counting on using the duration of Sekido's lengthy blathering to come up with something, but by silencing Sekido, the recruiter had put Amon on the spot. The similarity between the recruiter and Makesh threw him off further, for there was no way of guessing at his expectations. As a GATA man, the recruiter would surely value sentiments of devotion to the organization, but this was precisely what had disappointed Makesh the most. The thought of looking into the very same eyes and expressing just such sentiments filled Amon's heart with dread, even if he could force himself to accept that they were two different people. Then there was the problem of honesty. To answer the recruiter's questions truthfully, he would have to tell them about the corruption, but was this the right audience? Who was this nameless man anyway?

Amon's pause was getting awkwardly long, when to his relief, the waitress came over to take their orders. He asked for a chocolate mint cocktail and Sekido another martini. The recruiter ignored the waitress's attentive gaze until she noticed his glass of sherry still standing unsipped on the table and walked off. The whole time he just kept staring at Amon, the blue light on his sharp eyelashes casting grated shadows over his eyes. Something had to be said. Amon took a deep breath, and began.

"Last night just after 12:17 a.m. I received a charge from Fertilex for an action called jubilee that was incredibly expensive. After reviewing my LifeStream, I discovered that I had performed no such action and decided to contact the MegaGlom. I requested a refund, but made no progress due to problems with their customer service system. At work today, I contacted the Ministry of Monitoring to report a . . . mistake."

"So you doubt the GATA system?" asked the recruiter.

"No, no, no," said Amon, waving his hand through the air as if to sweep aside the possibility. "Far from it."

"Then how could you suspect there was a mistake?"

"You have to understand, the Fertilex agents kept hanging up on me and harassing me with spam. There were no other avenues of investigation." Sekido nodded as if to show his understanding, but the recruiter stared relentlessly. *Slice. Slice.* "In any case, I then contacted the Ministry of Access and the Ministry of Records. I was told that no mistake had been made, and soon after I received a call from a Fertilex agent who once again refused to hear my complaint."

"So you accepted the call even after learning that the withdrawal was appropriate? If so, it's hard to believe that you trust GATA as much as you claim."

"Of course I trust GATA. No more respectable organization has ever existed." This was just the type of comment that had irritated Makesh yesterday, but it was impossible to tell how the recruiter was taking it. He just kept staring, slitting space with his lashes, and staring some more. "But you see, what the officials said was contradictory. The Monitor I spoke with told me I hadn't performed an action at all, but my AT readout and bank account said that I had. The property description of jubilee from the Ministry of Access contradicted my LifeStream and my memory. Which one was I supposed to believe?" Sekido gave another understanding nod, but the recruiter just kept stare-slicing.

The instruments of the band stopped, leaving the singer to hum a few notes of breathy a cappella, before expending all her breath and fading into total silence. The crowd began to applaud. Sekido and Amon joined in energetically, while the recruiter only offered slow, intermittent claps. The two men looked towards the stage behind Amon, which he couldn't see from his vantage. It was the first time the recruiter had taken his eyes off him, and Amon felt slightly relieved. Now that the music had stopped, the waitresses had stabilized into sexy, hourglass form, as they carried away trays cluttered with empty glasses and half-eaten toothpicked appetizers. Amon could see the heads of the two demons peeking up above the backrests. The one with the gnarly horns was facing him and he watched it bring a cocktail to its mangled mouth, flick a grayish-green snake tongue into the black liquid, and lap up a blood droplet. A waitress brought Sekido's martini and Amon's brown cocktail with a thin wafer mint floating on top. He took a sip and tasted bitter-sweet syrupy cacao.

"Moving on," said the recruiter. "Sekido showed me surveillance segs from Barrow's residence. What I want to know is why you vandalized GATA property? And if you truly trust information sent to you by GATA, how do you account for your hesitation to crash the CEM?"

"Well . . . the thing about the anadeto . . . I . . . I was under a lot of stress. You see, I-I've admired Barrow for a long time and there's no one on Earth I wanted to crash less. But I knew I had to do it and. . . then I just sort of . . . lost control. And, as you know, Barrow is a very good speaker. Very . . . persuasive. So . . . I—"

"You're saying you suffer from a weak will?"

"No. Not that. It was more like an intuition." He wanted to say that the activist who'd called himself Makesh and looked nearly identical to the recruiter had planted doubt in his mind before the mission. By warning him about impending danger, he had opened Amon to the possibility that Barrow might be innocent. But something told him it was best not to mention the doppelganger.

"So all it took to make you think GATA is lying was a mere intuition?"

"Well . . . I wouldn't say lying exactly . . ." Amon was at a loss for words.

For years he'd envisioned this moment, when he would have a chance to prove he was qualified for greatness. But now that he was face to face with his long-imagined chance, nothing was going the way he'd hoped. Instead of sitting down in a GATA boardroom for a professional chat about his ambitions and skills, he was in this surreal jazz-bar being grilled about his entanglement in a conspiracy. He felt the same disappointment that had afflicted him again and again during the fake interview with Makesh yesterday, but this recruiter was for real; Sekido's presence proved it. The recruiter's questions were just as precise and biting as Makesh's had been, and all the answers Amon had planned out in his mind over the years—almost memorized without really trying—were of no use. *Quit your moping,* he told himself. *If you can't dodge his questions, you'll just have to spit it out the way you did yesterday. The ugly truth is your only chance.*

"Actually it isn't a mere intuition anymore," he said. "I now have evidence that GATA made a mistake."

"Is that so? Well then you can surely provide us with this so-called *evidence*, can't you?"

"Of course."

Amon sent the recruiter and Sekido copies of the segs for his missions against Kitao and Barrow, his talks with Fertilex and GATA officials, along with the files he'd received from Barrow and Monju.

A few seconds after the transfer was complete, the recruiter said: "I don't have time to look through all this. Just explain as briefly as possible what they are and what you think they show."

Taking a deep breath, Amon began. "This collection of AT readouts and LifeStream segments suggests that someone has been systematically tampering with GATA records in order to trick me into assassinating the identity of Chief Executive Minister Lawrence Barrow."

"Suspicion is a natural feeling," said a white man with short, orangish hair who sat in Sekido's seat and spoke with Sekido's voice. Amon's spine stiffened with a jolt of fright as his mind registered this sudden exchange of bodies. Wearing a black turtle neck beneath a green velvet jacket, the man's lips were delicately thin, his white cheeks dusted with freckles, his eyes pale green, his shoulders stooped. With the zen-garden epidermal texture, his freckles looked like orange jewels interspersed in sand dunes. "A healthy feeling, maybe even adaptational in fact within those societies of which we often read in the history books where the laws are unjust and the people no better than slaves, or serfs, or peons, or whatever terminology you and like-minded radicals choose to use. But the fact is, in this Free World of ours . . ."

Taken aback by his boss's rapid face change, Amon lost track of what he was saying. Over the seven years since they'd met, Sekido had only changed his face three times, yet this was his fourth face of the week and second of the day (maybe third if you counted that mask of lurid darkness on the phone earlier). *What's going on with him?* Amon wondered. *Is there some reason for this increase in frequency?* But reined in his thoughts before they could wander too far astray. *Now is not the time for speculating about individual eccentricities*, he told himself. *This is an interview. No! This is THE interview. Stay sharp!*

"I'm not talking about a feeling," broke in Amon, taking a cue from the recruiter and cutting off Sekido in the middle of whatever he was saying. "I'm talking about hard evidence. Before you doubt me, I urge you to look at the files."

The recruiter darted his eyes about and mumbled commands, apparently examining the files. Whether following the recruiter's lead or Amon's recommendation, Sekido began to twitch his fingers and do the same.

With the two men focused on their tasks, Amon stuck the middle and pointer finger of his right hand between two slats in the Venetian blind and pried them apart to peek through. There he saw a window with square panes set in a wooden grid. Through the glass was a gothic cityscape rendered in black and white, like New York in some noir classic, the little white flecks of aged film flickering in his vision like snow. As he looked out at the grim, gray skyscrapers, Amon could hear the band pick up their pace, the flutist doing syncopated stutters over grimy bossa swing. Someone at the back let out a whistle from between fingertips and the shrill laughter of dames pierced through the music.

"You've found some compelling evidence here," said the recruiter, drawing Amon's gaze back to the table. "But I have to wonder: Where did you get the segs not part of your own LifeStream?"

"From a personal connection of mine," Amon said evasively.

"You're going to have to be more specific," said the recruiter with a razor blink that seemed to warn of the danger in not complying. "This information obviously has very serious implications."

"We had hoped to traverse quickly through the preliminaries, hear your excuses for misusing work time today, and dive—if you will excuse my figurative verbiage—beyond the main interview, for the express purpose of removing the shroud over facets of the administrative significance in this conundrum capable of facilitating more efficient movement through the relevant processes without denying certain difficulties or, to put it more mildly, inconveniences inherent in the promotional outline of our advancement strategization plan, that have—"

Sekido seemed to be reaching a new pinnacle of incoherence when the recruiter pressed the start button on the turntable, put his middle and pointer finger near the center of the record, and began rewinding it rapidly, the reverse words speeding up into a high-pitched whirr. *Shrip-shrip-shrip-shrip.* "As I said at the beginning, I expect total honesty. If you can't provide straightforward answers, there will be no interview."

"I acquired the segs from Kai Monju," Amon blurted out.

"What?!" shouted Sekido, jerking back in surprise as though from an electric shock. "The PhisherKing?!" Even the recruiter's eyes went wide.

"Please don't misunderstand me," said Amon, cutting in before Sekido could initiate his next ramble. "After Fertilex brushed me off and the GATA officials dismissed my suspicions, there were unaccountable inconsistencies. Barrow's readout contradicted the info I got from GATA and the jubilee property contradicted what my LifeStream showed. I thought about seeking an investigation through GATA but I was afraid."

"Are you suggesting a conspiracy?"

"Conspiracy? I don't know. But I couldn't just dismiss it all as coincidence. Three cash crashes at GATA in one week plus my jubilee is too much. I never thought I would deal with a Phisher, but I had little choice for recourse. And it turned out I was right. Now we know that Barrow was assassinated and Rick committed suicide."

"Suicide! Who said anything about suicide?" bellowed Sekido, who had reverted back to the cornrowed black man in a beige suit.

"I guess you haven't watched that far yet. That's what one of the segs shows. Rick jumped in front of a train last night. I tried to tell you earlier on the phone, but I didn't get the chance."

"If you've in fact understood the situation correctly," said the recruiter. "Then who is behind it all? And why?"

"I have no idea." Amon paused to think for a moment before continuing. "But when I consider the meaning of jubilee, the return of property, and everything the activist I met yesterday kept saying about how terrible GATA is and how he wants to make a new society, I begin to suspect that this whole plot could be coordinated by terrorists, people who want to take away our freedom."

Amon felt strange saying "terrorist," an archaic word that smacked of pre-Free Era politics, but the words were just spilling out. The dual pressures of his yearning to confide and his hope to impress the recruiter with the honesty he had requested were bursting the barricades of his discretion from the inside.

"Who is this activist you speak of?" demanded the recruiter, his voice suddenly doubling in volume.

"I don't know who he really is, but he called himself Makesh Adani and . . . he looked just like you."

The recruiter frowned, turned towards Sekido, and both men began to mumble while twitching their fingers, apparently conferring by silent message.

Amon turned his head towards the crowd, as if to grant the two men a bit of privacy, but made sure to watch them out of the corner of his eye. The more time he spent with the headhunter, Amon reflected, the more he was convinced that he and Makesh were one and the same. Otherwise it was hard to believe that one of them wasn't violating the other's image rights.

When the two men had finished conferring, they turned back towards Amon and Sekido spoke first. "That this whole scenario is a complexity among complexities is an assertion difficult, if not impossible, to fully and without any reluctance deny. However, after a show of compliant sincerity on your part, albeit with a full realization of potential consequences and ramifications within the mode of contextual positioning unique to your personal milieu—if you'll pardon the French expression—we have hit upon new considerations, hitherto dubious, as of now, reasonable. Now to direct my locution more closely to the heart of—"

Shrip-shrip-shrip-shrip. The recruiter clicked off the turntable and released the record, which came to an abrupt stop.

"We appreciate your honesty and recognize the need for investigation. Until we have more information, we cannot be certain of your innocence, but have decided for the time being that we would like to conduct the interview as originally planned."

"Thank you very much," said Amon with a rush of relief. He bowed deeply to the tabletop, careful not to topple his cocktail. "I promise you that by the end of the investigation, my innocence will be assured."

The waitress returned. Sekido ordered another martini and Amon, feeling like a switch to something more savory, ordered the same. The recruiter's glass of amber liquid still stood untouched on the table, and the waitress left. Amon had just sipped down the sweet, grainy dregs of his chocolate-mint cocktail when the recruiter said: "To begin with, please tell us a bit about yourself."

It was a vague question, but Amon was ready for it. He had been ready for years.

"As I imagine you already know, I obtained a perfect concentration score and was admitted into the Liquidation Ministry seven years ago. During that interval my proficiency in detecting bankruptcy danger cases has steadily increased, and . . ."

As he was talking, Amon's AT readout caught his eye. To his surprise, his balance had gone up significantly—much more than the amount of his regular salary—which would have come in several minutes ago for his pay hour at 9 p.m. Guessing that Sekido had given him a bonus, Amon felt his confidence return and his words began to flow with renewed spirit.

"My liquidations are fast, do no harm to the targets, and have not garnered any media attention. Moreover, I believe my promotion to Identity Executioner reflects the ministry's trust in my . . ."

But Amon's tongue began to fail him when he looked more closely at his account activity. All he was doing was sitting, breathing, blinking, talking, sipping his martini, paying the seat charge, but his balance was dropping rapidly and steadily.

"You have anticipated my next question," said the recruiter. "Where do you see yourself in the future?"

"Without a doubt I'll be serving at GATA Tower, and if you'll be so kind as to give me the chance, I hope to . . ."

As Amon gave his answer, he used his hands hidden beneath the table to twitch open a more detailed breakdown. There he found a multitude of charges for strange ImmaNet services. According to his readout, he was playing slots, pachinko, and poker simultaneously at five different casinos. He had purchased worthless properties like black holes in the distant reaches of space, obscure words like "mazomany", and DNA strings for life forms that didn't exist. Several times he had bought real estate high and sold low. He was subscribed to a paparazzi search engine and was looking up the morning routines of celebrities. He now had memberships for a kick-boxing club in Chiang Mai, a go-kart track in Milwaukee, and three nail salons in Osaka. Nowhere did he find jubilee, but this brought little relief: the second-by-second charges for all these transactions had already consumed his bonus and the remainder of his replenished regular account; it was now eating away his savings.

"That's enough about your plans. Now tell me what you do with your free time."

"I'm dedicated to the principles of frugal living and . . ."

Once again, Amon was glad his emotions were hidden, as the icy flame of horror seared through his bowels. He was struggling to hold himself together as he talked about his efforts to channel his concentration talents towards humanitarian ends, when he noticed something unbelievable.

Glancing down at his lap, he saw one right hand and two left hands resting there. Both left hands protruded from the same wrist, partially overlapping with each other in a single spatial location. But while he could control one of them, the other was moving rapidly irrespective of his will. Amon recognized the movements as the gesture language he used for interfacing with the ImmaNet. He turned up the opacity of his desktop and saw a minimized window in the corner of his eye almost hidden from sight:

Order 12 raw blowfish: Cancel   Confirm

His phantom left hand did the command for *confirm*, the window disappeared and his balance dropped.

Just then, Amon felt a tingling sensation in his ears and mouth. Mindfulator was reminding him that someone was talking to him and that he should respond.

"Are you listening?" asked the recruiter.

"I'm very sorry," said Amon. "Could you repeat that?"

"Wasn't he just bragging about perfecting his concentration?" said the recruiter to Sekido, who shook his head.

Amon wondered whether he should say something about his hand, but the last thing he wanted was to admit he'd been infected and interrupt the interview, his only chance to rise at GATA. Virus protection on BodyBanks was almost flawless, except for rare cases of short range attacks, which coincided with epidermal stimulation and were easy to notice. He felt like a BioPen child who'd gotten all dirty with malware by rolling about in the muck of dubious websites.

"I'll repeat myself, but don't expect me to be so generous again. Why are you so eager for promotion?"

"I have confidence in my potential and want to use it to the utmost. The more responsibility I'm granted . . ."

The phantom hand in his lap kept wriggling like a beached fish. It was now trying to order a crate of rare wild mushrooms from the south of France. When Amon tried to cancel the order, only his right hand responded and he messed up the command. He could move his left hand, but the ImmaNet no longer tracked it. It had been cut loose from the digital world and appeared before him in the naked flesh, looking bulbous and hairy in comparison to the handsomely digimade contours of the phantom version.

"So you were saying about your contributions," the recruiter said impatiently.

"Um . . . well . . ." Amon scrambled for words as he scrolled backwards through his readout to try and pinpoint the moment he had contracted the virus. There was something. His balance had gone up suddenly just after 9 p.m., but there was no listing for a bonus or salary transfer from GATA. In fact, there was no listing for any transaction whatsoever. A large amount of money had gone into his account, but for some reason, his readout hadn't recorded it.

What?!

Abruptly, Amon leapt to his feet in the aisle, bumping the table with his hip, the glasses atop shaking, the turntable needle hopping off the record with a pop.

"What's going on with you, Kenzaki?" asked Sekido. "Are you feeling ill?" Now that he was standing up, Amon's hands were visible, and the two men stared at the convulsions of the phantom.

"Why haven't I been paid my salary yet?" Amon said, his flesh tantalized with cold fear.

"Well, Amon," said Sekido. "We were intending to trade words about that particular matter, for you see, with your new job, if you're accepted onto the team that is, you'll have a different, *ahem*, much higher salary."

"That's got nothing to do with it. Protocol clearly states that employees must be paid on time. You know that! Where's my fucking pay?" As he cast a challenging glare into Sekido's brown eyes, they changed to pale green and a visual transformation spread out from those two points over his body; a wave of white, freckled skin rippling across the black; his cornrows turning to short orange hair; his beige suit to the velvet green jacket and black turtleneck. Somehow, this metamorphosis jogged Amon's memory, and a detail in Rick's readout that he had overlooked suddenly leapt to his mind. Although Rick's final moments had occurred around 9 p.m., there was no record of him receiving his salary. His balance had simply dropped and dropped until he committed suicide.

"Shit!" he barked aloud. Now Amon realized why he had felt an itch when he sat at the booth and reached around to his back where Sekido had patted him. He removed a circular object that clung there. It was a leach with a ring of tiny red teeth on one side, its black body pulsating in his hand. Amon flung it across the room without looking and hissed, "You infected me! You fucking infected me!"

A sliver of clarity came to him in a flash. His boss had given him a parasite, a biological device that hacked into BodyBanks through the skin. It had infected him with a virus that seized control of the sensors in his hand and transmitted data that mimicked its motions, fooling the ImmaNet into registering actions he had never chosen. His biological hand was a worthless hunk of meat now; he could almost feel it festering there on the end of his wrist.

Clearly, the money sent into his account at 9 p.m., the moment Sekido touched him, had been compensation for credicrimes: hacking and infecting. The House of Blinding had made the transfer, but the Ministry of Records had hidden the transaction from his readout, just as it had hidden the deposit that paid for Amon's crimes during his mission against Barrow. Amon didn't doubt that it was Atupio—in other words Fertilex—that was funding the deeds of the Archivists and Sekido's betrayal. To silence Amon, Sekido had delayed his salary and done the same to Rick just before his suicide. No! Not suicide—could they have altered Rick's records too? Could it have been murder?

"What on Earth are you talking about?" said Sekido.

When Amon didn't respond, Sekido did some sort of hand gesture. Out of the corner of his eye, Amon saw the trenchcoated demons rise from their seats. As they lumbered down the aisle towards him, he noticed their great stature for the first time, their foreheads reaching the smoky cloud. There was no mistaking their heavy, plodding gait. The one stroking its chin-spike was Tororo, and the one with horns twisting up into white obscurity was Freg. Amon watched the actions of the phantom hand on his desktop. He could see it making all sorts of mistakes: opening the wrong window, closing programs accidentally, changing the names of files. The virus had not yet mastered some of the unique gestures in his personalized command language, although it was gradually learning by trial and error, and he hated to think what damage it might do when operating at full strength.

"I regret to inform you, Amon," said the recruiter pursing his lips, "that I've decided you're not the right person for the job. Please believe me when I say that I was truly impressed with your work history and skill set, but under the present circumstances, our interview will have to stop here."

"A conclusive finale to this genial conference of ours, that is to say, an ending of ginormous significance, has come to pass, and yet it would . . ."

Amon ignored Sekido and turned to face his approaching teammates, their contorted, monster shadows upon him under the blue light.

"Freg, Tororo. What are you doing?"

"Grr," growled Tororo and Freg laughed, revealing his yellowing, jagged braids of teeth stained black in patches presumably from the cocktail.

"Sorry Amon," said Freg, with a sympathetic look in his gaping, moldy eyes; his hand hovering over the duster at his hip. "Please come quietly with us. You know we've got to do this discretely."

So they had come to crash him.

"Listen to me. I'm not bankrupt. The AT readout they gave you is fake," Amon pleaded as he frantically wracked his brain for a way to escape and the spasms of his phantom hand threatened to make this lie of bankruptcy into a truth.

"Fake?" said Tororo, pausing for a moment to scan something in his view. "It looks pretty real to me. It's got the stamp of authenticity and everything." Freg nodded his assent.

"The Ministry of Records has been corrupted somehow. These men," said Amon, gesturing to the booth beside him "have conspired to cash crash Rick, Barrow, and Kitao, and now they've infected me with a virus to ruin me too."

"Men?" said Freg, with a frown. "What men? You mean Sekido-san?"

Amon did a double take on the booth and saw that the recruiter and his turntable had vanished. His glass of sherry still stood half full on the table, and Amon realized that he had not sipped it once the whole interview. For of course, a mere binary figment could never have picked it up.

"There was a man there that Sekido told me was a GATA recruiter . . . But I guess he was just a figment and . . . Please let me show you my records. They prove that I'm not even close to bankruptcy." Now he understood the desperation Barrow must have felt when he said something similar to Amon just yesterday and only wished that he had Barrow's liquid tongue.

"I will not authorize anyone—and neither of you is an exception—to listen to this magnificently, enormous, and whopping load of neurosis. He's as delusional as a syphilitic butterfly. I do not hesitate to remind you that he just now said 'men,' as though another living, breathing individual were in the booth here with myself, when it's clear to anyone with eyes, or in lieu of these, at the very least some sophisticated contraption of vicarious, visual simulation that—"

"Just let me show you my readout. I promise you'll change your mind about this."

"You're not seriously asking us to neglect our jobs, Amon, are you?" asked Tororo, contorting the blackish-red leather of his face into a scowl that Amon took for an expression of pity. "We always liked working with you, but we know you understand the call of duty better than anyone."

There was no denying his words. Before jubilee, say just the previous week, if the situation had been reversed, Amon would have dusted them already without hesitation.

"But I'm not bankrupt! I can't be! Just hear me out for a second. This mission is pretty strange, don't you think? Why would Sekido be here having drinks with the target? Why would he order you to compromise discretion by crashing me here in this crowded place? You know how frugal I am. Do you really think I'd go bankrupt so quickly without warning? And knowing my personality, do you think I'd deny my bankruptcy? Don't you think I'd be more ashamed than anyone? And don't you think it's odd that Rick crashed just yesterday? I bet you've never heard of Liquidators crashing, but two partners in two days, plus Barrow and Kitao? And you know what? Actually, Rick isn't bankrupt. He's dead. Sekido killed him and I can prove it!"

"Receipt of any files, data, or other information media from this bankrupt will result in the termination," said Sekido who was the cornrowed black man again, "without further delay or warning of any kind, of your employment contract, along with all attached benefits for—"

"We don't want to hurt you, man," said Freg, apparently taking a cue from Amon and interrupting Sekido. "But we can't violate protocol. You know that. So just take the duster out slowly," he gestured to the holster at Amon's hip, "and put it on the floor."

"Yeah, sure. But only if you look at my files first."

The two demons didn't respond. Amon knew they couldn't explicitly disobey Sekido, but their pause told him his plea had made an impact and they might be willing to give him a chance. He unclipped the holster with the gun inside from his belt and crouched down to put it on the floor, under the watchful eye of his teammates. But when he went to make a copy of his readout, the phantom hand immediately closed it. He tried several more times, but each attempt led to the same result. "I can't send you the file because Sekido infected me. Look!" He pointed at the ever more spasmodically wriggling end of his limb, a beached fish now in its death throes. "The virus has control of my left hand and keeps cancelling all my commands."

"Madness! Insanity! Delirium! Take note once more that not minutes earlier he said 'men' as though there was another being of the human sort present, and now behold! That out of control appendage of his is proof much more indubitable than any putative evidence taken from some readout, without a doubt non-existent or at least in a dubious ontological category, that he is having a breakdown of the nervous sort, not without—"

For the first time ever that Amon could remember, Sekido seemed to realize that his speech was going nowhere, cut himself short and said: "Dust him now!"

Slowly but decisively, Tororo began to reach for his duster.

Amon snapped the fingers of his left hand to be sure. As he thought, no transaction appeared on his readout.

With his right hand, Amon faked a punch towards Tororo's bulging gut, making him flinch, and drove a left uppercut square into his reddish-black nose. The band's song was just then rising to its climax in a sibilant shimmer of high hats and quivering pulses of flute, but he could still hear the crunch of breaking cartilage and bone. Amon saw that he hadn't been charged for assault; the BodyBank had detected the motion of his arm, but not the impact of his hand.

As Tororo brought his palms up reflexively to cup the black blood gushing from his nose, Amon reached for the demon's waist with his left hand to draw the duster from where it was hidden beneath the folds of his tattered trenchcoat. Stunned by the blow, Tororo began to stumble about, his shoulder barreling over a man standing on the edge of the aisle who then slammed into a table, toppling cocktails and sending mahjong pieces scattering onto the floor. Freg hesitated a moment in surprise before reaching for his duster, giving Amon just enough of a head start to whip Tororo's up first.

Freg's hand froze, fingers on the grip of the still-sheathed duster, as he looked up fearfully into the barrel aimed his way. The grimy bass, bossa drumming, and skittering flute began to drift apart in rhythmic space, the beat disintegrating as the instrumentalists faltered one by one. Amon could feel a crowd's worth of eyes on him, as they watched this tall man in a black suit hold up two huge demons, one bleeding and one armed. The singer stopped and the music went quiet, leaving behind the panicked whispers of the crowd. A hush soon smothered these as well, until, aside from the steady drip of Tororo's black blood, silence reigned. The whole room held its breath, waiting for Amon to make his move. His hand shook as he watched his account balance drop from all the actions of his phantom hand—purchase of bonds in collapsing dictatorships, a lease on a new hummer, the rights to racial insults hurled at aboriginals. Soon his dream savings would be down to half of what it had been that morning. He had to be willing to fire or Freg was going to dust him, but if he fired, the fines would bankrupt him legitimately and a different Liquidator would dust him. Whatever happened, it seemed his fate lay in the bankdeath camps.

Then suddenly Amon's duster went off and a hazy whirl of particulate flew tinkling at Freg, who toppled to the floor with a deep, reverberating howl. Amon stared in astonishment at the barrel as it kept firing round after round, the dust blasting straight down the aisle, past the patrons and waitresses cowering beneath tables, to hit the wall and disperse into the corners of the room. *Why is this happening? I'm not pressing the trigger.* Then he realized that the phantom hand must have activated the device remotely. Being an algorithm programmed to undertake the most costly actions possible, the virus had seized on the chance to get him fined. Before it could do any more damage to his account or the bystanders, Amon flung the duster away with revulsion as though it was a poisonous snake and watched it bounce beneath a table to his left.

Still holding his nose with his left hand, blackness trickling between his fingers, Tororo bent over to reach for the duster, as the cowering men and women scrambled out of his way. Amon charged down the aisle and clubbed him in the temple with his left fist, knocking him to the floor and away from the weapon. But Tororo sprang to his feet with surprising speed for a man of his size and put up his warped, red fists. He threw an underhand right for Amon' chin, which he blocked and countered with a kick to the side of the kneecap. Unfazed, the giant grabbed Amon's collar with his left hand, put the underside of his right elbow under his armpit, crouched low, and twisted around to hurl him over his shoulder—all in one fluid motion. Amon went aerial and slammed down hard atop a mat of prone bodies, someone's elbow jabbing into his back. Winded, he got up slowly and Tororo was quickly upon him, but Amon sprang away into the aisle and put up his dukes. Tororo came at him again with huge grasping hands, but Amon stepped back, keeping his distance from a man who could surely overpower him in a test of strength. Once Tororo's fists were up, the two men started doing footwork back and forth down the aisle, trading punches and kicks, deking and blocking. Amon tried to favor his disconnected left hand to conserve funding, but he was right-handed and could hardly defend himself against this giant with a single appendage. He had no time to check his AT readout but imagined he could see the fine for his violent crimes appearing as numbers in the air each time a blow connected—a billion yen roundhouse here, a trillion yen headbutt there—years and years of frugality disappearing in a concussive instant. Tororo was bigger and stronger, but the blood loss and pain of his broken nose seemed to be wearing on him, and although Amon never managed to land another direct hit in the same spot, his jabs occasionally pushed the giant's blockers into his face, making him cringe.

With a lunge, Tororo went low to grab at Amon's waist, but Amon backed off and pushed on the top of his head to send him tumbling chin-first to the floor. The course of their brawl had brought them back to Freg's inert form. The fallen Liquidator's duster was nowhere to be seen, but Amon spotted his own holster resting beneath a nearby table and kicked it spinning along the aisle towards the front wall. He chased it down, dodged past a waitress stranded with a tray of drinks, picked it up, drew the duster with his right hand, and did an about face.

Tororo was on his feet now, frozen in fear of the weapon as twin streams of blackness trickled from his nose and newly-split chin. Freg lay unconscious on the floor. The waitresses, patrons, and bartenders were all crouching low beneath tables, chairs, booths, and the bar. The musicians had abandoned their instruments on the stage, perhaps gone out a back door, perhaps dissipating into the smoke cloud that fed them. And taking cover behind a table flipped on its side, Amon could see the half-concealed form of Sekido in his Caucasian guise.

He wanted to go over and question him, to beat the answers out of him if necessary. But the minister might call in more Liquidators, and with the virus in his hand, it wouldn't be long before Amon went under. Now was not the time.

He opened the door and stepped out of Shuffle Boom.

The elevator arrived just as Amon staggered panting to the end of the corridor. Of the dozen or so people inside, two got off. Amon felt the eyes of the remaining riders glued to him as he boarded and took his place in the center facing the doors. Although he'd set his digimake to edit out emotion, he hadn't specified what to do about clothes, and the right lapel of his jacket was visibly torn, several buttons of his shirt popped.

With his two left hands, one of them convulsing, and the black blood spattered all over, Amon was an odd sight to say the least. Yet with his heart pounding, his nerves all juiced up on stress hormones, the last thing on his mind was appearances. He held his breath to fend off a sigh as the doors closed and the elevator began to descend.

He watched his account balance and noticed that it rose now and then, although no record of a deposit appeared on his readout. He supposed that Sekido—or more likely his employer Fertilex—was being forced to compensate him second-by-second for continuing to *infect* him, but that this credicrime was being illegally omitted from his feed just as when Sekido had stuck the parasite on his back. Sadly, this moderate income was not nearly enough to match the costs incurred by the actions of his phantom hand. On his readout, he could see a couple of instances where it had tried unsuccessfully to log onto a platinum search engine. Several seconds of such a search would have bankrupted him for sure, but the virus lacked Amon's password for making big online transactions and was unable to impoverish him in a single blow. Instead it kept whittling down his funds, bit by bit. Of course Amon wasn't supposed to be paying for any of these actions, as he hadn't chosen them. The virus was tricking the Monitors into registering them as volitional by wielding the sensors in his hand. He tried to contact the Ministry of Monitoring and inform them of this error, but found that his communication apps—FacePhone, and text—had been paralyzed by the virus. Its designers had likely built in this function in anticipation of such countermeasures, and Amon could only watch helplessly as his balance continued to drop ever more rapidly with the accumulation of unchosen services. Already, less than half his savings remained. At this rate he would be in debt within seconds and bankrupt before he reached the ground floor. His only chance was to find an antidote and quickly.

Amon tried to open an anti-virus app called Code Dr., but his left hand immediately closed it. He tried again and it closed it again. With only his right hand connected, Amon's interfacing was half its usual speed, and now that the virus had fully adjusted to his gesture language, the phantom hand was an even match. So try as he might, Code Dr. cancelled every command before he could initialize it. Forcing the virus into this stalemate was better than doing nothing because his left hand couldn't waste any more of his money while engaged in thwarting his right. But now he was being charged for *opening* and *closing* the programs over and over, on top of all the membership fees, etc. The pace of depletion had slackened, but his financial doom would soon be assured all the same.

"Sixth floor. The doors will open. Take care," said a high-pitched granny voice. As the doors opened and several people got off, an idea came to Amon and clicked the icon to activate eye-dialing. The phantom hand tried to close it immediately, but in the split second before it succeeded, Amon did an eye twitch to open Code Dr. As he expected, the virus algorithm prioritized deactivating anti-virus software, and while the phantom hand was closing Code Dr., Amon activated voice interfacing with his hand before re-opening Code Dr. with his eye. While his eye and the phantom went back and forth opening and closing Code Dr., Amon used gesture and verbal commands to go on the web, download another copy of the same app, and install it in a different location. He then opened the copy with his eye and the original version with his hand. Only able to do one thing at a time, the phantom closed the original, at which point Amon targeted the copy of Code Dr. on his left hand with an eye twitch and mumbled a voice command to execute "cure." The phantom hand did a wriggle to try and close the copy, but Code Dr. had already diagnosed that area of his body as infected, and didn't authorize the closure. His left hand had been completely disabled, along with the virus.

"Fifth floor. The doors will open. Take care."

As passengers got on and off, Code Dr. began to inject the most up to date medicine into his hand and the phantom squirmed more frantically than ever before, like an ant with one leg pinned. Amon was still unable to use his left hand, but at least the virus was neutralized for now, and he breathed a sigh of relief (not regret! don't get sucked into the regret!).

Yet this feeling faded immediately when the reality of his situation hit him: he was a hunted man now; Tororo and Freg were in no condition for a chase, but Sekido and his accomplices would surely call in others, for they couldn't let Amon roam the city with the information he possessed. He had to find a way to disappear.

Amon remembered many occasions when bankrupts had tried to evade him and Rick using all sorts of clever tricks. These had merely delayed the inevitable, for there was nowhere they could hide with their locations disclosed. But Amon's case was different, he realized, since he was not actually bankrupt and would still be hidden by blinding. Then again, Barrow's location had been provided when Amon went on the mission even though he wasn't bankrupt. This meant Amon's pursuers might have had a way to circumvent blinding. But he doubted this. Whatever resources and influence they possessed, this was too expensive. More likely they had watched Barrow by accessing the sensors in his residence and then used this data to fabricate a location file for Amon that mimicked the Liquidation Ministry format. *Stalking* and *surveilling* were immensely expensive infringements of anonymity rights, but Fertilex could surely afford it for a short time. And if they were willing to invest in spying on Barrow, they were likely watching Amon at that very moment through the sensors in the elevator. *Right!*

Taking a hint from one of the bankrupts he'd crashed, Amon accessed the blueprint for the elevator and sent his perspective feeling around inside for the access nodes that connected the interior space to the ImmaNet. A net of tiny dots spread across the ceiling represented mics, cameras, heat detectors, motion detectors and, amongst them, the nodes. Amon clicked on one to open its specs, copied its serial number into a search engine, and delved into the inner corridors of hackspace. There he found a cheap hardware crack, bought it, selected all the nodes, and pressed execute. This incurred hefty fines for *purchasing contraband, hacking, vandalism*, but Amon didn't even flinch; this was his only chance to get away.

Once the crack took effect, the nodes shut down and the elevator was disconnected from the ImmaNet. As the chamber descended, the appearance of the walls, floor, ceiling, and passengers began to jitter and peel away from the naked forms underneath, revealing cracks, stains, wrinkles for a split second until even the digital light was torn off. A visual echo of their bodies and the space around them was left behind in the tunnel above, where it floated like a stranger's apartment in the night.

"Fourth floor. The doors will open. Take care." The elevator stopped and the room began to jerkily rematerialize, pixel by pixel. Minuscule dots of skin, hair, clothing, wall, and shadow splattered their way back into place, gradually filling in more and more of the interior, as though god were machine-gunning the universe into existence out of that first dim chaos. The moment the doors opened, full network connection was established and the overlay caught up with the elevator; color, and texture pouring back into the space so that everything looked just as it had seconds before. Half the passengers got off, half remained frozen in fear and confusion, and a dozen boarded, unaware of what had just transpired. As soon as the doors closed, Amon's visual field wavered and shook, but remained just barely tacked to the naked world when he pressed the emergency stop icon. With the elevator stalled, he backed up against the doors, drew his duster, pointed it into the crowded chamber, and shouted: "This is a nerve duster. Do exactly as I say or feel the worst pain you can imagine. Got it?!" The passengers all backed up against the four walls as far from Amon and the weapon as possible, as if repelled from him by opposing magnets. Now that he had their undivided attention, Amon contined: "Give me exclusive rights to the digimakes you're wearing now!"

Immediately, file transfer windows began to pop up one after another, and Amon consented to them all before releasing the stop icon. The elevator dropped and the room was torn back up into the tunnel, leaving them in darkness once again. "Now start moving clockwise around the elevator. Go! Go! Go!"

Saying this, he slid the duster back into its holster, removed it from his belt, hid it in the inner pocket of his jacket, switched to a generic digimake template he had on his hard-drive, and set his height for average. He then joined the fray, milling blindly about. Almost immediately there was a jam and someone bumped him from behind. He found himself falling over into a heap of bodies, his left arm and right leg lodged somewhere under the tangled mass, so that he was pinned down.

"Third floor. The doors will open. Take care." Visibility flooded back into the room as the doors opened. Aside from two men squeezed into the corners, everyone in the elevator was rendered immobile in the tight pile-on. Seeing this, the salarymen lining up outside hesitated, thought better of boarding, and the doors closed.

Once back in darkness, Amon shouted: "On your feet! Now!" He could feel bodies yanking and bumping him this way and that as they all sought to pry themselves loose. Eventually the weight pinning his arm was removed, and he used his hand to pull on someone's ankle and draw his leg out before doing a pushup on his neighbors to get to his feet.

"Second floor. The doors will open. Take care." The elevator stopped and the room splattered into partial visibility. Amon could see now that the passengers all looked different than before. By depriving them of their own likeness, he had forced them to change their digimake. His plan was working. Concealed in the ImmaNet blackout, he had gone incognito and scrambled himself in with the others. Now it would be nearly impossible for Amon's surveillers to guess which one was him.

Doors opened. Light. Many already on board eyed the doorway eagerly, but as though afraid to get singled out by Amon, no one made a move. They just stood there panting, and the half-dozen salarymen who boarded gave them queer looks. The doors closed and the overlay began to jitter, but Amon deactivated the virus in the nodes before he could accrue any more fines. It had served its purpose well.

The elevator dropped, the newly-arrived passengers fiddled around online, and the others glanced furtively from face to face as if trying to discern which one was Amon's. Not one of the eyes paused on him and he imitated them, his gaze darting about as if he didn't know which one he himself was.

When the doors opened into the lobby, Amon poured out with the rest and slipped through the exit, where he melded into the crowd like a pixel into the adscape.

18

THE OPEN SOURCE ZONE

The black clouds that had been hanging over the metropolis finally opened up. First a sprinkle of Korean soap opera fell—crystal tears of drama that spattered onto the pavement into vaguely glowing spots. Then the InfoRain picked up its intensity. A concentrate of nuclear bomb tests, churning vats of milk, and powder for baby's bum encapsulated in each drop. In response, thousands of umbrellas unfurled upwards. Baritone documentary narrators, big band swing, and laugh tracks *pitter-pattered* sibilantly on the taut plastic; sumo bouts, transvestite pageants, and swirls of alphanumerics dripped off the round edges.

Amon ran through the wet streets. He kept to the edge of the curb where the crowd was thinner, the oncoming pedestrians clearing aside when they spotted his tall-charging form. To his left, headlights flashed by, one after another. The interior of the cars was hidden behind windshield glare until the hood was right beside him and the angle of light revealed the driver's face for a split second before vanishing into the oblivion of Tokyo night. To his right, other faces no more memorable streamed steadily past, a shroud of dead TV static obscuring their features from hairline to chin. Across the sidewalk, an enormous mall ran for blocks and blocks. Its outer walls were a jigsaw puzzle of miscellaneous women's merchandise glued seamlessly together—necklaces, bracelets, bras, underwear, perfume bottles, flowers, lipstick, purses, vases, dresses—this irregular cliff-face of products rising twelve stories. Windows of pink glass peeked out every few meters, the whole structure pulsating gently as though breathing.

The rain had not soaked through Amon's jacket yet, but he could feel the cool droplets on his head, and his skin was moist with sweat trapped under his clothes. His lungs were pumping to capacity and his hard soles clacked rhythmically on the wet sidewalk when he felt a tingle in his legs. He thought it might be the virus making a comeback, until he saw a window saying it was Mindfulator. The app was warning him he might slip into traffic and advised him to slow down or get into the middle of the sidewalk. He turned it off. Ignoring its advice was undoubtedly dangerous, but this time the risk was worth taking. Almost any risk was worth taking now if he could get to where he was going just a little bit faster.

Once out of the building in Kabukicho several minutes earlier, Amon had begun to walk. He had wanted to run—anything to get away quickly—but was worried that this would draw the eye of his surveillers. The fine for keeping the likenesses he had stolen was eating away his last bit of savings. So, once he had left behind the Neon Void, he sent them back to their original owners. All except one. This he put on. He didn't throw his perspective outside his body to see what he looked like. He didn't care. He just needed another skin to hide in and it hardly mattered whose.

For anyone watching from the elevator sensors, Amon had disappeared between floors four and three, when he had forced everyone inside to change digimakes and scrambled himself amongst them under cloak of the ImmaNet blackout. Now they would have to track dozens of people at once to find him, and this went beyond the crimes of mere *stalking, peeping, tracking*, into the legal category of *mass surveillance*, which carried exponentially higher fines since it cut against the very idea of anonymity. Amon knew just how much higher as he'd been deployed with Rick several years earlier to crash a paranoid CEO who'd gone bankrupt from keeping a constant eye on his whole board of directors. And after doing a quick online search for the estimated value of Fertilex and all its assets, he calculated that the fine in this case would be far too much even for the likes of the world's largest MegaGlom to afford before long.

His guess was that, once he gave back the stolen digimakes, the original owners would put them back on immediately, except of course the one whose digimake Amon had kept. With any luck, this person would lead his surveillers astray, for they would likely assume that only Amon had reason to refrain from looking like their very own self and would thus keep their eyes on the odd one out. Amon continued to wear this pilfered image for another few blocks before giving it back and returning to the generic digimake he had found in his hard drive. Once the owner reverted to their own appearance, Amon's surveillers might realize their mistake, but by then it would be too expensive to track everyone and Amon would be long gone.

After this, Amon began to consider what to do next. More than anything he wanted to go to the frugal sanctuary of his apartment, remain still, do a bit of blink reduction, settle his jittery nerves, and plan his next course of action. But they would surely find him there, whoever *they* were. Moreover, the trains to Jinbocho would be rammed with the evening boozehounds at this hour, and he couldn't afford all the touching. Until that morning, whenever he'd thought *I can't afford this*, it had meant *for the sake of my savings, I don't want to pay*. Now it meant something different. Now a ride across the downtown core on a crowded train could literally bankrupt him.

When the first few raindrops had begun to fall, Amon got an idea: he would find an open source zone. By credilaw, all properties were automatically put up for auction six months after they became public domain (just like Amon's likeness), the rationale being that unowned things obstructed economic growth. This meant open source zones, where the space itself was complimentary, could only exist for a limited time, although Amon had come across a few, as his targets occasionally took refuge in them. Going to an open source zone would only delay the inevitable, Amon knew, since he had no credit coming in, but a delay was better than giving up. Once he slipped into bankruptcy, his location would become known to GATA, and Sekido would hunt him down. Then all the evidence of corruption in his BodyBank would be seized and there'd be no way to get back everything he'd lost: his job, his life, and above all his dream, now on the brink of annihilation like a candle flame wavering under a breeze. He had no idea who he could give the information to or whether it would have any effect, but at the very least, he wanted to keep it out of the hands of his enemies as long as possible, even if merely as a fading act of defiance. It would buy him time to think (literally) and, who knows? He might even hit upon a way towards financial salvation in the meantime. After a quick web search, he'd found one to the south in Shinagawa and began to run towards it.

Now he just kept running and running through the InfoRain; past the hookers and the johns, the street corner buskers and the clubbers in their bling, past stoplight after mall, billboard after temple, past light itself into the darkness of the city. In mid stride, Amon cancelled the services his left hand had signed him up for one by one: premium news databases, venture charities, bodybuilding studios, virtual gaming worlds, earthquake insurance. Code Dr. had neutralized the virus but had not yet restored the use of his left hand, the phantom still hanging limp from his wrist, where it twitched occasionally like a dangling slug on a mild electric current. Even combining the interface of his right hand, eye, and voice, it took time to undo everything, as the list was long, and some services required that he fill out cancellation forms (incurring cancellation fees too!).

The InfoClouds began to pour. A billion-gazillion logos and celebrity endorsements and specialists explaining the facts of this and that plummeted all about at high velocity. They splattered into formless color and light before Amon's mind could register what it was seeing, the heavens a Gatling gun of subliminal admotisement fluid. The crowds kept blurring past; glistening globules of silent film factory workers cranking shafts and autumn leaves dribbling non-stop down their umbrellas. Amon's shoes stomped shallow puddles of five-second pressure-cookers that trickled off the curb into the gutter where a stream of the Japanese emperor sitting on the balcony of a wood lodge flowed. When a middle-aged drunkard lurched into his path suddenly, Amon saw a gap in the traffic and stepped into the gutter, splashing the emperor's wrinkled face across asphalt before leaping immediately back onto the curb and continuing on. Up ahead he saw a row of vending machines selling snacks, energy drinks, alcohol, umbrellas. He could feel the rain begin to penetrate his jacket, its cool wetness impinging on the warmth of his skin, a faint precipitainment glow on his swinging sleeves. He fought the temptation to buy an umbrella, dashing right past the machines. Now he was wallowing in debt and the price—even for the cheap, clear plastic ones on display—was absolutely unthinkable. He finished cancelling the last of his services, and was now only paying for breaths, blinks, sidewalk, running. But according to the Liquidation Ministry bankruptcy calculator, even with his balance dropping at the normal rate again, he only had a few hours of creditime left (give or take several minutes depending on evening inflation). His end was nigh, unless, that is, he could find another source of income.

Aw, fuck no, he moaned to himself when a repugnant but irresistible plan came to him. *Not that.* With a few clicks he put his body space up for auction to advertisers and configured his settings to automatically accept the highest offer. A second later, he noticed that everyone around was suddenly sending strange looks at his running form. Wondering why, Amon looked down to find that his body had become a traveling theatre of the obscene. On his chest, silver implements were inserted repeatedly into unidentifiable hairy mammals; around his shoulders, diapers for the elderly lay stretched out on a candlelit dinner table; on his belly, a peep cam view showed a woman's posterior coming down on a toilet; and on his palms, a spokesperson for vagina enlargement therapy demonstrated her enhanced capacity with an increasingly endowed array of unprotected young men. Amon didn't want to imagine what was playing on his forehead, back, and other parts that he couldn't immediately see. Radiating from his body, he could hear the crack of whips, the smack of flesh on flesh, guttural pillow talk, and moans of either ecstasy or pain—there was no telling which. Amongst this churning shell of porn and smut, the same logo recurrently appeared: inside an open safe, a tongue licked in a circle around its rouged lips, whereupon the safe locked shut. This was the trademark image of XXXTrust, the MegaGlom of perversion. What a fool he had been. He should have realized that the highest bidders were those with the most offensive content, and now he was signed in for a year-long contract.

Pedestrians and drivers glared at him with disgust. Some smirked and sneered. Some pointed and laughed. Others frowned and cringed, or turned away immediately as though he were a putrescent stain on the infoscape. *Don't they realize these ads have nothing to do with me?* he whined indignantly in his head, but knew he would have reacted much the same at the sight of such a repulsive, discreditable loser. The advertising remuneration was enough to cover the interest on the debt he had now accumulated, but not his action expenses, so that the principle continued to grow and thus the interest to increase, threatening to soon top the income. His exhaustion and fear felt almost like a blessing, as they numbed what would have otherwise been unbearable shame.

Amon was now thoroughly soaked. Above the hiss of traffic, the murmuring patter of InfoRain, and the porno babble that clung to him like raunchy pheromones of sound, he could hear the sloshing of his wet socks as his drenched shoes suctioned his feet with each step. All of a sudden, a window popped up and blinked in front of him. It was an automated notice from the Liquidation Ministry warning him that he was at high risk of bankruptcy. *As if I didn't know that already*, he thought and clicked it closed without breaking stride. The idea that another Liquidator was looking at his coded name in the Gutter, just as he had looked at other names on countless occasions, was somehow embarrassing, even though he knew his anonymity would hide him from his colleague. Never in his most rambling speculations had Amon imagined himself on the receiving end of his own trade. Now he was forced to imagine it, as the possibility stood before him, a financial reaper lurking somewhere in the infolight or darkness ahead.

As he moved ever further from Kabukicho, the crowds thinned out, giving him room to pick up pace. Soon he saw a bridge devoid of pedestrians up ahead and broke into a full sprint. This was obviously an expensive act, but every second counted now; the sooner he got to the open source zone, the longer he might extend his life . . . his pathetic digital life.

The bridge spanned a valley overshadowed by a huge highway overpass fifty meters above his head. The overpass traced the course of an InfoRiver running along the valley floor; monolithic cylinders of sheer concrete rising up out of the water to support it, as though linking shadow to thing. Rivulets of vibrant, multicolored InfoRain trickled down the sides of the valley into the river, like a brew of manifold universes melted down in acid. Halfway across the bridge, the overpass offered Amon a brief respite from the downpour, but he immediately began to choke on the foul air. A chemical stink permeated the surround; perhaps drifting down from the traffic, perhaps rising as vapor from the river, perhaps born of a more insidious pollution now woven into the soul of the metropolis itself. Quelling the urge to stop and catch his breath, Amon staggered coughing to the other side.

Soon he hit a main street and his navi-beam pointed to the right down a narrow alley. A wall to the left, the shuttered backs of stores to his right, Amon ran to the end where a fence cordoned off a factory yard. Turning right again, he continued down an even tighter alley bordered on his right by a stucco wall until he reached an uneven hole clipped in the fence. Ducking his head beneath the sharp tips of wires, he stepped through and found himself on a gravel path. To his left were flat warehouses, to his right cylindrical tankers two stories high with metallic staircases winding up them. After advancing straight ahead for a minute, Amon saw a gap in the warehouses where they opened up into a gravel square. The navi-beam stopped at a flashing circle in the center, telling him that he'd reached his destination.

The square was sandwiched between two warehouses and bordered on the other two sides by the tankers and another fence, beyond which Amon could see the InfoRiver valley and the highway hovering above. Dark forms huddled every few meters across it, crouching low with their feet flat on the gravel and their posterior bent against the back of their calves. Most kept umbrellas propped up against them with the handle resting on the ground, but a few—like Amon—were exposed and totally drenched. All of them hung their heads and remained utterly still. All of them were alone. Amon had never been to this place but had witnessed similar spectacles on missions before. Many bankrupts withered away their last moments in open source zones like this one. Soon, perhaps, it would be his turn.

Finding a spot as far from the others as possible, Amon crouched on his haunches in the same way. He felt like he was defecating, for this was the exact posture assumed when using an old-style Japanese toilet, little more than a hole in the floor. Although shitting position was tiring to keep up, it was the cheapest stationary posture aside from balancing on one hand, which Amon couldn't do.

Once he'd begun to catch his breath, he noticed MyMedic was having a fit. "Dehydration. Please drink water. Urination alert. Please find a bathroom. Low blood sugar. Please eat a well-balanced meal high in protein. Stress . . ." As Amon read each diagnosis and prescription on the list, he became aware of uncomfortable sensations and insistent urges spurring him to relieve them. The dry, pastiness of his tongue told him to turn his open mouth to the heavens and drink the InfoRain. The painful tingle of his swollen bladder told him to pee his pants right there. The ache of his stomach told him to backtrack to the main street and buy a snack from one of the dispensers. The heaviness of his eyelids told him to curl up against the wall of the nearest warehouse and sleep. The wet chill in his spine told him to go home and change his clothes . . . But of course, he could afford to heed none of it, and the app only succeeded in teasing him about his helpless misery, so he turned it off.

This reminded him that he had numerous applications running in the background that were slowly draining his funds. They had become such an integral and obvious part of his life, it had never occurred to him that these could be deactivated even in his most frugal moments. Now it seemed that desperation was pushing him beyond frugality, as he closed them all: PennyPinch, ScrimpNavi, Mindfulator, FacePhone . . . Next he sold all the worthless property accumulated by the phantom—strings of gibberish in fictional alphabets, real estate in the center of stars, hunting of extinct animals—the sale price only slightly higher than the fee for the action of selling them. Finally, he cancelled his apartment contract. A cleaning fee was immediately withdrawn from his account, but it was small, and he estimated that the savings on his minute-by-minute rent would pay it off in about half an hour. That was it for the Tezuka. All his stuff would be scrapped, not that he had much other than a SpillBot and a spare suit, but it felt strange to be homeless—nothing to his name but a BodyBank, a duster, and the info-soaked clothes on his back. (He wanted to pawn off his duster too, acknowledging that it was useless now that he lacked the werewithal to even draw it, but it was property of GATA and the fine for such theft would be more than it was worth.)

After this he crouched motionless for a time, the cool precipitainment relentlessly tapping at the back of his head, neck, and shoulders, oozing over every inch of his skin. His body was bored, so pretty soon his mind got antsy. There were so many thoughts he'd been too hurried to deal with, but now that he finally had an opportunity to recall them with Self-Capture, he didn't have the money to use it. They rose up all at once in a madly writhing clutter, a cerebral sandstorm that whirled out of control. Certain memories stood out, cycling again and again through his consciousness like a merry-go-round of faceless snakes, horrible but unreadable. It seemed at first that his cognition would be stuck on repeat until his last yen was spent and he left the Free World in unfathomable despair. But eventually his scattered experiences began to order themselves before his inner eye as meaning wove itself around the spool of unconsciousness and time. When at last the spinning stopped, he glimpsed his nascent creation—a story—and began to re-enact it from beginning to end on his private stage, hoping for even the faintest inklings of clarity.

It had all started when Fertilex and certain GATA officials began to collude. The psychological instability of the Minister of Records had been a convenient stroke of good luck, and they had waited patiently until he crashed, so as to take advantage of the power vacuum left in the Ministry of Records. Once influence over the Archivists had been secured, they forged a report of Barrow's bankruptcy using action and location data gathered through an illegal surveillance operation carried out in his residence. This report was then sent to Barrow's guards, leaving the Chief Executive Minister defenseless, and included in Amon's assignment folder alongside a forged AT readout. When Amon went on the mission, Archivists had edited out his credicrimes as Fertilex compensated him for them, making him into an unwitting identity assassin. Then, when he caught a glimmering of what was happening, Sekido had invited him to a bogus interview and gave him a parasite to bankrupt him into silence. The Archivists were used again to hide the credicrime of infection from his readout, and in case the parasite failed to crash him, another forged mission assignment was sent to Freg and Tororo. Rick must have been likewise manipulated. As Mayuko had told him, Rick had been offered an important mission the night he disappeared . . . the night he was murdered?

The most terrifying aspect of the whole scenario was that none of this would ever come to public light. The Fiscal Judiciary would assign fines for all these credicrimes to the individual perpetrators and the corporations they served, but when Barrow, Rick, and soon Amon, were brought in to the Archives for BodyBank removal and data upload, the double-dealing Archivists would declare that the AT readouts and LifeStreams of these three men matched. With the records verifying the legitimacy of their identity executions, no suspicions would be raised and they would go down in history as deranged dropouts of GATA society.

Once he'd gone as far as his limited knowledge would take him, Amon was overcome with shame. It should have been so obvious that Sekido had been manipulating him the whole time. The first sign was when he'd mentioned nothing about Rick's absence. With the attendance records at his fingertips, there was no way he could have failed to notice. In retrospect, he must have already known of Rick's death, but kept silent to have Amon dispatched alone, since one witness would be easier to suppress than two. The next sign was when Sekido delayed the start time for the mission. He clearly ought to have prioritized the objective of stemming the huge debt that Barrow would have supposedly been accumulating during the many hours that Amon waited over the objective of discretion. That interval had likely been used to surveil Barrow in order to gather data for the forged AT readout later sent to Amon. The third sign was when the readout from Barrow contradicted the one from the ministry. Instead of merely stalling, Amon should have trusted in Barrow completely, based on everything he knew about his character, and realized that the files from Sekido were counterfeit. Another chance to clue in was when he reviewed Rick's final readout. He should have paid attention to the fact that his friend hadn't been paid on time and remembered that only the Liquidation Minister could authorize salary disbursement. Yet despite all this, Amon had gone to the interview (which was foolish and naïve in itself) with his guard completely down, never suspecting that the itch on his back might be a parasite.

He wanted to bang his head against the gravel, as if that would beat out his gullibility, but he didn't have enough credit, although he was starting to think bankruptcy wouldn't be that bad. Then at least he could get a drink of water, a bento box, a change of clothes, and find somewhere to pee before the Liquidators arrived. *No!* He quelled this self-destructive impulse with the final remnants of his willpower and forced his attention back on his story, reflecting this time on the gaps in his understanding.

First he considered Rick. His friend must have been duped into performing some dirty deed, just like Amon, Freg, and Tororo. But what? And why had he jumped in front of the train, when he had the job, the girl, and the aspiration to live for? Then Amon considered all the money invested. The number of serious credicrimes perpetrated was unbelievable: bribery of Archivists, forgery of AT readouts, surveillance of Barrow, trespassing, identity murder, hacking, infecting, the violence of Tororo and Freg. Also, a virus sophisticated enough to crack into a BodyBank, mask itself under Amon's identity signature, and disable his communications required hundreds of man hours from a team of specialists plus compensation for the credicrime of designing it. The combined cost of the whole operation had to be several percent of the global economy, enough to threaten even Fertilex's financial stability. And for what? Where was the profit? He could see why someone might want to eliminate Barrow before the upcoming election, but did the political benefits really outweigh all these enormous costs?

Even more confusing were the doppelganging headhunters. Despite incredible similarity of features, physique, gesture, voice, and manner of speech, they seemed to be at total cross-purposes. The first headhunter, Makesh Adani, had been appalled by Amon's faith in GATA, the second by his lack of it. The first had warned him of impending danger, while the second lured him into a trap. And Amon thought he could sense animosity between them, for the headhunter at Shuffle Boom, who had remained deadpan all night, frowned only when Amon mentioned having met his look-alike. Were they different people or the same? And either way, who were they?

The biggest mystery of all was jubilee. It was hard to see how making Amon pay for it aided their scheme. On the contrary. This seemed to be a strategic error, since jubilee had awakened Amon's suspicions and kickstarted his investigation. And setting aside its effectiveness, what did it mean? What in the Free World did a political conspiracy and the cash crash of four GATA employees have to do with the return of property and freedom from debt? (Amon didn't overlook the irony:

that an action with such meaning had triggered his plunge into the deepest debt of his life.)

When no new insights came, he grew exhausted with such pondering and turned his focus towards the surround. A sharp pain had started in his lower back from crouching too long. He wanted to move around, but stayed right where he was. Keeping his eyes fixed on a speck of wet gravel a few meters ahead (which was complimentary to look at in the open source zone), he used his peripheral to watch the huddled forms around him. Fallen ones silently awaiting the inevitable. Amon didn't want to think of himself as one of them. He wanted to blame circumstances—not his own choices—for his seeming discreditability. But bankrupts had always tried to make excuses to Amon in their final moments, and he'd never been convinced . . . not even by Barrow. Why was his predicament any different?

Although he'd taken part in executing thousands of identities during his career, Amon had never tried to imagine what being severed of the digital world, of reality, would be like. Of course he must have glimpsed the naked world momentarily as a child when he still wore a training bank, for contact lens' displays had to be cleaned and certain parts of the suit replaced now and again. But since he hadn't been rigged up to record in these moments, he lacked segs to keep the memories fresh, and all he remembered was a feeling of unbearable boredom. It was as though the deficient character of such experiences accelerated forgetting, as though the monotony of information lack were a mental poison and oblivion the antidote. Now that he was staring into the pit of insolvency, now that the gravity of debt was palpable like a viscous darkness, he found himself trying to imagine bankdeath for the first time. The best he could do was visualize it as a tattered, incomplete shadow of the Free World. In naked existence, some essential aspect of consciousness would be missing, like looking into a broken mirror. It was utterly horrific, the idea of life without search engines and spatial mapping, without minute-to-minute weather reports and vital sign monitoring, without zoom and night vision, without audio-visual memory enhancement, without fathomless databases of pornography to suit any capricious desire in an instant, without ever-present human connection through silent messaging and FacePhone, without the wisdom of FlexiPedia and advice forums, without products and choices, and, most scary of all, without the Market. How could one even think of living without the Market? For Amon—and perhaps for all his Free brethren—such a life, an uncreditworthy life, seemed inherently self-defeating, like a heart pumping bloodless veins, just dry air eroding desiccated tunnels.

To stay liquid just that wee bit longer, Amon struggled desperately not to breathe and blink, his eyeline still fixed on the speck of gravel. Regulating his physiology used to be an exercise in frugality; now it was a matter of identity life and death. Above all, he made absolutely certain to keep his eyes open. He had not slept in a day and a half, and if his eyes closed, he would surely fall asleep, topple over, and wake up in a pecuniary grave. He knew his efforts were futile. However drawn out and infrequent he could make them, his breaths and blinks were steadily dwindling away his funds, marking the ineluctable approach of his black fate. Even still, he wouldn't give up. He would meet himself in that forest, even if there was no way to get there or forest to get to. His dream remained a concrete truth, even as it sunk in the mire of delusion.

Staring bankdeath in the face, Amon remembered one last way he could reduce his expenses: by turning off Spam Fortress. This would save on the minutely subscription for the app and the charges for each message blocked, but he loathed to even consider this prospect, more demeaning even than the sale of his body space. A quick glance in his junk folder revealed billions of messages, mostly from Fertilex customer service and the mailing lists his phantom hand had signed up for. Almost nauseous with dread, he completely deactivated it, allowing in not only email, but audio and video spam as well.

Immediately a skinny, balding man of middle age seated in a wheelchair appeared.

"Good evening, sir. My name is Goro Tanaka. I'm here to request your assistance." He bowed from the waist while still seated.

Amon couldn't afford to respond. He didn't want to respond. The spammer didn't pause.

"Having consulted with my colleagues and our board of trustees, after careful consideration of the information collected vis-à-vis official channels at the National Profitability Agency, we have decided that you are the ideal recipient of my inheritance.

"Please allow me to explain. I am the CEO and majority shareholder of several very successful corporations, but am afflicted with a rare, incurable genetic disease called Dufenhauser-Mahegel Syndrome that will soon claim my life. I have no children, friends, or family and have been searching for a capable young professional like yourself to take over my estate. I would be very grateful to have your assistance in making the credit transfer. Nothing on earth could make a poor, sick man like me happier.

"In order to facilitate your participation in this lucrative opportunity, we will require certain information and pecuniary support mechanisms offered voluntarily on your behalf. As a first step, we ask for your bank name, account number, FacePhone address, place of work, and all other data within your inner profile."

Beside the crippled man, a voluptuous woman appeared. She had long blonde hair dotted with blue sparkles and wore the absolute minimum clothing to not be considered nude: two navy blue stickers over her nipples and a g-string just thick enough to hide her nether region, which was shaved. Aside from her head, eyebrows, and lashes, she was completely hairless and glistened with a creamy lubricant that constantly trickled down her body.

"Having trouble with your erection, sweetie?" She straightened her index finger, which made a popping sound at the precise moment she said *erection*, and then put the digit between her lips. "No need to hide and feel ashamed. Our girls are powdered from head to toe with Manhood Dust, a powerful new nano-medication made to superpower your lust. One sniff or touch of these hot, dexterous sluts and you'll be twice as swollen and hard as usual with half the side effects and all the pleasure, all the excitement, all the orgasmic bliss. Now sixty percent off and always one hundred percent erotic. What are you waiting for? Just squeeze my breasts to make your first appointment."

A clean-cut salaryman holding a briefcase appeared.

"Fact: eighty-three percent of customers purchase products and/or services from the dealer who supplied them with one of their calendars. What does this mean for you? Calendars are a great way to promote your business. Right now we're having a blowout sale, over eleven thousand styles to choose from. Add your logo and make big cash." The man began to pull calendars out of his briefcase.

"The board has just informed me that the deadline has been fixed and that all applications for my inheritance must be submitted within the hour. For this reason I recommend . . ."

"What's the matter, honeypie? Feeling shy? I promise our juicy bitches will open you right up. Then you can spread them wide open. Why not . . ."

"Our most popular design is Grapefruit Sunset, now bundled with . . ."

As the three spammers blathered all at once, Amon kept his eyeline fixed and tried to ignore them, for purchasing anything—however intriguing—would be financial suicide.

When the salaryman noticed Amon's lack of interest, he put the calendars back in his briefcase, and closed it. When he reopened it, the case was full of aerosol cans that said "Water Repellent Spray." Withdrawing one, he pointed it at Amon, crouched down, and got right up into his downcast face, whereupon his sales manner suddenly changed.

"What? You don't want to stay dry?" he shouted. "Is there something wrong with you? You like to be a soggy rat. Huh pal? You like it? Just try one." Amon could see but not feel the spittle flying from the man's ferociously wriggling tongue. He wanted to buy a can just to make him shut up, but feared this would only encourage the spammers further.

While he continued to shout, Amon heard a whisper in his left ear: "Don't listen to that guy. He's just trying to rip you off."

Amon couldn't help but make a small investment in moving his eyes from right to left, so as to locate the source. He saw no one, until he noticed a vague form on his left shoulder and, turning his eyes to the limit, realized that a tiny, elderly man was perched there. Leaning on a mahogany cane with a gold, spherical handle, he wore a dark overcoat, his long silver hair tied back in a neat ball.

"The name's Togo," the man said with a bow. "I can see you're in a tough spot there, pal. But don't worry, you can trust me." When the little man smiled, kind wrinkles radiated from his mouth and eyes, giving him an air of integrity.

The salaryman began to violently shake his open briefcase in Amon's face, forcing him to view the inventory of cans; the woman strutted towards him, bringing her lubricated navel right into his eyeline; and the wheelchaired man rolled slowly closer—the spammers crowding their prey.

"Can I offer you some assistance?" asked Togo. Amon couldn't afford to respond, and hoped the little man could read the *yes* in his eyes. "If you sell me your preferences, I'll get these guys off your case."

A window appeared with an offer to buy Amon's preferences, which were stored in his inner profile. "Don't worry, you can trust old Togo," the man smiled again. It was a piddling amount of money and Amon didn't trust old Togo for a second, but he was in no position to refuse income of any kind and quickly clicked consent.

Thereupon Togo immediately leapt from Amon's shoulder to the salaryman's shoulder and whispered in his ear. The salaryman then put the aerosols back into his briefcase. When he reopened it, there were canisters the size of lipstick tubes and bundles of incense.

"Try this stimulant lip balm. Proven to flush out chemicals that block concentration and impede the frugal mind. Or how about this forest incense, with real scent of cedar." The little old man remained perched on his shoulder, smiling that warm smile and nodding encouragingly to Amon.

Three burly olive-skinned men in jeans and polo shirts pushed the salaryman aside, sending Togo flying headfirst towards the gravel, and began to shout at Amon in a language he didn't understand. They were holding gray packets about twice the size of a business card, one in each hand. The packets were covered in vibrantly-colored flowing script, but Amon had disabled InterrPet, so he couldn't read them. Waving them about wildly in his face, these swarthy hawkers barked guttural gibberish at him. When Amon remained hunched and staring at the gravel, they shrunk to the size of ants. Then two of them leapt into his eyes, their frantically gesticulating forms embedded in his visual field, and the third flew into his inner ear, where he continued shouting nonsense straight at Amon's eardrum in a mosquito-like high-humming voice.

With the three men out of his way, the briefcase man filled the vacuum and got right up into Amon's face again. "Don't pretend you don't want this lip balm and incense. I know you like frugality and forests, douchebag. So just pay up before I sic a whole army of spammers on you. Then you'll buy something. Mark my words. Is that what you want? Huh?"

The volume of the shouting inside Amon's ear increased, and he could see Togo back on his shoulder, apparently arguing with the even smaller man in his ear. It was so loud that Amon could no longer hear what anyone was saying. Even the sleazy moans that emanated from his very flesh were overpowered.

The wheelchaired man seemed to realize that his voice had been drowned out and soon a copy of him appeared. It spoke in unison with the original, together at twice the volume: "According to our financial speculators, these assets are expected to double in value each year for the next decade, so you can be absolutely assured that making a meager donation of your personal information is a wise investment."

In response, the other spammers doubled as well, prompting the wheelchaired copies to split once again, inciting the other spammers to quadruple, this exponential multiplication continuing like frantic cell division until Amon was surrounded by hundreds. A roar of clashing inducements surged around him, the pipsqueak voices in his ear now a piercing choir, the men in his eyes now blanketing everything in sight by standing on each other's shoulders in rows.

Craving to plug his ears, Amon's hand twitched involuntarily, but he quelled the urge before the movement could be registered. As the volume of the sales cries rose and rose, his lower back throbbed with ever more intensity. His right calf was just beginning to cramp up when a calm voice began to speak directly into his earspeakers. It was saying something about reforming his lifestyle and seeking help, although he couldn't hear it with any clarity over the racket. He guessed it was an action counselor recommended by the Liquidator overseeing Illiquidity Alert, and was reminded of how he'd always been irritated by the gutterfolk that ignored good financial advice. Amon thought of the other lost souls crouching around him, now hidden by the swarm of bodies. Could they too be undergoing this spam assault? The worse life was at rock bottom, he had believed, the more motivation there would be to climb back into solvency. Yet the discomforts of poverty that he was experiencing now—drenched clothes, heavy eyelids, empty stomach, dry mouth, swollen bladder, frozen eyes, sore back, cramped legs, isolation, abuse from swindlers, estrangement from the law, guilt, shame, lack of dignity—these synergized into a great anguish that overwhelmed his most primal self. Resisting the urge to scream and flail about in paroxysms of frustration took all his strength, not a modicum remaining for that treacherous shimmy towards liquid salvation. The self-control required of him went far beyond frugality, and he could only hope, for the sake of his conscience, that it hadn't been like this for the thousands of bankrupts he'd executed.

Soon the spammers were pushing and pulling each other aside, battling for his vicinity, and as the minutes went by, the maw of despair finally managed to take his soul between its teeth and began to gnaw him whole. A popup said that Code Dr. had restored the use of his left hand, but it was no good to him now. A single wrong move was liable to put the last nail in his coffin of debt. Most depressing of all, he realized that he wouldn't have known what to do with money even if he had it. All his dreams were shattered, the great leader Barrow gone, his best friend dead, his job lost, his money stolen, his plans failed, his questions unanswered. With paralyzed will, Amon lost all control of his respiration. Violent breaths quivered out as tears welled in his eyes. The ache of resigned melancholy and guilt pulsed a steady beat within every particle of his flesh, in time to a voice that taunted him. *You miserable lecher, you depraved hobo, you squandering loser.*

Which one will extinguish me, a tear or a sigh? he wondered. Looking over the brink of the precipitous downward spiral—an unimaginable realm of deprivation, entrapment, and want awaiting him in its depths— he could feel liquid gathering into a globule at the bottom of his eyelid, and the slight contraction of his diaphragm that signaled a sigh.

The white noise all around became silence, like an auditory tableau. Against the chill stream of rain washing over his cheek, he felt a trickle of warmth. It was a single tear, not the sigh spiral, that would do him in after all.

But somehow he didn't go bankrupt.

The rain stopped falling on him and he felt a warm hand on his shoulder.

Someone was offering him a leash. Consenting without hesitation, he looked up to see an umbrella held over him by Mayuko.

19

WAKUWAKU CITY, NIGHT

In total disbelief, Amon gazed up at the delicate, curving form of his savior. Beneath her white umbrella, Mayuko stood inside a bubble of plain air amidst the information downpour, the spammers like so much smoke wafting insubstantially around her. She wore a tight, light-gray t-shirt with sleeves half way to her elbows, khaki half-pants and white high-heeled sandals, a silver necklace of fine chain hanging around her neck. Although the whirlpools still hid her eyes, it was definitely Mayuko, for her hair—held up above her head with magenta clips—was that unmistakable hue, the darkest amber encasing a comet's glittering tail. She seemed to be saying something, but Amon couldn't hear it, deafened as he was by the pandemonium of sales pitches and his own stupefaction. At that moment, it finally sunk in that she was paying for all his transactions, and he reactivated Spam Fortress, whereupon the raging crowd vanished like a nightmare to the eye's opening. Now the dark forms of the illiquid were visible once more, crouching in the square like human shadows torn off and abandoned.

I can move again! Amon's whole being cheered and he tried to stand up too quickly, so that his cramped legs and hips seized up before he could straighten his back. Unable to rise beyond a stoop, the force of his upward thrust caught on his locked muscles and he lost balance, toppling face first towards the gravel. Mayuko stepped in to catch him, and he collapsed against her body. Too stiff to stand under his own power, Amon leaned on her for a while, nestling his forehead against her warm chest, his chin touching the top of her soft breasts. Relief rushed through him and self pity for everything he'd been through as he grasped her shirt on both sides of her waist with quivering hands, his body shaking from head to toe. Then, when Mayuko put her hand reassuringly on the back of his head, time seemed to freeze, but for the continuous murmur-patter of InfoRain and his silently dripping tears, the descent of liquefied desire-image and liquefied sadness somehow beyond time.

"Come on," she said after a measureless duration. "Let's get in my car." She took one step back, forcing Amon to support his own head. But when Mayuko started out of the square, he just wiped his eyes and runny nose pointlessly with his wet suit sleeve and stood there staring after her in a daze. His nerves were so frayed he couldn't help but sway back and forth on his feet, still trembling all over, his breath coming out in pants, until Mayuko walked back over to Amon, held her umbrella over him, and took his hand in hers. It felt warm and delicate to the touch. And with her guiding him, Amon lurched stiffly in a slouch out of the factory yard, back through the alleyway to the main thoroughfare, and then down a side street into a parking lot.

Mayuko stopped in front of her car, a beige sedan with a boxlike frame and big windows. She opened the front passenger-side door and ushered Amon inside before going around the front end and entering through the opposite door.

"What's going on, Amon?" she asked. "What were you doing in that yard?"

"I . . . It was . . . the meeting . . . they . . ." Amon rocked anxiously in his seat with his head lowered. "M-my job . . . I . . ." His voice came out almost as a whimper.

"It's okay," Mayuko consoled him. "We can about it talk later." Then after a pause, she gave him a sidelong glance of piercing distaste and said, "But can you turn off those awful videos?"

"Oh . . ." Amon felt the warmth of a blush in his cheeks when he looked down at the nectar-dripping orifices, ecstatic scowls, and intertwined flesh that flickered across his body. In the few hours since he sold his space, he had become so completely habituated to the raunchy audio that he'd forgotten it was even there. In the midst of all the vile images, Amon spotted himself on his left breast. He was thrusting a telephone pole fused to his crotch into an open manhole brimming with cottage cheese. As he'd always feared, XXXTrust was making good use of his likeness. (Beside this, a FillBot was penetrating the lubricated hole of a SpillBot with its hard rubbery protrusion.) "I-it . . . w-wasn't my choice. I put up my space . . . f-for auto-auction . . . You see, and . . . this . . . This just . . . happened to be the highest bid." He knew it sounded like an excuse, but the truth was the best he could come up with. The sad look he'd seen in her whirlpool eyes when she noticed he was in the Ginza club district appeared suddenly and vanished just as fast. Amon used Mayuko's money to pay the severance fee to cancel his one year contract with XXXTrust. When the porno vanished, he was in his gray uniform, darkened with iridescent InfoRain.

Then Mayuko looked him up and down with a frown. "You're wet," she said. Already the red, yellow, and green plaid of the seat was beginning to blot with InfoRain and a small puddle had formed at his feet. "Should I take you to your apartment for a change of clothes?"

"No!" he said, shaking his head a bit too vigorously. "Thank you. I . . . I can't go back there anymore. I vacated."

"Vacated? To where?"

"Nowhere. I'm . . ." Amon cringed in shame, unable to finish the sentence. *I'm homeless now.*

She deepened her frown lines, apparently in thought. "In that case, let's head to my place."

"N-no good. They'll . . . find us there too."

"What are you talking about? Who!?"

"Sekido and the headhunter. They . . ." Amon found words failing him again.

"My new place should be fine. No one except you and Rick know where I live. I never even gave the address to my company when I left their dorm."

"You don't understand. These men are very free . . . They-they can afford . . . They could be watching you."

"Do you think Sekido and this headhunter are so paranoid that they'd be spying on all your ex-girlfriends?"

Amon wanted to say that he didn't have any other ex-girlfriends, but Mayuko went on before he could start.

"Don't worry, I'm totally anonymous. You're always seeing my naked face, but I look like a completely different person to everyone else. Watching me wouldn't tell them anything. Or what? You think they can cut through the blinding and find me just like that?"

"Well, no . . ." He shook his head. *If they could do that*, he thought, *they would have found me hours ago.* "But . . ." Amon realized then that he had been forgetting to text. He considered typing his next message, but thought better of annoying her, even if it would reduce the strain on her funds. "I don't think we should . . . go there. The chance . . . might be small that they know where you live, but . . . we'd still be taking a risk."

"So what do you suggest?"

"I can . . ." He thought for a moment. "I can stay in a capsule."

"A capsule? Do you really think I'd let you squeeze into one of those? If you're set against staying at my place, why don't we find a proper hotel?"

"A capsule would be . . . much cheaper for you. And if they find you with me—"

"Don't be silly. I don't mind spending a bit of money for a friend in need. And if you go to a capsule, we won't be able to talk."

"But I could still . . . FacePhone you."

"Amon!" she cried, a glaze of unshed tears suddenly swirling atop her whirlpools. "Rick is gone! Gone! Okay?! And right after I heard that from you, you hung up on me. Now you're telling me you want to go to a capsule alone? I thought Rick would always be close by, that I could just click and see through his eyes or talk with him whenever I wanted. Then all of a sudden I got cut off. Now I'm never going to see him again. What if the same thing happens to you? Forget it! I'm not letting you out of my sight. Not until I know what's going on, okay?"

Mayuko's voice was cracking, and as Amon looked at her expression of grief and distress, all his objections deflated instantly. It felt wrong to use her money unnecessarily and being with her would put her at risk. But now that she'd saved him, the least he could do was keep her company until things were a bit clearer. And although his ingrained impulses told him a solitary life was more frugal, he had to admit that the idea of having someone else around was kind of comforting. "Alright. Do you know somewhere we can stay?"

She broke their gaze and nodded. "There's a weekly mansion in my neighborhood. I'll put in a reservation now."

When Mayuko clicked on the ignition, Amon said, "Could you hold on a second." She nodded and Amon took her folded umbrella before getting out of the car. He sensed that this was an awkward moment, but he couldn't wait any longer. Opening the umbrella, he walked to the corner of the parking lot, unzipped, and relieved himself for what felt like an eternity.

When Amon sat back in the wet seat, the car was already revved and Mayuko immediately pulled out of the parking lot. With her arms stretched forward on ergonomic rests, she steered by see-sawing her left hand side to side with her middle finger as the pivot, and adjusted acceleration by tapping her index finger. Heading back across the bridge over the valley, she turned left, ascended a winding ramp to the overpass looming above, and slotted into traffic.

They were whirring along the wet highway for not a moment when Amon let out a long quivering sigh. He still found himself worrying about the price out of habit, but now that he was in the cushy seat, away from the illiquid, the spammers, and the InfoRain, he had finally accepted that he wasn't going to crash. Suddenly he found the shaking had subsided somewhat and sat up straight.

As though sensing Amon was calming down, Mayuko glanced at him and said, "So, Amon, tell me what happened?" Her whirlpools stared at him as she entrusted the steering temporarily to her driving app.

"Well...um...I...." Amon's attempts to explain sputtered into silence, but he continued to meet her gaze.

"What?"

"I'm sorry. It's just . . . when I look in those whirlpools, sometimes it's like . . . I lose my train of thought and . . . especially right now . . . Now that I'm more relaxed, my tiredness is starting to creep up and I can't keep my head straight."

Mayuko didn't show any signs she'd heard him but, before long, her whirlpools began to implode on themselves. Amon watched as the whites and irises were sucked inside the pupils as though going down a drain, swirling into some dimensionless point in the center, until all that remained was a dot that soon faded and disappeared, leaving her naked eyes. It seemed like forever since he'd seen them, even though the last time was just yesterday morning in Rick's apartment. They seemed to break down the world beyond the windshield as she took over driving again, dissolving the road, the lights, the InfoRain into their component atoms of matter and meaning.

The traffic came on thick and they ended up bumper to bumper with a gothic limo shrouded in heaps of dust and congealed shadow. As they inched slowly ahead, Amon related all the events that had occurred after they'd spoken on the phone, from the meeting and his ensuing flight to everything he'd been able to guess about the situation. Mayuko accessed his LifeStream through his inner profile and watched it all unfold as he talked, nodding her head periodically to show she was listening.

When Amon got to the part where Mayuko had arrived and his tale was done, silence followed. Frowning, Mayuko kept her eyes on the road, see-sawing her hand and tapping for gas, signal, brake. She seemed to be going over everything in her head, and Amon watched the headlights whip past as he waited for her conclusion, remembering how careful and thoughtful she had always been. After a minute, she said, "I was thinking about the strange similarity between the two headhunters."

"Yeah?"

"Well, what if you're caught up in some kind of sibling rivalry?"

"How do you mean? Ohhh, I see. Like they're related?"

"Not just that. I mean, you saw the recent news about the Birla fortune, right?"

"Yeah," said Amon, "I watched a report when I was with Rick in Self Serve a couple days ago."

"So you probably haven't heard the latest developments then?" Amon shook his head. "The details of the late Birlas' will were released at a press conference last night. Most of the experts were expecting them to go with tradition and give the biggest portion of their assets to their eldest daughter, but Rashana only got forty-nine percent. Full executive control of Fertilex went to Anisha, along with the monopoly on sex, reproduction, cloning, and everything."

Mayuko paused and looked at him.

"Wow. Okay. The younger sister got majority share. That's a big story. So what's the connection?"

"Well it wasn't like Rashana got totally ripped off. Becoming the second richest person on earth isn't such a bad deal, right? But by giving her the short end of the stick, the Birla parents are basically declaring to the world and all of posterity that they trust Anisha more. The variety show pundits are all talking about how Rashana is probably feeling about this, you know, humiliated, envious. Anyways, I couldn't help thinking that it kind of reminds me of your two rich look-alikes. Maybe their relationship is something like that."

"Right!" Amon jumped in astonishment, but felt the seatbelt on his gut keep him in his seat. "Maybe they *are* the Birla sisters?" Amon looked at Mayuko and shook his head in exasperation. She just smiled knowingly, as though perhaps it had been obvious to her from the start.

The Birlas were a notoriously reclusive family, carefully protecting all audiovisual aspects of their identities. The wizened faces of the parents and founders of the MegaGlom had become iconic representations of the true entrepreneur, but no pictures of their daughters had ever appeared in popular media, not even of their digiguises, and it was anyone's guess what they looked like. Yet presumably since they were siblings, they shared a naked resemblance, which explained how the headhunters could look so similar without any image rights violations. Both sisters, it seemed, were using the sex change function on digimake and, given similar input, it had rendered them as men who were nearly identical.

"It makes so many things clearer," said Amon. "All the connections to Fertilex and like, why they were both Indian. Also their conflicting attitudes and all the cash they're throwing around. But some of it still doesn't make sense. Like I know the Birla sisters are super rich now, but when I think about all the people involved and add up all the expenses, it's got to be some percentage of the world economy invested in this. One percent? Five percent? Ten percent? I can't guess at precise figures, but I doubt even the Birla's can afford this. Fertilex would go bankrupt."

"Maybe they have partners."

"Maybe. But who?"

Suddenly the traffic opened up and Mayuko blasted ahead into an open stretch.

A bit dryer now and sheltered within the glass and metal shell, Amon felt his stress and anxious jitters gradually settle down. In their place came a kind of calm—a dull, restless, empty kind of calm with a tingle of fear lurking in the background, but a calm nonetheless. "It's so much better to be here in this car than out there in the rain," he said. "You know the urban legend about the application installed in every BodyBank that boils down your whole LifeStream and flashes it before your eyes just as you go bankrupt?"

Mayuko nodded.

"Well, I was starting to wonder whether that thing would go off."

"I'm happy you're safe," she said, smiling weakly but with a kind of raw melancholy in her eyes that aroused Amon's pity.

"Why did you come find me?" he asked.

After a moment's pause, Mayuko said: "Well, after you called, I watched the segs you gave me and was feeling really sad and confused about Rick. I could accept that he was gone, but no matter how many times I turned everything over in my mind, I couldn't believe he'd killed himself. Bankruptcy I could see. Rick was a clever man in many ways, but he was never particularly careful with money. Like this year, he told me his bonus was lower but he kept renting out that huge apartment and taking me out to nice restaurants and hotel lounges. I tried to refuse, but . . . Anyways, if anything he seemed happier these days than I could ever remember when we were growing up. Suicide just seemed impossible. Then I thought about his special mission and that you hadn't heard anything about it. How could that be if you were partners working in the same office? It was just too strange and I started wondering how this mission might have been connected to his end . . . Then I thought about Sekido. He's the one who assigns your missions, and I didn't really know what was going on, but you said you were going to have a meeting with him and I started to get worried that . . . well . . ."

Amon clicked his tongue and shook his head ruefully. "It's my life and I didn't realize it was that bastard Sekido ruining it. But you saw through him just like that. I'm such an idiot."

"Amon," she said, turning to look straight at him again. The conscious and unconscious layers of his whole mind seemed to separate in her eyes like water fissuring into hydrogen and oxygen. "Don't beat yourself up like that. You're not an idiot. You're just in denial."

"Denial? About what?"

"About GATA, about the AT market, about bankruptcy, about the camps, about our society, and about yourself. It's okay. To be a Liquidator you've got to tell yourself the Free World is fine and dandy. Otherwise the guilt would drive you nuts. Rick did the same thing to an extent. Everyone has to find ways of coping with their job." Mayuko's face contorted into a grimace for a moment, as though some deep-sunken pain had bobbed up to the surface. "But if you forget that everything you tell yourself about the industry you serve is just a fairy tale to get you through the work week without having a breakdown, then you lose your hold on the truth about yourself and the world. When that happens, people who are better able to stomach what's really going on can take advantage of you. So you might have been a victim of your own ambition, but you're not stupid, Amon. Even smart people have blind spots."

Amon felt anger rise up in him and gave Mayuko an intense stare. *Denial? How dare you?* he thought, but found the words refusing to go to his lips. The next moment something inside him shifted, releasing a pulse of overwhelming shame that impelled him to lower his head. Then he knew that she was right. There had been so many chances for him to see that the minister was stringing him along with the false promise of promotion, but each time he'd been blinded by his hopes for career advancement, by yearning for realization of his dream and by faith in the AT system. As a result he had crashed Barrow, an innocent man, a hero. Admittedly a nostie too, but maybe that wasn't such a bad thing after all. Now that it was clear Barrow had been telling the truth about his readout, maybe he had been telling the truth about nosties too. Sure, Amon had always been taught they were perverse rejects, only a notch above the bankdead. But had he not lived in the same building with them for years? And was his desire to meet the forest in the flesh not somewhat like what Barrow had called "the primary act?" Perhaps he had more in common with them than he cared to admit. And if nosties could be forgiven their quirks, then there wasn't the slightest excuse for Barrow's assassination. *How could I have let myself be tricked into doing that?* Amidst his self-loathing, Amon felt Mayuko's eyes on the back of his bowed head.

"Anyways, after I started to worry about you, I tried FacePhoning but wasn't able to connect. That was when I checked your inner profile and found you were in a factory yard in Shinagawa, crouching with illiquids."

Amon said nothing. He was getting drowsier by the second. The car turned, swinging his bowed head to the left against the door. He let it rest there, the smell of rubber in his nose, hoping for just a wink of sleep. But he couldn't relax on the soggy seat in his soggy clothes. After a few minutes passed, he lifted his head.

Outside the window he saw a dragon with long, streaming whiskers whip just above the roof of the car. Inside little cubbies in its undulating serpentine torso, people sat side by side, screaming with their mouths wide open. Having come off the overpass, Amon and Mayuko were driving along a four-lane road into a district that integrated theme park and condominium sprawl. It was Mayuko's neighborhood—Wakuwaku City.

The track for the dragon coaster snaked and spiraled upwards above the thoroughfare, threading its way through the knotted, aerial spaghetti of other tracks. Done up as warheads, griffins, desert caravans, sound waves, drilling braids of strobing psychedelic pinwheels, dozens of roller coasters whizzed straight at and around each other. They rose to peaks high above the roofscape. They plunged through tunnels bored diagonally in skyscrapers. They ripped along hallways past bedrooms, kitchens, and private Jacuzzis. They loop-de-looped low to bring the heads of riders skimming just above traffic.

The scaffolding that supported the tracks was bolted at the base to outer walls, reaching across streets from one building to the next to form a pervasive canopy of interlinking steel beams that blocked out the InfoClouds. The still-falling InfoRain was channeled down its structure to pour onto particular points along the street. Some sections of the scaffolding had been digimade to match the various rides they supported: scuttling spider legs beneath Arachnid Twirl, licking flames for Runaway Dragon, and one that had been completely edited out with the riders flying in sitting position through empty air.

Children inside stars spun through space like the movement of the cosmos in time-lapse photography, and couples strapped in transparent tubes rose and fell on wires like pistons through hydraulic cylinders. Merry-go-rounds hula-hooping skyscraper shafts and Ferris wheels crowning their rooftops rotated at a steady pace like massive horizontal and vertical cogs, some of the buildings themselves turning gradually like slow-motion dreidels.

Crowds queued along rope dividers for blocks, the lineups bending around intersections and narrow alleys. They waited for outdoor ski lifts and escalators that led to boarding zones on raised platforms, balconies, and rooftops. Stalls peddling various sorts of junk food were stationed between the ropes and the narrow pedestrian lane running along the curb. Even inside the car, Amon could smell hot grease, curry, caramel, and could hear screams of different volumes layered on top of each other—some growing louder as they approached, others fading as they retreated—a multi-track soundscape of exhilaration.

Mayuko turned down a ramp that ran beneath a skyscraper into a basement parking chamber and parked in the center of a circular pad. Once they were out, the pad lifted the car into a hole in the ceiling and they stepped into a nearby elevator. The elevator rose for mere seconds before the doors opened directly into their weekly-rental apartment.

Beyond the single stair of the entranceway was a white rectangular room. On the left was a wall of windows; on the right a wall with four faux-wood doors; on the far end a kitchen with narrow counters, a single sink, and a small fridge; in the middle a small white dining table with two wooden chairs. And between the table and where they stood, a black leather couch. Aside from a glass vase of white and black roses on the table, nothing was decorated: the dark, reddish-brown floorboards were without rug; the walls without paintings. They took off their shoes and entered.

Once inside, Mayuko opened a closet beside the entrance, taking out a white towel and a *yukata* robe patterned white and grayish-blue. "You must be wanting a shower," she said, and handed them to Amon, who nodded in thanks. She then opened the nearest door, ushered Amon into the shower room, and closed the door behind him. Amon undressed, put his wet clothes and duster in a plastic basket, and got in the shower. Steam filled the off-white plastic chamber. He stood there for a time on tired legs, struggling just to hold his head up, before finally succeeding in urging his arms to lather his body in soap. He savored the hot water as it ran down his flesh, washing away the rain, the sweat, the residue of fear.

After drying off, Amon slipped his arms into the yukata sleeves, tied a fabric belt around his waist, and returned to the living room. At that moment, Mayuko was at the entrance taking a white plastic bag from a man in a navy blue jacket that stood in the doorway. The man bowed low, displaying the top of his head, where the LVR Logo—swirling spirals of letters and numbers that coalesced into a leaping dolphin—was animated in the shave pattern of his buzz-cut, before Mayuko shut the door.

She brought the bag towards the kitchen and, as she was passing Amon, said "I got some dinner for you."

"Great! Thanks. I'm starving."

"You must be." Mayuko put the bag on the counter. Amon could see the neck of a green glass bottle sticking over the lip of the white plastic. Mayuko drew out a black bento box, brought it to the table, and placed it on top in front of the seat facing the window.

"You go ahead. I've already eaten."

Without wasting a moment, Amon sat at the table before the box and removed its transparent lid. The black plastic was divided into six square compartments in two rows of three with a different dish in each. Running clockwise from the bottom leftmost compartment were white rice; teriyaki chicken; slices of yellow pickled daikon; potatoes, carrot, and pork simmered in soy sauce; squid and salmon salad; and stir-fried eggplant. Amon drew his disposable chopsticks from their paper sheath, snapped them apart, said thanks for the food, and began to eat ravenously. He knew it was just fast food, but being used to vending machine fare—not to mention excruciatingly hungry after all the exertion on an empty stomach—it tasted like the most wholesome, delicious meal he'd ever had.

When he was finished, Amon realized that he could hear a muffled hissing. It appeared that Mayuko had slipped off to the shower while he was absorbed in eating. Now that his belly was full, he began to feel woozy and leaned back on the chair, listening to the sound of the water and feeling the cool A/C air from a vent above.

★

Amon awoke toppling headfirst to the right and stiffened all his muscles to catch his balance on the chair. Last he remembered, he had been reclining on the backrest and had closed his eyes for just a second. Now he could hear the muffled hum of a blow-dryer. Soon it stopped and a few moments later Mayuko came out. With her comet hair tied back in such a way that a strand of her bangs dangled along each cheek, she wore a smaller version of the same yukata as Amon, the liquid ripple of two curving forms beneath the fabric announcing she was bra-less.

"How about a drink?" she asked, drawing the tall bottle from the bag in the kitchen. Amon nodded, so she tonged some ice cubes from the freezer into two whiskey glasses and brought them to the table along with the bottle. The label said it was a kind of shochu called *awamori*.

"Since when did you start drinking awamori?" Amon asked, "I thought you were a wine girl."

"I've grown fond of awamori in recent years," she said, filling the glasses to the brim. "It's much lower in calories than wine or sake." Amon frowned. The Mayuko he remembered never used to worry about such things.

She placed the glasses on opposite sides of the table and sat down across from him with the black and white roses between them. They said cheers, clinked glasses, and brought their lips to the rim. The cool Okinawan rice liquor tingled Amon's tongue and went smooth down his throat before rocketing warmth from his belly to his head. They put their glasses down on the table simultaneously and Amon saw that hers was more than half empty. He had only taken a sip. They sat in silence for a moment while Amon stared at her and Mayuko down at the flowers. Her upper body above the table was a silhouette against the window and he gazed behind her into the night. The glass was fogged and he could make out nothing but distorted light and blurry shapes. Faint screams and rumbling wheels whispered in the background.

"What a nightmare this all is," Mayuko said eventually, still looking at the flowers.

"Yeah. Unbelievable."

"I want to be positive about this, you know. I mean you're safe and we're spending time together for the first time in ages. So I'm trying to tell myself it could be worse. But then I remember that someone is after you. And then I think about Rick . . ."

Amon said nothing. He stared at her as she absentmindedly fingered the loose bang dangling along her right cheek.

"We've known him pretty much our whole lives," she said, "and . . . what happened—it still hasn't sunk in, you know?"

Amon nodded. "Everything happened way too fast. Yesterday he didn't show up for work and today . . . Suddenly he's just gone."

"Do you think it's really true? Was Rick . . . murdered?"

"I don't know. The seg did say train suicide, but—"

"What?"

"Well, like you said in the car earlier, Rick was bad with money, but he was happy."

"How come you're so sure?" she said taking another sip of awamori. "I thought you two hardly talked anymore."

"We don't . . . didn't," Amon flinched slightly with a twinge of sadness when he corrected himself. "But even still, I picked up on little things, like the way he was always in a good mood when he showed up late in the morning. He'd be panting as though he'd just sprinted from the station. Then he'd bow a thousand times looking all embarrassed, and his hair would be digimade tousled as though he'd been too hurried for morning hygiene. But I could tell it was just an act. When he should have been feeling guilty, he seemed relaxed, almost carefree. I never understood why until that night at Self Serve."

"What? Did he say something?"

Not thinking about what he was saying, Amon had let something slip. And realizing that now was not the time to bring it up, he backtracked, "N-no. Nothing in particular. It was just . . . this feeling I got, you know? That his attitude kind of made sense for him. That's all."

"A feeling?" Mayuko didn't look up from the flowers, but she frowned, appearing unconvinced. Her hands seemed to have minds of their own. As her right index finger looped and unlooped her hair around itself, her left one ran around the rim of her glass, which Amon found odd as it wasn't a wine glass. He took another sip of his drink while the muffled theme park racket infiltrated their silence. Something was gnawing at him. He had to get it out.

"Listen Mayuko," he said staring straight at her eyes, which remained focused on the flowers, "I want you to know how grateful I am."

"For what?"

"For coming to get me from that yard."

"Don't be silly. It's not like I could just, you know, twiddle my thumbs and watch idly while you went bankrupt."

"No. Really. I don't know how to thank you enough. I mean, like, I know we didn't end things on the best of terms. And I know I wasn't there for you and Rick these last few years. But you came when I needed you the most. You saved me."

"Just forget about it," she said with a wry smile, which disappeared as she took another big draught of awamori. Her right hand still working her strand of hair, she shifted in her seat.

Taking another sip of his drink, Amon said, "So what do we do now?"

"Let's talk about that tomorrow. You look exhausted."

"I am. But the sooner we work this out the better, don't you think? Obviously we can't stay here forever."

"I've rented this place for a week, so there's no need to rush. Where else could you go anyways?"

"I have no idea, but . . . I don't want to burden you any longer than I have to. I mean, it's not just my actions. You're covering the interest on my loans too."

"It's okay, Amon. I just got a raise last spring and I've got a bit put aside. I'm totally fine to cover the both of us."

"That's not the point. It doesn't matter how much you've saved. That's money *you* earned. It's your freedom, not mine. Asking you to sustain an extra person is just too much. I feel like a mooch already."

"A mooch? That's ridiculous," her eyes still averted. "Have you thought about what's going on right now? You've been tricked into assassinating the CEM. Then you were hacked and attacked. Now people with lots of freedom to spend are hunting you. With Rick gone, I'm the only friend you've got, right? What are you going to do? Become one of those attention panhandlers, spending all day trying to get people to look at you just to buy a few rice balls? The interest on your debt would bankrupt you in seconds. And I don't care how much it costs. Not everything is about money in this world. So please, just accept that you're going to have to stay under my care for a while. At least until we can be sure you're not in danger."

She finished her glass and poured herself another. Amon still didn't feel right about the situation, but he couldn't think how to respond, so he joined her in looking at the flowers. The petals looked fragile but restless, as though eagerly awaiting the slightest draft to float into the air, drift away, and dissolve into nothing, like poised springs formed of the thinnest ice. Amon put his hand over his mouth and stifled a yawn. The effervescent warmth in his head and two sleepless nights worth of exhaustion had crept into the back of his eyes, turning everything in the room faint and unreal, as though color itself had been injected with a sedative.

"So what did Rick say about me at Self Serve?" Mayuko asked, looking up at him at last. Under the gaze of those incisive eyes, Amon was laid bare and knew there was no hiding anything.

"Just that . . ." Amon reached out and touched a white flower. To his surprise it felt soft and a white petal fluttered to the table. "I'm sorry I didn't tell you earlier on the phone. I wanted to but it didn't seem like the right time."

"Why? What was it?"

"He . . ." Amon gulped nervously, "He told me his dream was to have a family. He wanted to find a wife, have babies, and raise the kids himself. I told him he was being hasty, that he needed to shape up at work and plan carefully if he was going to afford that. But as you know, Rick is no good at waiting. The dream brought him too much joy. He was going to . . . propose to you."

The last sentence floated out over the table like a black mist, slipping over the edges and drifting to the floor, where it fed the shadows of everything in the room. Mayuko said nothing. She had just lifted the glass, but now her hand froze, holding it hovering barely above the tabletop as her fingers gradually tightened. Her lips began to tremble and her eyes glittered with moisture, peering into his with raw sorrow that seemed to beg him to somehow soothe the pain. Unconcealed by digimake, it was the most sincere expression of misery Amon had ever witnessed in his life, and he immediately regretted what he'd said. Part of him had wanted her to know the truth about her relationship with Rick, but maybe he should have kept it a secret forever, or at least until everything else had stabilized.

Quickly, she looked back at the flowers and the expression disappeared, a lifeless deadpan appearing in its place. Whatever she did, she didn't seem to be able to get comfortable. Her hands gripped the lapel of her yukata and released it. She brought her chair forward, gripped her bang, and rested her right elbow on the edge of the table. She sat up straight, put her hands in her lap, and pushed her chair back out. Finally her hands made their way back onto the tabletop and settled around the bottle. She topped up Amon's glass, which was still half full, poured her third, and said: "Looking back, it should have been obvious. But somehow I never realized he was that serious. I guess you're not the only one in denial."

"Why? You mean you weren't planning to marry him?"

"I liked Rick, of course. He was a good friend for such a long time and I never thought of him as more than that in the beginning, but I lost my confidence and . . . he always said such sweet things. He made me feel beautiful again." The awamori's spell appeared to be working, for without seeming to realize it, she was leaning her whole body slightly to the right, her words coming out half-slurred. Looking up again at Amon, she forced a smile, but the rest of her face grimaced, creating a commiserating contrast. Meanwhile, her fidgeting seemed to get worse and worse. She inserted the fingers of her right hand in and out of the hair tied up tightly on the top of her head while the fingers of her left hand opened and closed repeatedly on the tabletop, and she shifted in her chair almost constantly, her breaths shallow and quick.

"Are you okay?" Amon asked.

Mayuko finished her third glass of awamori and said. "I'm just upset . . . and maybe a bit tipsy, that's all. And this is the first night I haven't run on my treadmill in ages."

Frowning, Amon thought for a moment. "I remember you were always good at sports, but you were never really into working out. You just liked the fun of it. Now it seems like every time I talk to you, you're on that treadmill and you've got this look on your face like it's some kind of chore." In spite of himself, he stifled another yawn. "When did you start exercising so much and worrying about calories?"

"After we broke—" she stopped herself. "Around the time Rick and I started dating."

After we broke up, thought Amon, wondering what it was about that Mayuko felt the need to hide. She glanced at him with a look almost like guilt and saw that he'd noticed her cover up. Then something in her seemed to shift, and she shuddered. Her eyes lost their point of focus, her mind drifting off into some hidden theatre of tragic memories. Then tension built up in her face as she fought to maintain her composure, the muscles around her eyes beginning to tick, her shoulders to vibrate with long, shaking breaths.

Confused, Amon put his elbows on the table and hid his face in his palms. He didn't know why, but something about what she'd said was affecting him deeply. The feeling was unfamiliar, and it took him a moment to figure out what it was—remorse. As though it were a fine glass dust permeating the very air he breathed, his chest stung with every inhalation. *What does that night in Ginza have to do with her exercise?*

"But. You . . . I . . ." he mumbled, wanting to ask her many things, but they had never once talked about their breakup and he struggled to find the words. To make matters worse, a wave of numbing exhaustion and inebriation was spreading across his body, submerging his thoughts in murk before they could reach his tongue. He bowed down too far and laid his head on the table for a half-second, hoping to rally his clarity, when the whole room suddenly melted away into the darkness of sleep.

20

WAKUWAKU CITY, MORNING

Amon awoke to the sound of rumbling rails and exhilarated screams: Wakuwaku City's birdsong. He found himself lying on the couch. He had been tucked in beneath a thin summer blanket, his head resting on a firm pillow. His right eye read 11 a.m. He sat up.

On the floor beside him, his suit was neatly folded with the duster resting on top. He guessed that Mayuko must have had it dry cleaned while he slept. On the table he could see dishes laid out and realized that she'd made him breakfast. There was a jar of strawberry jam, a boiled egg, a cucumber and tomato salad, triangular chunks of sliced persimmon, two thick slices of white bread, and a pot of coffee. With no sign of Mayuko, he supposed she'd gone to work. Standing up, he went over to the table, sat down, and began to eat.

Spreading the jam on the toast, he suddenly remembered the end of his talk with Mayuko the night before and felt a stab of guilt. Here he was sitting in the apartment she'd rented, eating her food, subsisting on her salary. With no hint of resentment for all the pain he'd put her through, she had rescued him. Now she was covering the interest on his loans, second by second. If he stayed dependent much longer, it would be more economical for her to pay off the principal and bring him back to zero. But could she afford that? Either way, it was too much to ask.

Taking a bite of the jam-slathered toast, Amon saw that a black petal now rested at the base of the glass vase beside the white one he'd dislodged with his finger. The white petal seemed more withered and dry than the previous night. The black one still retained some moist fullness, but it was dotted with holes. Where had they come from? With each bite of toast, he was gnawing through a fallen flower, shamelessly mutilating its elegant form. At that moment, he decided his next move. He had to find a job and get back on his feet.

Amon was startled when the bathroom door opened and Mayuko stepped out. She wore the same white shirt and khaki half-pants as yesterday, her comet hair flowing loose to her shoulders. "Above the banner," she said, opening the door to her room. "Then the font will have to—" She stepped over the threshold and closed the door behind her, muffled words indecipherable. Fully immersed in her task, she hadn't noticed that Amon was up. He remembered then that her company didn't own an office and she was always working remotely.

After finishing the toast, salad, and egg, Amon ate the persimmon with a toothpick and finished his coffee. The tone of Mayuko's voice coming through the wall rose in volume and pitch, sounding impatient, and Amon guessed she was directing one of her assistants. He remembered the look on her face in the car when she'd talked about finding ways of coping with one's profession, and started to wonder if she was speaking from experience. Mayuko worked for Capsize Solutions, a young, independent corporation that specialized in buying bankrupt companies at a low price, repackaging them, and selling them at a higher price. Her job was the repackaging. As head of marketing, she coordinated the design of logos, mottos, promotional videos, uniforms, websites, customer service overlays—in short, the entire audiovisual identity—of these failed enterprises, so as to increase their value in the eyes of investors. Her imagination was a tool that made shattered hopes appear like opportunity, that painted over marketplace vulnerabilities and obsolete business models with a chic new look. Now he suspected there was more to her obsession with exercise than their breakup. Her very means of earning money had to be taking its toll. All the more reason to start making his own living as soon as possible.

After finishing his coffee, Amon stacked the dishes and took them to the sink. As he wiped his plate down with a sponge, he began to consider his employment prospects. There was no going back to GATA, that was for sure. If he could expose the hidden corruption festering at the core of government and industry, he might one day restore everything that had been taken from him, including his career. But he would need to gather more evidence and seek out well-placed allies. Such an endeavor would require time and funding, so the first step had to be rebuilding his savings. *My savings! My savings!* screeched an agonized voice through the lips of an open wound in his soul. *I sacrificed every waking moment of the last seven years for that savings, every breath and blink, and it all came to nothing.* This was the voice of despair, Amon knew. He could ignore its words, but not the ache of self-pity, shame, and loss it spoke up for.

Wherever he applied, he would enter the job market a clean slate: with no letter of recommendation and no experience. For if he mentioned his previous life, word might one day leak out to GATA and Fertilex, who would track him down in a flash. Lacking a past, he might try impersonating a fresh BioPen graduate, partaking in newbie training programs for newbie pay. Alternately, he could find a forge artist in hackspace and buy a professional profile that would communicate his skill set. *Aron Kenzaki. Security guard/database analyst.* Guised in a new digimake, he would send out resumes that reflected what he could do, if not who he was. Then he might have a shot at something better than a starting salary. But whichever path he chose—faking his youth or his past—he could never hope for the prestige and incentive he'd once had. And even if the deception was never discovered, always he would be hounded by the awareness that every one of his achievements was founded on lies. Compared to the life built of honesty and diligence that he'd lost, the future awaiting him seemed hollow and fragile, a porcelain manikin in a man's suit. *No, it would be worse*, he realized, for his empty existence would be further tainted by unease, maybe paranoia, as the specter of one day being tracked down haunted him forever.

Once he'd dried the dishes with a towel and put them into the cupboard, he turned around and noticed a grayish-silver light seeping through the window. Walking over, he stood with his face up to the glass and looked out. A faint, iridescent field of InfoRain still hazed all of space outside, but now that the condensation had cleared, he could see just how high he was. Looking down, an intricate system of suspended tracks and scaffolding tangled its way to the street below, a multitude of aerodynamic forms pulsing along knots of steel at high velocity. Inside crescent-shaped cracks and slivers in this curving structure, tight streams of specks and oblong dots that must have been people and cars squirmed constantly into view and then out again. According to ScrimpNavi, he was seventy stories up.

Mayuko is paying for a room with a view, he realized. And what a view it was. None of the surrounding buildings reached their apartment: the tallest one across the street stopped several stories short. With no obstructions anywhere, Amon could see the whole metropolis stretched out before him, an endless vista of info-slathered rooftops rising to varying heights, like the steps of a staircase disassembled and scattered at random, leading nowhere. Graphical inducements fluttered rapidly between the shafts like bouncing pinballs beckoning the gambler to his next game. To center right, he could see the lavender and baby blue immensity of GATA Tower looming over all, its tip swallowed in the swirling, hypnopromo of raining InfoClouds above. Poking up over the roofscape in its vicinity were the thirteen skyscrapers of The Twelve And One, their heights relative to each other just as difficult to ascertain from this vantage as any other. Labels popped up over particular swathes of buildings arrayed around these financial monoliths, indicating the names of districts: Chiyoda, Shibuya, Kabukicho, Jinbocho, Akihabara, Tsukuda, Tsukiji, Kiyosumi, Kanda, Ginza, Shinbashi. The list went on and on. Amon felt like he'd visited so many places in the last two days, but now he realized that it had been a mere speck of this vast amorphous adscape called Tokyo. Its roads and alleys and levels were too numerous and labyrinthine to traverse in a lifetime. Its veneer of imagery was too evanescent to observe even a minuscule fraction before the informational contours of the whole had been remade anew.

There was one area far to the left of GATA Tower that was unlabelled, and Amon wondered why, until he spotted a river running before it. From his vantage, the river looked like a thin silver thread peeking intermittently between roofscape cracks, but he knew that it was a mighty torrent when viewed up close. The Sanzu River, a massive watercourse, marked the border between Wakuwaku City and the District of Dreams on the opposite bank.

Amon had never before laid eyes directly on the District of Dreams, and allowed himself to gaze upon it for a time. To his surprise, it seemed well-maintained, the glass of the sleek skyscrapers sparkling clean as in any other area. The spectacle certainly didn't resemble the filth and squalor depicted in the reports from aid groups that worked in the pecuniary retreats, and he wondered how much of it was digitally rendered. A society stranded from the global economy could never hope to procure enough resources for infrastructure upkeep, and he seriously doubted that charity could make up the difference. Then suddenly he had a chilling thought. Perhaps it was like one of those dictatorships he'd read about in the history books, where the border lands were lined with grand mansions, sumptuous gardens, and bright lights while the inner towns went dilapidated, the people starved, and blackouts rolled ceaselessly.

Wakuwaku City and the District of Dreams were two manmade islands that covered the northern section of what was once called Tokyo Bay. Until Mount Fuji and neighboring mountains in the Southern Alps were hollowed out about a decade earlier, Japan had always lacked space for waste storage and it had been common practice to dump in the sea. Over decades, most of the bay was filled in with household garbage, rubble from demolished buildings, and nuclear waste, before being sealed in concrete. The resulting landmass was separated from the rest of Tokyo by canals and divided east to west by the Sanzu River, an artificial confluence of various rivers that ran out to sea.

The two islands were originally owned by rival MegaGloms (the land had since changed hands so many times, Amon couldn't recall which). Before the Free Era began, these MegaGloms rapidly threw up luxury condos all at once across their respective territories and competed with each other to attract buyers. The eastern island was integrated with the theme parks once running along the Boso Peninsula on the Chiba side of the bay. Officially it was called Minami Ward, but quickly became known as Wakuwaku City. With subsidies offered to residents for the inconvenience of living amidst rides and crowds, the units filled up quickly. Construction on the western half, however, was beset with numerous problems. Some of the contractors were found to be involved with the yakuza, funding mysteriously vanished, and crooked administrators set the prices inordinately high so they could skim a bit off the top. When the buildings stood in half-finished limbo for several years, tales about stretches of unclaimed urban territory began to reach the ears of the bankdead. Sick of huddling in the overcrowded shelters of areas like Ueno, many began to slip their way in. When the Fiscal Judiciary issued the controversial judgment that *removing* the squatters was the credicrime of *ethnic cleansing*, the property owners tallied these fines onto the already unmanageable debt from the construction debacle and decided to indefinitely postpone the grand opening. Instead, they struck a deal with the venture charities. Food and supply outposts moved shop, millions migrated from across Tokyo and Japan, and the District of Dreams became the most populous bankdeath camp in the world.

As he stared at the skyscrapers beyond the river, a strange bow-like shape began to take form across the infoscape skyline. Faint and ghostly at first, it gradually increased in opacity, until Amon could identify what it was: an InfoRainbow. Behind Mayuko's building, where Amon couldn't see it, the InfoSun was peeking out from the cloud cover, its infolight refracting through the InfoRain still falling all around, reverting the flickering images of both into their fundamental graphical elements. An arch of squirming pixels and inchoate color flecks curved against the cloudy InfoSky, its mid-section blocked by GATA Tower, its two bases by the jutting architectural sprawl below. This was Amon's first viewing of such a rare phenomenon, but looking directly at it hurt his eyes, so he turned from the window.

Sitting back down at the table, he began to wonder for the first time what had become of the many economic offenders he'd captured over the years. Surely they were scraping out a living somewhere in the camps, but were they happy? Sad? Bitter? Hopeful? Depending on which reports in bronze media you believed, pecuniary retreats were either slovenly hives of indolence or, as critics in the counterculture had dubbed them, the best of all possible slums. Whichever story was accurate, conditions were said to be harsh but tolerable due to the kind donations of Free Citizens, but what was it really like to live there?

In the past, Amon had always viewed the bankdead as radically other, almost like another species unfit for the financial pressures of the environment inhabited by true, hard-working humanity. But crouching in the rain with the other Illiquid, he had peered into the abyss of bankruptcy and seen that even he might slip in, that life was like the metropolis itself, with infinite branching paths and just as many distractions to obscure the way, some roads leading to misfortune in spite of our most conscientious efforts. All it took was a bit of bad luck and anyone could step into the pit of bankruptcy without warning, but did that mean they had earned such a fate? Our basic predicament was the same, whether bankdead or Free Citizen. Although Amon had met charity campaigners who profited from donations, he'd never met anyone who truly seemed to care about the bankdead, except perhaps Makesh Adani. Right! Makesh had offered him a job. Contacting him—no, contacting *her*—had seemed unimaginable before, especially since aid workers were generally low paid. But if the offer was still open, it was probably his best option. He would have no need to lie, for Makesh recognized his potential already and might offer him responsibilities commensurate with his capabilities. Furthermore, if Makesh was truly one of the Birla sisters, she had great wealth at her disposal, meaning Amon might hope for a more lucrative salary than he'd assumed, and perhaps a bit of protection.

Although he'd deleted Makesh's business card, he had the LifeStream from when he viewed it saved, so he could contact her at any time. But could he trust her? The other Birla sister, who collaborated with Sekido, was undoubtedly an enemy, and since Makesh had warned Amon of impending danger, perhaps she was an ally. Yet this was just a guess. Although the sisters appeared to be in opposition, familial bonds might take priority over petty disputes. Moreover, if they were in fact the Birlas, Amon could be sure that Makesh had lied about her name (and her gender for that matter), although he had no idea which recruiter was the elder Rashana, and which the younger Anisha. So, while there was a good chance he could count on Makesh, Amon needed to understand the woman's motives more clearly before putting his life in her hands.

Since the Birlas were highly protective of their audiovisual identities, Amon knew it would be a senseless waste of Mayuko's savings to try searching for images of their faces online. Later on, he decided, he would commission Monju for more information. The PhisherKing would definitely be interested in Amon's LifeStream of his meeting at Shuffle Boom, which contained evidence of GATA's collusion with Fertilex. It would be even more valuable if sold as a set with the recording of Amon's meeting with Makesh, for combined the two segs suggested that the Birla sisters were involved in Barrow's ID assassination, whether supporting or opposing it. But Amon had to get Mayuko's permission to borrow funding for the negotiation and resolved to speak with her before visiting Akihabara later that day.

Amon opened up his LifeStream and began to cut off still images. He hoped to use them as samples to pique the PhisherKing's interest and maybe secure a better deal. Aside from turning on Spam Fortress and opting out of the body-ad contract, he hadn't interfaced with his left hand since it was restored and this was his first time using it to execute several commands in a row. Severed from the ImmaNet, it had felt dead, like a lump of cold, useless flesh, and he was delighted to have it back online. Until, that is, he noticed something strange.

Overall, his left hand responded fine, but sometimes there would be a slight lag between when he moved his pinky and when the movement was registered. And coinciding with this, he occasionally noticed the overlay trailing behind his naked digit, producing a momentary double image. Amon guessed that Code Dr. had not yet returned full functionality to the appendage, but upon opening the app, he found a warning message that had been minimized and hidden in the corner of his left eye. It explained that he had been mostly disinfected, but that a malware trace still lingered. Code Dr. claimed to have downloaded the latest update and cured it, but Amon felt he could no longer trust the app after this failure and deactivated his pinky. Suspecting that the phantom finger might have performed some sort of unauthorized operation, Amon used his remaining nine digits to scroll back through his readout and quickly found a transaction from several minutes earlier that he didn't remember performing: *send text*. He then opened his sent folder and found an unfamiliar message. The subject line was blank and the address of the recipient was not in his contact book.

Upon opening it, he found it lacked a body entirely. All the transmission contained was a snapshot of the cityscape taken from up high. Studying it for a few seconds, he found a blurry arc of pixellation in the distance. His heart pounding with fear, he got up and looked out the window to be sure. There was no doubt about it. It was the exact same vista he'd just seen, InfoRainbow and all. Terrified and confused, Amon gazed blankly over the metropolis, trying to fathom what had happened. A merry-go-round ringing the shaft of an adjacent building had been shut down. With fading inertia, its turning gradually slowed, like a roulette wheel before the decisive moment.

Just then, the call of a loon warbled through the apartment, sending a chill down his spine. Immediately it sounded again just as Mayuko burst into the room.

"Did you invite anyone here, Amon?" her voice was calm, but there was fear in her eyes. "Some weird men in the lobby are asking for you."

"What?!" he shouted, getting to his feet. "Show them to me."

Mayuko tossed a ball, which expanded into a portal in the center of the room. Within the circular frame, Amon could see nearly a dozen men in a hallway of lime green marble. Standing erect and motionless like soldiers, they formed two lines of five each stationed one behind the other, plus a lone man standing out front of the rest.

The men in lines looked like *tengu*, with red faces, golden eyes, huge feathered wings, and horribly long cylindrical noses that got incrementally thicker towards the bulb-like tip. They wore black shawls, baggy black pants, and black boots with a separate segment for the big toe, like mittens for feet. Their clothes were soaked in InfoRain and a panel of interior designers in matching Hawaiian jumpsuits discussing investment in hot futures drip, drip, dripped off their long noses onto the lobby welcome mat.

The lone man in front wore a white robe that billowed to the floor, white gloves, and sandals of braided straw. Although of average height and build, his long, narrow face lacked features almost entirely. His ears were large and round like those of a jolly Buddha and a ladder of deep horizontal wrinkles ran from his bald pate to his hairless brow. But between brow and chin, where his eye sockets, nose, and mouth should have been, an utterly flat sheet of pallid skin stretched.

The man pulled up the drooping sleeve of his robes to expose his analog wristwatch and tipped his face towards it, as though checking the time despite having no eyes. "I said, I'd like to speak to Amon Kenzaki." A lipless slit suddenly appeared above his chin as though the act of speaking had ripped him a mouth. At the same moment, two perfect circles of pure white light carved themselves below his brow. These radiant eye-sockets seemed to open into the bright, empty lantern of his skull. Incongruously, he still had no nose or nostrils—a flat patch remaining in the center of his countenance—and his mouth didn't move when he spoke. Instead, his features kept repeating the same sequence of motions over and over. His head turned to the left to draw attention to his right eye-hole, whereupon the flesh above and below squeezed it closed. Once this wink was complete, his head would suddenly be centered and his eye open again. This reversion to his initial expression was instantaneous and lacked any transitional movements. He began the pattern anew each second and performed it exactly the same way every time, like some sort of freakish emoticon.

"My men are wet and I don't have time to wait around," he said. "So I'd appreciate if you came to speak with me right away, Amon. I know you're in there." His voice was faint and rattling, wavering at an eerie high pitch like the whistle of winter wind through a city of broken windows.

"Fuck!" howled Amon, squeezing his pinky in his right fist and shaking it violently. Flailing about the room, he felt the urge to chop it off with a knife from the kitchen.

"What's going on?" asked Mayuko, gripping him firmly by the shoulders in his frenzy and forcing him to face her. The look of urgency in her incisive eyes sobered him, and he released his finger, his muscles relaxing into resignation.

"You know that fucking virus I had?"

"Yes. What's wrong?"

"Code Dr. couldn't completely eliminate it, and the virus suppressed the warning message, so I only noticed just now."

"No! What did it do?"

"A few minutes ago, it woke up, took a snapshot out the window from my eyes, and sent it to someone. It must have taken them a bit of time to do the calculations with satellite pictures, but now they've managed to home in on this—"

"I've waited long enough," rattled the man, his slit-mouth unmoving. "Please respond immediately." He began to frown, his forehead wrinkles bending inwards towards the center to make a stack of Vs, his eyeholes narrowing to bright lines like vending machine coin slots. Then his expression snapped back to neutral, looping repeatedly as before. When his eyes were completely open, the full strength of their light was released, bleaching the marble of the hallway to a faintly green-tinged white and, when he squinted, the illumination was reduced so that the original lime color returned, the space around him blinking between two hues. The tengu all stood perfectly still behind him, the drip of InfoRain slowing.

"You've got the wrong address," said Mayuko. "There's no one by that name here."

"No nonsense, please. If you're going to continue being evasive, I'm afraid we'll be forced to carry out an inspection."

"Under whose authority? You're not Liquidators and I'm not bankrupt. There it is on my readout. I've just been compensated for a credicrime. You're threatening to break into my rented property."

"Let's not get sidetracked by irrelevancies. I know Amon is there and I insist on speaking with him."

"What should we do?" asked Mayuko after cutting off her audio transmission to the lobby. Staring into her wide, fearful eyes, Amon froze, the thumping of his heart loud and ominous.

Although the face of the freakish emoticon man continued to cycle between frowning and neutral, he rolled up his right sleeve as though to check his watch again, his shifting luminant holes pointing straight ahead. "I see you've made your choice." He walked towards the elevator at the end of the hallway and immediately the tengu began to march in step behind him. With a wave of his white-gloved hand, the doors opened.

"How can he do that?" Mayuko demanded. "No one invited him here!"

"They must have cracked the security system."

"But . . . You mean they can just barge right in here?"

"Does the door have a password?"

"Yes!"

"Change it now!" Mayuko nodded and did some finger flicks. "Make it as long and complicated as you can, and transmit it with heavy encryption by a server you've never used before." Not only would this keep the door closed, it would prevent anyone from sending their perspective inside the room without authorization.

The emoticon man entered the elevator first and stood in the center. Eight of the tengu filed in and lined up in twos on each side of him to form an enclosing box, while two of them remained stationed in the hallway. When the doors closed, the portal shifted its perspective inside the chamber. The man looked at his wristwatch and his features vanished, becoming blank flesh again. He then waved his gloved hand and immediately the elevator began to ascend.

When Amon looked through Mayuko's perspective and saw that she was done changing the password, he said, "Okay. Now activate the emergency stop button."

She did as he requested, but by the time the stopping mechanism engaged, the elevator had already reached her floor. The man waved his gloved hand and the inner door opened, but the outer door didn't budge. The men inside stood in formation before the thick, steel barrier—all that remained between them and the apartment.

"Please open up," said the man. "We don't want to damage this property."

Mayuko backed away from the door and looked at Amon with an expression of bewildered terror.

Amon put his finger to his lips to indicate that she should be quiet in case they might hear through the door.

WHO ARE THEY? texted Mayuko.

I THINK THAT WEIRDO IN THE MIDDLE IS THE HEADHUNTER FROM SHUFFLE BOOM, EITHER ANISHA OR RASHANA. HE PROBABLY PUT UP THE MONEY TO HAVE THE PARASITE THAT SEKIDO GAVE ME DESIGNED. THE VIRUS MUST HAVE SENT THE IMAGE TO HIM. NOW HE'S BROUGHT SOME MERCENARIES TO GET ME.

The man made a fist with his white gloved hand and did a knocking motion in the direction of the door. Immediately, they heard a thud from the entrance and Mayuko jolted away from it in fright. More thuds followed and the door shook repeatedly as the two tengu in front began to kick it at a steady pace in alternation.

Amon activated a Liquidator standard issue shape recognition app called KonTour. It traced white lines around the edge of bulges, folds, and billows in their clothes, searching for concealed weapons. It detected nothing, which was encouraging, but given how baggy the shawls and pants of the tengu were, offered no guarantees.

OH, THIS IS AWFUL, texted Mayuko.

HOW DO WE GET OUT OF HERE?

THERE'S A FIRE EXIT THROUGH MY ROOM. She rushed over and opened the bedroom door. WE'RE TOO HIGH TO CLIMB DOWN BUT THERE'S A RIDE ON THE ROOF. WE CAN PROBABLY FIND A WAY DOWN FROM THERE.

NO! Amon texted, as she made her way across the room to a thick whitish-blue door on the back wall. THEY'LL BE WATCHING THE EXIT AND TWO OF THEM ARE WAITING FOR US BELOW. IT WON'T TAKE THE OTHERS LONG TO CATCH UP WITH US IN THAT ELEVATOR ONCE THEY'VE CRACKED THE EMERGENCY STOP AND THERE COULD BE MORE LURKING ABOUT. HOW MUCH MONEY DO YOU HAVE IN YOUR ACCOUNT?

WHAT DOES THAT MATTER?

MAYBE WE CAN STAY AND FIGHT, texted Amon as he went over to the elevator, carried his shoes in from the doorway and began to change into his suit.

Grasping his meaning, Mayuko sent a figure to Amon and he went to the Fiscal Judiciary's website. There he found the credicrime database and did a search for "Liquidator abuse of authority." The thudding on the door was steady and rhythmic, boots striking the same spot in turn, and the sound was amplified as it doubled up with the recording coming through the portal. From their cold efficiency, Amon could see that these mercenaries were well-trained. He couldn't hope to take them all in a fair firefight, but given KonTour's result they were probably unarmed. Either way, if he waited until a hole opened in the door and went trigger-happy into the chamber, he could dust everyone inside before they knew what hit them. With any luck, the Judicial Broker would rule it as self-defense, given that the men were breaking into his friend's rented property. Then Mayuko would pay nothing and they might find a way to escape. Yet Amon wasn't authorized to use his duster except in the line of duty, and dispatching nine men would undoubtedly incur heavy penalties. When he found the list of credicrimes he was looking for, Amon watched their fines fluctuate with inflation. He then had PennyPinch calculate whether Mayuko's balance was enough. Amon was impressed by the amount she had saved: it rivaled his dream account, and just kept on growing rapidly as the compensation for the B & E continued to pour in. But it still wasn't enough. The penalty was stricter than he'd expected, and the assault would clean her out.

For a moment he considered cutting the leash and dusting them with his own funding, but what would that achieve? He might succeed in knocking them out, but it would mean instant financial suicide. Then Sekido could get into Amon's inner profile using the access privileges given to the assigned Liquidator or, failing that, wait until the Collectors took his cash-crashed body to the now-corrupted Archives for upload and a quick look through his LifeStream would reveal just how much Mayuko knew. She would become their new target, and there would be no one to protect her. They might as well just turn themselves in on the spot. No! They would have to find a way out.

As the man checked his watch, the tengu rotated clockwise around him so that two men with fresh legs could take over the kicking. The switchover was so smooth they didn't miss a thud. Already a slight dent had appeared in the outer door. Apparently the material was much cheaper and flimsier than it looked.

IS THERE ANY WAY TO SLIP INTO ONE OF THE OTHER APARTMENTS? texted Amon, buckling the duster to his belt and slipping on his jacket.

Mayuko shook her head. I DON'T THINK SO. THERE'S NO HALLWAY. JUST ELEVATORS THAT LEAD STRAIGHT INTO EACH ONE.

Like a cornered beast, Amon's eyes darted madly about the room in search of an exit, but there was none to be found. Just an elevator under siege, a door being watched, and a window that opened to a seventy-story plunge. Could he leap out and grab ahold of some ride scaffolding? Maybe, but it was madness to think he could climb to the ground without losing his grip, especially if a coaster rode over and shook the track. Amon felt his gut clenching with terror. He took out his duster, pointed it at the growing bulge in the door, and then put it away again. He ran his fingers over his buzzed hair and gritted his teeth. He wanted to scream and shout, but that would only tell his pursuers that Mayuko had company, and they would recognize his voice upon analysis. He knew he should have got a capsule on his own. Because of his presence she was in danger now, and his evidence was about to be seized. The only sane possibility was the fire escape after all. If he could just find a way for them to sneak out unnoticed. *Yes!* He remembered one of the tricks a bankrupt had tried to pull on him and immediately conceived a plan.

Amon did some quick calculations to make sure it was financially feasible. He knew that Mayuko was watching him through his perspective and, when he was finished, he turned to her, and shook his head. THIS ISN'T GONNA WORK. IT WOULD BRING YOU RIGHT TO THE EDGE OF BANKRUPTCY. AND EVEN IF WE HAD THE FUNDING, THEY'LL KNOW THE MOMENT THE DOOR OPENS.

BUT WHAT IF . . . YOU WENT OUT ALONE.

WHAT!? YOU CAN'T--

I CAN AFFORD IT FOR ONE OF US. AND IF I OPEN THE DOOR FOR YOU, THEY WON'T HAVE A CLUE.

NO WAY. Amon gave his head a single emphatic shake. IF ONE OF US GOES, IT'LL BE YOU.

ARE YOU CRAZY? WE DON'T HAVE THE MONEY TO FIGHT, SO WHAT ARE YOU GOING TO DO? JUST LET THESE WEIRDOS HAVE THEIR WAY WITH YOU?

Unsure how to answer, Amon froze and stared into Mayuko's incisive but deeply-troubled eyes.

PLEASE, AMON. I'VE JUST LOST RICK. I DON'T KNOW WHAT I'D DO IF I LOST YOU TOO. YOU'RE MY ONLY FRIEND LEFT AND EVERYTHING'S SO COMPLICATED NOW. I CAN'T FIGURE THIS ALL OUT ON MY OWN.

As Mayuko stared up at him with an expression of utter despair, Amon thought about what she'd said for a moment. If he gave in peacefully and did nothing to bankrupt Mayuko or himself, he could pretend that he'd borrowed a woman's voice to lie to the men earlier and she might slip away safely. Yet there was no telling what they would do to him, and in all likelihood Mayuko would be left to spend the rest of her days alone in the city. Her two closest friends would be gone and she would have no way of finding out what had happened to them. Not being a Liquidator, she didn't know how the bureaucracy worked, and even with the segs he'd given her, she wouldn't know the first thing about where to start. Amon tried to imagine her life after he disappeared—directing her subordinates impatiently for the same opportunistic company, coming home by herself to this same joyless theme park, wondering every moment she had why the most important people in her life had been stolen from her, running so much on that treadmill her body just melted away ... Was sacrificing himself to leave her in baffling solitude really the right thing to do? Could he really forsake justice and let Rick's murder sink unproven into the dark oblivion of time? And what about his dream, the goal to which he had dedicated his whole waking existence for the last seven years? Was he going to let a bunch of double-dealing technocrats just kill it and get away with it?

If he left and she stayed, there was still a chance the two of them could survive, for the men could never be certain Amon had ever been there. All they were going on, after all, was some photo from a barely functional virus. As far as they knew, the email could have been forged and sent to throw them off the trail. Or their calculations were off and they had homed in on the wrong room. Or the virus could have been transmitted to someone else and the picture taken from eyes that were miles from Amon. Their lead was too shaky. And if digiguised Mayuko insisted she had never heard of Amon, they'd have no choice but to accept their mistake and—

Boom! There was a loud noise from the elevator, as one of the tengu delivered an especially strong kick, and Mayuko and Amon flicked their heads towards it simultaneously. The dent was bulging out from the surface now like a steel egg, shaking and expanding with each impact. It would not be long before a hole opened up and the men could see into the room.

"Come on, Amon," said Mayuko, "can you think of anything better?"

Looking back into her moist, quivering eyes, Amon realized that he couldn't. Some macho part of him bellowed that fleeing was cowardly, that he ought to take a stand and protect her. She had saved him and he owed her more than he could ever return. But he needed her as much as she needed him now, and the greatest danger to her was his presence. It was the best chance they had. For her, for Rick, for himself, he had to go.

OKAY, WE'VE GOT TO MOVE QUICKLY. Without waiting for Mayuko's reaction, Amon glanced at the pulsing steel surface. Already the dent was as big as a giant's fist.

He gave Mayuko precise instructions and she went into the bedroom.

WHATEVER YOU DO, texted Amon, as he waited around the corner, DON'T LOOK AT ME. I'LL PASS RIGHT BY YOU, BUT I NEED YOU TO PRETEND I'M NOT EVEN THERE. NOT EVEN A GLANCE IN MY DIRECTION.

She nodded, opened the emergency door, and stepped out onto the fire escape landing.

"Stay put!" rattled the emoticon man, his voice drifting to their ears from the portal in the living room. "My men are stationed downstairs and we can follow you to any floor. Don't you dare waste my time!"

As Amon had suspected, they were watching the exit, but that wouldn't matter. With a digimake eraser he rubbed out his entire body from head to toe, charged across the bedroom, and dashed out the door past Mayuko.

21

TRAINSMIGRATION

Taking the stairs two, three, four at a time, the division between each step irrelevant in his haste, Amon bounded to the next landing. Spinning around, he half-stumbled up another flight and reached the seventy-first floor. There he saw the emergency door for the apartment directly above Mayuko's and gave its handle a quick yank but of course it was locked. *No time for that*, he thought, and kept on climbing.

Clang, clang, thump. Clang, clang, clang, thump. The sporadic rhythm of his feet on the metal grating beat out of time with the steady thudding on the elevator door. His ears were still half in the room with Mayuko and he made her perspective into a thin overlay. She stood beside the table looking at the dent. The steel egg seemed to be hatching now, with jagged shards of metal jutting from a small hole open at its peak. As though nothing were amiss, she went into the kitchen and filled the kettle, just as Amon reached the top of the stairwell wondering if she was planning to scald them.

On the left side of the roof he saw a raised block that resembled a small stage, where a thin man wearing a blue polyester jacket was strapping a bungee cord to a pudgy man in street clothes. On the far right, a square glass chamber that Amon guessed was an elevator stuck out over the edge. Two lineups bordered by rope barriers ran in parallel between the two, one headed for the bungee ride, one the elevator. Amon sprinted to the right along the outside of the nearest rope. As he approached the chamber, a glass platform crowded with thrill-seekers rose into it. When the platform became level with the roof, it stopped and the clear wall of the chamber slid open left and right from a vertical slit in the middle, whereupon the passengers poured off and got in line for the ride. When he reached the edge of the roof, Amon stopped beside the nearest rope, pushed in the people on the other side to make room for himself, and stepped over to join the front of the line for the elevator. As those around him began to board, Amon butted his way towards the doors, the absence that shoved and shouldered everyone aside getting strange looks. Then, just when he was about to step over the threshold, an arm swung down in his path like the barrier at a railway crossing.

"Sir," said the owner of the arm, another man in a blue polyester jacket who stood to the side of the door, "You'll have to go to the back of the line."

Most ride operators discouraged cutting ahead by adding an extra charge, but some hired attendants like this guy to keep the crowds flowing quickly and maximize profits. Irritated by this unexpected obstacle, Amon made a tight fist and was about to slug him when he thought of a cheaper way through. Quickly, he changed his digimake settings to turn himself visible only to the man. He then set the surface of his palm to play a LifeStream montage of every moment he had ever dusted someone—beginning with Freg and working backwards to his very first mission—before holding it up in front of the man's eyes. Immediately the man was transfixed, staring at the shifting images of person after person collapsing in horrendous agony, until Amon flicked aside his jacket, lowered his upraised hand, and gestured to his hip, directing the man's gaze towards the holster clipped there. Once he saw the weapon, the man's focus drew back and seemed to take in Amon's whole body for the first time, including his concrete gray uniform, and his eyes went wide. This was Amon's cue to step forward—the arm across the doorway no longer offering any resistance—and he got in the elevator with the others crowding in behind him.

Just as the doors slid shut, there was a vaporous hiss. White steam was rising from a kettle and brown granules filled a strainer set atop a cup. Mayuko was making coffee. When she glanced back at the elevator, Amon saw that the hole was about the size of a man's head now and was stretching steadily as booted feet slammed repeatedly into its rim.

The glass chamber was the tip of a long rectangular shaft that ran down the side of the building to the street far, far below. As the platform began to plunge down the shaft, Amon found himself enthralled by the vista beneath the slivers of transparent floor not blocked by the feet crowded around him. Sheer cliffs of rippling promovation wildfire on all sides and ramified coaster tracks inter-spiraling between them whipped past as though rocketing towards the sky, while the squirming specks of cars and pedestrians that he could see through scaffolding cracks grew larger and larger. His readout said *abuse of authority, intimidation,* and, repeated every second, *invisibility.* This last action was more expensive than the others. The fee for completely erasing something from the ImmaNet in a private space (such as the Liquidation Ministry) was high enough, but applying invisibility to the human body in public was strictly banned by credilaw since it could cause dangerous collisions, and nine times out of ten was used for some perverted voyeuristic offense. Moreover, unlike the other actions, he had it on continuously. Amon felt sorry that Mayuko had to pay these hefty fines. The total was nothing compared to what it would have cost to dust the men in the elevator, but it would send her into debt before long, unless he could find a hidden place to turn visible as soon as he got to the street.

Despite all this, Mayuko seemed to be coping well. The hole was now big enough for a toddler to crawl through, and the jagged shards of metal that projected dangerously into the center were gradually bending outwards. But she just sat at the table sipping her black coffee and breathing deeply as she patiently awaited them. Amon was impressed.

The continuous battering seemed to have softened the metal, for all of a sudden the hole expanded several centimeters in every direction and the thudding ceased. Seconds later, the long nose of a tengu poked out slowly through the mangled door, followed by his head and shoulders. Suddenly, hands boosted him by his legs from behind and he flew smoothly through the hole, slipping barely between the jutting blades as though escaping from a shark's jaw. Diving to the floor, he did a roll, sprang to his feet, and flapped his wings, flicking a color-wriggling splatter of InfoRain residue onto the walls. He then went over to the hole and kicked the shards outwards until all the sharp tips were bent flat against the door. When he was done, the remaining tengu immediately began to crawl in one by one and line up facing the way they had come. Once all eight were through, two stood on each side of the hole and took the hands that came out, helping the emoticon man into the room, wrinkled head first. Once he was standing with them, they did a simultaneous about-face, their golden eyes regarding Mayuko from the base of their long noses, like the crosshairs of sniper rifles. The bald man faced her too, if he could be said to face anything now that his featureless wall of pallid flesh was on again.

The platform stopped, the glass doors opened onto the sidewalk, and Amon got out with the other passengers. Unable to see his body, passersby walked straight at him and didn't give way, but he did his best not to bump anyone, sidestepping and dodging his way to the curb. The cars were stopped at the red light and he dashed across, carving through thin channels between bumpers and bounding over the line of shrubbery in the middle. Reaching the opposite sidewalk, he careened into a tunnel leading underground to Wakuwaku Station. Instead of the packed escalator, he took the stairs, leaping past and around the ascending salarymen from flight to flight.

Mayuko continued to quietly sip her coffee as she watched the men creep slowly towards her. When they were close enough, she could see up into the huge nostrils of the tengu, the inside lined with tiny black feathers. Soon she was surrounded, the tip of their long noses ringing her head, the emoticon man confronting her face to unface. Unable to meet his eyeless gaze, she stared down at the dark brown liquid in her cup, stirring it pointlessly with a little spoon.

Amon was still searching train routes when he reached the platform. The tail ends of the lines in front of each door were filing onto the train. "The doors will close. Charging on board is dangerous. Please wait for the next train," said a deep male voice. Galloping to the edge of the platform, Amon leapt into the half-empty car just as the doors slid shut. When the train began to move, he turned off his invisibility and stood there panting. Although his body had been erased and his footsteps muted, his interactions with other people had still been observable. If his pursuers somehow figured out that he'd slipped out the fire escape, as unlikely as this seemed, they might have been able to follow the recording of his trail of impacts using an app like God's Eye. But he had collided with nothing since leaving the glass platform, so they would have no way of knowing which way he went, nor would they know for certain it was Amon who had fled rather than someone else. If they somehow figured out that he had entered the station, they still wouldn't know which train he had taken (or whether he had taken a train at all). Now he was on a linear locomotive—the fastest ride out of Wakuwaku City—and, supposing the worst case scenario in which they did somehow manage to locate the car he'd boarded, by that time he would be far, far away, and the surveillance costs too great to track him down. It certainly wasn't over yet. Mayuko was still paying for everything he did—the line-cutting, the jaywalking, and now his ride on this super express—but he felt somewhat relieved to have slipped away undetected before the invisibility bankrupted her. Now there was little to bring her under suspicion and nothing they could do to find him. Or so he wanted to believe.

Over the encompassing infoblather and the muffled breakbeats of his spasmodic heart, Amon heard a voice. "Where is Amon Kenzaki?" said the man. The slit mouth and white holes reopened on his face. Mayuko could see his eye sockets more clearly now that he was up close. They seemed to open into a realm of pure luminescence somehow contained in his head. It was divided into countless hexagonal cells by a frame of golden beams, like some ephemeral honeycomb, the walls of this frame an iridescent membrane like soap bubbles.

"There's no one here," replied Mayuko. Her voice was calm, but the cup shook as she lifted it to her mouth.

Without moving their limbs or torsos, the tengu simultaneously rotated their heads around the room, their long noses like slow-motion helicopter rotors. Upon finishing a 360, they spread out and began to search the apartment. One looked under the couch while another opened the fridge and the cupboards. One entered each bedroom, one the lavatory, and one the shower room. Only one remained standing beside the emoticon man, the two of them wielding merciless stares.

The man's straw-sandalled feet seemed to glide over the floor beneath his white robes as he came even closer to Mayuko's seated form, his arms hanging loosely at his sides.

"We happen to know that he was here within the last hour," he rattled. "Tell us where he's gone, immediately." Eerily incongruous with his demanding tone, he beamed a broad smile. Through the lipless slit above his chin Mayuko saw a solid bar of bone that wrapped along the top of his oral cavity, as though his teeth had been welded together. Below this, resting within the pocked semicircular ridge of toothless gums on the bottom, was an oblong blot of faintly fluorescent orangish yellow and red, like a tongue viewed through infrared goggles. As his mouth opened, his eye-holes widened at the same rate, and within the golden soap-bubble honeycomb filling his skull, Mayuko could now see that each cell contained a woman. Naked, they reclined on their sides in empty space; their skin so pure and milky they nearly camouflaged into the white glare; silver grapes growing from their crimson hair; the delirious ecstasy in their eyes seeming to invite Mayuko into this paradise. When his smile and eyes widened to a certain diameter, his face flipped back to deadpan, and the cycle rebooted, widening smile to deadpan, smile to deadpan. When it was clear Mayuko wasn't going to answer, the man said: "I'll make you an offer to tell me."

A fund transfer window appeared before her, and Amon gasped at the number. He had seen it before, had almost memorized it in his anger and despair. Just to be sure, he scrolled to the section of his AT readout for 12:17:23 the night before last, and saw that it was indeed the exact amount of jubilee.

Mayuko clicked the decline button and said, "I don't know who you're talking about."

"Is that so? Then how about selling me your LifeStream for the last forty-eight hours." A window appeared with the same offer. This time Mayuko ignored it.

"Why don't you accept?" The man shook his head to show his disapproval. Or rather, the direction of his face blipped suddenly from in-line with his right shoulder to in-line with his left, displaying his noseless profile on both sides, the flesh folds of his huge ears tracing a deep and intricate maze. "I doubt you'll ever see money like this again."

Mayuko took another sip of coffee. "That is my private life and I'm not doing business with discreditable people like you. Now please leave." Her voice was amazingly calm.

"Who are you?" said the man. "Your name please."

"I asked you to leave."

Suddenly the illumination in the man's skull went out, leaving two shadowed holes below his brow. Then the spot on his face directly to the left of his left eye began to glow as though someone were holding a flashlight beneath the skin. This light moved in a straight line to the right, beamed brightly out of his eye socket, became a skin-smothered glow again when it reached the bridge of his non-nose, beamed brightly out of his right socket and vanished when it reached the patch of skin beside his right eye, like a photocopier. When the process was finished, the man's eyes lit up as before with the female-inhabited golden honeycomb matrix and he said, "Oh. I see now. It's you, is it? You're that girl. From his BioPen . . . Mayuko Takamatsu."

The room whipped from side to side as Mayuko shook her head.

"No. It has to be you. You do look a bit more worn out than in your youth, sure. But your hair. It has a certain glitter to it, doesn't it?"

Amon was agape with horror on the train as he watched this unfold. *How did he know?*

"Well, it seems that you've been wasting my time with lies, Ms. Takamatsu. I can't stand when people waste my time. But let's start from the beginning anyways, except this time I'd like you to try and answer as honestly as you can. Do you think you can manage that?"

Suddenly, it hit Amon what had happened. "Mayuko! Listen! He looked at your naked face. The Birlas can afford it. I saw one of them do it to a whole room. That means he knows exactly who you are and there's no way he'll believe that I wasn't there. So just tell him what he wants to know. We've got no choice."

Ignoring both men, Mayuko sat there silently looking into her coffee.

Suddenly, the emoticon man lifted a finger and the tengu kicked her dining table with the sole of his boot. It flipped over, the vase shattered against the back wall, black and white petals fluttered up and cascaded down, and Mayuko's coffee splashed out of her cup onto the floor. Still holding the wet ceramic handle in her right hand, she used her right arm to cradle her left elbow where the table had struck her.

"I don't want to waste any money making threats," said the man, "but I will if you force me to. Where has he gone?"

Don't you hurt her! thought Amon as he watched through her eyes from the crowded train. He squeezed his duster tight in his fist, itching to draw it on them. But while his eyes and ears were close by, his body was too far away for his dust to reach them. He wanted to get off the train and head back to the apartment, but the next stop wasn't for some time, and he could do nothing but shake with helpless rage. "Mayuko! What are you doing? Tell him where I am already. Quickly! Before it gets worse."

Still silent, Mayuko took another sip of the bit of coffee remaining in her cup.

Without another word, the emoticon man went irate. "When I ask questions, people answer! What? You're too good for my money? I'm making a generous offer here and you don't have the right to refuse! Speak, damn it! Speak! Tell me now! Where is Amon?"

The tengu plunged his right hand into his left nostril, reached past feathers deep into his nose until his arm was hidden up to the elbow, drew out a small handgun and pointed it at Mayuko. It was a miniature duster. But what kind? Nerve? Arthritis? Fairy? Surely not vegetable? Amon tried clicking it, and to his surprise details of the make and model popped up. He gasped. Access to the specs must have been left open for a reason: they wanted their targets to be afraid.

"Mayuko!" he shouted with urgency. "It's a piranha duster. Do you understand? Those nanobots will eat your flesh alive. Tell him already, please!" The tengu must have fooled KonTour by strapping the gun to his face and concealing it beneath his digital proboscis. Simply carrying such an illegal weapon incurred fines, and murder wouldn't be cheap even for the Birlas. But money aside, were these men really willing to go that far?

The emoticon man's expression was shifting again, but Amon couldn't make it out, as Mayuko's eyes were focused on the gun, its barrel and the nose of its wielder oriented identically. "Now you have a choice. Become a heap of bones or a wealthy lady. One or the other and nothing in between."

For a moment Mayuko's eye flicked over to the offer window, which still floated there unclicked. "I told you I don't—"

"Bullshit!" shouted the man. He began to gag as though vomiting, his mouth opening wide and his infrared tongue popping out. The contractions of the inside of his throat were visible at the back of the oral cavity, and his head popped towards her like a lunging snake spewing venom.

Gag, deadpan, gag, deadpan. "Don't think for a second that I can't afford to kill you. I can and I will unless you tell me the truth right now."

When Mayuko just kept staring blankly up at him, he grabbed her shirt, shouted "speak up!" and backhanded her across the cheek. A ragdoll in his grip, her head rolled to the side and her eyes fixed on the remains of the vase on the floor. Glass shards mixed with soggy petals lay soaking in a puddle, and the stem, barren but for a few white and black scraps, had rolled almost within reach.

Unable to move with the bodies pressing tight on all sides, Amon stomped his right foot hard into the floor and began to dig his fingernails into his scalp. This was what she got for rescuing him from the brink of bankruptcy. Fleeing had seemed like the only option, but with time closing in as the men rapidly breached the door, he had been too panicked to think clearly. He should have remembered how the activist had sundered the overlay at Sushi Migration and realized that her digimake was far from impregnable for the Birlas. He'd often pondered diminishing the overlay on GATA Tower to check its height relative to The Twelve And One, but this was just a fantasy. Peering beneath the digital veneer was not the sort of thing that regular people actually did. Not even the bankrupts he'd encountered, in their most licentious frenzies. Cost-benefit analysis was so deeply ingrained in all Free Citizens that affordability constructed the borders of possibility in their minds. And through his frugal training, Amon had built a narrow world indeed. Now that Mayuko was suffering for his limiting habits of thought, he saw what he had become and hated himself for it. If only he'd guessed that the men might look at her naked face or that they'd be packing weapons, he never would have left. He wanted to go back and fight—outnumbered, out-equipped, and out-financed as he was—but with the train blasting rapidly away, it was too late, and he bit his lip to fight back the tears.

"Pay attention to me!" said the man, grabbing her chin and forcing her to look into his eyeholes. They had grown so bright, Mayuko began to twitch. The cells had been totally whited out in the glare along with their inhabitants, but she could just make out thousands of tiny, delicate hands reaching towards her and hear faint, angelic singing. The man's wrinkled forehead expanded and opened like an accordion of mouths, sharp fangs bearing from the roof of each crease. Then his expression flipped back to neutral. The tengu beside him kept his duster sighted on her, and the others, having finished searching the apartment, began to gather around. The bulbous tip of their noses pointed straight at her, the veins that ran along these lengthy shafts pulsating with an aggressive vitality.

This is overkill, thought Amon. *All those mercenaries on an unarmed woman.* "Please, Mayuko!"

"Speak!" rattled the man, little dots of spittle blurring Mayuko's eyes as though from the forehead mouths. "Speak!"

"J-just listen," she said, her voice wavering with fear at last, "I-I don't know what—"

The man pushed her by the chin and Mayuko grabbed the sleeve of his robe to stop the chair from toppling, but one of the tengu kicked her wrist and she lost her grip, smacking into the floor back-first with a squeal. She tried to get up but a booted foot came down on each limb to pin her down and the tengu with the duster pointed it down at her. As her eyes began to shake, the room was totally blocked out by the muscular bodies looming over her, the ceiling mostly hidden by their canopy of noses. It was too much to bear. Amon wanted to look away, but the overlay followed his eyes and it was unthinkable to abandon her by turning it off.

"If you even squirm, my man will fire and you'll be nothing but bones. Now lie still! You've got one more chance to give me what you know before I take it."

The tengu beside the emoticon man put away his duster, stepped behind her head, and bent over her with a strange instrument. It was a thin metal rod with a suction cup on one end and thread-thin ectoplasmic tentacles of white neon wriggling out the other. Mayuko darted her eyes between the man and the instrument, her breaths quivering, her shaking body subdued by the four men stepping on her. "Do tell me soon and save me the expense of hacking you."

When Mayuko said nothing, the tengu attached the suction cup to her forehead and waved his palms in circles over her as though enacting an occult ritual. The neon-white tentacles began to wriggle into her mouth, eyes, and ears like slowly exhaled smoke reversing direction.

There was nothing more violating than being flesh-hacked. Breaking through the BodyBank security system remotely was next to impossible. Without some sort of access privileges, it could only be done by putting a sophisticated parasite in direct contact with the skin. Soon they would no doubt have full access to all her data. The virus Sekido had given Amon had probably been designed by the same technicians who had cracked the building security and would soon crack Mayuko's body. The lingering traces of that virus had taken over Amon's smallest finger and betrayed his whereabouts. Now Mayuko was suffering in his stead. The shame was too much. He couldn't stand up straight anymore and felt himself leaning with the motion of the train into the cocoon of bodies. He wished Mayuko had never rescued him from that factory yard. He wished he had never let her take him to that weekly mansion instead of going to a capsule on his own. He wished he'd never let her convince him to leave. The macho voice had been right. He was a coward. He was a pathetic, disgrace of a man. He didn't deserve to be standing. He ought to be lying on the floor of the train, trampled under the feet of the crowd. And thinking this way, his legs gave out under him, his head began to sink, and his visual field was swallowed in the black mire of suits. *Stop!* shouted another voice in his head, *Falling apart on her would be the worst cowardice of all*, and Amon forced himself upright with the faint remnants of his will, knowing it was true.

"Mayuko. I'm begging you," he said. "Just tell them where I am."

Mayuko did a gesture to switch on eye interface and closed her eyes to hide her commands. I CAN'T DO THAT, AMON.

"Why not? They'll kill you."

I'M AFRAID. I DON'T WANT TO DIE. BUT TELLING THEM IS ONLY GOING TO SPEED THINGS UP. ONCE THEY KNOW WHERE YOU ARE, DO YOU SERIOUSLY THINK THEY'LL JUST LET ME GO?

Immediately he saw that she was right. When she had given the men the information they needed, she would become their liability, since she knew as much as Amon did. Sekido would simply issue another fake bankruptcy report to have her crashed. Or perhaps the emoticon man would have her shot on the spot if murder was cheaper at that moment than bureaucratic trickery. Either way, if she told them where Amon was, they would both be doomed. Fearing for her life, Amon had panicked and failed to see this, but Mayuko, who had no combat-training, had somehow managed to keep her cool, and he was astounded by her bravery.

He realized then that she'd been right about something else too, although she couldn't have known it. If Amon had stayed alone in the apartment and she had fled invisibly instead, the men would have inevitably hacked him. Then they would have discovered the extent of her knowledge, just as if he had gone bankrupt. Their fates were inseparably bound and his fleeing alone had been the only chance either of them had, for now that he was loose he might still find a way to save her and himself.

THERE MUST BE SOMETHING WE CAN DO, she texted, as though reading his mind. YOU'VE ALWAYS BEEN GOOD WITH STRATEGIES, AMON. HELP ME.

At that moment, Mayuko glanced into the bottom left corner of her eye at her AT readout, and they both saw something strange and awful. There was a list of credicrimes committed against her by the men—breaking and entry, threats, intimidation, assault, hacking—but in the amount column, instead of a series of numbers, each one read "verdict pending."

"Oh shit. . . no!" said Amon.

WHAT'S GOING ON? WHY AREN'T I BEING COMPENSATED?

"They're appealing all of the sentences."

HOW? THE JUDICIAL BROKERS CAN'T SERIOUSLY DOUBT THEIR CULPABILITY.

"No, they wouldn't, but the Birlas must have powerful lawyers. I doubt they can win their case, since the evidence is obviously in your favor, but they'll be using every dirty legal trick they can think of to delay the verdict. In the end, the expense of appealing may be greater than the fines and that emoticon freak will probably have to pay both. But these lawsuits can last for hours sometimes, and if they can stall long enough, you'll be pushed right to the edge of bankruptcy. I've seen this kind of thing in AT readouts before. It's a ploy the super wealthy use to take away the freedom of their enemies."

OH NO, THIS IS AWFUL. YOU CAN'T BE--LOOK! I'M ALREADY DEEP IN THE RED. OUR DEBTS ARE TOO MUCH. WHAT ARE WE GOING TO DO?

The train began to slow to a stop. When the doors opened, Amon pushed his way out and headed for the stairs. He began to search train lines, looking for the fastest route to Wakuwaku Station. He found another train headed back that way, but stopped at the bottom of the staircase and stood there frozen. It wasn't an express like the one he'd come on and would take nearly forty-five minutes. By that time, their combined actions and interest would drive Mayuko bankrupt. The Liquidators couldn't technically crash her until all the credicrime verdicts were reached, but the blinding would still drop. Before he even got close enough to fight, Sekido would have Liquidators stationed on the other end. And in all likelihood, the men would hack Mayuko by then. One way or the other, they would both be caught. There was nothing to be done. It was over. Perhaps if he begged them, they would go easy on her.

As Amon was resigning himself to death of one kind or another, he heard the toot of a whistle. Turning his head, he saw a steam engine slowing down alongside his platform on the track opposite the train he had taken. It had a heavy frame of black iron, a dark wood panel interior, and luxurious seats upholstered in burgundy velvet lining both sides. He heard a rhythmic chugging, and as the train passed him his eyes caught black words across a copper plaque on the front: "Oneiro Express." Amon recognized the name immediately. The Oneiro Express was famous for running to Yume Station, the stop closest to the District of Dreams. In that instant an insight flooded his mind and Amon realized exactly what he needed to do.

He got in line to board the train and, before it came to a stop, he had already cast a figment of himself into Akihabara. The only listing for the PhisherKing was an address, but there was no rule saying visitors had to come in the flesh. Appearing before the rectangular pit, Amon found the elevator already waiting for him. The doors of the train and elevator opened at the same moment, as though the digital and naked worlds were beckoning him as one. He took a step forward, his body and its graphical copy in synch. Immediately, he heard a voice behind his back and turned around.

"Hello, Kenzaki-san," said Monju. He stood in front of the already closed doors. His bleach blond hair and dark trenchcoat rippled in an unfelt wind, his eyes gleaming strangely in the dim. "You took longer to contact me than I expected. Any fresh catch?"

"Here are some samples." Amon put the stills of his meetings at Sushi Migration and Shuffle Boom inside a glass orb and threw it to Monju, who caught it in a fish net that expanded from his palm like a magician's handkerchief. "These segs prove collusion between GATA officials and the Birla heirs. Interested?"

"Of course. How much are you asking?"

"I want to do another trade."

"For what?"

"I need information to blackmail this man." From Mayuko's LifeStream, Amon took frontal and profile stills of the emoticon man and flicked it like a card to Monju, who allowed it to slot between his knuckles. "Do you know who he is?"

Monju's eyes flickered rapidly in alternation from half-closed to closed for a second before he answered. "Yes."

Amon wanted to ask who, but he knew the info would cost him and had more important deals to make. "Do you have anything that might sway him?"

"I know of some information that will be very persuasive, yes, but the licensing agreement doesn't allow me to use it. I may be able to acquire the rights, although my connections are tight-lipped so the bait will be very expensive. Are you confident your segs will cover the labor?"

"I'm not sure."

"Then I may need a supplementary payment."

"To be honest, Monju, I've got no cash. But I really need your help."

"You're suggesting I take up a new hobby? Well let me think it over a few years. I doubt I'll start phishing for charity until my retirement."

"Listen to me. My best friend is being held at gunpoint with a piranha duster and that Birla freak is hacking her. They're committing all kinds of credicrimes against her but their lawyers are appealing every one. Once the court cases are settled she'll have plenty of cash and we can pay you whatever you need."

"How can you be sure she'll win?"

"The evidence is stacked in her favor. The lawyers are just stalling."

"Too risky. I need more reassurance."

"Look! I don't have time to explain, but once they get the info inside her BodyBank, they're going to kill her, okay! I need your help. I can do it on a loan. I'll pay double your usual rate. I'll owe you ten-thousand favors. I'll do anything. I don't want her to die! Not for me, please!" Amon was shouting, his whole body shaking, and through the film of overlay, he could see heads on the train turning towards him.

The PhisherKing stared at him for a few moments, his gold irises glinting between the scarlet and silver circles. "Alright, Amon. I'll do my best to get this man off your friend."

"Thank you!"

"But it may take a few minutes to acquire what I need, so try not to let her go bankrupt in the meantime. I wouldn't want to lose my pay."

"Of course!"

"And I'll need the segs in advance."

Amon tossed another orb to Monju containing his LifeStream since their last meeting, as well as his meeting at Sushi Migration.

"One last thing: remember our deal. That train is taking you to the right place. You'll have many opportunities to ask questions there. Don't betray me by giving up."

"I won't, I promise. Please take care of her."

"Yes. And I'll pray that the great Treasure Matrix takes care of you. Good luck." Monju smiled with his glass teeth and vanished.

Splitting his perspective between the train and the dim space behind Mayuko's closed eyes once again, Amon said, "Erase me."

WHAT?

"Before they hack into your account, search through your bodydrive for all the files related to me and delete every one."

YOU WANT ME TO TAMPER WITH MY LIFESTREAM?

"Not just your LifeStream. Your readout too."

BUT THE FINES WILL BANKRUPT ME.

"They won't, trust me."

WHY? HOW?

"Please just do as I say. Once they get inside your inner profile, they'll find out what you know and the exact route I took out of your place. But if you erase every trace of me, they'll be confused. They'll start to think that maybe you're not lying and your resemblance to Mayuko Takamatsu is just a coincidence."

BUT THERE'LL BE ALL KINDS OF GAPS IN MY RECORDS. WON'T THAT ALERT THEM THAT SOMETHING IS OFF?

"Maybe. But it'll take some time for them to notice the omissions. Then they'll probably think their hacking failed to access certain parts or something. This will just confuse them more. And that's all we want for now. We just want to buy time until the PhisherKing contacts you."

ARE YOU SURE HE'LL FIND SOMETHING?

"I don't know, but look, these Birlas are filthy rich and free. There's got to be all kinds of scandals in their past. If anyone can dig them up, it's Monju. So just do what I ask. I need you to find every trace of me, even from when we were kids. Quickly! Erase me!"

She didn't respond but he could see her doing a search for "Amon."

"Stop whatever you're doing," shouted the man, "I can see your eyes moving beneath those lids. Stop it now!" Mayuko screamed as the tengu pressed their boots down harder and her eyes opened wide. The hacker tengu continued to wave his hands over her face, guiding the flow of light into her orifices.

"Are you okay?" said Amon.

IT STINGS, she texted, the room disappearing behind her eyelids again. THERE ARE TINY SHARDS OF GLASS IN MY BACK.

"I'm so sorry." Amon shuddered with empathy. And when Mayuko had selected all the files about him, he said, "Before you erase them, there's something else you've got to do. Send me enough cash for about fifteen minutes and cut off my leash."

WHAT!? WHY?

"You remember I said not to worry about the fines for editing your records. The only way you'll be able to afford them is if you don't have to cover the interest on my loans. And if they open your readout, they'll see all the actions you're paying for. My identity will be encrypted, but they'll know you're leashing someone and it won't be hard to guess who."

BUT WITHOUT ME YOU'LL GO BANKR—

"There's no time. They could hack in any second."

BUT—

"No more arguments, please. I'm almost at my stop now."

WHERE ARE YOU GOING?

When he explained his plan, her incisive eyes lost their point of focus and whirled about in bewilderment. It was the first time Amon had seen them stumped. In the end, she cringed miserably, seeming to accept that he was right. Immediately, the credit appeared in his account and the leash was cut.

"What are you crying about?" shouted the man. She shrieked even louder this time when the tengu put their weight on her.

"Mayuko," said Amon. "I'm so sorry for everything. I wish you'd never come to get me."

DON'T SAY THAT. I'M GLAD WE HAD A CHANCE TO TALK. Then, after a pause. I'M SORRY I COULDN'T BE BEAUTIFUL LIKE THOSE GIRLS IN EROYUKI.

Amon felt her words bore into him, drilling emotional wounds at various points across his torso. Each of these raw holes welled up with remorse and overflowed, swelling and merging until there was no space between them and his whole body flooded with the feeling. It was the same remorse he'd felt the night before and Amon remembered Mayuko's slip of the tongue. Then all the observations about her he'd made since seeing her with Rick that morning began to take on new meaning. Now he saw why she hadn't changed her privacy settings to block him from her inner profile. Now he saw why she looked so tired these days, with new frown lines etched in her brow. Now he saw why she was always running and worrying about calories. Without intending to, he had betrayed this sensitive, irreplaceable being that had been closer to him than anyone on Earth. He wanted to tell her that she was wrong, that that night in Ginza was the most painful of his life, that he'd been alone ever since, that comparing her with those whores from Eroyuki was like comparing a slug stitched with flamingo wings to a flamingo, that if you peeled back layer after layer of who she was, delving into ever deeper sediments of self, you would find each one more beautiful than the last. But there was so little time.

"No," he said. "That's not right. I wanted to tell you last night."

I HEARD ABOUT YOUR DREAM FROM RICK ALREADY. I CAN'T SAY I UNDERSTAND, BUT I TRIED MY BEST.

"Not just that. The girl in Ginza too. I wish I had the chance to explain."

YOU DON'T HAVE TO, she texted. I CAN SEE IT IN YOUR EYES. Then Amon noticed a faint spectre of her floating there on the train watching him.

Of course. He should have realized. Those eyes left no corner of him unscoured, even those parts he couldn't see himself. Especially those parts.

A bitter yearning tore at his chest like fish hooks tugging him towards her, and he wanted nothing more than to have her there before him in the flesh, to feel her warmth in his arms, to have the smell of her comet hair in his nose. He stepped forward, pushing aside passengers in his way, to embrace this figment of his love, when the shift in vantage brought her surround more clearly into view. She had seemed to be standing upright on the train, but he realized now that he was looking down on her from above as she lay on the wooden floor in the shadow of her captors, a steady stream of tears flowing down her temples onto the mat of comet hair splayed about her head. The spectacle was so sad, Amon thought his heart would split open and weep pulses of blood.

Then he saw it. In spite of all her pain and humiliation, her mouth was drawn in the faintest suggestion of a smile, too subtle for the men to notice but impossible to miss for Amon.

ALL THE RECORDINGS OF YOU WILL BE GONE, BUT I'LL ALWAYS KEEP YOU IN MY MEMORY, AMON.

As the train arrived at Yume Station, the last stop on the line, Amon lost all control. His face cracked into a grimace and he began to shake the bodies around him with the spasms of his chest, his hands cupped to his face, the tears pouring out between his fingers.

"Goodbye," Amon croaked.

"Be safe," whispered Mayuko and broke their connection.

At Yume Station, Amon flooded off the train with the other passengers and descended the escalator in line. At the bottom was a concourse bustling with salarymen and office ladies weaving through each other in every direction. In each of their freely purchased movements, each toe pivot and advance, each link click and scratch of the head, Amon could sense their faith in the reciprocity of the market, in the recompense they would receive for the growth they created through spending on actions, and their hope of earning ever greater possibility, of being able to pay for expression of their deepest desires. These feelings Amon recognized only now that he no longer possessed them. There was one chance remaining; he could admit that much. Such faith and hope, there was none.

Crossing the ticketing line, Amon opened the image of Makesh Adani's business card saved in his LifeStream. He couldn't say which Birla he was contacting, and knew it was a long shot to think that she would still hire him after his blatant rejection. Only ten odd minutes remained until the interest on his debt ate away all the creditime Mayuko had given him, and even if Makesh arranged the interview in time, who wanted to deal with a disgraced, illiquid hobo? But with nothing to lose, he clicked the woman's FacePhone number.

After the seventh ring, the answering machine picked up. To save cash, Amon typed out his message, the words read aloud by software that perfectly mimicked his voice.

"Good day, Ms. Birla. This is Amon Kenzaki. Thank you for the sushi the other night. You may be surprised to find that I know who your parents are. Many things have happened since we met, and I've come to regret my decision to decline your offer. In fact, now that certain details of my situation have become clearer, I'm very interested in the opportunity you mentioned. Unfortunately, I'll be going away shortly. If the position is still open when I return, I'd be delighted to fill it. In the meantime, you're welcome to come find me in the District of Dreams. I hope to hear from you then. Take care."

The light at the upcoming intersection turned green just as Amon reached it. Was this bit of good timing an omen that his luck was turning around? Or were the gods mocking him with insincere mercy only now that his salvation was too late?

Yume Station was a central terminal that connected to the ports and factories in the west end of Wakuwaku City. The rides had faded away several stations back, leaving looming skyscrapers, low warehouses, and the massive metal spheres of power stations. Here, suited office-jockies walked alongside assembly line workers and mechanics in jumpsuits. The patchwork heavens were clear, each quilted segment composing a single video of triangular lips blowing smoke like a moving jigsaw puzzle. It would all look different soon. Amon wasn't there yet, but he was close enough. Already he could smell rank water, surely blowing from the Sanzu River.

There was only one thing left to do. Before he went bankrupt, he had to get to the bankdeath camps. He might die there, but so be it. Dying was better than being captured and drained of information, for that would mean the end of his chances to expose the corruption, to prove that Rick was murdered, to vindicate himself. It would mean the end of his dream. Yes, his dream was still alive. Its heart had stopped, but some relentlessly hopeful impulse in him had resuscitated it at the last moment. And so long as it still breathed, he would never give up. The forest was close. He could almost hear the surf.

Faint, wispy images half-materialized and then disappeared in the air about him. He thought he saw a dancing ballerina—or was it a puppet? A comb running through hair or a tractor in a field of wheat? A metal scrapyard or a closeup on human skin? Each time they vanished before his mind could grasp what they were. These were InfoGhosts, a rare phenomena said to occur only in that liminal state where humidity was high but not quite high enough to become mist. It was as though spirit voices had crept excitedly across the threshold between the digital and naked realms, eager for his imminent arrival.

To his dismay, the rate of inflation suddenly surged, the increased interest and higher action prices rapidly devouring his last bit of money. He wasn't going to cross the Sanzu River in time. He had to do it now.

Turning onto a small side street, Amon went down a narrow alley between condominium towers, crouched beneath a second floor balcony, and sat on the concrete ground with his back against the wall and his legs splayed out in front. He then put a hand on his chest, accessed his system registry, and recalled to mind the correct string. Finally, he entered the Death Codes into his own BodyBank, but paused a moment before initializing the command. Was this the right thing to do? He had thought it through, and there was no other way. Only an Identity Executioner like him could pull it off. By committing identity suicide, he would cash crash without going bankrupt. Then he could keep his BodyBank with all its evidence and his location would never be unblinded. Then he could escape. Then he would have a new kind of hope, however faint and fragile it might be.

Just before clicking "accept," Amon let out a sigh. For the first time ever, the expense of this action didn't bother him. On the contrary, it actually brought a small sense of relief. Blinking, breathing, swallowing, sweating: he wouldn't need to worry about these where he was going. There was fear in him, and regret, no doubt, as he wavered on the brink of the unknown, but mixed with this, he felt the bittersweet warmth of anticipation glowing out from cinders of curiosity buried too long beneath the ash of ignorance and denial.

He clicked execute.

The faces of passersby, the lips in the sky, the extravagant skyscraper façades began to jitter, slitting apart into mismatched doubles of themselves, quivering violently like singing crystals and then bursting into shards of abstract outline and chaos. A choir of footsteps, promo-musak, car engines were dissected too, syncopating and reverberating against each other until sound gave way to wailing static and soon cascaded into silence. Experience itself ruptured—the smell of exhaust fumes in his nose feeling like the hard ground beneath his feet, memories of lying snug in a warm bed tasting like cold metal on his tongue.

One world fizzled out, leaving Amon in darkness, lost and alone.

ACKNOWLEDGMENTS

Many thanks to Maiko Takemoto, Chris Molloy, Ashley Davies, Robert Priest, Marsha Kirzner, Eleanor Cruise, and Bec Miller for reading to the end of the early drafts and providing useful feedback.

Daniel E. K. Priest, whose lengthy online discussions and incisive yet delicately phrased critique saved me from producing a much shallower story.

Logan Fulcher for making it through two different drafts, giving great comments on both of them, and being my first ever fan.

Corey and Rowan McNamara, and Ginny Tapley-Takemori for their comments on part one.

Takafumi Kajihara for insisting on introducing me to everyone we met as "a novelist," even back when the manuscript was in a very rough state with no obvious hopes of being published, and for reading as much of it as he could.

Aaron Schwartz for his legal advice. Joe Grealy for his critique of my submission materials. Peter Tasker for scouring the manuscript with a financial eye. Amelia Beamer for her encouraging comments on chapter one and her advice. Dr. Kenichi Furihata for keeping me stably employed.

Finally, a special thanks to Meg Taylor and Wayne Arthurson, without whose support this story might still be languishing unpublished on my hard-drive, and to my agent Monica Pacheco and my editor Jason Katzman for taking a chance on a debut novelist with a long manuscript.